THE OUROBOROS CYCLE, BOOK FOUR

A SOJOURN IN BOHEMIA

THE OUROBOROS CYCLE, BOOK FOUR

A SOJOURN IN BOHEMIA

G.D. FALKSEN

WILDSIDE PRESS

To Nikki.

THE OUROBOROS CYCLE, BOOK FOUR

Published by Wildside Press LLC.
www.wildsidebooks.com

Ebooks available at wildsidepress.com

A SOJOURN
IN BOHEMIA

CHAPTER ONE

Christmas, 1898
Prague, Austro-Hungarian Empire

The clock struck twelve. It was midnight. December the Twenty-Fifth had passed and it was a new day. Doctor Varanus closed her book and set it to one side. She rose, took the shotgun from beside her chair, and returned it to its place above the mantelpiece.

"Well," she said, turning toward Ekaterine, who sat painting by the window, "this has been a surprisingly pleasant Christmas."

Ekaterine looked away from her work—a snowy street scene taken from outside—and shook her head.

"It isn't Christmas," she said.

"You are correct," Varanus agreed, pointing toward the nearest clock. "By my count Christmas ended just over a minute ago."

"Nonsense," Ekaterine replied, "Christmas isn't for another two weeks."

"Ekaterine," Varanus said, turning to her friend and sighing, "we are in the West. Here in the West, we use the Gregorian Calendar, and the Gregorian Calendar says that Christmas Day has finally ended with neither death nor bloodshed. And I consider that to be a successful Christmas."

She returned to her chair and her book, very pleased with the day's conclusion. Ekaterine simply looked at her and made a face.

"Doctor, you cannot truly expect *every* Christmas to result in misfortune. It has been five years since the…unpleasantness back home." Ekaterine euphemistically avoided mentioning the horrors of the recent civil war by name. "And five years before that your son's aunt fell to her death. Two tragedies in ten years do not make an ill-omened date."

"What about Barcelona two years ago?" Varanus countered.

Ekaterine sighed. "*Three* tragedies in ten years. That is still no reason to assume the worst about one day or another."

"She is right, *Liebchen*."

Varanus glanced toward the fireplace and saw her dearly departed Korbinian lounging on the Persian carpet before the fire, dressed in the black and crimson uniform of a Fuchsburger hussar. Having died in his uniform almost forty years ago, he seemed loathed to wear anything else.

Varanus gave Korbinian an irritated look. As she was the only person who could see and hear him, she could hardly respond without appearing mad to Ekaterine.

"Christmas has been full of tragedy for us, it is true," Korbinian continued, standing and walking toward her. He gently kissed Varanus's lips and said, "But not *this* Christmas, and that is something to be pleased by."

"I *am* pleased," Varanus said softly. "Did you not hear? I even put the shotgun away."

"Oh, *Liebchen*, what a wonder you are."

Varanus kissed Korbinian and returned to her chair and her book. Across the room, Ekaterine had resumed her painting. A quick glance told Varanus that it was coming along nicely. As one of the immortal Shashavani, her eyesight was keen enough to make out every detail of the work even from such a distance.

After a little while, Ekaterine set her painting aside and began sorting through a rather large pile of letters and correspondence that lay heaped in a basket nearby. Varanus tried her best to keep on top of the mail, but it really was a damned nuisance. There ought to be a law against sending society invitations to respectable persons, she mused. It never did anything but cause trouble.

"You know, you really should read some of these," Ekaterine called to her. "I seem to be the only person answering the post around here."

"That is why you're my social secretary," Varanus answered. "Is there anything interesting?"

"Very little," Ekaterine said, opening the next envelope with a silver knife. "Oh! Goodness!" she exclaimed, drawing out the embossed card inside. "We've been invited to a Christmas ball!"

"Ah…" Varanus said. She made a face. Perhaps she *was* proving a little slow managing her correspondence.

"This is most exciting," Ekaterine continued. "I wonder what I shall wear!"

"Ekaterine," Varanus interjected softly, "today was Christmas. Remember?"

Ekaterine paused a moment and drew herself up in a huff, acknowledging the date.

"You Latins and your wrong Christmas!" she declared, sounding deeply disappointed and throwing the invitation away.

"I am sorry—" Varanus began.

Suddenly, Ekaterine's expression brightened as her eyes fell upon the next letter. "Oh! This one's from our old friend Doctor Constantine!"

"Constantine?" Varanus asked. "That *is* a surprise."

Well, not too much of a surprise. Varanus had sent a letter to Constantine's London address when they had arrived in Prague, expressing pleasantries and inviting him to join them for tea if he ever happened to be in Austria-Hungary. Of course, she hadn't really expected a reply.

"How is he?" she added.

"Quite well it seems," Ekaterine replied, reading the first few lines of the letter. "He sends his best regards and hopes the letter finds you before Christmas, which technically it has."

Varanus simply rolled her eyes at this. "Nonsense."

"Good old Constantine," Ekaterine said wistfully. She lowered the letter and gazed off toward one of the gas lamps. "Can you believe that it's been ten years since we saw him in London?"

"Ten years," Varanus agreed. "Little more than the blink of an eye for us, but probably quite some time for him. I wonder how he is."

"I'll bet he's gone all gray," Ekaterine announced.

Varanus sighed and said, "Ekaterine, he wasn't *that* old when last we saw him."

"Still," Ekaterine said. She returned to the letter and continued reading. "Let me see here.… Constantine thanks you for your letter and hopes you're enjoying Prague. He says he won't be able to visit. He is leaving for America in the New Year. Something about a lecture tour. It sounds very exciting." She paused a moment. "Perhaps I should give a lecture tour in America. I'm certain I would be awfully good at it."

"You surely would be," Varanus agreed, only slightly sarcastically, "but one must wonder, is America ready for you?"

Ekaterine considered this and then concluded, "Probably not." She sounded rather proud of the fact.

"Anything else from Constantine?" Varanus asked.

"Um.…" Ekaterine continued reading for a bit. Then her eyes suddenly widened and she jumped to her feet. "Oh my word! He says that your son's in Prague as well!"

"What?" Varanus demanded.

"Well, Zizkov," amended Ekaterine. "It's very close by."

"What the Devil is he doing there?"

"Science, apparently," Ekaterine replied. "Constantine writes 'In his last letter to me, dated this past Autumn, Friedrich mentioned that he has taken up residence with some Bohemians in the City of Zizkov and is pursuing his experiments there. What marvelous coincidence that you happen now to be in Prague. I hope my letter arrives in time for you to reunite with your son for Christmas.' "

"Bohemians?" Varanus asked. "This is Prague; they're all Bohemians here. Well, the ones that aren't German."

"Oh, no, I believe he means Bohemian artists, not Bohemian Czechs," Ekaterine explained.

Varanus's face fell at this. Her son had a dreadful habit of associating with troublesome people. First it had been American wellness enthusiasts; now it was artists! What next?

"Good Lord, artists," she grumbled. "Well, there can be nothing for it, Ekaterine. We must find him first thing tomorrow and see what sort of a mess he's gotten himself into. Does Constantine give an address for him? Or must we wander around Zizkov, knocking on doors and asking for directions?"

"Oh yes, there's an address," Ekaterine replied. "Although knocking on doors sounds rather fun." She gasped with excitement. "We could go caroling!"

Varanus frowned at the mention of caroling and said, "I think that England was a bad influence on you, Ekaterine."

"But it introduced me to scones and Kent!" Ekaterine protested. "What could be bad about that?"

Varanus was about to reply when she heard the front door open and close. The sound was very faint, coming from the foyer of the townhouse they had procured, but Varanus's hearing was keen enough to notice. There followed two sets of footsteps in the hall, and presently the parlor door opened to reveal a pair of men.

The first was Luka, Ekaterine's cousin, who entered still brushing snow from his elegant dark moustache. He was dressed simply, as was his custom, and he seemed rather disdainful of his European clothes. He paused by the fireplace and a scowl crossed his face.

"Someone has moved my shotgun," he announced, sounding very displeased.

"Entirely my fault, Luka," Ekaterine announced playfully, rising and rushing to embrace her kinsman. "I picked it up and put it back when I heard you downstairs, entirely to spite you!"

Luka did not reply, but he grumbled softly and tried to hide a smile.

Ekaterine kissed Luka on the cheek and added, "Goodness, you're cold! What ever have you been doing? Standing in the river?"

"Standing in the snow," answered the second man, Lord Iosef Shashavani, as he stepped into the parlor.

Iosef was a beautiful man with dark hair and pale blue eyes, and he wore his fine suit with far more ease than Luka wore his. Iosef looked impossibly young, scarcely out of his teens, but in fact he had almost two centuries behind him. Though his face was emotionless, Varanus saw a lurking glint of sorrow in his eyes, one that had not left him since the death of his wife five years earlier. But whatever he felt within, Iosef kept it hidden from the others as he continued:

"I did tell Luka that he should wait in the carriage, but he insisted on standing guard for me."

"What sort of friend waits in a carriage while his sworn brother burgles a house?" Luka replied. He took a pipe from his coat pocket and began packing it with tobacco. "A poor friend, that's what."

"A sensible friend," Iosef said.

"Burgles a house?" Varanus asked. "Do I take it that the auction did not go as planned?"

"It did not," Iosef replied, the hint of displeasure in his voice. He reached into his pocket as if to draw something out, but instead he kept his hand there as he continued, "The late Herr Hoffmann's family had already sold much of his collection before the auction itself. The piece I require was not among the objects sold."

"So you robbed them?" Varanus asked, skeptically.

"Do not be absurd," Iosef replied. "I entered the house unseen, I examined their papers, and I found a bill of sale. It has told me everything I need to know."

"Cause for celebration!" Ekaterine announced. "I'll have the servants bring some wine."

"That will not be necessary," Iosef said.

Luka quickly held up a hand. "Let us not be hasty. Wine sounds like a very good idea."

Iosef looked at him. "You have snow on your moustache."

Luka made a face and quickly brushed at his face with his fingertips, trying to be both expedient and nonchalant.

"And where is your missing trinket, My Lord?" Varanus asked, returning to the subject.

"It was sold to a man named Mordechai," Iosef said. "He owns a curiosity shop and bookstore in the Old Town, so tomorrow I will pay him a visit and see what sort of arrangement can be reached."

"Do you intend to burgle him as well, My Lord?" Varanus asked. It was a cheeky question.

The corner of Iosef's mouth tilted upward into a slight smile, though the sadness in his eyes remained.

"Of course not, Varanus. One does not rob a man who sells books any more than one would rob a church, for they are both providing a great service to the community."

CHAPTER TWO

Iosef waited until evening on the following day to investigate the curiosity shop. Arriving after sundown was a necessity. As one of the Living—Shashavani gifted with immortality—his flesh burned at the touch of the sun. And given his relative youth, it would be at least a century more before his body became inured to the light.

The curiosity shop was located in a winding side street in Prague's Old Town, a short distance from the river. The air was thick with snow and the street was dark, but the light of the moon and stars gave it a pleasant quality like a scene from a painting gifted with greater sentiment than art. The windows of the shop were lit with a warm glow from within, and a weathered wooden sign above the door read "Herr Mordechai, Books and Curiosities" in bright, bold letters.

Iosef reached into his pocket for a moment and drew out the object he kept there. It was an amulet of sorts: a small, flat circle of aluminium, stamped as if by machine with the emblem of an eye encircled by a serpent devouring its tail. The reverse held lettering, imprinted as clear as if by a typewriter, but in an alphabet that Iosef neither knew nor had even heard tell of. He had discovered the amulet in the tomb of a deceased Turkish khan on the shores of the Aral Sea five years ago, only moments before the murder of his beloved wife Sophio.

He closed his eyes tightly at the recollection. The talisman was now all that he had left of Sophio, and he kept it with him always, even as he struggled to uncover its secrets. As if sensing his anguish, the wind began blowing hard against him, brushing through his black hair and stinging his cheeks with frozen kisses. He almost fancied that he heard the wind whispering Sophio's name in his ear over and over again: "Sophio, Sophio, Sophio". It was the same imagined sound he had heard the past five years whenever the sky was dark and his thoughts were left free to wander.

"Is this the place?" Luka asked, rubbing his hands together.

He had come with Iosef, of course; Luka would not have allowed otherwise. Indeed, it seemed that since Sophio's death, Iosef could find scarcely a moment when he was not kept company by either Luka or Varanus. Iosef suspected—indeed, he knew—that it was because they feared he might kill himself over the loss of Sophio. Five years was the blinking of an eye, and nothing compared to the century and a half that Iosef and Sophio had spent together. It was certainly not enough time to heal. But still, Iosef was no fool. He lived now for Sophio, as she would have wanted him to live. To take his own life, when she had died preserving his, would be an abomination.

"Indeed," Iosef replied, shoving the amulet back into his pocket. "Let us see if Herr Mordechai is willing to sell his new acquisition."

"And if he is not?" Luka asked, taking a long pull on his pipe.

"I would prefer not to resort to theft," Iosef said.

"But you will."

"We shall address that when we come to it," Iosef answered.

He went to the door and gently pushed it open, with Luka following closely behind him. The front room inside was almost as Iosef had imagined it. What might once have been a proper store front, with broad open space before the counter for visitors to admire wares on shelves, was now transformed into a tightly packed maze of bookshelves and display tables, all tightly woven around one another so that there seemed to be half a dozen paths to the back of the shop, and none of them quite large enough for one to pass through. The shelves were packed to bursting with books, most of them recent printings, but with the odd vintage treasure packed in with little care for the difference in age. The curiosities were held in viewing boxes or glass-fronted cabinets, and they proved to be all manner of things, from ancient skulls and exotic trinkets to items as mundane as pocket watches that must have caught the owner's fancy.

Luka took a look around, tapping his pipe out against the door frame, perhaps appreciating the rudeness in smoking so close to books. Most Shashavani had a great respect for texts, even those freshly printed; and though Luka still walked in the Shadow of Death, he was just as truly Shashavani as one of the Living.

"I am not claustrophobic," he said, "and yet...."

"Indeed," Iosef agreed, staring at the towering shelves. "It is quite enclosed, isn't it?"

The sounds of rustling papers and footsteps upon the floorboards came from the back of the room. A few moments later, a man appeared from between two of the bookshelves, quickly brushing dust from his sleeves as he came. The man was young, perhaps in his thirties, with dark skin and black hair. He was cleanly shaven and his clothes, while a little disheveled, were of impeccable quality. He seemed too disorganized to be a businessman and too fastidious to be an eccentric. A scholar, Iosef concluded, which pleased him.

"Gentlemen, gentlemen!" the shopkeeper exclaimed, first in Czech, then in German, as if gauging which language his customers preferred. Settling on German, he offered his hand first to Iosef and then to Luka and said, "Come in, please, do come in. How may I be of service?"

"You are Herr Mordechai?" Iosef asked.

"I am indeed," Mordechai replied, bowing his head. "And you gentlemen?"

"Prince Iosef Shashavani," Iosef answered. "And my…secretary, Herr Luka."

Mordechai paused a moment at the introduction, his smile never wavering. "Prince Shashavani, Your Highness, an honor. Your accent.… Russian?"

Luka made a face at the suggestion, but Iosef merely nodded.

"That will suffice for now," he said. "I must confess, Herr Mordechai, you are not quite what I expected."

"It is the lack of a beard," Luka explained, his tone ever so slightly jocular.

Mordechai laughed. "A beard? That will be a first. Most of my customers are surprised that I am Indian. From my name, they expect me to be an aged Ashkenazi gentleman. I try to explain that there have been Jews in India since before there were Christians there, but it is to no avail."

"Men are foolish," Iosef said. "It is no matter."

"No matter, indeed," Mordechai agreed. "Now then, what may I do for you gentlemen? Is it to be books or curiosities?" He motioned to the shelves and cases. "As you can see, I have an ample supply to please all comers."

"Curiosities," Iosef replied. "I understand that you recently acquired a number of items from the Hoffmann estate. I am interested in one of them."

"Ah!" Mordechai said. "Of course. Come, come."

He motioned for Iosef to follow him and led the way to the back of the room. Behind the bookshelves and the cases of mysterious trinkets was a sort of parlor that extended from the main room of the shop, adorned with a large desk, several cabinets, and even more books waiting to be read, stocked, or sold. A closed door led further into the building, perhaps to a private study or to the living quarters of the shop.

Mordechai paused and opened a ledger on a nearby desk.

"What precisely are you interested in, My Lord?" he asked. "I recall that the Hoffmann estate included a marvelous collection of Grecian pottery that has come into my possession. Would that be of interest to you?"

"No, I fear not," Iosef replied. "I am interested in one item, in fact. A small talisman composed of aluminium, stamped as if by a machine on one face with the symbol of the Greek ouroboros surrounding an eye and with sigils of an indeterminate nature on the other."

"Ah," Mordechai said, clearly recognizing the description. He frowned slightly.

"In fact," Iosef continued, "Herr Hoffmann had agreed to sell it to me…before his unfortunate heart attack two weeks ago."

Mordechai nodded and sighed with regret. "A most tragic event. And under the new moon. An ill omen, surely."

"You have the item in question?" Iosef asked.

"Yes, indeed," said Mordechai. "I know just the piece you seek."

He removed a key ring from his pocket and unlocked a drawer in the desk. Opening the drawer, he drew out a small disc of silver metal and held it up for Iosef's inspection. The object was almost identical to the one in Iosef's possession, and he leaned in to study it carefully, astonished at the sight of it.

"That is it," he agreed. "How much do you want for it?"

"Regrettably, nothing," Mordechai said. "It's not for sale."

"You wish to keep it?" Iosef asked.

Mordechai made a face and replied, "Oh, no, not at all, Highness. I have no wish to keep the thing."

"Because it is an obvious fraud?" Iosef asked. "Clearly a product of machine production."

"Clearly it is," Mordechai agreed, "barring some incredible craftsmanship on the part of ancient peoples." He indicated the amulet in his hand. "Allegedly this was taken from the tomb of a Slavic king. And truly, if a high chief of the Polans had command of such quantities of aluminium and such precise craftsmanship, I would be astonished, but still.…"

"It cannot have been created when the tomb was built," Iosef said, echoing the facts about his own talisman, "and yet it cannot have been placed there at some later date."

"Quite so," Mordechai said. "As a scholar, I assume it to be the work of great wealth by its owner and remarkable skill by its creator, and I fear that there can be no other explanation."

"And still you will not part with it?"

"I would gladly be rid of it," Mordechai replied, "but I fear it has already been sold. Indeed, I hope that the buyer will be arriving sometime today…or rather tonight. I sent him a letter about the acquisition before the Christmas holiday, and he replied by telegram with assurances of his impending departure. I hope he arrives before the year is out!"

"So it is not for sale?" Luka asked, moving forward. It seemed he wanted to expedite the matter. "Perhaps some arrangement could be made."

"Gentlemen, I assure you, I am happy to sell," Mordechai said. "It is simply that there is already a buyer, and I have agreed to sell to him." He raised a hand to stop any dispute. "Ah, but when my client arrives, if he would like to sell it to you, then by all means, let him do so. I have my obligation; after that, it is none of my concern."

"I suppose that is reasonable," Iosef replied. "And you expect your client tonight?"

"I have expected him for the past three nights," Mordechai explained. "It is entirely in his hands now." He unlocked a drinks cabinet and withdrew a crystal decanter. "But…if you gentlemen would care for some Cognac, you are welcome to wait for him with me."

"I would certainly not refuse," Luka said to Iosef. He quickly joined Mordechai as the shopkeeper began filling three glasses with fine French brandy.

Being Georgian, Luka had very exacting standards when it came to wine, but he had developed a fondness for brandy and its various refinements over the years.

"I suppose not," Iosef said, taking a seat at the table with them. "If I may inquire, Herr Mordechai, who is your buyer for the piece?"

"A Prussian gentleman, Count von Raabe," Mordechai answered. "A bit of an occultist, truly, but a learned man. I daresay he seeks the amulet for its historical merits as much as wanting a piece of pagan exotica."

"And what is its history?" Iosef asked.

It was a matter that struck a chord with his curiosity. He had studied the Kara Keçi Turks who had created the amulet he possessed, but discovering another that had been dug up from a Slavic tomb had surprised him. Perhaps there was a connection that he did not yet understand.

"Well, obviously, it was forged in honor of the Horned Serpent," Mordechai explained. "You are familiar with the Horned Serpent, are you not?"

"I…fear not," Iosef admitted, taking his glass and sipping the Cognac.

Mordechai paused, perhaps sensing Iosef's hesitation at admitting ignorance.

"Oh, there is no shame in that, My Lord," he said quickly, taking a drink of his own. "It is very esoteric. But tell me, are you familiar with the Black Goat—"

"Of the Kara Keçi Turks?" Iosef finished. "Yes, I am acquainted with the history of Arslan Khan and his forebears."

Arslan Khan had been the ruler of the Black Goat Turks in the early thirteenth century, and he had very nearly conquered the rising power of the Mongol Empire before his untimely death at the hands of the Mongol general Jebe. Had Arslan Khan assumed control of Genghis Khan's great horde, there was no telling what horrors the Kara Keçi might have inflicted upon the world.

Mordechai nodded and drank from his glass of Cognac, perhaps a little impressed by some strange nobleman recognizing the name of the Kara Keçi.

"If you are familiar with the Kara Keçi, surely you know of the Roman cult of the Dark Faun," he said to Iosef, measuring his words carefully. It was surely an esoteric subject and not one to be addressed among unenlightened company.

"Or course," Iosef reassured him. "The cult of the so-called Magna Mater that allegedly inflicted the Plague of Cyprian upon the Romans."

"And the Plague of Justinian after it," Mordechai agreed. He seemed pleased at having a companion familiar with the topic. "Ah, but I do not mean to distract us with talk of the Dark Faun. As I said, the connection that most interests me is that of the Slavic Horned Serpent, Veles as it is often known. And as my talisman came from a Polish Slavic tomb, I would assume it to interest you as well."

Iosef considered this for a moment. "I must confess, I am not familiar with this 'horned serpent'," he said. "Should I be?"

"Ah, well..." Mordechai replied. It seemed that he believed it so, though he was hesitant to say so to such a distinguished customer. "Well consider, Highness, the Dark Faun may not have made contact with the Black Goat cult in a timely fashion, but the Horned Serpent of the Slavs holds many similarities to the Kara Keçi cult, including blood sacrifice made to the head of a goat; and as neither the Turks nor the Slavs left written records, we cannot dismiss the possibility that the two cults were connected to one another."

Iosef sat back in his chair and studied his Cognac, unable to conceal the smile of curiosity that crossed his lips.

"Herr Mordechai, you have certainly caught my attention," he said. "If we are to wait for your elusive buyer, perhaps you would care to tell me more about this 'Horned Serpent' and its manifold secrets."

CHAPTER THREE

While Iosef and Luka attended to their business at the bookstore, Varanus took Ekaterine to find her son. The address provided by Doctor Constantine was located in a particularly low part of the city, a winding expanse of streets with crumbling buildings that loomed over the claustrophobic pathways below them. A few of the houses were old, dating back at least a hundred years to when the region had been rural land outside of Prague. The rest were far newer: tenements and townhouses erected to house Zizkov's rapidly growing population, and run by landlords who cared little for their working class tenants.

"It reminds me of London," Ekaterine announced, as they picked their way through a torch-lit alleyway and past a snoring drunk who lay huddled in a doorway against the cold.

"How curious that your keenest memory of London should be Osborne Court," Varanus said.

Osborne Court had been a particularly corrupt and rotten rookery in the heart of London's Spitalfields, where Varanus and Ekaterine had operated a small charitable clinic during the unfortunate year of 1888. It was certainly an apt comparison to the neighborhood that Friedrich had taken for his residence, and that fact troubled Varanus.

They continued along to Friedrich's address, which proved to be a decaying townhouse of what appeared to be considerable age. Its windows were greasy and in some places broken, stuffed with rags and newspaper to keep out the cold. Behind them, warm lights flickered and danced against the frosted panes. Varanus shivered at the sight of it. This was not the sort of place she wanted her son to be residing.

Sighing, she walked up to the door and gave it a few strong knocks with her fist. At first there was no answer, but presently the sounds of footsteps came from within, and the door opened to reveal a fair young woman only barely out of her teens. She was dressed rather more finely than Varanus would have expected given the location. But, she realized, the girl's dress was stained in places and fraying; it had not been properly cared for in several months at least.

"Who are you? What do you want?" the girl asked, her voice revealing a very fine Hungarian accent. Though she seemed startled and a little frightened by the sight of them, the girl maintained the poise of nobility.

"I am looking for my son," Varanus replied, advancing into the decrepit foyer despite the girl's protestations. "Perhaps you are familiar with him: Doctor von Fuchsburg?"

The girl looked astonished. "Friedrich? You are Friedrich's mother?"

Ekaterine joined them and closed the door against the cold, shivering slightly.

"She is," she confirmed. "And I'm his aunt, and we are both very eager to find him." She quickly extended a hand to the girl. "I'm Ekaterine Shashavani. And you are?"

"Erzsebet," came the reply.

"Lovely to meet you, Erzsebet," Ekaterine said. "Do you have a family name?"

"No," Erzsebet said quickly, drawing away.

While Ekaterine did her best to exchange pleasantries, Varanus took a moment to study the house. The foyer had long ago seen better days. A nearby doorway led into an adjoining parlor, from which came the smell of smoke and alcohol and the sound of violin music being played in a manner that was both too rapid and too syncopated for prevailing styles. A rickety staircase led to the upstairs part of the house, and from that direction Varanus smelled the faint odor of chemicals left to burn.

"Erzsebet, who is it?" called a voice from the parlor door.

Varanus turned and saw another woman, several years older than Erzsebet, who had just joined them. Her hair was dark and wavy, left in far greater disarray than Erzsebet's more precise arrangement, and her clothes were dotted with flecks of paint, which also stained her hands and fingertips.

"Visitors for Freddie, Zoya," Erzsebet answered. "They claim to be his family."

"Is that so?" asked Zoya, slowly advancing toward them. She did not appear hostile per se, but she did seem rather skeptical about being visited by two well-dressed women of obvious means, which was to be expected given the neighborhood.

"Yes," Varanus replied. "I am his mother."

"And I'm his Aunt Ekaterine," Ekaterine added cheerfully, offering Zoya her hand.

Zoya turned toward Ekaterine, and suddenly she stopped and stared. Gazing in wonder at Ekaterine, she exclaimed, "You!"

"Me?" Ekaterine asked, quickly looking over her shoulder in case there was some other person concealed behind her.

Zoya did not reply. Instead, she reached out with her fingertips and touched Ekaterine's face. Varanus frowned and made a move to stop her, but Ekaterine did not seem to mind, appearing more curious than anything. She allowed Zoya to tilt her head from side to side, smiling all the while.

"Oh muse…" Zoya said. "The light! It adores you!"

"Does it?" Ekaterine asked.

Zoya suddenly took Ekaterine's hands. "I must paint you, muse," she announced.

There was a pause as Ekaterine considered the strange statement and then said, "Yes, all right."

"Ekaterine, do you really think—" Varanus began.

"Come, muse!" Zoya exclaimed, gently pulling Ekaterine toward the parlor.

"Now just a moment!" Varanus protested.

"Farewell, Doctor!" Ekaterine replied. "I'm off on an adventure! Don't wait for me!"

And with that, she vanished into the parlor along with Zoya, into the smoke and the wailing of the violin. Varanus was about to follow when a man suddenly appeared on the upstairs landing, drawing her attention.

She saw her son Friedrich standing at the head of the stairs, wearing a soot-stained smoking jacket over an open shirt and a pair of rather worn trousers. Friedrich was not quite as Varanus remembered him, for the passage of ten years had clearly weighed upon him. Now in his mid-thirties, he looked thin and tired. He seemed not to have slept, and Varanus doubted that he was eating properly. And worse than the gauntness of his cheeks and the dark circles under his eyes was Friedrich's hair. Still the same shade of fiery auburn as his mother's, it was now shaggy and unkempt, while Friedrich's handsome face was marred by a bushy tangle of beard that seemed absurdly cultivated.

"Mother?" Friedrich exclaimed in astonishment. He began to descend the stairs, at first slowly but then with hurried steps as he rushed to embrace her. Reaching the bottom of the steps, he caught Varanus in his arms and swung her around, laughing with delight. "Mother! It is you!"

"Put me down, Friedrich," Varanus said, doing her best to hide a smile at his exuberance.

Friedrich quickly set Varanus down, still smiling at her.

"Mother, what are you doing here?" he asked. Then, just as quickly, he motioned to Erzsebet. "And have you met my friend Erzsebet? Erzsebet, this is my mother, the Princess Shashavani."

"Kindly call me Doctor Varanus," Varanus interjected. She had little interest in being addressed by something so tawdry as a courtly title.

"We have already met, after a fashion," Erzsebet said, but she bowed her head to Varanus with all proper deference to rank. That, coupled with her dignity in so low a place, all but confirmed her background. "And it is an honor to meet you...Doctor."

"Where is Aunt Ekaterine?" Friedrich asked.

"She was stolen to be painted," Varanus replied.

Erzsebet cleared her throat and explained, "Apparently Zoya has found her new muse."

"Aunt Ekaterine?" Friedrich gasped. "That is...wonderful, if unexpected."

"Who can say with Zoya?" Erzsebet said, shrugging. She looked at Varanus and asked, "You are Friedrich's mother? Truly?"

"She is!" Friedrich answered.

"I am," Varanus agreed.

"You are simply so youthful," Erzsebet explained. "My own mother would be envious. I would not imagine you to be a day over thirty...if you will pardon my saying it."

Thirty? Varanus thought. What nonsense was that? She had been physically *twenty-five* for the past quarter century.

"I am an adherent of wellness," Varanus explained. "I...milk bathe, you see. And...eat...cereals."

In truth, she knew little about the cult of wellness and its various remedies for old age and disease, but it seemed the sort of excuse a person could give for unnatural youth.

"Oh, I see," Erzsebet replied. The girl was clearly confused by the explanation, but she had the good sense not to inquire further. "Well...I shall go and tell Stanislav that there are guests, though I imagine he knows already, with the arrival of Zoya's 'muse'."

"I daresay," Friedrich answered, giving Erzsebet a smile. "Mother and I will join you all presently."

"Do hurry," Erzsebet said. "Ilya arrived from Russia last night."

"No!" Friedrich exclaimed. "I thought they deported him to Siberia!"

"Siberia?" Varanus asked.

"No, no, he was convicted of revolutionary activity, but he escaped," Erzsebet explained. "I am certain he will be happy to tell you of it himself."

"With embellishments," Friedrich agreed, sighing happily. "1899 will be a marvelous year, I am sure of it! Now then, go along and we will join you all very soon."

"Yes, of course," Erzsebet said. She bowed her head to Varanus. "Again, an honor...Doctor Princess Shashavani."

"Mmm," Varanus answered, nodding. She waited until Erzsebet had gone, before turning to Friedrich and shaking her head. "What a peculiarly earnest girl."

"A wonderful young lady, you'll see," Friedrich assured her. "Hungarian nobility, you know. Her family tried to marry her to a man twice her age whom she despised—some political thing—so she ran away with her lover at the time: my good friend Stanislav."

"I see," Varanus replied.

"He's a musician," Friedrich explained.

"Ah," Varanus said. That would the violin music.

"And a revolutionary."

"Of course he is." Varanus sighed. Her son had fallen in with a most peculiar crowd of people: not only artists, but also politicals. She could not imagine what sort of a bad influence they might be. Smiling at him, she said, "Alistair—"

"Friedrich, Mother."

"Yes, Friedrich," Varanus agreed.

Alistair had been the name Varanus gave her son when he was born. "Friedrich" had been imposed upon him by his aunt Ilse, who had raised him after he had been so cruelly stolen from Varanus shortly after his birth. It was always a trial to remember to call him by the wrong name, which he had for some reason adopted as his own.

"Friedrich, how are you?" Varanus asked. "What ever have you been doing?"

"Asia," Friedrich replied.

"Asia is a place, Friedrich, not an activity."

"I do beg your pardon, Mother," Friedrich amended. "I should have said, 'I have been being in Asia.' "

"Much better," Varanus replied. At least it was grammatically correct. "And what have you been doing in Asia?" she asked.

"Visiting distant relations," Friedrich replied.

Varanus sighed at this. It was obviously not the real answer. Friedrich was simply referencing an old fanciful tale about his paternal grandmother being a great khan somewhere north of Afghanistan. It was the same story that Korbinian had told Varanus's grandfather when he had been courting her, and it was not at all plausible.

Instead, she placed her hands upon her son's waist. She felt his ribs and hipbones through his smoking jacket, and this did little to reassure her about his health.

"You…you haven't been eating, have you?" she asked.

"Now Mother—"

"Or sleeping!" Varanus looked at the deep circles around Friedrich's eyes.

"I...." Friedrich frowned. "I have been very devoted to my work of late, that is all. Surely you understand."

Varanus wanted to protest, but on that point she could not. She understood the draw of science, which demanded one's attention beyond all considerations of hunger or exhaustion. So long as one could stand and the pangs of hunger were not too great, the work was more important and could not be interrupted. But she was immortal, Living Shashavani; Friedrich still walked in the Shadow of Death, and he needed both food and rest. She would not have her only child working himself into an early grave!

"Nonsense, Alis...Friedrich," Varanus replied. "Even in the midst of scientific discovery, I know how to eat a meal."

It was a lie, but a necessary one.

"And you, Friedrich, are not eating enough," she said. She touched his cheek and frowned at the rough red hair that covered it. "And this beard!"

"I thought it was rather artistic," Friedrich replied, stroking his chin proudly.

"It is dreadful, Friedrich," Varanus replied. "You must shave the damned thing immediately!"

"I will do no such thing, Mother!"

"Oh, but Friedrich, it does not suit you!"

In all truth, she doubted that such a thing would suit *anyone!*

"Nonsense, Mother, I think I look very dashing with it," Friedrich said. "And I will not shave it off."

"But Friedrich—"

"I am not a child, Mother." Friedrich laughed. "You cannot tell me when to shave!"

At that moment, they were interrupted by Ekaterine, who danced back into the foyer with light steps, looking very pleased with herself as she removed her hat. She stopped short at the sight of Friedrich and smiled in delight.

"Alistair!" she exclaimed.

"Friedrich," he corrected, though his face lit up at the sight of her, and he looked at her in a way that was not at all proper for a nephew to look upon an aunt. The fact that she was not actually his aunt was not a point of consideration.

"Yes, of course, Friedrich," Ekaterine amended. She patted his cheek and sighed. "Oh, but Friedrich, this beard of yours is simply dreadful. You must shave it off at once!"

Friedrich frowned to hear this, but he did not immediately rebuff the suggestion as he had done with Varanus. Instead, he said:

"Oh, but surely… I think it's rather artistic. Don't you agree, Auntie?"

Ekaterine removed the pins securing her hat and answered, "Friedrich, art is measured in paint, not whiskers."

"You don't find it a bit dashing?" Friedrich ventured.

Ekaterine sighed as she removed her hat.

"Friedrich, only three sorts of men grow beards: fathers, sailors, and those who have given up on life. And being neither of the first two, I should hope that you are not among the third."

Friedrich laughed at the statement, but then he stroked his upper lip and said, "Well, perhaps it is not right for me. But what about a moustache? I think I could wear a moustache very well."

"Nonsense." Ekaterine sighed and placed her hat and hat pins into Friedrich's hands. "Hold these for me, will you?"

"Well, yes, of course—"

"Friedrich," Ekaterine said, "there is only one man in this world who may grow a moustache and that is my cousin Luka. All other men who attempt it are surly charlatans, and I would dread to think that you are one of them."

"Oh, I see." Friedrich was silent for a few moments, holding Ekaterine's hat in one hand. He stroked his chin. "Well…I shall go and shave then. Do excuse me, Mother, Auntie. Go on into the parlor. I'll join you shortly."

Varanus stared open-mouthed as Friedrich hurried back up the stairs in search of a wash basin and his razor. When he had gone, she turned to Ekaterine, who was shaking out her hair so that it fell about her shoulders in a wild and unruly manner.

"How did you manage that?" she demanded. "I've just asked him the very same thing, and he refused me at every turn!"

"Oh, Doctor," Ekaterine said, giving Varanus a warm embrace, "you must learn that there are some requests that a young man will surely refuse when made by his mother that he will still agree to when asked by a maiden aunt. And shaving is one of them."

Varanus sighed and shook her head.

"I don't know which is worse, Ekaterine," she said. "That my son is so troublesome or that you indulge him."

"He's not troublesome; he is young," Ekaterine corrected. "People eventually grow out of that. As for indulging him, that is something aunts never grow out of."

"Hush," Varanus replied, laughing at this. Then she paused a moment and gave Ekaterine a serious look. "Ekaterine, why have you taken off your hat?"

"Didn't you hear?" Ekaterine asked, taking Varanus by the hand and leading her toward the parlor. "I'm going to have my portrait painted!"

CHAPTER FOUR

Varanus followed Ekaterine into the adjoining parlor, which was broken and decaying like the rest of the house. It was deceptively cozy, Varanus had to admit, with a warm fire to keep out the chill and gas lamps that were kept well lit despite the cost. But still, it was a poor and unkempt place. All the furniture was broken or otherwise damaged, there were empty wine bottles in all of the corners, and the furnishings, such as there were, were all threadbare.

There were half a dozen people in the room. The girl Erzsebet was sitting beside a man with a bushy, unkempt beard who was playing the violin by the window. Another fellow lounged on a sofa nearby, scribbling bits of poetry onto sheets of paper before tossing them on the floor, evidently dissatisfied with every last bit of his own work. Two more men sat across the room, shouting at one another in a mixture of Russian and German, though no one else seemed to care. And finally there was the strange painter, Zoya, who had her easel set up by the fireplace and was busy stirring up the fire to what Varanus assumed to be the "artistically necessary" degree of intensity.

Zoya turned to Varanus and Ekaterine as they entered and hurried over to them, taking Ekaterine by the hand and pulling her toward a chair by the fire.

"Come, muse, come!" she exclaimed. "The light will not last forever."

"How very peculiar," Varanus mused.

"Isn't it fun?" Ekaterine asked, in what it seemed she thought was agreement. "I've never been an artist's model before!"

"Indeed," Varanus said.

She stood to one side and watched the room. Nearby, the two arguing revolutionaries carried on, easy to hear and difficult to ignore.

"Revolution is simply impossible in Russia!" one of them insisted, his accent German. "Marxism is not made for such a rural country!"

"That is absurd!" came the retort, the speaker clearly a Russian. "What is needed for revolution is oppression and tyranny. And you tell me, my friend, what nation in all the world is as oppressed as Russia?"

"Marxism requires a proletariat!" said the German.

"There is a proletariat!" answered the Russian. "And we are more aware of the need for revolution than you here in Austria!"

"Nonsense, you have nothing but peasants! And you cannot have a revolution with peasants!"

Varanus sighed and ignored them. Arguing about peasants and revolution? What sort of people had her son fallen in with?

She turned her attention back to Ekaterine and the painter. Zoya had directed Ekaterine to the chair and was busy adjusting her hair. Ekaterine sat through it without complaint, unable to take the grin of amusement from her face. Finally, Zoya backed away slowly, holding her hands out toward Ekaterine.

"Do not move," she said. "Do...not...move...."

"Mmhmm," Ekaterine answered.

"Ekaterine I cannot believe that you are humoring this," Varanus said.

"Oh, she is having fun, *Liebchen*," Korbinian murmured in Varanus's ear.

Varanus turned and saw Korbinian leaning against the wall nearby, his arms folded. Varanus simply shook his head at him. There were far too many people around for her to give an answer. But yes, he was right: Ekaterine was having fun. And why shouldn't she? She had no business in Prague; she was simply there accompanying Iosef and Varanus. It might be good for her to have some sort of diversion, though being an artist's model was not quite what Varanus would have had in mind.

"Does the light still adore me?" Ekaterine asked, as Zoya began to paint her.

Zoya's eyes darted from the canvas to Ekaterine, mimicking the rapid movements of her brush as it covered the canvas in dabs and strokes of paint. She did not even break the darting of her eyes as she replied:

"Oh yes, muse, it most surely does. And by firelight... I wonder...I wonder how you look in the sun."

"Radiant," Ekaterine answered.

"Cheeky," Varanus said.

She walked to the easel and studied the painting. Although there was little to be seen yet, there was something almost coherent forming on the canvas. But the method of painting was simply bizarre to Varanus's eyes, for it seemed to involve laying fragmented bits of color all over the canvas in the hopes that viewed together they might be mistaken for some greater whole. It almost reminded Varanus of certain works by Claude Monet, but altogether more chaotic.

"Your style is very...unique," she said to Zoya.

"Thank you," Zoya answered. Her tone, though it was distant and focused, suggested that she interpreted the word as a compliment.

"Is it Impressionist?" Varanus asked.

She knew little about artistic movements and cared about them even less—why quarrel over methodologies of art when scientific questions were so much more important?

"Impressionist?" Zoya exclaimed. "Do not speak to me of the Impressionists, Madam! Superficial sentimentalists scrabbling about in the dark with their *brush strokes!*"

"I thought that the Impressionists were all about light," Ekaterine interjected. Varanus suspected that her friend knew more about European art than she did. Ekaterine had always been eclectic in the subjects she found it worth her attention to study. She might never be a great scientist, but she was a truly remarkable dilettante.

Zoya made a face and grumbled, "The likes of Monet and Renoir and Bazille wouldn't recognize light if it shone into their eyes!"

"I believe that is what light generally does," Varanus said.

"Even Seurat!" Zoya cried, never once stopping the mad tapping of her brush. "Such genius! Yet wasted, wasted!"

"I've never met the man," Ekaterine replied, acting like she was expected to have done so. "I'm afraid I couldn't say."

"Seurat…" Varanus mused. "The name is familiar. I'm certain I saw a painting of his when we were last in France. Something about a river."

"Well they do have a lot of those in France," Ekaterine agreed.

"Paintings or rivers?"

"Both?"

"If you aren't an Impressionist, then what are you?" Varanus asked.

She felt Korbinian appear behind her and whisper in her ear, "There appear to be quite a lot of dots on the canvas. Perhaps she is a *Dottist.*"

Though rather funny, Varanus considered it to be a rude statement and she did not relay it.

"I…" Zoya replied, drawing herself up proudly as she continued to dab at her canvas, even in the midst of a tirade unable to break from her work. "I am a Chromoluminarist!"

"A what?"

Zoya pointed at her canvas with her palette so that she would not have to distract her brush hand.

"A Chromoluminarist. I take color and light and through them I show Truth."

Well, Varanus thought, *it is certainly grammatically correct and accurate by degrees.*

"I consider myself to be a disciple of Van Gogh," Zoya continued.

"Who?" Varanus asked.

"Who? *Who?*" Zoya exclaimed. This at least was enough to pause her painting, though only for long enough to say the words; and then she was at it again, her hand working like a thing possessed while she carried on her conversation. "Not ten years in the grave and already forgotten!"

This loud statement was enough to draw the attention of the others in the room. The arguing revolutionaries stopped their heated debate long enough to laugh heartily and raise their glasses in toast to something or other—Varanus could not make out what. A moment later, they were bickering again. Across the room, the violinist's music paused, but not for long. Of them all, only the poet on the sofa paid any real mind, for he laughed aloud and said:

"Hardly forgotten, dear Zoya! I daresay your beloved Dutchman is better known in death than he ever was in life!"

"Oh be quiet, Karel!" Zoya snapped. "What would you know of it?"

The poet named Karel called to Varanus and Ekaterine:

"She only considers herself a disciple of his because she saw a few of his paintings on display in Belgium and took a fancy to them! And don't let her tell you otherwise! She's never even met the man!" He pointed his pen at Zoya and said, "Besides your paintings don't even look like his! All your factories and shop girls and the struggles of the working class! You're practically a Realist. You should call yourself a disciple of Millet."

"How dare you, Karel!" Zoya snapped. "If I were not working—"

Varanus and Ekaterine exchanged looks, neither enjoying the angry mood that had suddenly imposed itself upon an otherwise perplexing environment.

"Well, I don't believe that you're a Realist at all," Ekaterine said. "You're an absolute *Goghite* if you ask me."

Varanus rolled her eyes at the statement, but at least it did the task of diffusing the situation. Zoya immediately turned her back on Karel and looked at Ekaterine.

"Truly?"

"Absolutely!" Ekaterine said. "Now, you must tell me all about Chromoluminaries."

Varanus as about to explain the error in the word, when she saw Friedrich appear in the doorway. Leaving Ekaterine and Zoya to the painting—thankfully just as Zoya began to launch into a rather dis-jointed lecture about "color, light, and truth"—she hurried to her son and gave him another looking over. He was still exhausted and starved, dangerously thin, but at least he had shaved off his dreadful beard, and he looked much better for it. His cheeks were a little hollow, and his face was certainly showing its age—a fact not at all helped by his lack of food and rest—but at least he was clean and tidy now.

"Hello, Mother," Friedrich said, kissing her on the cheek. "Have you met everyone?"

"I have seen everyone," Varanus replied.

Friedrich quickly pointed around the room. "Erzsebet you have already met. With her is Stanislav, the violinist. And Zoya. Then Karel, our resident poet. And finally our Marxists, Wilhelm and Ilya. Ilya's just arrived from Siberia, I am told."

He exchanged a wave of greeting with Ilya.

"So I heard," Varanus said. She lowered her voice and said, "Friedrich, I…I am worried."

"Worried?" Friedrich asked.

"About you, Friedrich," Varanus explained.

"But why? I mean, I know I haven't slept much recently, but still—"

Varanus took Friedrich's hand and asked, "Has something happened to your estate?"

"Fuchsburg?" Friedrich seemed confused at the question. "Not at all. It's being perfectly well managed. The servants are quite capable of keeping it all under control in my absence."

"Do you need money?" Varanus asked.

"Money?" Again, Friedrich sounded confused. "Aunt Ilse may have taxed the family funds a bit while she was managing them, but I've had ten years to rebuild them. I am comfortably well off." He laughed. "I could hardly have traveled into the heart of Asia otherwise, could I?"

"But then why are you here?"

"Prague?" Friedrich asked.

"In this place!" Varanus exclaimed, softly so that the others could not hear them. "Friedrich, this is one of the poorest neighborhoods I have seen since my stay in London, and this house is a shambles!"

Friedrich shrugged. "It's very reasonable. And the neighbors don't complain about my work or the hours that I keep."

"Friedrich, there are rats!"

"Rats are very good animals," Friedrich replied. "And they're very useful for my work."

"And what is your work, precisely?" Varanus asked.

"I…" Friedrich hesitated. Then he smiled. "I can't tell you, Mother. Not yet. Not until it's finished. But once I have achieved what I am trying to achieve, I will tell you everything." He grasped her hands tightly. "And Mother, you will be so proud of me!"

Varanus sighed and said, "Friedrich, I am proud of you already. And I will be even more proud of you when you tell me what you are doing in your laboratory."

Friedrich laughed and embraced her.

"Oh, Mother," he said. "It is almost ready, I am sure of it. And when it is, I will show you the fruits of my Great Work." He clapped his hands. "Now, let's join the others and have a little wine, *ja?*"

Varanus hesitated and eyed the arguing Marxists. "If it will make you happy, Friedrich, then yes."

CHAPTER FIVE

"You are very generous with strangers," Iosef noted, as Mordechai refilled their glasses. The Cognac was quite good and certainly expensive. Did the bookseller hope to impress visiting nobility with the quality of his cellar?

"It is not any stranger that comes to me curious about the Kara Keçi and their Black Goat," Mordechai replied. "I consider myself a scholar of the esoteric, and I know one of my fellow scholars when I see him. I would consider it beneath my honor to welcome you with any less hospitality."

"All the same, my thanks," Iosef said.

"Of course."

Iosef took another sip of his drink and then said, "Now then, Herr Mordechai, tell me of this 'Horned Serpent' you mentioned."

"Surely you are familiar with Veles," Mordechai ventured.

"The Slavic god of the underworld, yes," Iosef answered. "Though I do not understand its connection to either the Black Goat or the Dark Faun."

"You see the Dark Faun and the Black Goat as different gods?" Mordechai asked, his tone sincere in its curiosity.

"They must be," Iosef answered. "We know from Ibn Fadlan that the Kara Keçi Turks were making sacrifices to their 'Black Goat' as early as the tenth century, but they did not make contact with the Eastern Romans until some hundred years later. Even assuming that the Dark Faun cult of Imperial Rome survived the Christianizing of the Empire, the Kara Keçi could not have encountered it until well after Ibn Fadlan's mission to the Bulghars, who were very clear in their tales of the sacrifices made to the Black Goat. Whatever similarities exist between the two must be coincidence."

Mordechai nodded and took another drink. "A reasonable supposition," he agreed, "and one that I ascribe to myself, though one must confess the occasional moment of paranoid speculation. What if the two were the same?" He asked this question mirthfully, clearly disbelieving it even as he presented the possibility.

"Then the Black Goat would have to be real," Iosef replied, chuckling. "And as we can safely dismiss that possibility...."

"Quite so," Mordechai said. He lounged back in his chair, enjoying the company of another scholar. "But surely you accept that the Slavs may have made contact with the Kara Keçi during the earliest era of the Middle Ages?"

Iosef sighed. "Taking into account that the Mordvins and the other tribes of the Volga region presented some barrier between the two, I suppose I can accept the *possibility*, yes. With reservations." He paused. "Do you suggest that Veles is somehow connected to the Black Goat? A Slavic offshoot of the Kara Keçi cult?"

"Or perhaps a Slavic origin to the Turkic god..." Mordechai suggested playfully. He spread his hands. "We cannot know for certain, but there are...similarities between the two."

"I hardly consider horns and beards to be of particular uniqueness," Iosef noted dryly. "The Kara Keçi worshipped a goat. The Slavs associated Veles with cattle. The two are not the same. And what is more, we are told that Vladimir of Kiev erected a statue to Veles, along with the other Slavic gods. Hardly an indication of some foreign transplant."

Mordechai raised a hand and replied, "Ah, but do not forget: the Veles statue was kept separate from the others. I think it very much suggests an *uncertain relationship* between the Slavic gods and their Chthonic cousin. But that aside, we are speaking of the Horned Serpent, not of Veles proper."

"And what is the difference?" asked Iosef.

Mordechai considered his answer for a few moments. He took another sip of Cognac and explained:

"Veles, as you clearly know, was the ancient Slavic god of the underworld, cattle, and wealth. The enemy of great Perun the sky god, and a god of trickery and magic. Now as far as is known, the worship of Veles was quite mainstream among the Slavs. But you see, there is evidence of a cult within the Slavic faith that worshipped Veles as the Horned Serpent, a dragon-like creature depicted with the horns and beard of a goat, who was feared and worshipped as a sort of demonic force demanding blood and sacrifice in exchange for his great riches."

"Pagan blood sacrifice to a god of agriculture and gold?" Iosef mused. "Unsettling, perhaps, but surely nothing too unexpected."

"It is said," Mordechai explained, "that the Cult of the Horned serpent chose the icon of a goat's head—a goat, not a cow—as their centerpiece of worship and that they bled their victims when they sacrificed them. There are stories written down about whole villages put to the sword, of men and women slaughtered like cattle to the glory of Veles, who is called the Horned Serpent." Sipping some more Cognac, he added, "Of course, much of this is relayed to us by Christian missionaries who say that both Veles and the Horned Serpent were manifestations of the Devil, so the authenticity is dubious."

Iosef chuckled softly. He had suspected as much. The image of the Devil as a horned god had been inherited from the early days of the Church, when it had struggled against such imagery among the pagan Celts. No wonder that Veles, so often depicted as a man with the horns of a bull, had been perceived as such. And no wonder that the missionaries would have related tales of bloodletting and death among the pagans they so ardently hoped to convert. It was a simple thing to murder a man over a question of faith when one believed him guilty of atrocities.

But he said nothing about this, and instead remarked, "Indeed, the source is, alas, dubious. A chilling tale, surely, but one must doubt its authenticity when related by German men speaking about the Slavs they hoped one day to conquer."

"Oh, but it was not only the Slavs…" Mordechai said, raising a finger. He leaned forward into the flickering firelight. "Indeed, there are tales that came out of Poland regarding the Germans of the Teutonic Order, who were invited to conquer the Baltic Coast on behalf of the Polish King and who then decided to stay and would not give up their conquests."

"Oh?" Iosef asked curiously.

"Oh, indeed," said Mordechai. "They say that there was a secret order within the Teutonic Knights that made sacrifice to the head of a goat and that they prayed to it in the name of God to grant them victory over their pagan enemies. And moreover—"

Mordechai paused as the bell over the door rang. He smiled in surprise and quickly finished his Cognac.

"Ah!" he exclaimed. "That will be my client. Gentlemen, if you will excuse me for just a moment."

"Of course," Iosef replied.

Mordechai withdrew from the office and vanished into the narrow passage between the bookshelves. From the front of the store, Iosef heard him greet the new arrival:

"Ah, My Lord! Welcome, welcome, do come in! There is some Cognac waiting in the back room."

There was a pause as the front door closed, and then a man could be heard to reply, "Thank you, Mordechai. Your hospitality is appreciated on this bitter night."

The voice was crisp and precise, and while it resonated with a typically Prussian tone of authority, the man sounded genuinely friendly in the way he addressed Mordechai. A curiosity, for what nobleman spoke in friendly tones to a shopkeeper?

"I would have arrived sooner, but...the Christmas holiday," he continued.

"Of course, My Lord," Mordechai replied.

There was a pause and then the newcomer asked, "You have guests?"

"A scholar from Russia and his secretary," Mordechai said. "We were sharing some conversation and a glass of Cognac while I waited for you, but if you would prefer, I can send them away...."

"No, no, quite unnecessary. You know me, Mordechai: I enjoy meeting new people."

As he spoke, Iosef heard the footfalls of the two men returning through the bookshelves.

"And you have the artifact?"

"Yes, as I said in my telegram," Mordechai said. "The Hoffmann family seems to have had little faith in the salability of a number of items in the late Herr Hoffmann's collection. The Polish amulet was one of them."

"Splendid!"

Mordechai appeared in the back room again, followed by a tall gentleman in a snow-dusted overcoat. He was in his mid forties, quite handsome and distinguished, with pale blond hair and penetrating eyes. He carried himself with the customary Prussian dignity, but even so he smiled warmly at Iosef and Luka.

"Gentlemen, if I may make introductions..." Mordechai said. "Prince Shashavani, Count von Raabe."

The Prussian clicked his heels together and bowed to Iosef.

"Your Highness," he said.

"Please...Iosef," Iosef replied, returning the nod but extending a hand. "What cause is there for such formality among scholars?"

"Wisely reasoned." The Prussian gentleman touched a hand to his heart and said, "Julius," before shaking Iosef's offered hand warmly and with a firm grasp.

"And Herr Luka," Mordechai said, indicating Luka, who had resumed his seat without waiting for the others.

"Evening," he said, taking another drink.

"My secretary," Iosef explained, as he and Julius sat.

"Is he?" Julius asked, giving Luka a skeptical look. "Well. A gentleman is always in need of a good secretary."

Mordechai quickly poured another glass of Cognac and handed it to Julius before returning to his chair.

"Prince Shashavani and I were discussing the matter of the Horned Serpent when you arrived, My Lord," he said to Julius.

"Is that so?" Julius asked, sounding sincerely intrigued. "A subject of great interest to me, I must confess."

"I in turn must confess that I knew nothing of the Horned Serpent before tonight," Iosef replied. "Though Mordechai tells me that he regards it to be an offshoot of the Turkic Black Goat."

Mordechai quickly held up a hand and corrected, "*Of common origin*, surely, whatever that origin may prove to be. And likewise, I do not think we can readily exclude the Antlered Maiden of the Ugrians from that evaluation."

"Oh, God preserve us," Julius said with a laugh. "Let us avoid that particular question, Mordechai, or else you and I shall argue about it and nothing else until dawn!"

"I suppose that is true," Mordechai agreed.

Julius turned to Iosef and said, "Prince Shashavani, if you will pardon a moment of business...."

"Of course."

"Mordechai, may I see my purchase?" Julius asked, holding out his hand.

Mordechai quickly retrieved the amulet from his pocket and handed it to Julius, whose face lit up at the sight of it. Julius took the amulet and raised it to the light, examining it carefully.

"Beautiful..." he whispered. After a few moments of study, he quickly closed his fingers around the object and tucked it into his coat. "Do forgive me: I am fascinated by pagan antiquities. I could stare at it for hours."

"I quite understand," Iosef said. He paused a moment and then decided to make a calculated admission. "In fact, I had hoped to purchase it myself, but Herr Mordechai would not relent on the matter. I wonder if you might be inclined to sell it now that you are the owner."

Julius smiled politely but shook his head. "Out of the question, I fear."

"I have possession of considerable means," Iosef added. "I am certain there must be some arrangement."

"No, I must refuse," Julius said. "My interest is not financial, you see. I am not only a scholar, I am also an archaeologist. I have made a lifelong study of the pagan cults of Europe, and the Slavs and their Horned Serpent are of particular importance to my work. I hope one day to write quite the extensive book about it. And to that end, I have made it a point never to relinquish any of the texts or artifacts I have acquired.

I should rather be a pauper in a shepherd's hovel than sell any article of my work before it is completed."

Having spoken so forthrightly to Iosef, Julius cleared his throat and took another drink. Iosef must surely appear young enough to be Julius's son, and however seriously Iosef might carry himself and form his words, it was inevitable that older men would address him in such tones. It was a point of irritation for Iosef, but one that could easily be managed.

"Then perhaps you might permit me to study it in your company for my own research," Iosef said.

"Ah, I see!" Julius exclaimed. "You wish to examine it for your studies?"

"Indeed."

"I see no reason why not," Julius said. "Perhaps we could even compare notes." This was spoken rather like a teacher offering guidance to a young student, which was to be expected. He took another drink. "What is your interest, may I ask? I thought you were not acquainted with the Horned Serpent."

Iosef placed his hand in his pocket for a moment, and his fingertips brushed the smooth metal surface of his amulet with its sharp-cut letters and symbols. An ember in the fireplace crackled, and it seemed to whisper "Sophio.... Sophio...."

"I have one of my own," he said. "Acquired from a tomb on the shores of the Aral Sea. I am curious to compare it with any others of similar design."

Julius's expression lit up, and he grinned at both Mordechai and Iosef.

"Ah, ha! Now it becomes clear! A tomb for one of the Black Goat Turks, no doubt!"

"Yes," Iosef said, after a moment's hesitation.

Julius turned to Mordechai and exclaimed, "You see, Mordechai! The Black Goat and the Horned Serpent. There is a connection!"

"*That* has never been in dispute," Mordechai reminded him.

"You and your Siberian origin theory," Julius scoffed. "Until an amulet is found in Perm or Yugra, I will not believe it!" He looked back at Iosef and asked, "So you are a scholar of the Black Goat, then?"

Nearby, Luka coughed a little too loudly. Iosef glanced at him and only barely hid a smile. Luka, even more than Iosef, was an ardent realist. The very suggestion that some nonexistent pagan demon was a subject worthy of study was the sort of thing to make him laugh—or to choke on his wine, as had nearly been the case.

"I have…recently come to study the Kara Keçi Turks and by extension some aspects of their faith," Iosef answered. "But I am more intrigued by the curiousness of the amulet itself."

"You mean that it is aluminium," Julius noted, "a metal not available to the ancient world."

"Precisely," Iosef said.

"But clearly, it was," Julius countered with a smile. "Somewhere, at sometime in the distant past, some ancient people discovered aluminium in sufficient quantities to produce these beautiful—and no doubt expensive—pieces of jewelry. It may confound our reason as to how or why it could have been so, but we cannot deny the evidence."

"I suppose not," Iosef agreed.

Julius finished his glass of Cognac in a long gulp and said, "Well, Prince…Iosef, I believe I have a solution to suit us both. I see no reason why we cannot share our knowledge. Let us agree to meet sometime in the near future, and we can examine both artifacts together." He gave Iosef a warm smile and added, "And perhaps I might teach you some of the intriguing things I have learned while studying the Slavs and their Horned Serpent."

Iosef sighed softly, recognizing Julius's tone and expression, which had assumed a hint of the paternal.

He thinks me a naive student he can educate, Iosef thought. It almost made him laugh. Still, it was an easy means of gaining access to Julius's knowledge and to the amulet.

Iosef was shaken from these thoughts by Luka, who—under his breath and concealed behind that act of drinking his Cognac—commented in Svanish:

"Yes, and after that, we can tell ghost stories." Luka scoffed at the very notion. "I shall notify Ekaterine. She would be delighted to attend."

"Don't give her any ideas," Iosef answered softly.

CHAPTER SIX

January, 1899

Varanus drummed her fingers against the desk as she peered into her microscope, irritated beyond all measure.

"Well, I have learned two things," she said to Ekaterine, who sat reading some uninteresting Gothic novel by the window.

Ekaterine looked up from the book—something by an Irishman titled *Dracula*—in the midst of a giggle. She paused and turned to Varanus.

"We shouldn't eat the biscuits?" she asked.

It was a piece of biscuit that Varanus was using for her examination.

"No," Varanus said, sighing at Ekaterine. "And do put that thing away," she added, referencing the book. "You shouldn't read rubbish."

"It's rather funny," Ekaterine said. "It's about a vampire in Transylvania."

"Don't be absurd, Ekaterine," Varanus told her. "Vampires are Serbian. Transylvania is in Hungary and populated by Romanians." She paused and returned to the matter of greater importance. "This is the most powerful microscope that I have ever engineered, its lenses expertly crafted at great expense, and yet I can discern that there are things still to be seen far beyond its reach."

"How...exciting?" Ekaterine ventured.

Varanus frowned. "Frustrating," she corrected. "As much as I enjoy a challenge, I fear this is rather on the verge of impossibility. There must come a point where a thing cannot be magnified any further, and I fear I am staring at that point as we speak. I have reached the very limit of optics."

"It *sounds* exciting," Ekaterine said.

"The thrill of discovery is, alas, marred by its inability to progress further," Varanus replied. "I hoped this new microscope would be sufficient for my studies."

"And...?"

"It isn't."

Ekaterine sighed and set her book down. "What is it for? Other than examining biscuits, I mean." She paused and suddenly her eyes opened wide with realization. "It's for the water, isn't it?"

"Of course it is," Varanus replied, a little surprised that her friend had only just realized it.

"Doctor!" Ekaterine exclaimed in protest. "It's forbidden! I thought all of that was behind you!"

"Scientific progress is never behind one," Varanus said, "only ever ahead, waiting to be discovered."

"If you keep pursuing this matter, you may die!"

"Science has been known to result in death," Varanus agreed, "but I escaped execution the last time. I am certain I have nothing more to fear in that regard." She glanced back at her microscope and added sullenly, "An inability to achieve the results I require, on the other hand...."

"*Doctor!*" Ekaterine repeated, rushing to her side. "You promised!"

Varanus sighed. Though she remained committed to her work, Ekaterine's distress troubled her. And she did understand why. Five years prior, she had taken samples from the waters of life, which gave the Shashavani their immortality, and subjected them to countless tests to discern their nature. When the heads of the Shashavani Order had learned of her transgression, she had been imprisoned with the possibility of execution—before a timely civil war had given everyone more important things to think about. Varanus had never been able to take more samples since, and it seemed Ekaterine had assumed that she had "learned her lesson" and abandoned her illicit research.

"But one does not give up on scientific discovery so easily, does one, *Liebchen?*" Korbinian's voice murmured in her ear. Startled, Varanus looked to the side and saw him sitting on the edge of the desk. Korbinian smiled at her and continued, "Still, you cannot blame your friend for worrying so. You may now have friends on the Council that rules your order, but even they would balk at treating the source of their power like some chemical to be sampled in a beaker."

"Perhaps," Varanus murmured under her breath, though she knew that he was right.

"What was that?" Ekaterine asked.

More loudly, Varanus replied, "I promised that I would not take the water in secret. I remain confident that I will eventually convince the Council to support my experiments. The question of our nature is vitally important, Ekaterine."

"I know that," Ekaterine said. "But why bother yourself about the matter of a microscope before permission is given?"

Though she tried to hide it, Ekaterine's tone sounded as if she doubted such permission would ever be given.

"Because as soon as I have that water in my grasp again, I intend to unlock the secrets that previously eluded me," Varanus explained. "There were *things* in that water just clear enough to be noted but too small to be examined. From what little I saw, I can anticipate how powerful a magnification would be required based on the examination of other objects." She looked at her microscope and grimaced. "Now all that remains is to find a microscope capable of the task, which I fear this one is not."

Varanus paused as her ears detected a faint noise from the direction of the foyer. It was too quiet for Ekaterine to notice, but as Living Shashavani, Varanus had no difficulty hearing it. She listened more carefully and heard the distinct sound of the front door being opened.

"I do believe we have guests," she said, rising from her chair, "though I wonder who it may be. Are you expecting anyone?"

"Not until next Thursday," Ekaterine replied, looking puzzled.

"Who are you expecting on Thursday?" Varanus asked.

"Friedrich's friend. I'm having my portrait painted again." Ekaterine sounded very pleased.

Varanus sighed and shook her head. "Artists, Ekaterine? Not in the house."

"She's a very clean and well-behaved artist," Ekaterine insisted.

"There's no such thing," Varanus replied dryly.

But her curiosity had been pricked by the new arrival, and she hurried out into the upstairs hall. Crossing the length of the townhouse, Varanus came to the landing above the foyer and saw that the footman they employed had just answered the door and had shown in their mysterious guest.

The stranger was tall and dignified, and his elegant clothes spoke of his great wealth and station as did his poise. He was fortyish, blond, and rather handsome to Varanus's eyes, so she took a moment to admire him on point of principle. The stranger looked around the foyer with an appraising look as the footman took his hat and coat, and after a moment, his eyes turned upward and he spotted Varanus watching him. A smile crossed the stranger's lips, and that smile grew broader as Varanus placed a finger to her lips for silence.

"I shall inform the Prince of your arrival, Your Lordship," the footman said. "If you would care to wait in the sitting room—"

"No, I will wait here," the stranger replied, his tone authoritative but not unkind.

"As you wish, My Lord."

The footman bowed and withdrew from the room. When he had gone, the stranger approached Varanus until he stood just below the landing, looking up at her with mischief in his clear blue eyes.

"Good afternoon, *Fräulein*," he said, bowing his head politely.

"Good afternoon to you as well, *Fremder*," Varanus replied, smirking a little.

She began walking along the landing toward the staircase, running her fingertips along the wooden railing. The stranger turned and walked alongside her on the floor below, matching her step for step but never taking his eyes from her. The smile had not left his lips since the footman's departure, and it grew a little as they walked.

"It is not often we receive visitors," Varanus said. "Had I known, I would have dressed for the occasion."

Having been at her work, Varanus wore only a simple skirt and blouse, certainly nothing appropriate for entertaining. Surely one of Ekaterine's tea gowns would have been more presentable, even in front of a stranger. And her hair was in disarray, only some of it successfully tied back with a ribbon, the rest falling about her shoulders in a most unkempt manner.

"Nonsense," the stranger answered. "If you will pardon my saying so, I think I prefer you as you are."

"Wild and untamed?" Varanus asked, amused at the stranger's lack of decorum. It was such an uncommon thing to find in a German aristocrat.

"As Nature intended," the stranger replied.

Varanus reached the stairs and descended, carefully watching the stranger as he turned and continued to walk along parallel to her, never once looking away.

"I doubt very much that any of us are as Nature intended," Varanus noted. "Only rarely does one find bears wearing shoes, does one, *Fremder?*"

"If you will pardon me again, *Fräulein*, you are hardly a bear, not by even the furthest stretch of the imagination."

"You will recall, I haven't pardoned you yet for the first time," Varanus replied.

She came to the foot of the stairs and walked to the center of the foyer. The room, like all the rest of the house, was carefully shrouded against the daylight by thick curtains, but the gas lamps burned brightly and kept away the shadows that flitted about in the corners. The stranger followed her as she walked, keeping a respectful distance.

"So I did notice," he said. "I fear that I have gambled upon your being especially charitable, *Fräulein*. You have kind eyes." There was a pause as his own eyes twinkled with mischief. "If you will pardon my saying so."

"Perhaps you should tell me your name, Sir, and then I will feel more inclined toward forgiveness."

The stranger bowed slightly and answered, "I am Julius Johan Graf von Raabe, and I am at your service, *Fräulein*, at least until Prince Shashavani deigns my company."

Graf von Raabe. A count.

"Babette Varanus Shashavani," Varanus replied, offering her hand, which Julius took with gentle fingers and held longer than was appropriate. Again, Varanus found herself amused.

" 'Babette,' " Julius said, as if testing the word. " 'Varanus.' What an interesting name."

"It's Latin," Varanus replied.

"Well that explains it," Julius agreed, smirking. "And you are a Shashavani like the Prince? You are perhaps his…"

"Wife," Varanus replied.

"I see…" Julius said. Still smiling, he released Varanus's hand and placed a finger to his lips. "I must confess, Princess, I had not expected that."

"No doubt you mistook me for one of the servants," Varanus suggested. "Perhaps Princess Shashavani's social secretary."

Julius chuckled and said, "Nothing of the sort, Highness, I assure you. I thought perhaps you were his sister."

"Alas, the Prince's sister is upstairs, reading a book about Romanian Serbian Hungarians."

Julius raised an eyebrow. "That sounds rather convoluted."

"Well, it's by an Irishman," Varanus explained. She motioned to the upstairs. "I could fetch her if you like."

"Oh, I would hardly wish to disturb her in the midst of Irish literature," Julies said. "And besides, you have yet to pardon me for my rudeness, so you certainly cannot leave yet. I would be distraught at the thought that my offending you had gone unforgiven."

"Very well, you are pardoned for complimenting me out of turn, Count von Raabe," Varanus said.

The corner of Julius's mouth turned up in another smirk.

"Forgiven so quickly?" he asked. "Are you so eager to be rid of me."

Varanus paused a moment to consider this and answered, "Not yet."

Julius chuckled. He looked away for a moment and glanced around the foyer. "It is rather dark in here," he noted. "I confess, I had not expected that. Is this the fashion in Russia?"

"Oh yes," Varanus replied. "Princess Shashavani and I are starting a whole new trend. Naturalism as the absence of natural light. It will be in vogue all across Europe by 1900, you will see."

"How very Romantic," Julius said. "But tell me…I thought that *you* were the Princess Shashavani."

"We…um…" Varanus answered. "It's complicated."

"I enjoy complications," Julius assured her.

"My sister-in-law is a princess by blood; I a princess by marriage. In Saint Petersburg they call us the Princesses Shashavani, and they can never tell us apart."

Julius looked into Varanus's eyes as he replied, "I find that most unlikely. You do not seem to be the sort of woman one would ever mistake for another."

Varanus gazed back into Julius's eyes for a few moments, finding them rather pleasant to observe. Despite her intentions to the contrary, Varanus found the rest of the room slowly slipping away into darkness and shadows, leaving only the two of them standing there, gazing at one another. Even the beating of the pulse in Julius's throat, tantalizing though it was, could not distract Varanus from his clear blue eyes.

"Shall I pardon you again, Count von Raabe?" she asked softly.

"I would be most grateful," Julius said.

The noise of the footman approaching in the adjoining hall broke Varanus from whatever reverie seemed to have taken both of them. She glanced toward the doorway as the footman entered. He seemed surprised at the sight of her—Varanus only rarely left her rooms except on business, and the servants almost never saw her—but he quickly bowed his head to her before addressing Julius:

"My Lord, Prince Shashavani awaits you in his study. If you would care to follow me…."

Julius nodded. He turned toward Varanus and said, "An honor to meet you, Your Highness. I hope we shall speak again."

"That would be most agreeable, Count," Varanus answered.

Julius smiled softly and then turned to follow the footman. Varanus almost gasped at the sight of Korbinian standing directly behind where Julius had stood a moment before. A trickle of blood crept from the corner of his eye as he slowly approached Varanus.

"Having fun, are we *Liebchen?*" he asked.

* * * *

Iosef was in his study when the footman arrived with his guest. At the sound of footsteps, Iosef marked his place in the book before him with a strip of cloth and closed it. He rose and turned toward the door a moment before it opened.

The footman looked startled at the sight of him standing. The young man had only been with them a few months. Perhaps he had not yet become accustomed to the peculiarities of his employers. Perhaps this was for the best.

"Count von Raabe, Highness."

"Of course," Iosef replied, as the footman ushered Julius von Raabe into the study. "Thank you, Pravec. That will be all."

The footman nodded. "Very good, Highness." Having performed his duty, he quietly withdrew and closed the door behind him.

There was a long silence as Iosef and Julius studied one another. After a few moments, Julius smiled and bowed his head to Iosef.

"Good afternoon, Prince Shashavani."

"Ah," Iosef corrected. "Iosef, if you please, Count von Raabe."

"As you wish, Iosef," Julius replied, "if you will afford me the same courtesy."

"Of course, Julius," Iosef said. "And how are you?"

Iosef did not normally engage in pleasantries, but it seemed a satisfactory approach.

"Quite well, quite well," Julius answered. "In fact, I have just met your wife."

"Indeed? And how is she?"

It was a sincere question: absorbed by his studies, Iosef had not spoken to Varanus since the day before.

"In high spirits," Julius said. "And apparently your sister is enjoying a book about Romanians. No…Hungarians. No, wait.…"

It took Iosef a moment to recall that Varanus had taken to passing Ekaterine off as her sister-in-law, but he blinked twice to bring that memory back into focus and nodded.

"Ekaterine is prone to reading whatever takes her fancy," he said. "Recently she has become enamored of tales about the Goths…though why that would involve Hungarians I cannot imagine." He waved the matter away. "Regardless, it is good of you to come, Julius. I see you received my letter."

"Oh yes," Julius said. "I was very pleased to receive your invitation."

"But surely," Iosef replied, "we already spoke of collaboration when last we met."

"True," Julius said, "but we are both aristocrats, my good Iosef. The high and the mighty say much. Adhering to it is…less certain."

"I thought that Prussians were famous for honesty."

Julius chuckled a little. "If you ask the Austrians, I think you will find it to be quite the opposite."

"I suppose they have ample enough reason to suspect Perfidious Brandenburg," Iosef said. "First you ally, then you declare war, then you ally again. You cannot fault the Austrians for being suspicious."

Julius stared at Iosef, surprised by his candor. Surely Julius was not accustomed to being spoken to in such a way by one he mistook for a youth. But after a moment he laughed.

"Entirely the fault of Bismarck, I assure you. Pardon me for speaking ill of the dead, but with that wily fox gone from the government, I daresay the world may find in us the truest of allies."

"Of course," Iosef said. Then, to assuage any insult from his earlier words, he added, "Do forgive my bluntness, Julius. I do not mean to speak ill of your country."

"Ah, it is nothing," Julius replied, though he smiled at Iosef's apology. "Indeed, scholars must be honest with one another. Too often they succumb to the politician's duplicity and cannot be cured of it."

"Alas, it is so," Iosef agreed. "A man may come to love his position more than he loves the work that brought him there."

"I say let them leave the universities and quarantine themselves in Berlin," Julius said. "They will be better received there."

"So politics is a prison for those too arrogant for scholarship?" Iosef almost laughed, but his capacity for laughter had become too dulled, not only by time but also by the weight of loss that still hung upon him and clouded his thoughts.

Julius sighed and said, "I wish that it were so. Instead, such men are to be found everywhere doing everything, and that is perhaps why so little is ever accomplished."

It was clearly a joke, so Iosef made himself smile at it. In truth, there was humor in it, but again sorrow and age together robbed Iosef of such amusement. But Julius seemed pleased that his joke had been well received, and he grinned.

"Would you care to sit, Count von Raabe?" Iosef asked.

"Julius," came the reminder. "And yes, I would be grateful."

Iosef pulled a second chair to his desk and motioned for Julius to join him. Even seated, Julius maintained his Prussian dignity, his back ramrod straight and his chin held high; but such was his pleasant joviality that this seemed more an indication of liveliness than an affectation of pride. Iosef approved of that. Men should be dignified because it pleased them, not because they hoped to put others to shame.

Julius's gaze fell upon the old leatherbound book that Iosef had been reading and he said, "Ah, ha! I see you have been perusing the works of Stanislaw Kaminski. A most interesting man, if I may say so."

"You may indeed," Iosef agreed. He picked up the book and examined it for a few moments. "And 'interesting' is one way of putting it. His account of witchcraft in Christian Poland is intriguing, certainly, but his accusations toward the Teutonic Knights are nothing short of scandalous."

"Scandalous indeed," Julius said, chuckling. "At least they would be were they true."

"You disbelieve the great Kaminskus Magnus?"

Iosef found enough good humor in himself to offer a jest, which seemed to please Julius further. Iosef made a note of this. Maintaining friendly terms with the Count would make it easier to siphon his knowledge about the amulets and the cults that made them. And, Iosef reflected, there was something pleasant in conversing with another man of letters.

"I do indeed!" Julius remarked. "A brilliant alchemist, it is true, and certainly his study of witchcraft is an intriguing look into the vestiges of paganism lurking in the Polish countryside, but I fear that the very suggestion of devil worship and sorcery among the Teutonic Order is ludicrous! These are the same absurd charges levied against the Knights Templar by Philip IV, and as men of intellect and learning, we ought to dismiss them just as readily."

"I suppose one should not be surprised to find a highly placed member of the Polish court accusing his king's enemies of such things," Iosef said. "The knights had just conquered Danzig and cut Poland off from the sea."

"Quite so," said Julius. "Under such circumstances it is easy, even preferable, to look at an enemy at the height of his power and accuse him of all manner of horrors."

"Not that the knights were any stranger to horrors," Iosef noted dryly. "As I recall, bloodshed came easily to them in the subjugation of Prussia."

Julius shuddered a little, but he nodded his agreement.

"Yes indeed," he said. "The knights massacred the pagans, and the pagans massacred the knights.... It was a very different time." He looked grim and saddened by such thoughts for a moment, and then he smiled. "But thank God such things are no longer done these days."

No, Iosef thought sardonically, *today we are honest enough to admit that we are killing our neighbor for his land rather than pretending it is because of his god.*

But he kept his thoughts to himself. "Thank God indeed," he agreed. "Now then, shall we examine the amulets?"

"A splendid idea!" Julius replied, producing the object in question from his pocket and placing it upon the desk.

Iosef opened the small drawer that held his amulet and reached for it. He shivered instinctively as his fingertips brushed the smooth metal. The thought of Sophio's death came to him again, and for a moment he could only stare ahead as the shadows whispered her name to him.

Sophio, Sophio, Sophio.

Iosef blinked a few times to compose himself. Each time he closed his eyes, he saw Sophio in her last moments: aflame and burning into ashes. But somehow the familiarity of such horrors helped calm him and silenced the whispers.

Regaining his senses, Iosef quickly drew out his amulet and placed it beside Julius's.

"Ah, yes," Julius said, leaning over to examine the two objects. "Practically identical." He paused and looked up. "Could we have a little more light, Iosef?"

Iosef glanced toward the oil lamp that sat on his desk. The wick was burning very low, and the room had indeed grown dark. As Living Shashavani, his keen eyes barely noticed, but a mortal like Julius would certainly be troubled by the encroaching shadows.

"Certainly," he said, turning up the lamp and pulling it a little closer so that Julius might take advantage of the light.

With fresh illumination, Iosef also began examining the amulets. Julius was correct about their being identical. The front face of each was stamped perfectly with the ouroboros and eye.

"If these were made by hand rather than machine—" Iosef remarked.

Julius looked at him a little disdainfully at this, and though he said nothing, his eyes all but scoffed at the suggestion.

"—then they must have been made at the same time," Iosef continued. "Or else one copied from the other."

"Or both copied from a third," Julius suggested, almost giddy at the thought. "I would be most excited to discover a third amulet...."

"Yes," Iosef agreed, "perhaps found in Perm or Yugra as Herr Mordechai suggests."

"*Mein Gott,* do not encourage him," Julius protested. "He is Yugra-mad, convinced of some *urheimat* for the Black Goat cults located in the furthest reaches of Arctic Siberia. I fear he takes the legends of the Reindeer Queen far too literally."

Iosef paused a moment, unfamiliar with the name. "The Reindeer Queen?" he asked.

Julius sighed and shook his head. "A fanciful tale to frighten children. Allegedly, a now forgotten Uralic tribe believed in a demon goddess who rules over the land of the dead at the northernmost reaches of the world. It is said that those who freeze to death in the wilderness are carried to her kingdom in the tundra and made to serve her for eternity. It is as lurid as it is absurd, and considering that the only 'evidence' we have for the tale's existence are some ghost stories told by Cossack adventurers in the seventeenth century, I am inclined to dismiss the whole thing as nonsense!"

"That would seem the most prudent action," Iosef agreed. However open he was to legends and mythology, the story certainly had the feel of an explorer's fabrication.

Returning to the amulets, he turned them over and examined the back of each. Both were stamped with letters written in an alphabet he neither knew nor had ever seen other than on the amulets.

"What do you make of these characters?" he asked.

"A message, clearly," said Julius. "Perhaps a prayer or incantation of some sort. It seems rather an expensive medium for a recipe or a bill of sale!"

He laughed at this, no doubt amused at the thought of rare aluminium being used for the same simple purposes as clay tablets.

"Indeed," Iosef said. He examined each line of letters in turn, looking from one amulet to the other. Although he could not discern their meaning, he could still recognize patterns. "The first two lines are identical," he noted.

"So they are," Julius agreed, gasping softly.

"The third one is different," Iosef continued. "The fourth is the same. The fifth different..." He frowned slightly and narrowed his eyes. "I wonder what is to be made of that."

Julius shrugged and grinned. "Ignorant of the language, we may never know. But I tell you truly, Iosef, I predict that you and I shall have a tremendous amount of fun trying and failing to work it out."

Such was Julius's enthusiasm that Iosef could not keep himself from smiling a little.

"I suspect you are right about that, Julius," he said, "on both counts."

CHAPTER SEVEN

Friedrich felt bad about the rats. They were such pleasant little fellows, always scurrying about in their cages, chattering to one another, grooming and playing. It made him regret killing them.

Not that he actually did the killing—that was the fault of the cancer and the poison—but he regretted his hand in it. He winced each time a rat squeaked when he injected it with a new formula. Every day as he checked on the cages, he silently prayed that there would be no more sickness, that the latest subjects would show improvement. As often as not, he was met with corpses. And even those that did show improvement inevitably developed tumors and died.

At first he had relied entirely on the local rat population, which was abundant in that part of the city. But as his early tests each ended in failure, Friedrich had hit upon the idea of breeding successive generations of test subjects himself, both to ensure a large enough supply and to prevent the rats from dying of any local poisons or diseases—which, he assured himself, was the entire reason for the failure of his formulae. Now months later, he had come to realize that perhaps it was not the local diet that was at fault.

Sighing quietly, Friedrich removed the morning's two dead specimens from their cages and carried them to his desk on a metal tray. He had been reading late the night before, and it took him a few moments to clear enough room from the mass of papers for his work. He set the tray down and rubbed his hands a few times to bring the feeling back into his fingers. It was cold in the garret apartment that served as his workroom, but at least it left him undisturbed by his guests on the floors below. And though the disrepair of the house was an inconvenience, at least the dismal state of the neighborhood meant that no neighbors would care much about the lights he kept burning late at night or about the occasional assortment of smells, fires, and explosions that were bound to happen in the pursuit of scientific discovery.

Rubbing his hands a little bit more to make sure they had the necessary dexterity, Friedrich selected a scalpel from the pencil case he used to house his supplies. He had found it the best way to protect them when not in use. A burst of morning sun shone in through the nearby window and momentarily blinded him. When it had receded behind the clouds, he rubbed his eyes with the back of his hand and fought back a rush of fatigue. He had fallen asleep at his desk again shortly before sunrise, leaving him with only a couple hours of rest to fortify himself.

Friedrich glanced back at the cot that served as his bed, which was crammed into one corner. It was too short for him, of course, so he had extended it with a few piles of books below the footboard. It did the job, but he doubted that it was really the best substitute for proper accommodations.

Don't be so fussy! Friedrich chided himself. *The Work! The Work! Better a few years of exhaustion and starvation than to give up the search for the greatest secret in the world!*

And having assured himself with his morning affirmation, Friedrich shook his head, blinked a few times, and looked back at the dead rats on his desk.

"I am sorry my little friends," he whispered. "I wish you had not died, but know that your sacrifice will one day conquer death itself."

The corpses stared back at him, unmoving, unspeaking, and silently judging him.

Why did we have to die? their eyes demanded. *Why did you fail us? You promised to find the secret ten years ago, Friedrich! Why haven't you done it yet? Why do you always fail?*

As he began cutting, Friedrich knew that he had no answer, only the fleeting hope that it might one day be so. One day there would be a rat who would look back at him, alive, and thank him for being made immortal.

* * * *

Friedrich woke as the door opened. He did not remember falling asleep. Momentarily confused, he grabbed a nearby scalpel and lunged to his feet before he had properly regained his senses. In that instance, he felt certain of danger and of nothing else. There was an instinctual determination to survive this as yet unseen threat, a voice whispering to strike first before death could crush him in its hungry jaws....

"Good morning, Friedrich."

It was Zoya, who stood in the doorway, her hair and hands mostly clean of paint. She eyed the scalpel in Friedrich's hand and smiled at him, though her eyes were hesitant.

"Bad dreams?"

Friedrich looked down at the blade in his hand and quickly tossed it onto the desk.

"I…I do not recall," he answered. "I didn't realize I had fallen asleep again."

"You and your sleepless nights," Zoya said, stepping into the room and closing the door behind her. "They'll be the death of you."

Friedrich laughed. "Nonsense. If that rats haven't killed me yet, I have nothing to fear from a little fatigue."

"Mmm," Zoya answered. "Your rats." She walked to the nearest cages and examined the rats as they scurried about behind the bars. "What ever do you do with them, Friedrich?"

"I have conversations," Friedrich said, the hint of a grin tugging at the corner of his mouth.

"Before or after you cut them open?"

"A bit of both," Friedrich admitted.

Zoya laughed. "Do not feel badly about it. I scold my paintbrushes when no one is watching."

"Pleased to know I'm not the only madman in the house."

"What would a madhouse be without the mad?" Zoya answered, smirking at her own joke. "But at least we are a respectable madhouse."

"Because of the drunks?" Friedrich asked. "Or because of the socialists?"

"The drunks, of course. Any respectable man might be a drunk. Indeed, most of them are. But a socialist…he might be sober."

"God forbid," Friedrich said, laughing. "Sobriety will be the death of us."

"Now you sound like Wilhelm," Zoya said.

"He's not a complete fool," Friedrich replied. "Stanislav likes him."

"Stanislav likes everyone," Zoya countered, her smile growing as she approached Friedrich slowly, one careful step at a time. "He even likes Karel."

"I like Karel."

"Then you're more the fool," Zoya said. "He's a self-righteous bourgeoisie pretending to be an artist, and I'm surprised you even give him the time of day."

"You give him the time of day," Friedrich replied.

"He's pretty. That doesn't mean I like him."

"He is pretty," Friedrich agreed. "Stanislav thinks he has a poet's soul, and he pays rent once in a while, so he's welcome here."

"Even if his poems are dreadful?" Zoya asked.

Friedrich nodded. "Even if his poems are dreadful. But they aren't dreadful, are they?"

Zoya sighed. "Not entirely, no."

Friedrich poured himself a cup of water from a glass decanter. Then, remembering his manners, he quickly cleaned a second cup with his handkerchief and filled it as well. He offered the first one to Zoya.

"Thirsty?"

"Parched," Zoya said, taking the cup. "After all, I need my voice for when our guest arrives." She looked at the clock on Friedrich's desk. "And that won't be long now, I wager."

"Guest?" Friedrich asked.

"Good Lord!" Zoya exclaimed. "Your aunt, Friedrich. Don't you remember?"

Despite the chastisement, Friedrich smiled at the news. "Really? Aunt Ekaterine is coming here today?" he asked. Then it hit him. Of Course! Zoya was painting Ekaterine's portrait. "The painting."

"Yes."

"Aren't you supposed to go to her house for that?"

Zoya frowned. "Apparently artists aren't welcome in respectable houses, so she's coming here for the portrait." She shrugged. "Still, it saves me a journey."

"I suppose that's a small mercy."

"I'm not accustomed to small mercies, Friedrich. I wouldn't know one if I encountered it."

Friedrich considered this and nodded. "Of course."

Zoya paused a moment and then grinned. "Smile, Friedrich," she said. "Your pretty aunt is coming. It's a reason for us both to smile."

"That's the truth," Friedrich agreed. "An odd observation, but a true one."

"You've never taken fault with my odd observations," Zoya said.

"No, nor will I." There was a pause as Friedrich wondered just how much time he had to make himself presentable. "When is Auntie arriving?"

* * * *

Ekaterine arrived promptly at the stroke of ten. She made a point of being punctual. There was no point in making appearances among the people of the outer world if one did not meet a proper schedule. She had the Shashavani reputation to uphold, even if no one else understood the significance.

She knocked on the door of Friedrich's dilapidated town house and waited politely to be seen in. It took two sets of knocks before the door was answered, but Ekaterine was in no hurry. The Doctor and Lord Iosef might have business in Prague, but she had none. It was no trouble to wait a few extra minutes for the amusement of having her portrait painted. Indeed, the entire trip was little more than a holiday!

Eventually the door was answered by a bleary-eyed man with dark hair and a beard. He rubbed his face a few times before he managed to ask:

"Hello? Who are you?"

"I am Ekaterine Shashavani," Ekaterine replied, smiling warmly and offering her hand.

"Oh," the man said, sounding a little confused. "I am…drunk."

"Splendid!" Ekaterine shook the man's hand and, as she did, pushed her way inside the house. "I'm here to have my portrait painted. Isn't that fun?"

"*Da?*" the man replied. It was more of a question than an answer.

"Goodness, Auntie!" came a cry from the top of the stairs.

Ekaterine turned and saw Friedrich standing on the upstairs landing, looking rather unkempt but still a little handsome. A little. He did need to shave again, poor boy. The artist, Zoya, was at his side, and Ekaterine raised a hand to greet her.

"Hello Miss Chromoluminarist," Ekaterine said.

"Muse!" Zoya exclaimed, and she rushed down the decaying stairs to greet Ekaterine. She stopped a few steps away and examined Ekaterine closely. "Yes…yes, this will do. You are bright with the sun, Muse. It pleases me."

Surprised at the comment, Ekaterine glanced behind herself, looking for the source of the comment. "The door is still open."

"All the same," Zoya said.

Taking Ekaterine's hand, Zoya pulled her toward the parlor. Ekaterine looked toward Friedrich, who was now hurrying down the stairs toward them.

"Hello Alis…er…Friedrich!" she called. "Wonderful to see you! Your mother sends her greetings…oh!"

Ekaterine found herself pulled into the parlor with such force that she nearly lost her footing. She followed Zoya to a chair by the fireplace, near the easel and the table of painting supplies. The fire was burning low, barely as bright as the morning sun that trickled in from behind the shuttered windows. There were people lying half asleep on the sofa, the chairs, and the mattresses spread across the room. Ekaterine recognized some of them from her prior visit with Varanus; but there were a few assorted others whom she had not met before. It seemed that Friedrich's home was a sort of flophouse for those of the artistic and revolutionary persuasions.

She waited as Zoya opened a few windows to let in the sunlight and stoked the fire with an iron poker. The sudden influx of light brought about cries and oaths from the local sleepers who were caught in the brightness. In particular, Ekaterine recognized the Hungarian girl, Erzsebet, lying in the arms of the violinist, Stanislav. As the morning light washed across them, Erzsebet blinked a few times. Presently, she pushed away Stanislav's arms and sat up, rubbing her eyes.

"By the fire, Muse!" Zoya exclaimed, leading Ekaterine to the chair by the fireplace. "Yes, yes, the light will be perfect for you!"

Ekaterine sat and carefully arranged her skirts. She enjoyed the extravagance of these European dresses, though she had to confess a certain sadness at how they had changed in the ten years since she had last worn them regularly. They lacked the complexity that had previously entertained her. And the sleeves were dreadful.

But no matter. She was someone's muse. That was entertainment enough for her short sojourn in Prague.

"Like this?" she asked, sitting by the fire and striking a pose with her chin on her palm.

Zoya looked at her and sighed. "So very bourgeois. Still, it cannot be helped."

"Better bourgeois than aristocratic?" Ekaterine ventured. Truly, she had little interest in the mores of the modern world and equally little knowledge of prevailing political views.

One of the half-slumbering revolutionaries scoffed. "Better an aristocrat than a bourgeoisie!" he grumbled. "Aristocracy will collapse on its own! The bourgeoisie must be torn down!"

"Go back to sleep, Wilhelm!" Zoya snapped, as she continued posing Ekaterine.

Ekaterine glanced toward the doorway and saw Friedrich enter, looking a little sheepish at the state of the place.

"Do forgive the mess, Auntie," he said, joining her. "I fear things can become rather chaotic when the wine is flowing."

"It sounds like I have been missing all the best parties," Ekaterine replied, smiling at him. Friedrich was quite handsome and it was nice to smile in his company, but he was still Varanus's son and that made it unthinkable to do anything else.

"You could always join us some evening," Friedrich told her.

"And miss a delightful evening with Mister Stoker?" Ekaterine asked. She gasped at the thought. "Unthinkable. He has become my favorite comedian. Even Miss Radcliffe is jealous."

"Well, anyone who could supplant Ann Radcliffe..." Friedrich ventured with a little uncertainty.

Ekaterine did not blame him for his half-heartedness. During their mutual stay in London ten years ago, Friedrich had ventured into the realm of the Gothic novel in an attempt to impress her. But since the whole ordeal had been overshadowed by murder and bloodshed, Ekaterine did not think it fair to consider the attempt any real success.

Suddenly, the sound of loud meowing interrupted them both. Ekaterine looked down and saw a sizable cat with puffy white fur at her feet. It was probably an Angora from Turkey, if Ekaterine judged it right. It looked at her with big blue eyes and made noises like it expected her to pet it, or feed it, or conquer the world in its name; in all likelihood, any of the three would have sufficed in a pinch.

"Why hello there," Ekaterine said softly. She carefully reached out and stroked the cat's fur. When it responded with pleased sounds, Ekaterine gently pulled the mass of fur into her lap. "And what is your name? I am going to call you Tinatin."

"That's Jadwiga," Zoya said, in the midst of mixing her paints.

"Jadwiga?" Ekaterine asked. She didn't necessarily dislike the name, but it was hardly a fitting name for a cat!

"Stanislav named her," Friedrich explained. "She's named for the Queen of Poland in the fourteenth century. A magnificent monarch."

"That sounds like a marvelous pedigree," Ekaterine agreed. She stroked the cat, who replied with an approving purr. "But her name is Tinatin, and I shall be adamant about that."

By now, Erzsebet had joined them. She yawned softly and asked, "Who is renaming the cat?"

"Jadwiga," Friedrich said.

"Tinatin," Ekaterine corrected.

Friedrich sighed. "Jadwiga."

"Tinatin."

"Zoya," Friedrich said, "please tell Aunt Ekaterine—"

"I take the side of my muse," Zoya answered. "Tinatin it is."

"But—" Friedrich protested.

Zoya glanced at Ekaterine and nodded. "I like the cat. It adds a...*je ne sais quoi*. Very feline."

"Literally speaking, yes," Ekaterine agreed, unable to hide a giggle.

Zoya paused and then directed with her paintbrush.

"Erzsebet, why don't you sit by the muse while you both enjoy the fire. That's right.... Her, the cat, you, the wall. There's a theme here. I don't know for certain what it is, but I'll have it sorted out eventually."

"Oh!" Erzsebet exclaimed, sounding surprised and a little frightened at being addressed directly. She slowly knelt next to Ekaterine. "Like this?"

Ekaterine took the girl's hand and smiled at her. "Marvelous. Just like that."

This seemed to reassure Erzsebet, and she gave Ekaterine a quick smile in return.

Zoya paused a moment and looked at them in the midst of her painting. "Perhaps a little to the right…" she ventured.

"It's perfect," Ekaterine answered. Having successfully settled both Erzsebet and the cat into a comfortable pose, she was in no mood to displace either of them.

Zoya looked at her and sighed, though the frustration was accompanied by the hint of a grin.

"Oh, Muse, you'll be the death of me."

CHAPTER EIGHT

Early Spring, 1899

Varanus had retired to the parlor to read, as she often did in the evening. Tonight she had a series of papers she had collected over the preceding years regarding the properties of Röntgen rays, advancements in the study of radiant matter, and in particular, new elements discovered through a careful examination of uraninite ore. Varanus made a note to secure a quantity of uraninite before returning home—after all, there was plenty of it mined there in Bohemia from the mountains along the German border. She was curious to see the reality of this "polonium" and "radium" and to study their properties firsthand. And with her examination of the Shashavani condition slowly stumbling into forced inactivity, perhaps the science of radioactivity would offer her a sufficient diversion.

She looked up from her reading and rubbed her eyes. The room was very dark, even for her sight. It must be quite late, for the fire had burned down until it was now little more than coals. Varanus had turned the gaslights down for privacy when she first arrived in the parlor, and in the absence of the firelight, their illumination was feeble and flickering.

What hour is it? she wondered. The windows were heavily curtained so they gave no indication. It might be well into the small hours for all she knew.

Varanus reached for the pocket watch that dangled with her ring of house keys from a chain at her waist. She checked the time and found it to be a quarter to midnight. Not at all late by her standards, but still.... For all she knew, the whole house had already retired for bed. Well, most of the house at any rate. Ekaterine would still be up, giggling by candlelight at some literary absurdity, and Lord Iosef's hours were as unpredictable as those that Varanus kept. And after all, he did have a guest.

She did not hear the door as it opened, nor did she hear the steps of the person who entered, muffled as they were by the heavy carpet. But still, Varanus *knew* that someone was there. She turned in her chair and looked toward the doorway. She saw a figure there, silhouetted in black against the flickering shadows of the hall, looming in the darkness, ominous, sinister, and indistinct.

"Good evening, *Fräulein*," Julius said, as he advanced into the parlor. He kept his aristocratic poise, but still he smiled warmly at the sight of her. "I hope I have not disturbed you."

Varanus smiled a little. "Not at all, *Fremder*. I was reading by firelight."

"What precious little there is of it," Julius noted.

"All the more reason for a distraction," Varanus said.

She reached for a poker by the fireplace and stoked the fire. Though reduced to coals and ashes, the fire blossomed at the poker's touch, pushing back the darkness with a gentle amber glow.

"Have you and my husband finished for the evening?" Varanus asked.

"Only just," Julius answered. "The art of translation is as arduous as it is rewarding." He motioned to the vacant armchair next to Varanus. "May I sit?"

Varanus laughed softly and replied, "Of course, Count. To think that you should need to ask by now. This has rather become our weekly ritual, hasn't it?"

"I suppose it has," Julius agreed as he sat in the adjacent chair. The dim light of the fire warmed his face as he smiled at Varanus and glinted in his clear blue eyes. "During the day I have my conversations with your husband, and at night I have my conversations with you, *Fräulein*. And truly, I cannot say which I enjoy more."

There was something in his tone that hinted he did know, but that he knew better than to confess it. It was hardly appropriate for a man to admit to enjoying the company of his friend's wife more than that of his friend, but the hint of it made Varanus laugh softly. That was the thing with Julius: she could never quite tell if his decorum was sincere or playful, and she found the uncertainty quite enjoyable.

"Well, I won't tell Lord Iosef," she said. "Your secret is safe."

Julius chuckled. "Thank you, *Fräulein*," he said, using the name he had called her by when they first met. It had become something of a joke between them over the past few months: the *Fräulein* and the *Fremder*, the Maiden and the Stranger, even though neither was true.

"I would not want His Highness to object to my visiting his wife in private every evening," Julius continued. He paused and the corner of his mouth twisted into a smirk. "Oh dear, that sounded rather dreadful, didn't it?"

"Only slightly," Varanus said. "And besides, it isn't every night. Only once or twice a week. I hear even the crowned heads of Europe do that."

"How right you are, *Fräulein*," Julius said, gently inclining his head toward her. "If an evening rendezvous is proper for the House of Habsburg, twice a week must be acceptable for us."

The two of them looked at each other and shared a quiet laugh. Varanus rested her chin on her hand and smiled at Julius.

"You are a wicked man, Count von Raabe," she said. "If these past weeks had not taught me otherwise, I might believe that you meant something untoward."

"Heaven forbid," Julius replied softly, though his tone and his smile said quite the opposite. "I am a gentleman, of course. A gentleman does not make insinuations in the house of a friend."

"He does other things," Varanus agreed.

"Like have conversations," Julius answered.

Varanus grinned at him. After a moment's pause, she asked, "Would you care for a drink, Count?"

"Julius," he corrected. "As I am ever reminding both you and His Highness, it is simply Julius. And yes, I would enjoy a drink, as long as you will join me."

"Of course, *Julius*," Varanus agreed.

She started to rise from her chair, but Julius quickly stood and stopped her.

"Allow me, please," he said, flashing a smile. "I like to be of use."

Varanus could not hide a smirk as she replied, "Thank you, Julius. There should be a decanter of brandy on that table there."

It was probably Luka's, but he would survive her using it. As Julius faded into the shadows in search of the drinks, Varanus turned her eyes toward the low-burning fire. She gazed at the embers as they popped and danced upon the hearth, and she felt herself smiling again. She did very much enjoy her conversations with Julius, however they might joke about them.

"Ah, I have found it!" Julius announced from the darkness. His words were soon accompanied by the soft clink of glass upon glass and the sound of pouring liquid.

Varanus glanced in Julius's direction and caught sight of his chair. There was Korbinian, seated just as Julius had been only a minute before. Korbinian's face was pale, his eyes were sad, and a single droplet of blood trickled down his cheek.

"Are you enjoying yourself, *Liebchen?*" he asked.

"I am," Varanus answered, her voice barely a whisper. Despite herself she was angry with Korbinian for having interrupted the pleasant stillness of the evening.

"And what a charming man is the Count von Raabe, yes?"

"We are only having a conversation."

Korbinian smiled sadly. "I am told that is what the Habsburgs do."

"Are you jealous, my love?" Varanus asked softly.

"*Liebchen*..." Korbinian murmured. "Of course. What man could not be jealous of you?"

Varanus felt herself shiver as Korbinian continued to look into her eyes with his mournful gaze. He seemed not quite sad and not quite angry, but altogether troubled. Jealousy indeed.

"Ah, and here we are," Julius said, almost making Varanus jump with surprise. He stepped around the now-empty chair and offered a glass of brandy to Varanus before sitting and taking a sip of his own.

"Thank you, Julius," Varanus said. Her voice was distant, distracted by the vision of Korbinian, so she quickly blinked a few times to right herself. Korbinian was clearly in one of his moods, and that was no concern of hers.

"Truly," Julius continued, "though it is pleasant to jest about it, I would never seek to cause disruption between you and the Prince. Such a charming household should never be troubled by romantic intrigues."

"It is very gentlemanly of you to make that clear, Julius," Varanus said. "But in truth, I do not think he would much mind."

"For one so young, he has a very broad-minded view of his wife," Julius mused. He sounded concerned about this. "It is not my place to pry, of course, but...."

Varanus laughed. "It is not a loveless marriage. You need not fear that I am a beleaguered woman pining away in silence and propriety."

"Good," Julius said, his smile quickly returning. He reached out and placed one hand atop hers. "For were that the case, I would be obliged to do something about it."

"As a gentleman?" Varanus ventured, smirking.

"As a gentleman," Julius agreed.

Varanus took another drink and considered how best to explain her relationship with Iosef in terms that would make sense to a mortal. In the meantime, Julius did not withdraw his hand, and Varanus found no reason to object.

"Iosef is a man of intellect rather than passion," she explained. "I find that his mind is moved far more often than his heart."

"But surely..." Julius countered. "A young man in the full bloom of youth...." His eyes twinkled. "And with so beautiful a wife.... I doubt even the Pope could restrain himself were he privileged to be your husband."

"At his age, I think health more than restraint would be the cause of inactivity," Varanus replied sardonically. She and Julius shared a grin at this, which she enjoyed. "No, truly, Iosef and I share a marriage of scholarship more than anything else. We have affection for one another, but it is hardly the fiery passion of youth." She took another drink and said, "You must have wondered why a man so young chose to marry a woman old enough to be his mother. A woman already married once before."

"I did not think it polite to ask," Julius answered. "And besides, were it not for the fact that I trust your word implicitly, I would insist you were exaggerating. You look older than the Prince by a matter of years, not decades."

"Milk bathing," Varanus replied without missing a beat.

"Not blood?" Julius asked. "I understand that one Hungarian countess found it very efficacious."

Varanus almost laughed aloud at the suggestion and at Julius's complete ignorance as to its deeper significance.

"Nonsense," Varanus said. "I can barely stand the sight of blood. I certainly wouldn't do anything like bathe in it."

But as she spoke of bathing in blood, she found her mind turning quite unexpectedly to the events that had transpired in the Shashavani valley five years earlier. She had bathed in blood then: her own and her enemies'. And for a moment she found herself quite unable to breathe as flickers of memory danced before her eyes.

The touch of Julius's fingertips against her cheek brought Varanus back with a start. Her hands clenched into fists, and it took all of her self-control to keep from shattering the glass she held.

"Babette?" Julius asked, his voice soft and pleasant like honey. "Are you alright? You seemed to have vanished for a moment."

The moment of panic gone, Varanus quickly took a deep breath and laughed.

"Oh, you must forgive me," she said. "I fear the brandy has gone right to my head."

Julius smiled at her and said, "That's not true."

"No, it isn't," Varanus agreed. "But I assure you that I am well. Just a momentary thought."

"Of course." Julius withdrew his hand, allowing his fingertips to stroke Varanus's cheek. He placed his hand atop Varanus's again and gave it a gentle squeeze. "But if you are troubled by something, I do hope you will tell me."

"I am troubled by one thing," Varanus said. "Not your fault at all, Julius, but kindly do not refer to me as 'Babette'." She let a moment pass before she explained, "I much prefer 'Varanus', if you don't mind."

"Of course, *Fräulein*," Julius replied. "Varanus it shall be. It is a very good name. I enjoy saying it."

Varanus gave Julius a pleasant smile. "And Julius...."

"*Ja?*"

"You are still holding my hand."

"So I am," Julius answered. He looked into Varanus's eyes and slowly raised her hand to his lips. "Shall I stop?"

"Not on my account," Varanus said softly.

CHAPTER NINE

That same night Friedrich was in his laboratory at the top of his crumbling house, feeling the weight of hopelessness pressing down upon him. After months of experimentation and a decade of work, he found himself faced with yet another failure. Again the rats were dead, riddled with tumors and physically distorted by the solution he had given them. Indeed, these latest results were among the most hideous; their bodies seemed to have gone mad, devouring themselves through rapid overgrowth and cellular collapse. And it was all the more frustrating that these had been his most promising subjects. These rats had shown real signs of improvement. For weeks their aging had slowed, they had become more active and revitalized, and the oldest ones had even shown signs of returning youth.

Until the tumors and the decay set in.

Friedrich sat hunched over his desk with his face in his hands, struggling not to weep or to scream with despair. He had been so close! He had seen the results that he had been struggling to find for the past eleven years! But again it was for nothing! It always seemed that the closer to success he came, the more horrible the ultimate fate of his subjects. He was at his wits' end; and worse, he simply could not bring himself to try again. It was not just the repeated failure that left him exhausted, but also the sheer cruelty of it all. His test subjects were only rats, but still he had murdered them. And for what? A few days of youthful vigor? Even an animal had the right for its death to carry some meaning, and without a success, all of their deaths were meaningless. Could he really continue killing them in some vain, arrogant hope that one day something might come of it? What if these poor beasts had been men? Could his conscience have borne the weight of that? Surely not!

Friedrich rubbed his face and sighed. He had almost forgotten how it felt to *not* be exhausted. Perhaps that was the trouble: he was too tired to think clearly. He was making mistakes.

"Friedrich?"

Friedrich turned at the sound of his name. He saw Erzsebet leaning in from the hallway, one hand raised to catch his attention. She was always very polite about respecting his privacy, unlike the others. But she was the youngest, so perhaps that was to be expected. She had not yet learned to take his generosity for granted.

"Erzsebet, what is it?" Friedrich asked, slowly rising from his chair.

"Oh…" Erzsebet replied, suddenly at a loss for words. "I just wondered if you meant to join us tonight. Stanislav asked about you, so I thought I'd check on you."

Friedrich smiled and quickly brushed off his waistcoat. Like much of the room, his clothes were covered in chemicals and soot. Accepting the opportunity for a distraction from his recent melancholy, he joined Erzsebet at the door.

"Yes, I suppose I have been a bit reclusive tonight," he said.

"*Tonight?*" Erzsebet asked, incredulous despite her polite tone.

"All month," Friedrich admitted. He sighed. "The work has been very demanding."

Erzsebet smiled at Friedrich and took his hand. "Come," she said. "Zoya wants to paint my portrait tonight. Why don't you sit with me while she does?"

Friedrich glanced back at his desk, then at the cages of the rats, whose numbers had diminished considerably since last year. There was a twinge of guilt and shame at his repeated failures. And he suddenly realized how badly he needed to get away. Why shouldn't he spend an evening with his friends instead of laboring on with an experiment he knew was doomed to failure?

"I think I shall," he said.

* * * *

There was a party in full bloom in the parlor when Friedrich and Erzsebet arrived. The whole house was in attendance, along with several others Friedrich did not recognize—his guests invited so many people to visit he could scarcely keep track of who was who. Karel was reading delightfully bad poetry to a pair of shop girls in the corner. Stanislav was arguing with Ilya and Wilhelm in the center of the room, along with three other men and a woman Friedrich recognized as fellow revolutionaries. A few hangers-on were drunkenly reenacting *Parsifal* by the fireplace, their loud tones competing with the arguments of the socialists and with Karel's poetry.

Zoya had sought some sort of refuge near the one gas lamp that worked properly, and she was setting up a backdrop for Erzsebet's portrait complete with ostrich feathers and the cat Jadwiga—or "Tinatin" as Aunt Ekaterine had taken to calling her. Zoya was clearly the only member of the party close to sobriety, and Friedrich could also tell that she was more or less infuriated by the intrusion of the drunken troubadours into the region of the fireplace, which she so often claimed as her personal workspace.

"There you are!" Zoya exclaimed at Erzsebet. "Where have you…?" She paused. "Oh, good, you've brought Friedrich. Perhaps he can talk some sense into that boyfriend of yours." She called across the room to Friedrich: "Those actors are ruining my light, Stanislav's revolutionaries are ruining my peace, and Karel is ruining.… Well, he's ruining everything, *as usual!*"

Karel pointed a finger at Zoya and replied, "*Sic transit gloria mundi*, my dear Zoya!" before returning to some sentimental ode to beauty that seemed to have engrossed the shop girls.

Friedrich gave Zoya a nod. She might pretend that all the noise was a mere inconvenience, but Friedrich understood the artistic temperament, so similar is it to the scientific. The clamor of intoxication was worse than a distraction: it was practically a wall against which the artistic mind had no hope of prevailing.

He quickly dropped onto the sofa next to Stanislav and was struck by the full force of the drunken argument.

"Wilhelm," Stanislav said, waving his hand to articulate his point, "we are all revolutionaries here, aren't we?" He put an arm around Friedrich's shoulders and grinned. "Even Freddie here."

"Of course we are, of course we are," Wilhelm replied, a little too drunk to be fully coherent. "But you are talking about nationalism, Stanislav! And nationalism is the enemy of revolution!"

"That is nonsense," Stanislav answered. "All I am saying is that the Czech people have a right to be free from the Austrian yoke. How is that nationalism?"

"Because you put your country before your cause," answered one of the other socialists—a Frenchman named Nicolas. "A bourgeois Czech is the same as a bourgeois Austrian. A worker in Bohemia is the same as a worker in France."

"I know many Austrians who would claim differently," Stanislav answered. His tone was playful, but there was an edge behind it.

"Your true comrades are the working class, not anyone else of any nation," insisted Veronica, a visiting Englishwoman of Stanislav's acquaintance. She had apparently joined them for a few weeks while on her way to agitate for social reform elsewhere in the British Empire. "Socialism will free the world, Stanislav, not nationalism. In nationalism there are only chains."

"I do not question socialism!" Stanislav insisted. He paused a moment to fill a glass of something from an almost empty bottle. He pressed the glass into Friedrich's hand. "I am glad you joined us, Freddie. You had better drink fast!" Then he turned back to the others and said, "But consider this, my friends: I want to live in a socialist republic as much as any of you do. But I want to live in a Socialist Republic of the Czechs, not of the Austrians, or the Russians, or the English, or the French!" He pointed at each of his fellows as he named their nationalities. "For too long we have been ruled by foreigners; and when the revolution comes, I intend to see our Austrian overlords overthrown just as surely as our class enemies are overthrown. If that is nationalism, then I am a nationalist!"

Friedrich gave Stanislav an encouraging slap on the shoulder, but he knew better than to get involved in the argument. However generous his purse, he was an aristocrat. He took a quick sip of the drink he had been given and found it to be some bitter concoction that went down hard and felt delightfully warm afterward. Friedrich quickly finished his glass and poured himself another.

"But don't you see, Stanislav?" Ilya protested. "When the revolution comes, there will be no need for nations. There will be no Republic of Czechy any more than there will be a Republic of Austria or a Republic of Russia. That is bourgeois thinking. There will be only a single socialist state. A republic, perhaps, but perhaps not! For democracies are so easily swayed by the wealth and deception of the bourgeoisie!"

"But there will only be one socialist state," Wilhelm insisted. "And we will all live there in harmony, whether German, or Russian, or French, or Czech."

"Or English," reminded Veronica, lest the Continentals forget the rest of the world.

"*Ja, ja*, Miss Wilson: also the English," Wilhelm agreed with intoxicated enthusiasm. "Even the Poles!"

Friedrich cleared his throat and said, "Wilhelm, I know you mean well, but the way you say 'even the Poles' doesn't really inspire confidence."

The Poles had every right to be part of the revolution, even if their county had been carved up a hundred years ago. Indeed, being without a state, it seemed logical that they had even more of a stake in the revolution than the Germans or the Russians!

"And what language will we speak in this universal socialist utopia of yours?" Stanislav asked.

"What?" Wilhelm asked in confusion.

"What language?" Stanislav repeated. He grinned at Friedrich like the two were conspiring in some secret plot against the others. He tapped his glass against Friedrich's and took a drink. "Come on, tell me."

"Well, I…" Ilya stammered.

"We needn't have just one," Nicolas said.

"Of course we must," Stanislav insisted. "One state, one language. The bourgeoisie use our many languages to cause division and confusion. A universal state must have only one, unless every nation will have its own socialist county and therefore its own language...."

Stanislav grinned at Friedrich as he spoke.

"Sneaky devil," Friedrich said, raising his glass in a toast, which Stanislav mimicked with his own glass. They both quickly drank and refilled.

"German!" Wilhelm announced suddenly. "Marx and Engels wrote in German. It is logical that our new state should use the same language."

"Here, here," agreed one of the other revolutionaries.

"Nonsense," Veronica protested. "The language of our new state should be the language of the country where the revolution first begins. And that country must be—"

"*La France!*" Nicolas announced proudly.

"Russia!" Ilya answered. "For what country is so oppressed as Russia? It is there that the revolution will surely begin, so it is Russian that all true revolutionaries must speak!"

"You see?" Stanislav asked. "Russian? English? German? French? But not Polish, or Irish, or Croatian, or Czech. This is why I must be both a nationalist and a revolutionary. Because it is so easy for you whose nations rule other nations to say that we will all be equal under your banner. But it is much harder for us who are under the thumb not only of the bourgeoisie but of *your* bourgeoisie. Tell me Wilhelm, if the revolution began in Warsaw would you throw off your German-ness and become part of a Polish socialism? Or you, Nicolas? If the revolution began in Indochina, would you so gladly renounce France and embrace your Asian brothers?"

The others were silent, looking annoyed at Stanislav's line of questioning.

"No?" Stanislav mused. "So I ask again, comrades, what language will we speak in this post-national utopia?"

"Latin," said Erzsebet.

Friedrich looked up, surprised at hearing her voice. The revolutionaries looked surprised as well. Young Erzsebet stood a few feet away, addressing them timidly but with conviction.

"What?" Ilya demanded. "Latin?"

Erzsebet paused for a moment and glanced back at Zoya, who gave her a reassuring wink.

"Latin," she repeated. "It is a dead language. It is simple enough to learn and so many intellectuals know it, but still no nation uses it. So it wouldn't give preference to anyone."

"Of all the…" Wilhelm began.

But Stanislav laughed aloud. He bounded to his feet and rushed to Erzsebet, pulling her into his arms and kissing her.

"My darling girl, putting us all to shame! Here we are arguing, and she is the one to give us an answer." He sighed sadly. "If only it were so simple."

"Isn't it?" Friedrich asked, rising from the sofa and joining them. He put a hand on Stanislav's shoulder. "It seems to me she's rather answered your question." He threw a glance at the other revolutionaries. "And provided the answer none of you could. I think that's cause for praise, really."

Stanislav coughed a little, looking frustrated at having been up-staged, both in front of Erzsebet and in front of his revolutionary friends. But he gave Friedrich a sincere smile and slapped him on the ribs.

"How right you are, Freddie. After all, we are men, not beasts. Compromise is our gift from nature, as savagery is theirs. It does not matter who provides the answer, so long as an answer is given, yes?"

This last question was directed toward Ilya and the others. There was a moment of hesitation before camaraderie and inebriation won out, and they all raised their glasses with a resounding "Yes!"

"…et Filii et Spiritus Sancti," Karel intoned from across the room. He glanced up at the loud shouting. "What?"

This brought laughter from the others, even Zoya, who still looked irritated at everyone and everything for disturbing her work.

"Oh, never mind, Karel," she said. "Erzsebet, come here will you? There will be plenty of time to give these fools sensible answers they won't remember in the morning. But I have a portrait to paint, and I think the actors have finally passed out. Now come along before they sober up and start reciting again!"

The command was half serious and half in jest, and it made Erzsebet laugh. She took a step toward Zoya and then turned back.

"Oh, Freddie, will you sit with me for my painting?" she asked.

But a thought had taken Friedrich. It was what Stanislav had said. Men, not beasts. What if that were all the difference?

"Um…" he said, stammering as his thoughts and his speech collided. "Just…um…. Five minutes, Erzsebet…Zoya. I only need five minutes…."

And with that, he stumbled to the door, his head spinning half from the sudden revelation and half from the five—had it been five?—drinks he had downed in his brief time in the parlor. As he went, he heard one of the revolutionaries ask:

"He's an odd one. Is he mad or something?"

"Don't mind him," Wilhelm replied. "He's just a scientist."

* * * *

In a daze, Friedrich rushed back to his laboratory. His head swam and his ears sang from the heavy drink he had imbibed. It would pass soon; it always did. But there had been enough of it in so short a space of time that, coupled with fatigue, it had left him rather tipsy. But in that hint of inebriation, he had found the key to his failure!

Not beast, but man! Of course the rats had succumbed to cancer and decay. Surely their bodies were weaker than that of a human, of a more highly developed creature almost two hundred pounds heavier than they! Just because their primitive forms could not withstand the rigors imposed upon them, it did not mean that man could not!

Friedrich stumbled against the door frame and shook his head. It was not really the drink so much as the exhaustion the plagued him so, but it was all the same. He had found the solution!

Stumbling to his work table, Friedrich measured out a syringe full of his latest formula. Already the blur of momentary intoxication was leaving him. It always did. He was so often the last person drunk and the first person sober. But sobriety would bring with it doubt and hesitation. What he needed now was action.

Rolling up his sleeve, Friedrich jabbed the syringe into his arm and injected a full double dose of the solution into his body.

Come what may, he thought, *let me be the test.*

Either he would be proven right or he would die. Either way, he had long passed the threshold of hesitation. No more experiments, no more failures, no more dead rats.

Death or immortality. That was all he would accept.

* * * *

It was with high spirits that Friedrich returned to the parlor a few minutes later. His head swam a little from the heavy drink, but true to form, the worst of the intoxication had passed. He would soon remedy that.

The revolutionaries were already far more into their cups, shouting at one another in incoherent debate and often pausing to tearfully embrace each other as comrades and toast their impending revolution. Stanislav jumped to his feet and embraced Friedrich when he entered. Friedrich hugged his friend back, tightly and with joy. None of the others would understand, but he had accomplished something wonderful tonight.

Friedrich took the bottle from the table and drank deeply from it before passing it to Stanislav and walking to Zoya's side. Zoya was already laying down the preliminary brush strokes for Erzsebet's portrait. It was more conventional than her usual style, a sure sign that she had been drinking. But of course! They had all been drinking, for what else were artists and revolutionaries to do when they were not changing the world?

"What do you think?" Zoya asked.

Friedrich studied the painting and then studied Erzsebet.

"Magnificent," he declared.

"Her or the painting?" Zoya asked.

This gave Friedrich pause, for he had not really considered the option of one or the other.

"Both?" he ventured.

Zoya chuckled, then sighed. "Oh Freddie. Still...I suppose there is only one person you have eyes for, no matter who poses in front of you."

Friedrich blinked a few times, slightly confused. It was not just the drink. He suddenly felt very warm. The injection had done something as well, filling his veins with heat and muddling his thoughts.

Zoya sighed. "Go and stand next to Erzsebet."

"Shouldn't it be Stanislav?" Friedrich asked.

"Stanislav is too busy with his friends," Zoya answered, casting a glanced toward the revolutionaries, who were even now in the midst of another argument. "Erzsebet wants a man in the picture. God knows why." There was a moment, and then Zoya's irritated expression softened a little. "It may as well be you."

"Right," Friedrich answered cheerfully. He hurried to Erzsebet's side as the edges of his vision began to blur. Was it the drink? Or the chemicals? He could not tell. But something was happening. Whether death or success, he had accomplished *something*.

Erzsebet looked up at Friedrich and smiled at him. Her eyes were wide and very pretty. Friedrich smiled back. She was like his niece, really. They all were, to be honest. He was the oldest, and he had to take care of them. It was why he had invited them into his home, decaying as it was. Well, into his private home: he could hardly risk their safety by housing them at the respectable Prague address he maintained for public purposes. This was a safe place where the police would never find them. They were all going to do great things, and they needed someone to take care of them until they did. But then there was the work, and it demanded so much time....

And why was his head spinning? Why was his blood on fire?

"Freddie?" Erzsebet asked softly, her expression growing concerned. "Are you well?"

Friedrich quickly smiled. "Of course," he answered, patting Erzsebet on the shoulder. "Now then, smile for Zoya."

"I'm not a photographer, you know," Zoya answered, looking as much amused as she was exasperated. "You don't have to pose. Just stand as you are. Just like that, Erzsebet, keep smiling." There was a short silence as she drew a few brush strokes. Then she looked at Friedrich and asked softly, "Are you sure you're well?"

Friedrich grinned. "Zoya, my dear, I am better than I have been in years."

CHAPTER TEN

A few days later, Julius surprised Varanus by calling on her at break-fast. Iosef and Ekaterine were there as well, and all three of them were busy reading—Varanus her scientific papers, Ekaterine another gothic novel, and Iosef an old manuscript of uncertain origin. They were not often in the same place at the same time, but a shared breakfast did allow them a few minutes each day to acquaint one another with any news of note.

She looked up from her work as their footman entered and unobtru-sively approached Iosef.

"Count von Raabe is at the door, Highness," he said softly. "I in-formed him that you and the family were at breakfast and that he could call again later, but he asked that I extend his special request to you."

"Of course, Pravec," Iosef said without looking up from his work. "Ask the Count to join us."

"Certainly, Highness."

The footman went out and promptly returned with Julius, who was rosy-cheeked and dressed for the brisk weather, and who smiled warmly at the sight of his new friends.

"Count von Raabe, Highness," Pravec announced.

"Thank you, Pravec," Varanus said. She gave Julius a friendly smile and inclined her head in greeting. "Count von Raabe, please join us. I will have some breakfast brought for you."

"Oh, thank you, but no," Julius replied, his tone warm and jovial. "I fear I cannot stay long."

"We certainly did not expect you this early, Count," Ekaterine said. She smirked and pointed at the heavy curtains. "Certainly not before evening. You have the treat of seeing our lightless dining room. Entirely my own invention, I might add."

"Of course," Julius replied, bowing his head to her. "The talk of Paris, I believe."

Ekaterine looked surprised. "Really? Who told them?"

Iosef suddenly looked up from his papers as if only just noticing that Julius had arrived. "Julius," he greeted, rising to his feet. "Is it Tuesday already?"

Julius laughed, but softly enough not to be impolite. "No, Your Highness, I fear I have called on you quite out of schedule."

"No matter," Iosef replied, sitting again. He motioned to an empty chair. "Come, sit. Have you eaten?"

"I have already dined," Julius replied, remaining by the door. "As I was telling the Princesses Shashavani, I cannot stay. I depart for Germany on the afternoon train."

"That's quite sudden," Varanus exclaimed. She had come to enjoy her late night conversations with Julius. It was most inconvenient to learn that he was leaving so suddenly, like a thief in the night.

"A thief under the cover of broad daylight?" Korbinian mused aloud from across the table.

Varanus looked and saw him seated in an empty chair beside Ekaterine, the same chair that Iosef had offered to Julius. There was a faint hint of blood upon his lips, but he seemed far more composed than he often did of late. Perhaps the hour had something to do with it.

As if in answer to her thoughts, Korbinian added, "I simply cannot abide a late night, *Liebchen*. Or the things one does in the dark."

What an absurd thing to say. She had hardly done anything at all. Yet.

"Running away from us so soon?" Ekaterine asked playfully. "Normally I don't terrify people away for at least six months."

The corner of Julius's mouth made a momentary grin before he asserted his Prussian composure and answered them all:

"No offense is intended, I assure you. I am required back at home for my family duties. I would have mentioned it some weeks ago, but I fear that I have become so engrossed in our work, Highness, that I rather lost all track of time."

"Is there some sort of emergency?" Varanus asked.

"Nothing of the kind," Julius assured her. "But you see, around this time of year my family hosts a sort of soiree at our home in Prussia. To celebrate the equinox as it were. It is all a great deal of fun. My wife is in command of all such matters, of course, so the arrangements are out of my hands; I fear I forgot how fast it was approaching until my son telegrammed me this morning asking when I planned to return!"

"An equinox party?" Varanus asked, almost laughing.

"An equinox party!" Ekaterine exclaimed. "Oh, that does sound like fun!"

Julius smiled. "I am pleased to hear that you find the idea exciting. In addition to rendering my most humble apologies for my sudden departure, I came here today to extend an invitation to your household to join us this year. It is only a small country affair, I grant you, surely nothing to compare to the great balls of Saint Petersburg, but I would be honored to have you join us as my guests."

Ekaterine gasped with delight and clapped her hands softly. Varanus smirked a little at her friend's excitement, but even though the party did not capture her enthusiasm, she was curious to learn more about Julius and his family. And besides, a trip to the country might be a nice escape from her continued frustrations over her work.

She glanced at Korbinian, expecting him to offer some comment on the matter, but suddenly he was gone, leaving only an empty chair. Indeed, his sudden disappearances were almost as unsettling as his unheralded arrivals.

"Hmm," Iosef mused, putting down his manuscript. "The equinox. That is…next week?"

"Yes," Julius replied. "But I invite you all to come for the week itself and to stay longer, if you prefer." He motioned to Iosef. "There are some texts I would like to show you, if you are interested. And you might enjoy taking a turn around our old Teutonic ruins. They are quite sublime."

Ekaterine gasped again and exclaimed, "Ruins!"

"Ekaterine, restrain yourself," Varanus told her, though she was unable to fully conceal a chuckle at Ekaterine's excitement. Who else could become so excited at the thought of visiting *abandoned* buildings rather than ones still in use?

"Marvelous ruins, Princess," Julius assured Ekaterine. He paused and turned to Varanus. "So you will all join us?"

"Yes, I think we shall," Varanus answered.

"And how many shall we prepare for? Is it only the three of you? And your servants, of course."

"Of course," Varanus agreed.

She paused for a moment, wondering if she ought to invite Friedrich along. It might do her son some good to get away from his decaying house and his nest of artists. Respectable company might be beneficial; well, as near to respectable as the aristocracy was ever likely to get.

But as she thought about it, Varanus realized that it was probably not a good idea to let Friedrich out in public at the moment. Last she had seen him, he had looked terribly unkempt, not to mention unhealthy. And who knew what sort of bad habits his recent lifestyle had impressed upon him. He needed a month on the Riviera, not at some polite society gathering.

She quickly put on a smile and said, "Yes, just us three. Everyone else in the family is…elsewhere."

* * * *

It was fitting that Varanus thought of her son, for he had spent a hellish night in his lab, feverishly examining himself for any sign of improvement. It was the same as it had been for the past several days: every hour looking in the mirror, measuring the lines and the weathering of his face, the luster of his hair, the tightness of his skin. Indeed, searching for any possible indication that the serum had worked.

But as with each hour before, each day before, he could detect no change. And worse, the very fatigue of sleeplessness and stress left him both looking and feeling older still. Was that the case? Had the mixture done the opposite work and was it slowly aging him, insidiously working its way into the fibers of his body, decaying them from within?

Friedrich's drunken enthusiasm that first night was now long gone. In its place was anxiety, which burned through his veins just like the intoxication of drink and the fever of the serum. Had he failed? Had he made a mistake? What had he been thinking?

Perhaps he had miscalculated the dosage. The rats had all showed at least some change within the first two days, some of it remarkable. But as Friedrich examined himself yet again, he found no indication of anything.

"I have failed," he whispered to himself. "I have utterly failed."

Friedrich's eyes fell upon his ledgers and papers and the countless piles of notes and formulae he had amassed over the course of his ten years of work. It had all been a failure. Each new thing he tried, each subtle alteration, each grandiose redesign failed. And Friedrich was so tired. He simply could not will himself to try again.

"What a mess I have made of it all," he murmured.

He had been so happy to learn that his mother was in Prague, for he had been certain that he was on the verge of success. What a stupid plan it had been: to solve the riddle of aging and death and to deliver the gift of immortality to her when she was still young enough to enjoy its blessing. And if, as he suspected, Mother had already uncovered the secret of youth, then he could have revealed his own success to her as a *fait accompli*, providing beyond a doubt that he was worthy of being her son.

But success eluded him yet again, as it always did.

Mother would be so disappointed in him when she found out. Perhaps it was a blessing Father was dead already so that he could never know what a fool his son had turned out to be.

If it was a test, then he had surely failed it. But why should he even believe that? There was no great mystery to be uncovered, no elixir of youth waiting for science to uncover. Mother looked young because she was fit and healthy and because she had mastered the art of appearance, like any aristocratic lady was expected to do. It had been naïveté that had driven Friedrich to even entertain another explanation.

Solve the riddle of death? Friedrich chided himself. *What a stupid notion!*

Ten years of work and all of it wasted.

Friedrich pulled open the desk drawer and took out his pistol—one of the new automatic Mausers he had bought the previous year. He held the weapon, feeling its weight in his hand just as he felt the weight of his failure pressing down upon his shoulders. Almost without realizing what he was doing, he raised the pistol and pressed the barrel to his temple.

How simple it would be to pull the trigger and end it all, to put a hole through his stupid brain that preferred flights of fancy to real science. He would be free of it all: of his failure, of his foolishness, of his memories of childhood, memories of Aunt Ilse and of the things she had done to him. Memories that he could never escape while he still lived.

His finger slowly pressed against the trigger, feeling the resistance of the smooth metal. Press. Press. All he had to do was press a little harder and it would all be over.

No. No, that was the easy way out. The coward's way out.

Friedrich pulled away from the Mauser and set it back down on his desk with a heavy thunk. Slowly, he lowered his head into his hands and felt his entire body shake with a silent scream of anguish. He had wasted ten years of his life with this immortality nonsense, and he would have to live with that shame.

Friedrich reached blindly for the bottle of brandy that he kept next to the lamp on his desk. He uncorked it and took a long drink. The warmth of the alcohol flooded through him.

"People die," he whispered to himself. "They grow old and die and you have to accept that." He looked at his papers again, seeing in the spidery writing all the self-righteous fervor of a dilettante pretending to be a doctor. "Give up this fairytale and do something useful for once."

And then, with the first real certainty he had felt in years, Friedrich tore open the door of the iron stove and cast his notes and formulae into fiery oblivion.

CHAPTER ELEVEN

Varanus and the others arrived in Königsberg by way of a rather lengthy train journey. She was very grateful for the state of modern transportation and doubly so for the fact that the Germans had been thorough with laying their railroads. A journey by horse or carriage would have taken days and been far less comfortable.

They were met at the station by Julius, who was as cheerful as ever despite his Prussian dignity. He waited for them next to a curious four-seated motorwagon, which was parked alongside a more conventional horse-drawn carriage.

"Your Highnesses!" Julius called, raising his hand to greet them as they emerged from the station. "Welcome to East Prussia!"

Varanus smiled at Julius as he took her hand warmly.

"Good day, Count von Raabe," she said. "And how are you?"

"Much better now that my dear friends have arrived," Julius answered. He shook Iosef's hand as he joined them. "Prince Shashavani."

To Julius's credit, he did not comment on the fact that both Varanus and Iosef wore dark glasses, wide hats, and veils to shield themselves from the sun. Once nightfall came there would be no need of them, but until sunset had finally finished its business, it was a necessary precaution.

"Yes, hello Julius," Iosef said, as he studied the city. "A very interesting piece of country you have here. And my compliments to your railway. It has proven to be most agreeable."

"Thank you, Highness," Julius said. "But it is surely nothing new. You must have railroads aplenty in so vast a land as Russia."

"Of course we do," Varanus said.

"Do not believe a word of it," Ekaterine told Julius. "Why, I have half a mind to move to Germany simply to ride the train every day."

"Yes, thank you, Ekaterine," Varanus interrupted, before Ekaterine could spin off on some wild fancy about becoming an engineer or something.

Julius winked and motioned to his automobile. "Well, this is *very* new and quite exciting. A Benz Viktoria. I thought you might enjoy a tour of the countryside while there is still some light. Oh, and there is a carriage for the servants and the luggage, of course."

"How thoughtful," Ekaterine said. She nudged Luka and grinned at him. "That's where you'll be traveling, Mister Luka."

Luka gave Ekaterine a look out of the corner of his eye and grumbled.

* * * *

The drive was pleasant, if a little brisk. There was still enough light to view the windswept countryside as the Benz Viktoria rattled along the road. The land that Varanus saw was mostly fields and meadows, here and there broken by a copse of trees. It was all very green, nature coming to life once more after its winter confinement.

Throughout the drive, Julius chatted away as usual, speaking with an easy joviality that seemed so out of place with his straight-backed Prussian posture. Varanus listened as their host made mention of certain points of interest, mostly involving quirks of topography or local legends. It was all rather parochial, especially as they drew further and further away from the city and the landscape became increasingly rural.

"It's very pretty," Ekaterine remarked to Varanus.

"Well, it's green," Varanus said.

"And flat."

"Yes, very flat, Ekaterine," Varanus murmured. She shook her head at the absurd statement.

"It rather reminds me of Blackmoor, come to think of it," Ekaterine said.

Varanus shuddered a little at the mention of her family's ancient home in England. There was something about their visit there ten years ago that troubled her. She could not bring herself to remember it clearly, and that troubled her most of all.

"No it does not," she answered.

"Blackmoor was very flat," Ekaterine insisted. "And this is very flat."

"It's not at all the same," Varanus said. "It is green here. I think the only time we saw anything green in Blackmoor was on a painting."

"Blackmoor?" Julius asked, sounding intrigued.

"My family's ancestral seat in England," Varanus explained. "We visited there a few years ago, and the land is very flat." She looked at Ekaterine and said firmly, "But it was not at all like this."

"If you insist." Ekaterine sighed and raised her hands in acquiescence.

Julius looked about to comment when they rounded a copse of trees, and he suddenly pointed toward the coast.

"Ah ha!" he exclaimed. "There it is, Castle Valkenburg."

Varanus turned in her seat and looked. There, silhouetted against the orange and purple sky, she saw a gothic fortress built of brick. Once stalwart and imposing, it was now abandoned and majestically decaying. Varanus counted down silently in anticipation of Ekaterine's reaction.

"It's beautiful!" her friend exclaimed, gasping with excitement. "It must be simply filled with ghosts!"

Julius chuckled and said, "I cannot speak to that, Princess, but it *is* full of my family's history. That is Castle Valkenburg, once the jewel of the Teutonic Order, now just an old ruin."

"There is no such thing as 'just a ruin', Count von Raabe," Ekaterine corrected.

Varanus sighed and shook her head. "Yes, there is."

Julius continued, "My ancestor, Heinrich von Valkenburg, took his name from the castle when it was given into his keeping by Albert, the first Duke of Prussia, in the sixteenth century. And it has been in the family ever since." Julius winked. "Though we now have much more comfortable accommodations, I assure you."

"A pity," Ekaterine said. She sounded genuinely disappointed that they would not be spending the night in the ruin.

"Von Valkenburg?" Iosef asked, entering the conversation without even the slightest indication that he had been listening. "Not Von Raabe?"

If Julius was surprised by Iosef's sudden question, he gave no indication. Instead, he laughed a little and replied:

"Well, you see, we Von Raabes are very new aristocrats where the German nobility is concerned. My grandfather, Jacob Raabe, was a merchant, if you can believe that. But during the war against Napoleon, he raised a free company of soldiers, paid for, equipped, and led by himself. Apparently he had a knack for it. After the war, he was rewarded for his patriotic service with the title of count and a small estate here in East Prussia, which you shall soon see."

"And the Von Valkenburgs?" Varanus asked.

"My mother's side of the family," Julius answered. "They were Jacob Raabe's neighbors when he and his wife and children settled into their new home. And very welcoming neighbors too, I am told, which was kind of them. We aristocrats can be a little…inhospitable to the newly elevated."

He spoke cautiously, perhaps measuring his words to be certain that he did not offend his guests, who were surely of much older lineage than he was. It almost made Varanus laugh, though Julius would not have understood why, so she was careful not to do so.

"I have always considered nobility of character to be more important than nobility of birth," she said. "Don't you agree, Iosef?"

Iosef raised an eyebrow at her. "Indeed." He looked at Julius and said, "I have no doubt that your grandfather was just as worthy of his position as I am of mine."

This seemed to please Julius, who smiled and raised his chin a little higher at the compliment. "Thank you, Your Highness," he said.

"Iosef," came the reminder.

"Of course, of course. Thank you, Iosef."

Ekaterine was still staring at the ruined castle as they passed it. She turned back and asked, "And what became of the Von Valkenburgs?"

"I am certain they're not ghosts, if that's what you are wondering," Varanus told her, though she spoke in Svanish to avoid offending Julius with Ekaterine's gothic nonsense.

"I'll bet they are," Ekaterine insisted, also in Svanish.

"Well, you are looking at them," Julius answered. When both Varanus and Ekaterine looked from side to side in search of the elusive missing nobility, he quickly explained, "That is to say, I and my family are all that remains of them. You see, the Von Valkenburgs of Jacob's time had been the victims of great tragedy. Having survived the war unscathed, the family was struck with an outbreak of fever that took both sons and left only a single daughter to pass on the inheritance."

"How dreadful!" Ekaterine exclaimed.

"Alas, it was more or less the end of the Von Valkenburg line," Julius said sadly. "But it was shortly after Jacob von Raabe and his family had moved to their new estate and, full of Christian feeling, they helped nurse their neighbors back to health. Despite the tragedy—indeed, perhaps because of it—the two families became very close, and when my father and my mother came of age, it seemed only natural for them to marry."

"And here you are," Varanus observed.

"And here I am."

"Curiously enough, something very similar happened to my family during the Crusades," Varanus said. She had no intention of telling the tale, but the coincidence was amusing enough for her to remark about it.

Julius did not pry when Varanus did not elaborate, but he smiled.

"Clearly this friendship was preordained," he said, to which they shared a laugh.

* * * *

Though Varanus would not admit it aloud, Ekaterine had been right about the superficial similarities between their visit to Blackmoor and their current journey: the vast open plain, the sunset arrival by train, the medieval history lingering at the fringes of modernity. But this was an altogether more pleasant visit as well, with green grass instead of the blasted heath of her forefathers. And Julius made a far more agreeable host than Varanus's English relations.

It was dark when they finally reached the Von Raabe estate, but the headlights of the automobile and the glimmer of the moon revealed an elegant stately house of the eighteenth century, which was both dignified and welcoming.

Julius stopped the motorwagon by the front steps and helped the others down from their seats. He caught Varanus's eye when it was her turn, and he smiled, his hand lingering on hers for a few moments even after she had alighted. Then he quickly motioned to the door.

"Come, my friends," he said. "Welcome to my home." As he led them up the steps, he checked his pocket watch and nodded with satisfaction. "And we are on time. Splendid."

"On time?" Varanus asked, as she pulled her veil up onto the brim of her hat where it would appear to be just another adornment. With the sun now fully set, there was no need of it, and Iosef had similarly removed and concealed his own protection.

"You will laugh because I am a Prussian," Julius replied, speaking as if it were an invitation, "but we are very punctual here."

"Nonsense," Varanus said. "Who ever heard of a punctual Prussian?"

Julius sighed and shook his head. "Dinner always begins promptly at six, but tonight we have decided to delay in anticipation of your journey." He chuckled. "After all, what sort of hosts would we be, eating before our guests arrived?"

"What sort indeed," Varanus agreed, as Julius led them inside.

They were met in the front hall by Julius's family, who waited to greet the new arrivals at the foot of the stairs. They were led by Julius's wife—whom he introduced as Augusta—a striking woman in her mid-forties with chestnut hair, perfect poise, and a ready smile much like her husband's. Though she kept her Prussian formalism, there was the same glimmer of warmth in her voice and her manner as Julius made introductions.

Next came the four children—three sons and a daughter, all somewhere in their twenties: Paul, Karl, Albrecht, and Mechtilde. Like their parents they were attractive and fair-haired, standing tall with great dignity but only just managing to hide their excitement at meeting strangers. Varanus stifled a laugh at the sight, but she found it charming as well as amusing. It was a very pleasant change from most of the aristocratic company she had been forced to endure over the years.

The dinner that followed was pleasant, though its content tended toward fish a little more than Varanus liked, perhaps due to their proximity to the coast. Like her grandfather before her, Varanus had little tolerance for the smell of the sea or the taste of its bounty. But there was plenty of far more agreeable fare as well, and it was all quite delicious.

The conversation was light but friendly, with a great deal of small talk to avoid offending anyone's sensibilities. But still Varanus did not fail to notice when Augusta remarked, quite innocently, that while Paul and Karl were both married, Albrecht and Mechtilde were still unattached.

"And have you any children, Princess?" Augusta asked Ekaterine.

"I'm not married," Ekaterine replied.

"Oh?" Augusta exchanged a smile with her husband. "Well, we simply must do something about that."

"There will be a great many eligible young men at the soiree tomorrow," Mechtilde said to Ekaterine. She spoke softly and in confidence, but Varanus had no trouble hearing. "I will point them out to you."

"Oh, that sounds like...." Ekaterine paused, wondering what was the proper thing to say. "Fun?" She did not sound convinced.

Varanus met her friend's gaze and shook her head.

"And do you have any children, Prince Shashavani?" Augusta asked Iosef.

Iosef had been looking at one of the table lamps with a certain intensity, and he quickly glanced up at hearing himself addressed.

"Uh...no," he answered, flashing a little smile.

"Just the one," Varanus quickly amended.

Despite her stated age and Iosef's apparent youth, it would have seemed odd if their union had not produced *any* children. Why else would his family have permitted it? And the last thing they needed was to alert suspicions and have strangers prying into the affairs of their illusionary family.

Iosef glanced at her out of the corner of his eye, but he clearly trusted her judgment in the matter and agreed:

"Yes, our son. He is...two."

"Little Koba," Ekaterine added with a grin. "He is simply darling. He has his father's eyes and his mother's hair and his auntie's—"

"Propensity for starting mischief," Varanus remarked dry. She quickly turned her attention back to assuaging the Von Raabes. "He is too young to travel, of course, so he is at home in Russia."

"It must be terrible being away from your child," said Karl's wife, whose name might have been Anna, but Varanus had not really paid attention to her at the time and so could not be sure. She looked at Karl and smiled. "I don't think we shall travel at all when we have our first child. Not for several years."

"No, no, don't give up so quickly," Ekaterine interjected. "Once they start walking, you can put them on a lead and take them anywhere—"

Varanus cleared her throat and interrupted Ekaterine. "You must pardon my sister-in-law, her German is not very good."

She glanced at the others, expecting the family to be upset at Ekaterine's manner of speaking, but in fact they seemed genuinely entertained.

"Nonsense, that sounds like a rather good idea," joked Paul. "Marie," he added, addressing his wife, "we must try that with our two children when we return home to Hannover."

"We must," Marie agreed. "We will call it the 'Russian method', and it will be very popular."

And they all laughed and nothing more was said about it.

* * * *

After dinner, as Paul and Karl went off with their wives to play cards, Augusta took charge of the remaining company:

"Mechtilde, why don't you take Princess Shashavani for a tour of the house?" She motioned to indicate Ekaterine. "Oh, and Albrecht, go and keep them company."

"Goodness, yes, you simply must see the house," Mechtilde agreed, taking Ekaterine's hand and pulling her toward the hall. "Come along, Albrecht, keep up!"

"Adventure time again!" Ekaterine announced to Varanus as she was whisked away.

Varanus sighed and shook her head. Why did strange women have to continually steal her friend? At least they weren't artists this time.

"Now," Augusta said to Iosef and Julius, "I know that the two of you will be spending most of your time here looking at old books, so for tonight I am going to put a stop to all that nonsense before it can start." She took Iosef by the arm and smiled at him. "If you will permit me, Your Highness, I intend to monopolize you myself tonight. I think perhaps a tour of the library. We have some old manuscripts that an ancestor of mine brought back from the Holy Land—he was a Templar, you know. I think they might interest you...."

Iosef exchanged a look with Varanus to which she shrugged. Iosef turned back to Augusta and gave one of his narrow smiles.

"That sounds agreeable, Countess von Raabe," he said.

"Oh please, do call me Augusta."

As Iosef and Augusta, too, vanished into the depths of the house, Varanus looked at Julius and smirked.

"If I did not know you to be a man of propriety, Julius, I would think that you and your wife are trying to marry my sister-in-law to your son."

"Perish the thought," Julius replied with a grin. "Although...."

Varanus gave him a look. "And now your wife has just run off with my husband. I might almost believe the two of you are trying to get each of us alone."

Julius offered her his arm, which she took, and he led her out through one of the other doors.

"And does that trouble you, Varanus?" he asked.

"Of course it doesn't trouble me," Varanus replied. "But I am surprised that it does not trouble her...or you."

Julius was silent for a few moments as they went on their way, perhaps considering the best reply.

"My wife and I love each other very much," he explained, "and we share a great affection. But we have been married for almost thirty years now, and from time to time one enjoys an escape from the familiar. My wife is very fond of men younger than I. Men like your husband."

Varanus coughed a little to stop a laugh. The very idea that Iosef might be considered "young" as he neared his second century was rather funny.

"And this doesn't bother you?" she asked.

"Not at all," Julius said. "As you can see, I have my heir, a spare, another one, and a daughter. So there is little reason to fear a difficulty of inheritance. The Von Raabe lineage is safely ensured, so why shouldn't my wife enjoy a few...*conversations* with a younger man?"

"How broad-minded of you," Varanus remarked.

Julius led Varanus into a cozy little sitting room with dark green paper and paneling. There was a fire burning upon the hearth and the lights were low, the shadows pleasantly enfolding; it immediately put Varanus in mind of their evenings in Prague, which, she realized, must certainly be the intention. It made her smile slightly.

"Broad-minded?" Julius mused, as they sat facing one another in a luxuriously upholstered *tête-à-tête* chair. "Perhaps. I do like to think of myself as a modern man."

"Better to be modern than archaic," Varanus agreed smugly.

"But..." Julius added, running his fingertips across the back of Varanus's hand, "we do have an agreement as well. What is permitted for the goose is permitted for the gander."

"A splendid policy," Varanus said, leaning forward and fixing Julius with her eyes. With the room so pleasantly dark, the light from the fire glinted in Julius's eyes and made a soft glow around his golden hair. "Perhaps Iosef and I should implement it."

Julius reached out with his other hand and stroked the soft skin beneath Varanus's chin, making her smile and inhale deeply.

"Nothing like a weekend in the country for trying new things," he murmured, as he leaned forward and kissed Varanus's lips.

CHAPTER TWELVE

Varanus had planned to spend the next day in seclusion until night-fall in order to avoid the threat of sunlight, but she arose from meditation to find that the Von Raabes had already taken the necessary precautions. She found the house curtained and dark, lit by countless lamps and candles that were being set out in anticipation of the evening's festivities. She had previously confided in Julius regarding her and Iosef's sensitivity to sunlight—a "hereditary condition", the medical study of which had first brought them together—but she had not expected the household to have taken steps to accommodate them. And when she arrived in the dining room for breakfast, the sole comment on the matter came from Mechtilde, who proudly showed her and Ekaterine the family's emulation of their new "Russian fashion". It was enough to make one laugh, but at least it was convenient.

The guests began to arrive in the late afternoon. By that time the decorating of the house had been completed, and again Varanus was taken by surprise when she returned downstairs after some work on her latest medical monograph. The theme of the festivities truly was that of a pagan spring, or at least of an aristocrat's imaginary fancies of one. There were wreaths of fresh-cut boughs and bouquets of flowers everywhere, which tickled Varanus's nose with their intoxicating scents. When the guests arrived, they did so wearing horns and crowns of flowers, which stood out curiously against their conventional evening dress.

The sight of it all amused Ekaterine tremendously. She had long ago become convinced that all Latin Christians were secretly pagans, and she made it quite clear that this soiree was further proof. Varanus could do little but sigh as her friend descended the stairs in her most outlandishly colored gown, with flowers in her hair and a pair of small antlers that one of the Von Raabes must have given her. She soon left Varanus behind and began flitting about the thirty or so guests, introducing herself as "the Queen of the May" and imparting her blessing on each of them.

"I see that Ekaterine is enjoying herself," Varanus heard Iosef say to her, as she surveyed the crowd in the house's sitting room.

Varanus almost jumped at his voice. She turned and saw him standing in the doorway wearing a pair of horns like most of the other men.

They did rather suit him, she reflected, but it was still a strange thing to see. It was like he had been transformed into some sort of satyr by the festivities.

"True," Varanus agreed, glancing back at the party. "Well, why not let her have her fun?"

Those assembled were unquestionably a collection of aristocrats, most of them local nobility from Prussia and Pomerania, if their accents were an indication. It was almost amusing to see them drinking, chatting, and even dancing in their festive adornments to music played on a phonograph. Varanus did find it odd that they had elected not to enjoy a small orchestra, but perhaps the intent was to maintain as intimate an environment as possible. This was more a private entertainment for friends than a display of ostentation.

"Indeed," Iosef said. "The past year has been strangely peaceful for us. Why shouldn't we enjoy ourselves?"

Though the way he spoke, it was clear that the enjoyment would belong to other people. And that was to be expected. Varanus still saw pain in his eyes, and she knew that the loss of Sophio was still weighing on him, as it had for years.

"A wise philosophy, My Lord," Varanus agreed. "Why…I haven't killed anyone in months. It is peculiar, but not unpleasant."

"Quite so, Varanus. Peace is certainly peculiar."

Varanus paused for a moment before she spoke next, her voice low so they would not be heard:

"My Lord, how are you…faring?"

Iosef glanced at her. He put on a smile that Varanus knew was forced and said, "I am well enough, Varanus. And that is all that need be said on the matter."

"Of course." Varanus knew better than to press her mentor, especially with the pain of Sophio's death so fresh. She quickly changed the subject. "I see that Countess von Raabe is in high spirits tonight."

Iosef made a soft noise of irritation. "Indeed."

Augusta, like the other Von Raabes, was busy mingling and entertaining her guests. But seeing that she had been observed, she flashed a smile in Iosef's direction and gave a discreet nod.

"I do believe you have an admirer," Varanus said.

"I had noticed."

"Did she trouble you much last night?"

Iosef chuckled. "She attempted to seduce me over a particularly enthralling Coptic manuscript, but I evaded her. Politely, of course."

"Of course," Varanus agreed. "I do apologize for your tribulations, My Lord."

"There is no cause for you to apologize, Varanus," Iosef told her. "Whatever your motivations for coming here, I came of my own choice. I intend to plumb the depths of Julius's knowledge and to avail myself of his library during our stay. If I must outmaneuver the advances of his wife while I do so, it is a small price to pay."

"She is still quite attractive," Varanus teased.

Iosef smiled genuinely at this, though it was faint. "I have no interest in younger women," he said.

"Of course."

"And what of your dalliance with Julius?" Iosef asked.

Varanus blinked at him, surprised at the observation.

"*Pardon?*" she demanded.

"I am not unobservant, Varanus," Iosef replied. "Nor do I speak in judgment of you. Julius is a handsome man, I suppose, and he certainly has a ready charm about him. You have accompanied me on my long journey to find hidden knowledge that I do not yet understand and which may not even exist, and for your patience I am grateful."

"It is not a student's place to be patient or impatient with her teacher," Varanus reminded him.

"Even so," Iosef said, "I grasp blindly for shadows while you enjoy the affections of flesh and blood. I think perhaps the student has more clarity than the master." He paused and looked across the room toward Julius, who was in conversation with an old bearded man. "Ah, and I believe that will be the Polish antiquarian Julius mentioned to me."

"More shadows, My Lord?" Varanus asked.

"Indeed." For a brief moment, a smile flashed across Iosef's pale lips. "Perhaps this time I will catch one. Excuse me, Varanus."

"Of course, My Lord."

Varanus frowned as she watched Iosef cross the room. There was still so much anguish in his every movement. No one else could see it, of course. Iosef was too subtle for that. But Varanus saw it. She saw it in his eyes and in the too-controlled form of his posture, calculated to hide any hint of depression. At a glance he seemed perfectly content, if a bit distant, and that veneer of contentment was what gave him away, like a smiling mask that was not quite right.

They very thought of Iosef's loss saddened Varanus, as it did whenever she reflected on it. She quickly looked away from him and at Julius, smiling to herself as the two men greeted each other cheerfully and Julius made introductions with his aged companion. As Iosef and the antiquarian began speaking, Julius turned his eyes toward Varanus and smiled at her. He nodded politely, but there was a glimmer of mischief in his eyes, and the sight of it made Varanus feel pleasantly warm beneath her high collar.

As she traded knowing looks with Julius, she caught sight of something familiar out of the corner of her eye. She already knew that it was Korbinian even before she turned and saw him drinking wine beneath the mounted head of a stag, which had been adorned with laurels and flowers for the occasion. Korbinian had been silent since leaving Prague, and seeing him now gave Varanus an unpleasant turn. Blood trickled from his eyes and mouth, and he was ghastly pale, just as he had been for months whenever he had shown himself.

It troubled Varanus to see him so affected, but at the same time it angered her. Nothing was wrong, and no one had died in almost a year, certainly no one she cared about. And that was a pleasant change. So why was Korbinian behaving so monstrously? Could he really be so jealous of her? But that was absurd!

Across the room, Korbinian smiled at her and softly mouthed the words, "What man could not be jealous of you, *Liebchen?*"

Varanus was suddenly shaken out of her thoughts by voices in the hallway behind her. More guests had arrived, and she was still standing in the doorway, blocking their path. Varanus quickly stepped to the side, but she did so casually as if she simply fancied inspecting one of the wreaths. There was no cause to be rude, after all.

But the speakers did not enter, instead lingering in the shadows just beyond the door where they would not be overheard by the others. Curious, Varanus glanced into the hallway and saw two men standing there, both of them somewhere in their forties, both of them tall and handsome and noble of bearing. They wore cavalry uniforms, which were curiously set off by the horns and flowers in their hair. The men spoke in hushed tones, but Varanus had no difficulty understanding them. From their accents she surmised that one man was Hungarian and the other likely Austrian.

"Yes, but have your men found any trace of my daughter?" the Hungarian demanded in a low voice.

"Possibly," the Austrian said, his tone far more relaxed than that of his companion.

"*Possibly?* That is the best your spies can do?"

The Austrian bristled slightly. "They are doing their best, Istvan. I have an interest myself, you know. Do not forget, she is supposed to be my wife."

"Well…. That will not happen if the child is not found, will it? And she will have earned herself a whipping before I give her to you."

"Poor child." The Austrian chuckled. "Whipped both before and after her wedding. Perhaps she will learn something from it."

The Hungarian chuckled too, but his tone was humorless. "That has not been my experience with my daughter," he said. "Now then, what have your men discovered?"

"My men have not yet found her," the Austrian answered, "but it seems that the violinist is in Prague. Some sort of radical. It is possible that she is still with him. If that is so, Prague is where we will find her."

"Find the violinist, find the girl," the Hungarian mused. "And have they found him?"

There was an uncomfortable pause.

"Not yet, no. But it is only a matter of time. They know that he is in Prague; they simply have not located his hideout. These revolutionaries, they have bolt-holes everywhere. You never know where they are staying."

"I am becoming impatient, Franz," the Hungarian pressed, his tone both angry and desperate. "It cannot be difficult to find *a musician*. They are not known for their subtlety."

However cordial their conversation until now, a sense of discontent suddenly fell across them. The Austrian bristled at the Hungarian's words, and the Hungarian, perhaps realizing that he had overstepped himself, grew uneasy.

"You are in no position to be impatient, Istvan," the Austrian told his companion. His tone remained friendly, but there was an edge to it. Of the two, he held the position of power.

The Hungarian quickly bridled his anger. "Of course, Franz. Forgive me. I…. My paternal outrage has gotten the better of me."

This seemed to satisfy the Austrian, and he answered soothingly, "Fear not, Istvan. There is no need for forgiveness between friends. What man could possibly take offense at the words of his father-in-law?" There was little sincerity in his voice, and it was clear that the son-in-law, and not the father, held the position of authority between the two of them. But having asserted his authority, he then continued with the matter at hand: "My men are making inquiries. They have drawn upon the assistance of the police as well, but, of course, I would prefer to avoid calling too much attention to the situation."

"Of course."

Varanus kept herself inconspicuous as the men finished their conversation and entered the sitting room. She doubted very much that they even noticed her in passing, which was just as well.

She turned back to the room and saw Ekaterine hurrying toward her with a glass of Champagne in each hand. Varanus sighed at the sight of her friend dressed up like a faery queen. What made it all the worse was the fact that the antlers and the floral crown actually did suit her, which Varanus found most intolerable.

"Hello, Doctor!" Ekaterine exclaimed in her native Svanish, handing one glass to Varanus before taking a rather long drink of her own wine. "Isn't it a splendid party?"

"It's…colorful," Varanus replied. Indeed, what else could one say about a scene that most closely resembled a theatrical interpretation of some pagan Bacchanal. "Are you enjoying yourself?"

"So very much!" Ekaterine said. She made a wide, slightly tipsy sweep of her hand to encompass the room. "I'm meeting so many new and moderately interesting people."

"I see."

"And Mechtilde has been introducing me to eligible young men whom I have no interest in knowing! It is such fun!" Ekaterine grinned. "*And* I'm the Queen of the May, as you may have heard."

Varanus sighed. "You certainly are enjoying yourself, and entirely too much."

"There's no such thing."

"You keep insisting that," Varanus said, unable to hide a smile at her friend. "I am skeptical."

"Nonsense," Ekaterine replied. She finished her glass and, looking around for an empty place to put it, quickly hid it behind a stuffed pheasant on a nearby table. Taking Varanus's arm, she asked, "And what have you been doing all evening, my dear Doctor?"

"You mean what have I been doing for the past hour?" Varanus asked.

"Yes," Ekaterine answered brightly.

"I have been wandering from room to room, admiring the ambiance." Varanus smirked. "Of which you, apparently, are a part."

Ekaterine gasped excitedly. "I rather like the idea of being part of the ambiance. Like an artist's model!"

"Dear God, no," Varanus said with a sigh. "You've done enough of that while we were in Prague."

"And soon to continue upon our return," Ekaterine assured her.

Varanus shook her head. Then she took another look around the room and its "ambiance" and shook her head yet again, this time deeply and slowly and with rather more resignation.

"Flowers, antlers, and wreaths," she remarked. "I wonder who thought of all this."

"I think it looks rather nice."

"It *does* look rather nice," Varanus said. "I simply wonder whose idea it was. I never imagined Prussian aristocrats as being the sort to transform a perfectly decent sitting room into some manner of Druidic grotto."

Ekaterine grinned. "It simply goes to prove my theory."

"Theory?"

"That you are all pagans here in the West," Ekaterine announced proudly. She leaned in and lowered her voice, whispering in Varanus's ear, "Which I've known all along."

"Are you drunk?" Varanus asked.

Ekaterine gasped and pulled herself up into a huff, which she could only maintain for a few seconds before giggling. "The Queen of the May is never drunk, Doctor. I am intoxicated with my own divinity."

"Divinity and Champagne are such good companions, aren't they?" Varanus mused, finally taking a drink. It was rather good.

"The best of companions," Ekaterine agreed. "Like us!"

"Ah, but which of us is divinity and which one is the Champagne?" Varanus asked.

Ekaterine did not reply but rather pointed at her antlers, as though that answered everything. Varanus rolled her eyes.

"Such a pity Luka couldn't join us," Ekaterine said.

"That is what he gets for not pretending to be an aristocrat." Varanus paused. "Where is he, by the way?"

"Downstairs drinking with the housemaids," Ekaterine replied nonchalantly.

"Of course he is," Varanus grumbled.

It was not uncommon for Luka to spend his idle moments with a mixture of wine and romantic companionship, but Varanus would be very annoyed at him if he stirred up trouble during their visit.

"Well, I must be off," Ekaterine announced. "A queen's work is never done."

"Do say hello to the peasants for me," Varanus said, exchanging a smirk.

As she watched Ekaterine flit away to her next source of amusement, Varanus caught sight of Julius approaching, now in the company of the two officers whom Varanus had recently overheard. A glance told her that neither of the men recognized her, so it seemed likely her eavesdropping remained a secret. And that was just as well, since their business was of no interest to her.

"Princess Shashavani," Julius greeted her, smiling warmly. "I hope you are enjoying our little soiree."

"As I said when you asked me an hour ago, it is a splendid affair, Count," Varanus replied.

The two of them paused for a moment exchanging a knowing look. Varanus still remembered the pleasant warmth of Julius's soft lips when he had asked her the first time and the intoxicating reverberations of the pulse in his throat....

Stop that, Varanus reminded herself. Julius was a friend, not someone to be eaten, though he would probably be quite delicious, she concluded.

Before their lingering stare could become too obvious, Julius motioned to the other two men and said:

"Princess, may I introduce you to two of my oldest friends? This is Colonel Graf von Steiersberg," he indicated the Austrian man, named Franz, "and Count Istvan Erdelyi, both of them my honored guests from Austria-Hungary."

Erdelyi smiled and quipped, "Yes, together Franz and I are both halves of the Empire."

"A pleasure, gentlemen," Varanus replied, carefully studying them.

The two men were quite polite, and they shared Julius's aristocratic dignity, but there was something about them that was not altogether likeable. They lacked Julius's geniality. Their smiles were less pleasing, their pride something more like arrogance.

"Franz, Istvan," Julius said, "this is the Princess Shashavani, the very charming wife of my new friend. I believe I mentioned the Shashavanis before."

Von Steiersberg chuckled and said, "Do not be mistaken, Princess. Julius speaks of you and your husband constantly. His 'new friends', as if his old ones are no good for him."

At this, the three men laughed together, and Varanus only thought it polite to join in.

"Well, it is wonderful to meet Count von Raabe's *old friends*," she remarked, smiling pleasantly and quietly hoping to end the conversation.

She rather suspected that Erdelyi's missing daughter was none other than Friedrich's young friend Erzsebet. The mention of a radical violinist with whom she had fled all but confirmed it. Nor was it much of a coincidence when Varanus took a moment to think about it. Aristocracy was a close-knit institution, crisscrossed all across the continent with ties of marriage and camaraderie. If she had bothered to spend any real time hobnobbing with the notables in the Empire for the past year, she suspected that she would have encountered either Von Steiersberg or Erdelyi long before now.

She would have to write Friedrich a letter warning him. The affairs of his artist friends were of no real interest to her, but she did not want him becoming caught in the middle of things.

"Well, I certainly hope that I at least will be seeing more of you and your husband," Von Steiersberg said. "Julius certainly will."

Again the men laughed.

"I don't quite follow," Varanus said.

"Oh, I should explain," Julius told her. "Franz has a house in Prague for when he is there on business, and he has generously allowed me the use of it. So, you…and the Prince will have to call on me there after our collective return to Bohemia."

He grinned at her and winked ever so slightly, which made Varanus smile at the insinuation. But her smile was suddenly interrupted as she chanced to look past Julius and saw Korbinian standing in the center of the room, his face and clothes wet with blood, as the other guests flitted about around him, ignorant of his presence.

Suddenly the candles burned low and the room grew dark. Soon there was nothing there but Varanus and Korbinian and the blood. And the shadows, which seemed to writhe about the two of them, caressing Varanus's face with their formless fingers, smearing her hands with Korbinian's freshly spilt blood. A ringing noise filled Varanus's ears, drowning out the talk and the laughter and the gaiety, a sound not quite like that of buzzing flies nor of an Edison bulb a moment before its filament snapped.

And through the noise, she heard Korbinian's gentle, loving voice whisper over and over again:

"Are you having fun, *Liebchen?*"

Suddenly, the sound of Von Steiersberg speaking interrupted the vision and dragged Varanus, silently screaming, back into the waking world.

"Do not make yourself too comfortable on your own, my friend," Von Steiersberg was saying to Julius. He exchanged a look with Istvan, and the two of them shared a little smile. "I suspect that business will bring me to Prague very soon."

"Well, the more the merrier!" Julius announced, his cheerful tone so contrary to the anguish and shivers that Varanus was even then struggling to conceal behind decades of discipline. "Won't that be a delight, Princess?"

Varanus stared into the empty space at the center of the room where Korbinian had recently stood, now without any trace of him or his cascading blood. It was all she could do to nod in agreement and put on a smile.

"A delight," she managed to say without her voice shaking. "An absolute treat, I'm sure."

CHAPTER THIRTEEN

The morning after the soiree was a late one, for the revelry had lasted well after midnight. Many of the local guests had already departed before sunrise, ferried back home by their exhausted coachmen; but the dozen or so who remained enjoyed a late breakfast together a little after noon. And having refreshed themselves for the day, the guests were then taken on a tour of the nearby Valkenburg castle, complete with a picnic luncheon.

The sky was gray and overcast, which Iosef regarded as a favorable sign. Though it might threaten rain, it meant that he was free to go about unshrouded, keeping his veil atop his wide-brimmed hat in case a sudden parting of the clouds threatened the burning of the sun. Sunglasses were still necessary to shield his eyes, but aside from a mild tickling of the skin, he carried through the day unscathed. It was a testament to the regimen of limited sun exposure that he had carried out almost daily for two hundred years. Another century and he would be completely free of the sun's threat, but that was still some time off. And, of course, Varanus was still obliged to go about fully veiled, as both her youth and the laxity of her sunlight regimen kept her flesh vulnerable to the light. Fortunately, as a woman, a veil did not appear too out of place: certainly nowhere near as strange as if Iosef had been forced to wear it.

Valkenburg was surprisingly intact for a ruin. True, its outer walls were crumbling, but the inner keep still stood despite more than a century of abandonment. It was a fortress that had been built to withstand the elements as well as armies. As Iosef strolled through the central courtyard with the others, he found himself casting his eyes skyward, as if tempting the sun to reveal itself.

Adrift in contemplation, Iosef reached into his coat pocket and felt for the amulet. Its cold touch against his fingertips brought him back to clarity, as it always did: back to the world and to the one thing it now lacked. The one voice that ever whispered:

Sophio, Sophio, Sophio.

"How are you faring, my brother?"

Startled, Iosef looked and saw Luka walking alongside him. His sworn brother seemed rather cheerful, in his own way. The man puffed on his long-stemmed pipe and had a half smile about his lips. Evidently he had had an enjoyable evening.

"I am well," Iosef replied, quickly pulling his hand away from the amulet and folding his arms. "I am merely in contemplation."

"Of course, brother," Luka said. He took another puff of smoke. "Strange people these Prussians. Disciplined and also cheerful. I don't know what to make of it."

"I suspect it is only these Prussians who are cheerful," Iosef said.

"Mmm," Luka mused. "That would make far more sense." He took a long breath of smoke and exhaled. "Why are we here, brother?"

"To see the castle," Iosef answered.

Luka snorted. "I mean why are here in Germany? I understand the Doctor's motivation.... I do not understand yours."

"We are here because I want to learn what Julius von Raabe knows about a subject of mutual interest."

"More of your 'black goat' nonsense," Luka grumbled. "Why has it so captured your fancy, Iosef? You cannot believe that such a thing is real!"

"No, I certainly do not," Iosef said. He placed a hand on Luka's shoulder and looked into his eyes. "Come now, Luka, you know me better than that. I do not believe in demons or phantoms. The Black Goat is not real. The Horned Serpent is not real. But the people who worshipped them were real. The amulets are real."

"That damned amulet again." Luka swore and shook his head. "It is playing tricks with your mind."

"Not *the* amulet," Iosef corrected. "The *two* amulets. Almost identical, yet one was found in Turkestan and the other in Poland. These are rare and precious things, not trinkets to be distributed through trade and barter. Who made them, Luka? Where did they come from? From the steppes of Turkestan or from the Polish plain? It cannot have been both."

They turned down a ruined cloister that ran along the main keep. The cloister's roof had almost entirely collapsed, revealing the gray sky. A flock of crows sat perched along the top of the ruined wall. As Iosef and Luka approached, the birds flew into the air with a chorus of angry caws.

"There is some peculiar mystery behind all of this," Iosef continued. "There is a connection—of culture, of faith, of mythology—that I do not yet see. And I will find it."

Luka was silent for a time. "Iosef," he finally said, "discovering the origin of that piece of metal will not bring her back."

Iosef stopped short and looked skyward, inhaling a deep breath of air.

"This is not about her," he said.

"Of course it is," Luka replied. "Ever since you returned from Turkestan, you have been obsessed with that amulet." Luka circled around and stood before Iosef, staring into his eyes. "It is not her, Iosef! It is not some fragment of her that you can keep with you! Some mystery to unravel to bring her back!" He grabbed Iosef's shoulders and looked at him, torn between anger and despair. "She is gone and you remain and you must accept that, Iosef."

Iosef was silent as he stared back at Luka. He had heard this before over the past five years, many times and with increasing regularity. He did not blame Luka for it. Five years were barely a moment for him, so short a time that it truly felt like Sophio's death had happened that very day—and yet, also so far away that it seemed a hundred lifetimes ago. But his pain was Luka's pain, he knew that. And though he hid his suffering well, he knew that Luka saw it every moment of every day that the two of them passed company together.

"I am aware, Luka," he said softly.

He stared past Luka at the haze of fog swirling about the far end of the cloister. Even in the wisps and clouds, he still saw Sophio: her dark hair that flowed like water about her shoulders, the bloodless alabaster of her cheeks, the glimmering black jewels of her eyes.

"But when Basileios took her from me, there was no part of her left for me to mourn over. The fire saw to that. That piece of metal is all that I have. It is the only thing that remains." Iosef blinked slowly, anticipating a tear that would not quite form in his eye. "I know that it is nonsense, but it is a comforting nonsense. I beg you, Luka, let me have my foolish obsession. Let me grasp at smoke and find nothing, and in that nothingness let me find my peace."

Luka did not reply, but he looked away and frowned. Iosef desired to be alone with his thoughts and with his grief, and he knew that Luka understood that. Luka always understood. But that did not mean he liked it.

And so, without another word, Iosef stepped past Luka and continued down the crumbling hallway and into the fog, as the crows circled above him, softly cawing:

Sophio. Sophio. Sophio.

* * * *

"A curious name, 'Valkenburg'," Varanus remarked to Julius, as she strolled with him through the ruins of the castle keep. Somewhere behind them, the rest of the luncheon party lingered in the courtyard, being regaled by Ekaterine about her adventures in Siberia and "uncharted Kent".

"It is Dutch, actually," Julius explained, smiling in acknowledgement of the curiosity.

"A Dutch name for a German castle?" Varanus asked, poking Julius with her fingertip. "How does one accomplish that?"

Julius chuckled. "It was named for a knight of the Teutonic Order, Claes van Valkenburg, who died valiantly in battle against the pagans that occupied these lands. He was hacked to pieces by the chieftain's bodyguard as he slew their leader with his bare hands."

"With his bare hands?" Now it was Varanus's turn to chuckle. "Had he dropped his sword?"

"Oh, you mock!" Julius protested.

Varanus glanced over her shoulder to be sure that they were out of eyesight from the others, and she leaned over and kissed Julius on the cheek.

"I *do* mock," she said, which made Julius laugh. "But come now…a valiant Teutonic crusader losing his sword in the midst of battle? It is a little absurd, you must admit."

"I did not say that he had lost it," Julius replied.

"Oh, I see. He 'chose' not to use it."

An absurd display of warrior prowess, no doubt. And just as surely invented by some later hagiographer seeking to inflate the dead knight's accomplishments.

They passed into a large hall filled with broken stone and the remnants of habitation. This had probably been the place where the garrison had taken its meals, as witnessed by the great hearth built into one wall that was clearly meant to bring light and warmth to an otherwise cold and gloomy chamber. Varanus saw a flock of crows watching them from a second-floor balcony. She smiled at the sight of them. Such pretty creatures. They often reminded her of…someone.

Varanus looked around, admiring the remains of what had once been a majestic structure. How tragic that it had fallen into such neglect.

Suddenly, the fluttering of wings drew her attention back to the crows as they took off in a torrent of black feathers. And in their place, she saw Korbinian on the balcony, his arms folded and resting on the stone balustrade. Blood trickled from his eyes like tears as he watched her watching him.

"According to the legend—" Julius said, carrying on with his story in ignorance of Varanus's distress.

Varanus looked back at him, feeling her own heartbeat for the first time that day. "What?" she asked breathlessly. She quickly cast a glance at the balcony and found it empty save for the crows, who had never left it.

Julius looked surprised. "The legend of Brother Claes's death."

"Oh, yes, of course," Varanus said. She put on a smile. "Please continue."

If Julius took note of her peculiar behavior, he said nothing about it, instead returning to the story like nothing had happened:

"According to the legend, this land was inhabited by devil-worshippers. Not that a reasonable man believes such stories, of course," he quickly added. "But the chronicler who wrote the tale down does clearly note that this tribe was unlike the other Baltic pagans. They did not share the same gods, and they were feared and hated even more than the crusaders."

"Ah, and so the Teutonic Order, unable to tolerate coming second, sought to redress the matter," Varanus quipped. "I see."

Julius laughed softly and placed his hand on hers where it rested upon his arm. He let it linger and she did not complain.

"You are a devilish woman, my dear Varanus," he said. "Imagine, mocking my ancestors so."

"At least my ancestors never lost their swords in a fight."

"I am coming to that." Julius waved an admonishing finger at her and then tapped it against the tip of her nose. "If only you will allow me to finish."

Varanus wrinkled her nose at the touch, but it was gentle and the touch made in jest. "Continue," she said.

"These 'devil-worshippers' were said to burn horned effigies and to worship the very smoke of their unholy fire." Julius shook his head. "Obviously, some form of agricultural deity now lost to the ferocity of the crusaders. But the legend says that bathing in this smoke made the tribesmen impervious to steel and utterly unfeeling of pain, so that when the knights came against them, the knights' metal swords were rendered useless, unable even to bruise the flesh of their enemies, while the tribesmen, gifted with demonic strength, clove the knights' armor to pieces with a single blow."

Varanus couldn't help but scoff at such superstition. "Smoke bathing?" she asked. "Clearly I must take it up."

"You *must*," Julius agreed, sharing a laugh with her. "It will be all the talk of Saint Petersburg."

"Milk bathing is good for my youth and complexion," Varanus continued, grinning, "but sadly it does nothing against swords."

"And a woman of your station must surely be threatened by the blades of long-dead knights almost constantly," Julius noted.

"How ever did I manage until now?"

They laughed again, loudly and with great delight. Varanus pulled Julius's arm against her and rested her head on his shoulder for a moment. He looked at her and smiled.

Beyond the great hall, Julius led her through a wide corridor and into the heart of the castle: the crumbling, rain-sodden remains of its once great chapel. It was an austere house of worship, fitting for a military order, although Varanus suspected that whatever treasures it had once held were long-removed to more secure and inhabited places. The windows were done in elegant stained glass, although most of them were broken. The sunlight that drifted in from the clouded sky shone feebly through the glass, filling the misty air with fragments of blue and red and green that could never quite form a coherent picture. The roof was broken in several places, leaving pieces of shattered slate in heaps on the stone floor.

Julius led Varanus down the center of the nave, motioning to the room's decaying grandeur with one hand as he continued his tale.

"Of course, the knights won in the end."

"Rather a foregone conclusion," Varanus remarked.

"And poor Brother Claes had died," Julius said. "But for his sacrifice, he was given a saint's funeral and laid to rest in the ground beneath this very chapel. Um...." He looked around and then pointed to a set of decorative flagstones ornamented with bits of mosaic tile. "Just there, I believe."

"Charmingly morbid."

"The remains of the tribe scattered, of course," Julius continued, "and in order to secure and subdue this fertile land, the Order built this castle and named it Valkenburg in honor of Claes's sacrifice."

"And then your ancestors took their name from it," Varanus teasingly reminded him. "A Dutchman lends his name to a Teutonic castle, which then lends its name to a German noble family."

Julius tried not to laugh, but a titter of mirth escaped him, and he quickly coughed in a desperate attempt to maintain the dignity of his family.

"I feel certain there is an historian in Amsterdam laughing at us this very moment," he said. "At least I can take pride that my patronym is thoroughly German: Von Raabe, the raven."

"Mmm," Varanus mused. She smirked and ran her fingertip along Julius's temple. "No, too blond to be a raven. I think you should adopt the Valkenburg name and become a Dutchman."

Julius caught her hand and gently kissed the tip of her finger. "I think not," he said, smiling at her.

Varanus smiled back, but her eye caught a figure standing some distance behind Julius, next to one of the columns that supported the ceiling. She looked properly and saw Korbinian again, leaning against the smooth stonework, his face dripping with blood that splattered in droplets against the floor, only to vanish like the rain.

Varanus quickly looked back at Julius and then just as quickly looked away, worried that he might discern something of what she had seen in her face. But she concealed her distress well, and Julius took no note of it as they resumed their walk, slowly approaching the chancel and the altar. Beyond the columns, Korbinian walked along with her, matching her step for step despite his longer stride. He never once took his blood-stained eyes from her.

Finally, Julius stopped before the stone altar and placed his hand upon it, running his fingertips across the smooth surface.

"A block of stone," Varanus mused, trying very hard to ignore Korbinian as he lingered just at the edge of her sight.

"More than a block of stone," Julius corrected. "This is the heart of the castle. Its soul and purpose. Though I realize it does not look like much now, this altar—indeed, this church—represents the final victory of the Teutonic Order over the pagans who once occupied it. For here, on this very spot, was the shrine where those tribesmen once bathed in smoke and sacrificed to their gods."

Varanus looked down at her feet. "*Here?*"

"More or less," Julius said. He placed his hand against the small of Varanus's back and gently drew his fingers in circles, making her skin tingle pleasantly even beneath the layers of heavy fabric. Varanus smiled and rested her head against Julius's chest, allowing him to pull her into his arms. "There was a great tree here, according to the legend. It was the centerpiece of the tribe's entire religion, and they would burn their fires directly beneath its branches."

"I imagine it was stained black with corruption," Varanus said.

Julius looked at her, his expression puzzled. "Yes, that is precisely what the legend says. How did you know that?"

"An inspired guess," Varanus answered. "It seemed thematic. And besides, smoke tends to stain things."

She began idly toying with the buttons on Julius's waistcoat, using it as a distraction to avoid thinking about Korbinian, who surely still lurked somewhere nearby, just out of sight.

"Logical," Julius agreed, "but I think I prefer the thought of you brimming with divinely inspired genius."

"Do not be absurd," Varanus said. "My genius is my own. God has nothing to do with it." She glanced at the altar again. "So where is the tree now? I suppose it must have been chopped down."

"Chopped down," Julius agreed, "dug up, cloven into pieces, burned to ashes, exorcised, and finally cast away on the wind. All that remains are the roots, rotting away somewhere down there. They built the altar directly on top of it, so that the light and the glory of God might cleanse the land and bring forth its bounty."

"And how is that proceeding?" Varanus asked.

Julius chuckled. "Well, we eat a lot of fish around here."

"I had noticed," Varanus remarked.

She took a deep breath and looked around, finally summoning up the courage to look for Korbinian. If she had been alone, she would have admonished him for his peculiar, bad behavior of late, but alas he no longer seemed to come to her except when she was in company.

But there was no sign of Korbinian anywhere, only the ruins of Valkenburg's decaying chapel. That was just as well.

Varanus looked back at Julius and smiled. "Count von Raabe, I do believe we have become separated from the others," she said. "This is most distressing."

Julius looked this way and that and gasped. "My goodness, you do seem to be right about that, Princess. Not a soul anywhere. I do apologize. I shall attend to the matter immediately."

"And how do you propose to do that?" Varanus asked.

Julius smiled at her. He lifted Varanus's veil just enough to reveal her lips and ran his fingers across the smooth skin of her cheek.

"I think I shall start by doing this…" he murmured softly, leaning in and pressing his lips to hers.

CHAPTER FOURTEEN

In the days that followed the destruction of his scientific papers, Friedrich was surprised to find himself easily reconciled with things. Admittedly, he had been overdramatic with how he had handled the culmination of his repeated failures, but perhaps that was to be expected after a decade of exhaustive, even fanatical, devotion to a cause that could never have ended in success. The very notion of granting immortality to the human body was, of course, absurd. It simply couldn't be done, which Friedrich knew he would have realized if he had only allowed himself to honestly consider the fact once during the past ten years.

And though he had first been seized with a deep bout of depression, his despair passed with surprising quickness—aided, naturally, by Stanislav's good cheer and more than a few stiff drinks. His newfound lack of purpose was nothing short of liberation, freeing him from the chains of obsession that had tied him to his desk night after night, producing nothing but pointless fantasies and scientific drivel. Now that was all done and gone. He was a free man again. And while it was true he was rapidly approaching forty, he still had some of his youth left. He might do something useful with himself. He might even marry! He still had his looks, which were returning to him more and more each day that he spent not chained to his desk and his beakers. And after all, both sides of his family aged gracefully. Aunt Ilse had kept her looks well into her forties…right up to the night of the accident. And Mother looked no older than Friedrich, though that could only be the result of good breeding and care. Whatever fantastic illusions Friedrich had previously harbored, he knew that his mother was not immortal.

And now, pleasurably aimless, Friedrich found himself finally enjoying life again. He had reintroduced himself to Prague society and was accepting invitations to things again—though the letters had to be received at his official address in Prague, which was located in a far more respectable neighborhood but which he only visited every few days to keep up appearances.

"More respectable," he mused. Almost anywhere would be more upstanding than the unruly warren that harbored his laboratory. But he

was not about to abandon his friends just because they weren't the sort one could take to a soiree or a ball.

Deep in his thoughts, Friedrich lowered his cup of coffee and cast an eye around his table at those same delightfully not-respectable people. They were in a local coffee house favored by Stanislav and the revolutionaries, which at the evening hour was filled with people all chatting or arguing, until the walls reverberated with the almost deafening sounds of camaraderie.

There was Stanislav with his arm around Erzsebet. Zoya and her sketchbook, making a study of the crowd. Wilhelm, Nicolas, and Ilya arguing. Karel reciting poetry that no one with half a brain wanted to hear. All was right with the world.

"The revolution will not begin in Russia!" Wilhelm shouted.

In reply, Ilya raised his hands as if pleading for divine intervention to knock some sense into him. "What people in all the world are so oppressed—"

"It is not the oppression of a people but the oppression of the soul!" interrupted Nicolas.

"Nonsense," countered Stanislav. "The souls of my people are oppressed, along with the rest of them!"

"But there is no soul," protested Karel. "Only the immortal longings of a mind unable to free itself from the shackles of terror at its own mortality."

Friedrich sighed and took another sip of coffee. Well, all was as usual, that was for certain.

Zoya leaned over to him and whispered, "I would stab them all into silence, but I only have the one pencil, and I'm afraid it might break."

"What, and ruin the show?" Friedrich replied, grinning.

"There is that," Zoya agreed. "Though if this keeps up much longer, I fear the Revolution will either break out here and now or else dissolve into civil war before it has even begun."

"Revolutions often do that," Friedrich noted.

He coughed loudly as a cloud of particularly pungent smoke wafted past him from Wilhelm's cigarette. He had never much cared for tobacco, neither for the staleness of the odor nor the heaviness of the smell that seemed to linger in the air long after its passing and assailed one's nose like a swarm of gnats. It had been bad enough as a child, but with each passing year, he seemed to have less and less tolerance for unpalatable smells. For that reason he never allowed smoking in the house, but in the cafe he suffered at the whim of the local breeze.

Zoya glanced at him, noticing his distress. "The smell?" she asked.

"Oversensitive nose," Friedrich replied, a little embarrassed. As a child, Aunt Ilse had been especially impatient about his finickiness with smells and tastes. "No cause for concern."

"Pssh," Zoya scoffed. "If it's bothering you, it's bothering you. Don't pretend otherwise."

She pulled a cigarette tin out of the carpetbag she used to carry her supplies. Opening the tin—which curiously smelled less of tobacco and more of roses and frankincense—she produced a handmade cigarette rolled in old newspaper, lit it from the lamp on the table, and passed it to Friedrich.

"Here," she said, "this should help."

Friedrich chuckled, very confused. He pushed the cigarette away. "I don't think actually smoking is going to make the stench any less intolerable," he said.

"Smell it," Zoya insisted.

Friedrich took a hesitant sniff, but to his surprise the cigarette smelled like the tin it had come from.

"Smells like perfume," he said in astonishment. He took the cigarette and waved it under his nose. It was actually rather pleasant, if a little strong.

"It's incense," Zoya explained, returning to her sketching. "I make them myself. It wards off bad smells. You don't even have to smoke it. Just let it burn and clear the air."

Friedrich sat back and waved the curious cigarette a few times, dispelling some of the tobacco stench that had hung about the table.

"That's rather clever," he noted.

"Mmm hmm," Zoya agreed as she sketched. "One might even think I have half a brain."

"On the mantelpiece in the parlor?" Friedrich quipped.

Zoya smirked at him. "Of course. The boys share it between them. I'm really just holding it for them."

Friedrich laughed and drank some more coffee. He really had missed all of this.

"Freddie…" Zoya said, still engrossed in her sketching.

"Hmm?"

"Do you think it's safe for Erzsebet to be out in public like this?" Zoya asked.

Friedrich looked at Erzsebet, who was quietly sipping her coffee as she watched Stanislav and his comrades arguing about the soul and whether it was more oppressed than Russia. She seemed to be enjoying herself sitting at the periphery of the conversation and observing rather than becoming embroiled in it.

"Why wouldn't she be safe?" Friedrich asked. "She's with all of us. No one is going to bother her, not with Ilya waving his hands about. I wouldn't come within ten paces of the table with him carrying on like that."

Zoya tilted her head and gave Friedrich a look. "I don't mean 'is someone going to bother her', Freddie. But she is on the run from her family. Stanislav too, you'll remember. I don't think either of them should be in public right now, and least of all her."

"Well, I suppose there is that," Friedrich agreed. He leaned across the table and patted Stanislav's arm.

"Hmm, what?" Stanislav asked, breaking away from the argument. "What is it, Freddie? We're in the midst of something momentous."

"I have no doubt," Zoya muttered. She poked Erzsebet with the blunt end of her pencil to get the girl's attention and flashed her a smile. "Chin up, if you please. I'm going to do something rather angelic with your profile."

Though startled, Erzsebet quickly smiled and placed her chin on her hand. "Like this?"

"Marvelous," Zoya replied.

"Stanislav," Friedrich said, "do you think perhaps we ought to be getting home?"

"Home?" Stanislav exclaimed. He laughed and shook his head in bewilderment. "But the evening's just started!" He gave Erzsebet a kiss on the cheek and asked, "You don't want to go home yet, do you darling?"

"Um…no?" Erzsebet replied. Her tone was a little distant, and she stared off into the crowd, her eyes darting around as if looking for something she only half imagined she had seen.

"You are a wanted man," Friedrich reminded him. "It may have been over a year, but Erzsebet's father must still be searching for the two of you."

At this, Erzsebet's face turned pale, and she pressed herself deeper into Stanislav's arms, her eyes still staring at the far end of the cafe. Stanislav gently stroked the back of her neck to comfort her and gave Friedrich an angry look.

"Good God, Freddie, don't frighten her!" Stanislav shook his head.

"I'm not trying to frighten anyone!" Friedrich protested.

"It's the first time she's been out in weeks," Stanislav said. "Let her enjoy herself."

He looked at Erzsebet and smiled. She smiled back at him, but then she quickly returned to watching the crowd.

"I don't know why you insist on being out either," Friedrich said. "Count Erdelyi is a man of some influence, you know. I don't want either of you getting caught just because you can't stay indoors for more than five blasted minutes!"

Stanislav wagged his finger at Friedrich. "Old Erdelyi isn't going to find us here, and I'll tell you why. He's already searched Prague once. I have it on good authority that while we were hiding in Salzburg last year, his men were scouring Bohemia for us. As far as he knows, we're not here!"

"Sneaky," Zoya commented, though her tone did not readily convey whether this was a compliment or a snide remark.

"I will tell you what Erdelyi's doing right now," Stanislav continued. "Either he thinks I'm a fool and I stayed here in the Empire, in which case he'll scour Hungary and Austria before he even imagines looking here again; or else he thinks I'm clever and he'll assume that I've fled the country. Paris, maybe. Either way, Prague is the safest place to be right now."

As he spoke, Erzsebet suddenly stiffened and shook her head. "No," she said. "No, it isn't."

"What?" Stanislav asked, suddenly alarmed. He was echoed almost simultaneously by Friedrich and Zoya.

Erzsebet pointed across the room to a pair of men who were seated at a corner table, drinking coffee like everyone else. But as Friedrich watched, he saw the men cast glances in their direction with deliberate interest.

"Your father's men?" Friedrich asked.

At that distance he could not hear what the men were saying, so he had no way of knowing if their language or their accents were Hungarian.

"No," Erzsebet whispered. "But I recognize them. They serve Count von Steiersberg."

"The man you were supposed to marry?" Stanislav exclaimed. "How did *they* find us?"

"Clearly by looking where the Count wasn't," Friedrich said.

"We should leave," Zoya said, packing her things away hurriedly. "We should leave now."

"What if they follow us?" Erzsebet asked, her tone frightened and barely above a whisper.

"They'll do that no matter when we leave," Friedrich said. "Better now when there's a crowd."

As they hurried to their feet, the revolutionaries halted their argument and stood as well, looking confused. In the heat of their dispute, they seemed to have missed the entire conversation taking place next to them.

"Is something wrong?" asked Nicolas.

"We're leaving," Stanislav said. "Meet back at the house. Make sure you aren't followed."

He nodded toward the men at the table, who had stood as well. It seemed that, having been discovered, they saw little need for secrecy or pretense now.

"Secret police?" Wilhelm asked.

"Near enough," Zoya said.

She grabbed Erzsebet by the hand and pulled her toward the back door of the cafe. Stanislav was right behind them, followed by Friedrich and the revolutionaries. But Von Steiersberg's thugs were close behind them, moving through the crowd with all the slipperiness of eels, somehow weaving past clusters of patrons without stopping.

"Keep going," Friedrich said, giving Stanislav and the others a push toward the door. "I'll see what I can do to slow them."

He turned and approached the men with a ready smile and his hand outstretched. He didn't really expect them to fall for his pretense of good will, but at least it would confuse them.

"Gentlemen!" he exclaimed. "Klein didn't say to expect you for another week."

Friedrich hurried forward the last few steps and blocked the men as they passed the counter, hemming them in between it and a packed table. There was no way for them to go around except by backtracking, and their angry expressions told him that they knew as much. Go back, or go through.

"What?" one of the men demanded.

"Klein," Friedrich repeated, grabbing the man's hand and giving it a firm shake. "The advertisement in the newspaper. You are here about ostrich feathers, aren't you?"

The man growled and tried to push his way past Friedrich, while his companion began working his way back the way they had come. Stanislav and the others had almost reached the door. Only a few more moments....

"Oh, that's not you then?" Friedrich asked innocently. "Dashed sorry. Here, let me get out of your way."

He bobbed back and forth, feigning an effort to get out of the way, while firmly planting himself in front of the man each time. In a moment he would have to attend to the fellow's companion, but this would do for now.

Of course, the man was no fool, and he did not play along with the game. As Friedrich continued to plant himself in the man's path, the fellow grabbed Friedrich by his coat and flung him against the counter. For a moment, Friedrich was dumbfounded. It was rare that he ever encountered someone capable of bodily throwing him in any capacity, let alone with such force. But as the ruffian rushed toward the back door, Friedrich pulled himself to his senses and grabbed the man.

He was rewarded with a solid blow to the jaw that, once again, landed harder than he had expected. But this time Friedrich did not allow himself to be stunned by his enemy's unexpected strength. Having allowed the other man to throw the first punch, Friedrich grabbed him by the collar and repaid him with a solid punch of his own.

The ruffian stumbled sideways from the blow, but Friedrich's grip kept him on his feet. The man recovered quickly, though blood trickled from his nose and the corner of his mouth. He grabbed for Friedrich's throat, snarling and hissing, and Friedrich struck him two more times to lay him out.

For a moment there was silence around him as the patrons of the cafe stared at the remains of the altercation. Friedrich smiled awkwardly and ran a hand through his hair.

"I think he was drunk," he explained. "Something about a…business. Good evening."

Hoping that no one would remember him if the authorities investigated—which was unlikely anyway in that part of town—Friedrich bolted for the back door. There was no sign of the second man. He must have reached the alleyway already. Hopefully the others had made their escape.

But as Friedrich ran out the back door, he saw that it was not the case. The second ruffian was there, aiming a revolver at Stanislav, who stood a few paces away, shielding Erzsebet with his body. The others stood around him, no one moving lest they provoke the man to shoot.

Friedrich drew the Mauser pistol from inside his coat and leveled it at the attacker. He slowly approached, taking each step as quietly as he could. Though armed, he did not relish the thought of shooting a man, not after the fight in the cafe. A brawl might go uninvestigated; a man shot would immediately draw the police.

"Drop the pistol," he said.

The ruffian tensed slightly and tilted his head.

"I said drop the—"

Friedrich did not quite understand how he failed to see the man turning in place, but suddenly the ruffian had reversed position and now stood with the revolver pointed at Friedrich. Startled, Friedrich blinked rapidly as his body tensed.

"What was that?" the ruffian asked. "Drop the…?"

And Friedrich knew that he was going to be shot. But while his mind hesitated with terror, some instinct of action seized him. Not quite understanding what his body was doing, Friedrich tilted sideways as his free hand snatched the ruffian's hand. The revolver fired, narrowly missing Friedrich's head and dazing him with the sound of its report.

The two of them struggled as the man fought to realign his aim and shoot properly and Friedrich fought to disarm him. Suddenly he saw Stanislav race to join him, grabbing the man from behind and pulling on his arm.

"Shoot him! Shoot him!" Stanislav cried.

But Friedrich's senses were returning to him. Murder was the last thing they needed. Instead, he hefted the Mauser and struck the ruffian across the temple, laying him out cold.

There was a short silence as the man's body tumbled to the pavement.

"Or you could do that," Stanislav finally said.

"I thought it went rather well, considering," Friedrich replied.

"The other one?"

"Knocked him out in the cafe."

"What do we do with them?" Stanislav asked.

Friedrich was shocked at the question. "We leave them, obviously! What do you expect to do? Lock them in the basement? *Kill them?*"

"Well...." Stanislav's expression showed that he did not much like the idea, but he certainly entertained it.

"If we kill this man, then the police will be after us for murder. An altercation, a fistfight, that they may not care about."

"What if they report back—"

"Report back what?" Friedrich demanded. "That they found you? They clearly expected to. Why else would they be in Prague in the first place?"

Stanislav nodded. He looked over his shoulder at Erzsebet, who was watching them with a mournful, resigned expression.

"You have to get out of Prague," Friedrich said, walking back toward the others alongside Stanislav. "If Von Steiersberg tracked you here...."

"It is only two men," Stanislav insisted. He knelt and checked the man on the ground to be certain that he was unconscious.

"Two men will lead to more."

Stanislav shook his head. "I'm not running. And I'm not making Erzsebet run either."

"I don't know what you expect to do," Friedrich said.

Stanislav paused and put a hand on Friedrich's shoulder. "Freddie, I appreciate your concern, but I have been forced into hiding more than once before. We will simply lie low for a while and have someone spread the word that we've left the city. They will look for us, they will find nothing, and they will move on."

Friedrich sighed. "I wish I had your optimism, Stanislav."

"I am a revolutionary, Freddie," Stanislav reminded him, "and more than that, I am a Romantic. Optimism is what keeps us going."

CHAPTER FIFTEEN

Deeply concerned by the events of that night, Friedrich remained indoors for several days, avoiding the public in case the police were looking for him after the fistfight. Most of the others had the good sense to do likewise, though Ilya and Wilhelm insisted on leaving to get word from their socialist comrades. But Stanislav did not join them. He and Erzsebet knew better than to let themselves be seen while Von Steiersberg's men were on their trail.

But as the week passed without incident, Friedrich began to doubt his earlier uncertainty, and he ventured back into the world. He avoided the one cafe, of course, but elsewhere there was no indication that the police were after him, nor did he notice anyone watching or following him. He knew that Stanislav's friends had begun spreading the word that he and Erzsebet had left Prague—some stories said they had gone to Russia, others to France, and still other to Switzerland. Perhaps after the brawl, Von Steiersberg's men assumed that the stories were true and that their quarry had fled immediately and had similarly given chase.

By the week's end, he had come to believe that the danger was, after its brief appearance, finally gone. So he was surprised when, taking breakfast in the parlor on Friday morning, he heard a firm hand knock at the door.

"Who can that be?" Stanislav asked, looking up from his meal.

"I have no idea…" Friedrich answered.

He slowly stood and reached for his pistol, which he had worn on his person every day since the brawl at the coffee house. Across the room, Zoya suddenly looked up from the book she was reading and began fumbling about in her bag for her diary.

"Is today Friday?" she asked.

"I believe so, yes," Friedrich replied.

Zoya sighed in relief. "It's your lovely aunt come for her portrait. And right on schedule."

"Oh."

Pleased at the notion of seeing Aunt Ekaterine again—it had been two weeks since her last visit—Friedrich hurried into the front hall and opened the door. Though he opened it only a crack at first to verify the identity of the visitor, he was delighted to see Ekaterine's pretty face and bright eyes smiling back at him from beneath the brim of a wide blue hat.

"Auntie!" Friedrich exclaimed, opening the door. As he did so, he saw his mother standing next to Ekaterine, eyeing the street with a displeased expression. "Mother?"

Varanus looked at Friedrich as he opened the door. She seemed pleased to seem him—relieved, even, as if she had doubted his safety.

"Hello Alis…Friedrich," she said, stepping into the foyer and taking Friedrich's hand in hers. She gave him another, more definite look and smiled. "You're looking very well. Good. Are you sleeping more? Eating properly? Of course, you must be and I am very pleased about it."

"Uh…thank you," Friedrich said, absently feeling his cheeks blush at the compliment. Well, at least Mother was happy. "Come in, come in. We're having breakfast."

"We have already partaken," Varanus replied, sounding dubious at the prospect of breaking bread with Friedrich's friends.

"I am here to have my picture painted," Ekaterine announced, entering the house in a happy flourish. She took Friedrich's hand and gave him a kiss on the cheek, for which Varanus gave her a disapproving look.

"Yes, Zoya mentioned it," Friedrich said. "She's just through—"

"Is that my muse?" Zoya called from the parlor.

"It is!" Ekaterine called back. "And I am coming, my…painter?" She looked at Friedrich and Varanus and shrugged as she walked toward the parlor door and began removing her hat.

Varanus sighed. "She insisted on returning in time for her appointment. And, I suppose, it was time for the rest of us to leave the hinterland as well."

"I did say that I could return on my own," Ekaterine reminded her, pausing at the threshold.

"And allow you to travel on the train by yourself?" Varanus looked horrified. "Perish the thought."

Ekaterine pulled herself up into a huff, brandishing her hat and hatpin like a shield and sword. "If some strange man had accosted me along the way," she announced, "I would have punched him on the nose and thrown him out the window!"

"Yes, that is what concerned me," Varanus said. "I'm not worried about you looking after yourself, Ekaterine, so much as what sort of damage you might do along the way."

"I think it's quite appropriate for ladies to defend themselves against unruly men," Friedrich ventured, smiling at Ekaterine. He was sincere in the sentiment, but he did enjoy the way Ekaterine returned the smile when he said it.

Varanus shook her head and took Friedrich's hand. "Of course it's *appropriate*," she said, her tone slightly annoyed. "Were it up to me, any man found taking liberties with a woman would be strung up like a hog and beaten soundly—unlike a hog, since pigs are really such nice animals and don't deserve that sort of treatment."

Friedrich chuckled at this, and Ekaterine openly giggled with delight.

"But," Varanus continued, looking directly at Ekaterine, "I am led to believe that such things are against the law when undertaken by private persons, and we really should avoid upsetting the law while we're abroad, don't you agree?"

"Of course, Doctor," Ekaterine said, trying very hard to look serious. "And I haven't beaten any strange and unruly man like a not-hog in months!" She winked at Friedrich. "Well, in weeks at any rate."

Varanus shook her head. "Go and have you portrait painted."

"Have fun, you two!" Ekaterine said, patting Friedrich's hand and waving to Varanus as she vanished into the parlor.

"Fun," Varanus murmured. Then she looked at Friedrich and smiled. "I am very glad that you are well, Alis...." She caught herself again. "Friedrich. I am very glad that you are well *Friedrich*."

"And I you, Mother," Friedrich said. He embraced her and found himself strangely happy to see her again. It had almost become his instinct to worry about her safety after the events that had befallen them ten years ago. But she was well and he was happy for it.

Varanus paused for a moment. She seemed troubled, and Friedrich quickly took her hand.

"Is something wrong?" he asked.

Varanus paused, seeming to consider her words before she asked, "Friedrich, are you familiar with a Count Erdelyi?"

Friedrich frowned at the name. He knew it very well.

"Erzsebet's father."

"I was afraid of that." Varanus's brow furrowed for a moment, though only slightly. Despite her evident concern, the very muscles of her face seemed disinclined to display the sentiment that troubled her. "Friedrich...."

"Yes?"

"Ekaterine and I were recently in Germany visiting a mutual friend. While we were there, I happened to overhear something that concerned me."

"About Count Erdelyi?" Friedrich asked. He felt panic rising in his chest. Had his mother become involved with the Count? Was she in danger too?

Varanus seemed to sense his distress, and she quickly placed a hand on his cheek to calm him. "It is no cause for concern, I promise you," she said, "but I overheard a conversation between him and a man named Von St—"

"Von Steiersberg," Friedrich finished. He looked away, breathing heavily. His mother *was* in danger, whether she knew it or not!

Varanus looked troubled by the news, but she did not seem surprised. "I thought so," she said. "Count Erdelyi and Count von Steiersberg know that your friends are in Prague, and they have sent men to find them."

Friedrich was silent for a moment.

"Those men have found them, in fact," he finally said.

"What?"

"There was an…an altercation a few days ago," Friedrich explained. "Some of Von Steiersberg's men found us at a coffee house and—"

Varanus's eyes flashed with anger. "Are you alright?"

"Oh, yes, of course," Friedrich answered quickly. He did not want to distress her. "There was a bit of a rough-up, but—"

"Did they hurt you?" Varanus asked, her tone more demanding than questioning.

"They tried," Friedrich answered, "but I saw them off."

Varanus inhaled and then exhaled slowly. She pressed Friedrich's hand tightly between her own.

"Were you hurt?" she asked.

"No, not really," Friedrich began.

"*Were you hurt?*" Varanus repeated more emphatically, looking into Friedrich's eyes as she spoke.

Friedrich suddenly felt himself convulse with guilt at his own words. What a brute he was to cause her such distress. How dare he trouble her with such concerns!

"Not at all, Mother, I assure you," he said.

Varanus looked visibly relieved at his words, but still she frowned. "You mustn't become involved in this sort of thing," she insisted.

"I wasn't hurt," Friedrich said.

"That is not the point," Varanus answered. She sighed. "Well, it *is* the point, but still…. I do not want you getting yourself involved in all of this nonsense."

"It's not nonsense, Mother," Friedrich replied. "Erzsebet does not wish to marry Von Steiersberg. Her father tried to force her, so she left. What more is there to be said about it?"

Varanus glanced away, staring at a corner of the foyer. She looked displeased by the emptiness of the corner, which was odd but not worth commenting on.

"Not much, I suppose," she acknowledged. "But still, these people you've involved yourself with, Friedrich.... I don't want you getting hurt...."

Friedrich smiled at her with as much comfort as he could muster.

"I am not hurt, Mother, I swear it. And I won't be. And as soon as Von Steiersberg's men have left the city, there will be no cause for concern at all, I promise you."

Varanus exhaled slowly and nodded. "I...trust your judgment, Friedrich." She sounded only half sincere.

Friedrich smiled and held Varanus's hand tightly. "Are you certain you won't join us for breakfast?" he asked.

"No, I fear I cannot," Varanus said. "I have an appointment this morning that I am very interested in keeping, now more than ever. But we should have dinner together, just the two of us. And soon, now that you are looking rather more...well."

Friedrich knew that she meant "more presentable", which was certainly true, but he appreciated her not putting it so frankly. He must have been frightful to see when she first visited him in Prague, especially with that horrible beard. But now that he was finally fit to be seen in public again, it would be nice to spend time with his only surviving family.

"I would like that, Mother," he said, grinning at the suggestion. "Tomorrow, perhaps? I know a delightful place near the Wenzelsplatz."

Varanus smiled, pleased at the news. "Tomorrow, then," she said. She reached up and brushed Friedrich's cheek, wiping away a speck of something only she seemed to see. "You really are looking much better, Friedrich. I am glad that you are finally sleeping properly."

Friedrich laughed and embraced her. "Thank you, Mother. I am quite well, I assure you."

"And no more of this getting into fights nonsense," Varanus reminded him. "Your revolutionary friends might enjoy a brush with the law, but I don't want you getting involved in that sort of thing."

Friedrich was about to protest, but he knew better than to make an argument of it. "Of course, Mother."

He saw Varanus out the door and gave her a parting wave. But as he went to join the others in the parlor, he caught a glimpse of himself in the hall mirror and suddenly remembered his mother's words. Frowning, Friedrich studied his reflection, gently pushing the skin of his face this way and that to get a better look at it.

"Oh God..." he murmured, as his stomach twisted with a sudden realization.

He did not merely look healthier; he looked *younger*. Younger by five years at least, possibly as much as ten. Having become so accustomed to seeing himself exhausted and gaunt from his poor habits, he had not thought to differentiate between the fading of the dark circles under his eyes and the fading of the very lines and wrinkles that had begun to form here and there. It was not merely the color that had returned to his skin, but its very liveliness as well, its firmness and elasticity. The structure of age was still there—the strong cheekbones, the sharp chin—but the skin and the muscles beneath it were those of a man at the very peak of vitality, upon the threshold between youth and maturity.

"No..." Friedrich gasped.

He had done it. *He had done it!* There could be no mistaking the signs. That night of drunken risk-taking had actually fulfilled its purpose. The last formula had been correct. It had made him younger.

Friedrich ran a hand across his mouth, shivering at this realization as if from a chill. He felt sweat beading upon his forehead and on the back of his neck. He was suddenly faint. He had never actually considered what might follow. Would he succumb to an insidious cancer? Would his cells begin to decay inside his very body?

On the verge of toppling over from a heady mixture of astonishment, triumph, and fear, Friedrich steadied himself with a hand on the wall and forced himself to keep ahold of his senses.

"Pull yourself together," he whispered to his reflection, staring himself directly in the eyes.

If he were going to suffer the corruptive effects found in the previous formulae, they would have begun to manifest themselves by now. Most of the rats had fallen victim within days, if not hours. Perhaps he had been right about needing a larger, stronger body to withstand the cellular distortion. Or perhaps the successful formula was simply free of all such side effects. This was incredible! To think that he had been right all along!

And then the cold feeling appeared in the pit of his stomach again.

"Oh God.... My notes!"

Friedrich rushed up the stairs frantically and made for his laboratory. It was much cleaner now than when he had been working. The rats were all gone, of course. He had set the ones who still lived free when he had abandoned the work.

"My notes, my notes," he mumbled, searching through every last drawer, pile of paperwork, journal, and heap of rubbish. "Oh God, let something of my work remain!"

But of course, nothing remained. Only fragments of failures and lists of unimportant scribbling.

Friedrich sank to his knees in front of the stove that had obliterated his life's work and clutched his head in his hands. He had succeeded and yet utterly failed. Unable to realize his triumph through a haze of premature despair, he had destroyed any hope of reproducing his results and sharing whatever scientific fountain of youth he had discovered.

CHAPTER SIXTEEN

Varanus left Friedrich's decrepit home for a much more fashionable neighborhood across the river, located in the shadow of the glorious Prague Castle. Her destination, the Von Steiersberg house, proved to be an old and majestic building, something bordering on a palace. This was the sort of place she wished her son was inhabiting during his stay in the city. And if it was true that he had not fallen on hard times, why had he chosen his current decaying domicile instead something far more fashionable?

After announcing herself to the footman at the door, Varanus was shown into an opulent sitting room and waited patiently for her host. It was only a few minutes before Julius arrived, smiling at the sight of her. Varanus rose as he approached her and extended her hand in greeting, but she suddenly halted when a second man entered behind Julius.

Count von Steiersberg.

Varanus was surprised to see him. Of course, there was nothing odd about it. It was his house after all. But she had always assumed that, though Julius was staying as a guest, his host would not in fact be there with him.

"Princess Shashavani," Julius said, taking her hand warmly. Though in the presence of his friend, he felt no need to conceal his familiarity behind a veil of formality.

"Count von Raabe," Varanus replied politely. She looked at Von Steiersberg. "Count von Steiersberg, it is a pleasure to meet you again. Thank you both for your kind invitation."

Von Steiersberg bowed stiffly, but his tone was friendly as he replied, "You are most welcome, Princess Shashavani. Sadly, I will not be here for long." He motioned to Julius. "I am simply seeing my dear friend settled and attending to some business in the city before I depart for Vienna."

Varanus smiled. "Of course. I would thank you for offering Count von Raabe accommodations, but I fear that might be regarded as self-serving."

"Oh?"

"Because otherwise my husband and I would have offered him a room in our house," Varanus explained, "which might be regarded as presumptuous. It would appear you have saved us a guest."

"Stolen one from you, surely," joked Von Steiersberg, and the three of them had a pleasant laugh at this.

But while the conversation that followed remained light and appropriately superficial, there was something in Von Steiersberg's manner that troubled her: something lurking around the edges of his tone and in the way his eyes looked at her. She was not entirely certain what to make of it until, quite unexpectedly, Von Steiersberg asked:

"And how is your son, Princess Shashavani?"

"My son?" Varanus asked.

"Friedrich, your eldest," Von Steiersberg said, his smile never wavering. "From your first marriage."

"What about him?"

"Why, it is only that I understand he is in Prague," replied Von Steiersberg. "One naturally assumes that you have had word of him. I thought it would be polite to inquire."

Varanus was silent for a moment, her eyes darting between Von Steiersberg and Julius as she considered her reply. Von Steiersberg might be entirely innocent in asking, but under the circumstances, it seemed unlikely.

She felt her pulse quicken—to the point where she actually felt it—as Korbinian stepped from behind Von Steiersberg and into the empty space between him and Julius. Korbinian's face was pale and his eyes were bloody with tears, but he seemed remarkably composed when compared to how he had recently revealed himself.

"What a question," he murmured, his voice echoing from the corners of the room. "To inquire after strangers is so very presumptuous, especially after one's servants have tried to beat them." He shook his head like an aging master of etiquette despairing at the declining morals of a younger generation. "And when he was so rude just to be here...."

That much was true. Varanus could hardly ask Julius discreet questions about his friend when that same friend was in the room with them.

"I must say, this is quite the surprise," Julius remarked. "I wish I had know that your eldest was here, Princess. I would have extended an invitation to him as well." Julius paused and asked rather slyly, "Is he married at the moment?"

"No," Varanus answered, the corner of her mouth tilting into a smile. Julius was clearly speaking in jest, but there was still a degree of sincerity behind the question.

"Neither is Mechtilde," Julius said, again keeping his tone mirthful while still allowing the remark to carry the option of seriousness.

Von Steiersberg laughed aloud at Julius's words and Varanus chuckled. She glanced at Korbinian to see his reaction, but Korbinian was gone again. There was nothing left but shadows.

"Regrettably, Friedrich is ever engrossed in his studies," Varanus said, dismissing both Julius's concern at a missed matchmaking opportunity and Von Steiersberg's…well, whatever he had hoped to accomplish by mentioning Friedrich in the first place. Had it been a threat? A test to see if she was involved with Friedrich's foolish friends as well?

Whatever the reason, Varanus was insulted by it. But two could play such a game.

"If I may ask, Count von Steiersberg, how goes the search for your errant fiancée?"

Von Steiersberg turned pale, and he tilted his head as he studied her. "How did you know about that?" he demanded.

"I thought it to be common knowledge," Varanus answered innocently. "Someone made mention of it at the soiree. Count Erdelyi perhaps. She is his daughter, is she not?"

"She is," Von Steiersberg confirmed, his voice little more than a growl.

"I do apologize," Varanus said. She looked at Julius. "Should I have not spoken of it?"

"I have known since the beginning," Julius said. He quickly raised his hands to calm Von Steiersberg. " And we will find her, do not fear."

"Of course I will," Von Steiersberg snapped. "I have loyal men scouring Europe in search of her!"

Varanus raised an eyebrow at this revelation—though she already knew it, it was prudent to feign ignorance. Julius looked similarly surprised, and he exclaimed:

"Franz, no! You swore that you would leave it to the authorities!"

"I know what I said, Julius," Von Steiersberg replied, "but this is my wife we are speaking about!"

"Not yet," Varanus heard Korbinian murmur in her ear. But when she turned her head to look, she saw him lurking just behind Von Steiersberg, watching Varanus over the count's shoulder. His crimson lips smiled. "She is his fiancée, not his wife."

Varanus smiled slightly at this, but the look in Korbinian's eyes chilled her and made the smile fade away again. He had found his humor again. He had not found his warmth.

"Count," she said to Von Steiersberg, focusing her attention on the man's face while Korbinian's pale visage hovered just where she could not quite look away from it. "I do apologize if I have caused you distress. If there is any assistance my husband or I can render in the search for your fiancée...."

Von Steiersberg clearly did not expect this. He looked at her, confused. "Pardon?"

Varanus did her best to present an expression of wide-eyed innocence. She had meant to provoke Von Steiersberg—partly to see his reaction, partly to unbalance him after his own probing remarks about her son. But she did not intend to let him realize her hostility.

"My husband's family is influential throughout the Russian Empire," she explained. "As you are investigating the matter privately, we may be able to offer some assistance."

Von Steiersberg looked dubious at the offer, but Julius smiled a little.

"That is a most generous offer, Princess," he said.

"Anything for a friend's...friend," Varanus replied.

Julius frowned and said, "Still, I must caution both of you against taking any sort of rash action in this matter. I do feel that the proper authorities ought to be left to manage this. Who knows what sort of danger might arise otherwise!"

"It was a kidnapping, was it not?" Varanus asked. "Again, it was only briefly mentioned to me at the soiree. I cannot clearly recall the details."

Von Steiersberg and Julius exchanged looks and coughed over their words for a few moments.

"Essentially, yes," Julius replied.

"Erzsebet was *lured away* by a young man of questionable character," Von Steiersberg explained. "She may have gone willingly at the time, but I am certain that she now regrets the decision. I only hope that she remains *unharmed*."

Varanus cleared her throat softly to avoid either laughing or commenting, whether at the euphemism for Erzsebet's virginity or the great certainty that it was gone, given away far more willingly than it would have been on her wedding night.

She quickly laid a hand on Von Steiersberg's arm, still consciously keeping her eyes away from Korbinian, who had begun to circle the three of them as he observed the conversation.

"I understand your concern, Count von Steiersberg," she said. "And surely time must be essential in this. I do not mean to pry into so private a matter, but is it known where she might be?" She paused long enough for it to seem that a thought had just come to her. "Vienna, perhaps? Is that why you are departing so soon?"

"Uh...no," Von Steiersberg said.

He studied her, his face friendly but his eyes suspicious. Of course he did not trust her sincerity: he knew, or at least suspected, that her son was in league with Erzsebet's lover. But if Varanus could keep him unbalanced with what appeared to be sincere goodwill....

"No," Von Steiersberg continued, seeming to make up his mind about her. "No, I have it on good authority that the kidnappers were until recently here in Prague—"

Varanus gasped softly and Julius exclaimed, "My God! So near?"

"—but that they have fled to Rome. And from Rome, they must surely plan to continue to…well, to God knows where." Von Steiersberg exhaled. "You understand why I must depart so abruptly."

"Of course!" Julius cried. "Honestly, Franz, I wish you had told me all of this sooner."

"So that you could caution me to leave this in the hands of the authorities?" Von Steiersberg asked sourly. "Which authorities should I now consult, Julius? The Austrian or the Italian? Or both? I am certain they will coordinate very effectively."

Julius sighed. "Your point is understood, Franz. Does Istvan know you are doing this?"

Von Steiersberg hesitated. It was brief, but long enough that Varanus knew his reply would be a lie.

"No, certainly not. He is troubled enough by what has befallen his family for him to worry about finding Erzsebet. I have undertaken this task myself."

"I despise people who lie," Korbinian murmured in Varanus's ear. "Don't you?" There was a pause. "I wonder if Count von Raabe hates it too."

Varanus did not answer him. Instead, she gave Von Steiersberg her most sincere of sympathetic looks and said, "I am certain we all understand Count Erdelyi's distress. If such a thing had befallen my child...."

"Quite so," agreed Julius. "I can only imagine if Mechtilde had been lured away by some strange man."

"Again, if my husband or I can help in any way—" Varanus continued.

"And Friedrich," Korbinian murmured in her ear. "What does he say to that?"

"Or my son," Varanus added. "He possesses many friends throughout Europe. If there is a city where these villains have fled with your daughter, I am certain Friedrich knows of a person who may investigate on your behalf."

As she expected, Von Steiersberg stiffened at the mention of Friedrich. It confirmed what Varanus suspected. He knew that Friedrich knew

Erzsebet. He knew that Friedrich had suffered an encounter with his thugs earlier that week. Even with Von Steiersberg leaving Prague to pursue some Roman fabrication, Friedrich might still be in danger.

But Von Steiersberg kept a sincere expression as he smiled with relief. His eyes betrayed his true sentiments, of course, but everything else looked honest. He was a good liar, that was certain.

"Thank you, Princess Shashavani," he said. "If there is anything that your husband's family—or your son—can do to aid me in my search, I will send word at once."

Another threat? Varanus wondered. *Or simply a dismissal.* It was so difficult to be certain sometimes. When a person veiled his words, one had to assume they were veiled always. That which seemed innocuous was safer to be assumed a deception.

Von Steiersberg glanced at a nearby clock and frowned. "I have a train to meet," he said.

"Yes, of course," Julius said. He put a hand on Von Steiersberg's arm. "I will see you out. And thank you for your hospitality."

Von Steiersberg nodded and gave Julius a slight smile. "Do not worry about me, Julius. I will sort this out. Erzsebet will be where she belongs very soon."

"Of course she will, Franz," Julius said softly. "Do not worry so. Erzsebet will be safely home with her family, and soon. I am certain of it."

"I shall trust my actions more than your feeling, Julius," Von Steiersberg answered. "But…but I do thank you for it."

"Let me see you to your coach, Franz," Julius added, walking with Von Steiersberg to the door. "And, of course, my thanks for your hospitality. If there is ever anything I can do for you.…"

"Oh, there will be, Julius," Von Steiersberg said. "There will be." He gave Varanus a parting nod. "Make yourself comfortable, Princess Shashavani. You are a welcome guest in my house."

Varanus gave him a smile. "Good luck to you in your search, Count von Steiersberg."

She waited until Julius and Von Steiersberg had departed before slowly exhaling. She had not expected him to be there when she called upon Julius, and while his presence had proven enlightening, it was trying as well. But as Varanus sank into the soft cushions of a nearby sofa, collecting her thoughts, she felt Korbinian's presence looming above her. Slowly, Varanus tilted her head back and looked up at him as blood dripped from his pale face.

"He knows that you are lying, *Liebchen*," Korbinian said. "I wonder what he will do about it."

* * * *

After Von Steiersberg's departure, Varanus enjoyed a pleasant lunch with Julius on an upstairs terrace, overlooking the house's garden and shielded by an overhanging canopy suspended on wooden posts. It was likely to protect against the risk of rain, but it also provided Varanus with a much needed shelter from the sun. She had become accustomed to wearing a veil when out of doors, but she did not like it, and she relished any opportunity to escape its haze.

Though spring remained elusive, the day was warm enough for comfort—well, for Julius's comfort; as one of the Living, Varanus hardly even noticed the slight chill in the air. And from the vantage of the terrace, Varanus enjoyed a magnificent view of the city.

As she dined, she looked off toward the town of Zizkov, on the far side of Prague, and wondered after her son. Was Friedrich safe? Why ever had he allowed himself to become embroiled in such nonsense?

She was startled from her thoughts as Julius reached across the table and put his hand on hers. Varanus looked at him and smiled.

"A charming day for a picnic," she said.

"A charming day for charming company," Julius replied. He grinned and then gave her hand a gentle squeeze. "I must thank you for your offer of help to Franz. Our troubles are not your troubles, but they matter greatly to us."

"Of course," Varanus assured him, taking his hand between both of hers. "The disappearance of a child or a fiancée is equally distressing. I can only imagine how the Countess Erdelyi feels."

Julius coughed softly rather than replying, and his expression told Varanus much: Erzsebet's mother was not overly worried about her daughter's disappearance. But was it because mother and daughter shared no love for one another, or because Countess Erdelyi considered it better for the girl to be missing but safely away from her own family? It was interesting, if only from a purely analytical standpoint.

"Do you believe the girl was kidnapped?" she asked.

Julius sighed and glanced away. "Ehh.... Istvan and Franz are both my dear friends," he said as an explanation.

"That is not quite an answer."

"Franz is my age," Julius said. "Young Erzsebet is not yet as old as my daughter Mechtilde. And while I know that the union of a young woman with an older man is both respectable and desirable, still there is a part of me that balks at the knowledge that the number of years between them is greater even than Erzsebet's own age."

"Indeed," Varanus murmured. "There is a point where respectability becomes something else entirely."

Julius smiled and summarized his thoughts on the matter as politely as he could manage:

"Let me simply say that there is a reason why, between my and Istvan's daughters, it was Erzsebet who became engaged to Franz, and not Mechtilde. There are certain things a father will not accept, even for a good match."

"I think that sounds very sensible of you, Julius," Varanus said. "Had I a daughter, I would certainly not want her entwined with a man twice her age or more." She quickly added, "However good his family."

"We are agreed on this point," Julius said. There was suddenly a twinkle in his eye. "And speaking of sons and daughters...."

"Oh yes?"

"I have a daughter, you have a son." Julius grinned. "And both of them unmarried, as far as I know."

"As far as you know?" Varanus asked teasingly. "Might Mechtilde have become affianced while you were away?"

"It would not surprise me in the least," Julius answered, his expression as utterly serious as he could manage despite the grin that grew even wider. "Young people these days, they are always doing just what you least expect."

"How true."

"And your son—"

"I have two," Varanus reminded him. Even though Iosef's alleged son and heir was entirely fictitious, it was important to keep up the charade.

"If one of them is not old enough to travel, he is certainly not old enough to marry," Julius reminded her.

"Friedrich, then," Varanus said.

"Yes, your mysterious German son who is in Prague and yet missed his invitation to my beautiful soiree." Julius gave Varanus a hurt look at having been made a poor host through the error of omission. "I should very much like to meet him."

"Possibly," Varanus answered, keeping her tone playfully aloof.

"*And* I should very much like him to meet Mechtilde," Julius added, "provided that you found her to be acceptable company for the introduction."

Varanus rested her chin on one hand and studied Julius. "Count von Raabe, did you invite me here to discuss the matter of a marriage alliance?" she asked.

Julius paused and laughed. "Forgive me. I certainly did not."

"Then why am I here, Count von Raabe?" Varanus asked innocently. "In this very charming villa with this very charming company?"

Julius stood and took Varanus's hand, leading her to the edge of the terrace. As they stood there, he placed his arm about Varanus's waist and motioned to the city below them.

"Why, to enjoy this magnificent view, of course," Julius replied. He smiled and ran his fingertip along Varanus's lip. "And to enjoy the company."

"The *charming* company," Varanus reminded him, smiling softly.

"The very charming company," Julius agreed.

He pulled Varanus into his arms and kissed her. Varanus pressed herself against him and smiled, sliding her hands beneath his coat and running her fingers along his back. At her touch, Julius held her tighter, his lips pressing against hers with a fervor that made Varanus heady with delight. The wind blew against them, its fingers tossing Varanus's hair. She smiled and drew away from Julius, who gazed into her eyes. He brushed her hair and Varanus shook her head, letting her auburn tresses fall about her shoulders.

"You are radiant like the sun," Julius murmured, tracing the line of her ear with his fingertip, then gently running his palm along her cheek.

Varanus sighed softly and pressed her lips against Julius's throat, feeling his warmth, inhaling the headiness of his scent.

Tasting the heat of his sweet blood as it pounded beneath his soft skin.

"Tell me more," Varanus whispered.

Julius lifted her into his arms and kissed her again.

"Glorious like the dawn," he said, carrying her from the terrace and into the adjoining bedroom. "Mysterious as the shadows of twilight. I would have you light my darkness from dusk until dawn, my flame-haired goddess."

Varanus laughed aloud with delight, throwing back her head and letting her hair cascade toward the floor.

She and Julius fell together onto the bed, lips pressing together, fingers struggling to undo every button they could find. Varanus stripped Julius of his coat and vest and tore open his shirt. Julius pulled away her jacket, and together they freed her of her blouse. Varanus breathed heavily, feeling her corset tight against her as Julius ran kisses from her bosom to her collarbone.

Varanus loomed over Julius, gazing at him hungrily. She saw him smile at her, his eyes burning with desire. She felt the strong muscles of his chest, undiminished with age, firm beneath her hands, flexing at her touch.

"My goddess of the dawn," Julius whispered, as he took her face in his gentle hands and pulled her down to him. "Come here and let me worship you."

CHAPTER SEVENTEEN

After spending so much time in seclusion, Friedrich was delighted to be out and about again. As he sat at dinner the following evening, he reflected on how nice it was to spend time with family. It was something that he had sorely missed for the past several years. Of course, he had taken Varanus to his favorite restaurant near the Wenzelsplatz in New Town. He suspected that one of the taverns or coffee houses he frequented with Stanislav and the revolutionaries would not have been well received.

He was pleased to see his mother in high spirits, and at first they simply chatted about trivialities as they began the meal. Ten years was a very long time to fill. They had corresponded during that time, but the letters had been infrequent and slow to arrive from either direction. Much of that was Friedrich's own fault: the result first of his extensive travels and then of his scientific obsession.

"You say you traveled in Asia?" Varanus finally asked, as their initial conversation lulled.

"Yes!" Friedrich exclaimed, a little louder than he intended. He quickly leveled his tone as some of the other guests looked at him with distain. "I did. A few years ago."

"It must have been very exciting," Varanus said. "I fear I have not yet ventured beyond Persia. Well, barring...." She quickly stopped herself and smiled. "Forgive me. Tell me about your travels."

Friedrich took a long drink of his wine and considered how to compose his tale. He certainly could not begin with the most important revelation he had discovered: Mother would never believe it, and her incredulity would complicate the questions he had for her.

"It was after Aunt Ilse's death that Christmas Eve," he explained. "As you remember, I was—"

"Conflicted?" Varanus asked.

Her tone was sympathetic, but surely it could only be sarcasm. Who could possibly be conflicted about the death of a beloved aunt? Granted, Friedrich *was* still deeply unsure about how he felt after his aunt's death, but he could hardly confess as much. It was horrible to think the he could both feel sorrow and relief at the death of the woman who raised him.

"Troubled," Friedrich replied. "At first I tried to distract myself with work, but I found the castle a little too…." He paused, searching for the word. "Disquieting."

"So you traveled?"

"Around Europe, first," Friedrich said. "Doing my duty as Baron of Fuchsburg. Being in the right places, being known to the right people."

"Courtly intrigue," Varanus summarized.

Friedrich smiled at this. "Hardly intrigue. I was never very good at that. I ended up spending more time at universities and taverns than at court. And eventually I just grew tired of it all."

"So you went to Asia."

"As one does." Friedrich paused long enough to eat another piece of his meat before he continued. It gave him time to consider how to approach the story. "Did…did my father ever tell you about my grandmother?"

"You mean the story about her conquering some province in Sogdiana and becoming a great khan among the Ozbeks?" Varanus asked. Her tone made clear her incredulity at the story. It amused her, surely, but she did not consider it seriously.

"That is the one," Friedrich said, keeping his smile lively while his heart sank. She would not believe him, whatever he told her. And that was to be expected. Of course his mother, a woman of reason, would not accept fanciful tales. He should have known better.

Varanus smiled slightly at some distant memory. "Your father told me the story many times," she said. "I found it most entertaining."

She studied Friedrich for a little while, her smile playing about her lips. Then she looked past him as something behind him caught her attention and she frowned. Friedrich glanced over his shoulder to see what so interested her, but he saw nothing other than a few other diners. When he looked back, Varanus had returned her attention to him and was smiling, a little too confidently. Something had upset her, and Friedrich had no idea what it was.

He took another look to be sure that nothing was amiss before he resumed his story: "Well, I suppose I got it into my head that I would see if there was any truth to the tale. I went to India first, to Malabar, and then I went north. Eventually I found myself in Lahore doing God knows what, and I managed to buy passage with a trade caravan bound for Samarkand. I suppose I fancied I would chase down the story and find out the truth, even it if was nothing more than my grandmother's bones."

"And what did you discover?" Varanus asked. "It sounds terribly dangerous and…exciting?"

Even if she held no faith in the family legend, she did seem genuinely interested in Friedrich's tale. It made Friedrich happy, though at the same time his delight was tinged with the knowledge that too much of the story would render the whole thing dismissible as absurd. Better to tread lightly and tell the breadth of his tale rather than the substance. After all, it was the first time he had enjoyed dinner with his mother in ten years. Surely that alone was more important than the truth.

"Well, it was not exactly easy," Friedrich admitted. "The merchants were not happy at the prospect of traveling with an infidel, but gold is gold. In the end, I think they accepted the likelihood that I would either die along the way or cease to be their problem once they reached their destination."

Varanus chuckled. "That sounds like merchants, truly. They are the same sort of men I am forced to entrust with managing my properties in France. If only I too had the opportunity of fleeing their company at the first sight of Samarkand."

"If only businessmen were so easy to avoid," Friedrich agreed, laughing aloud. He sipped his wine and smiled at his mother. Ah, but there was still more of the story to tell. But how much more? He wished to tell her all, but he would have to stop before she thought him mad. Eccentric was agreeable; insane was not.

"You went via Afghanistan, I presume."

"Naturally."

"It must have been very hard on you," Varanus noted. "That is rough country, even in the company of a well-stocked caravan." She paused and quickly amended, "Or so I have been told."

"It was very hard going," Friedrich agreed. "And to be honest, I fear.... I fear I may have caught a touch of fever along the way. I had a most peculiar dream somewhere along the road."

He was not entirely sure why he had thought to mention it, but it was true enough. The memory of it, however vague, still haunted him.

"Truly?" Varanus asked, reaching for her son's hand. She sounded concerned, almost distressed at the thought of him taking ill, even so long ago.

"I am much recovered, of course," Friedrich assured her. "But while I was sick, I had the most fantastical dream. It seemed almost real, I swear to you."

"Oh?"

"I dreamed that in Kabul the caravan took on another traveler," Friedrich said, weaving the fantasy of the tale with his tone and the waving of his hands. "A flaxen-haired maiden dressed in blue silk, if you can believe that."

"I can believe that you have a fruitful imagination," Varanus replied.

Friedrich smiled. "Well, in my dream, we traveled out of the highlands of Afghanistan, and we were followed by a pack of bandits who stalked us for several days."

"It must have been terrifying," Varanus said, not sounding particularly frightened. The benefit of hindsight, surely. After all, it had only been a dream and Friedrich was still alive, so what cause was there for concern?

"I must have been quite feverish," Friedrich admitted. "I recall distinctly that I dreamed I had arisen from bed one night, found my new friend strangely missing, and actually wandered out of camp to find her."

"Your noble impulse, no doubt."

"Well, yes," Friedrich admitted. "Even in a dream, I could hardly allow her to go wandering off on her own, could I?"

For some reason, his mother chuckled at this. She looked at him and seemed genuinely pleased.

"At the end of the dream, I found my strange new friend—Olga I think she called herself—in the camp of the bands I fancied were following us." Friedrich took another drink of wine. He very much enjoyed wine. It was a constant comfort to him. He had learned that much while Aunt Ilse was still alive. "And, if you can believe it, I imagined that I saw her fighting the bandits, killing them to a man to protect us."

Varanus laughed, but it was a happy laugh, filled with good humor. "In the grips of a fever you imagined a woman slaughtering men who would do you harm?"

"Well...yes," Friedrich said. He suddenly felt embarrassed. It was hardly a dignified thing for a man to dream about, being saved from death by the interventions of a woman.

"And...?" Varanus asked.

"And? Well, after she had killed the bandits, she saw me and...." Friedrich paused and laughed softly. The rest of the story was the most absurd. "Well, she looked into my eyes and told me to sleep, and I awoke." He snapped his fingers. "Fever broken, my senses restored to me."

"What did your companions say?" Varanus asked.

"It was they who confirmed that I was ill," Friedrich explained. "They had no recollection of the woman. They said I was feverish, and I had simply imagined her."

"That must have been quite the conversation," Varanus noted.

"Well, after I stopped insisting that they were wrong," Friedrich said, "and they insisted that if I carried on they'd leave my behind, we resolved the whole matter quite well."

"Compromise is so often the best resolution for disputes," Varanus agreed, though again she revealed a moment's look of distress at the mention of Friedrich being threatened with abandonment. She quickly concealed it behind her otherwise undisturbed expression, but it had been there for a moment. "And what happened then?"

Friedrich almost told her the truth, fantastical though it was. But as he opened his mouth to speak, he thought better of it. She would not believe him, and she would think he was insane. *He* almost believed himself insane.

"Then we continued on to Samarkand," he lied. "A magnificent city."

Well, he had gotten there eventually. And he had found it to be magnificent when he finally arrived.

"I shall have to visit sometime," Varanus said. She paused. "Speaking of maidens...."

Friedrich quickly took another drink, expecting what was to follow. "Yes?"

"Have you considered marrying, Alis...Friedrich?" Varanus asked.

There it was again. "Alistair." The name Varanus had given him before he could even recall being someone. The name he did not remember, yet it still echoed to him whenever she said it. But at least she was trying to use his proper name. His Von Fuchsburg name. The name Aunt Ilse had given him.

"I have," he replied, his tone ambiguous. "But I haven't found anyone suitable yet."

Well, that wasn't exactly true, but he suspected that Mother would be angry if he mentioned Aunt Ekaterine. And that was probably for the best. It was never a good idea to entangle two houses too closely together, unless one was a Habsburg. Although Aunt Ekaterine was more than a little magnificent, and the way she smiled was....

"That is a pity," Varanus said, interrupting his thoughts. "Of course, I would never want to pry, but as your mother...." She smiled. "I may have a few possible suggestions, when you decide to begin looking for an attachment. After all, every man wants to be married eventually."

"I'm not entirely certain that's true," Friedrich said. When his mother frowned, he added, "Not speaking of me, of course. I simply cannot wait for...um...nuptials."

Varanus sighed but she smiled at him. "I do not ask that you marry, Alis...Friedrich," she said. "I only ask that you give me some grandchildren. And surely, that is but a little thing to ask."

"Of course, Mother," Friedrich said. "I promise you that I will. Eventually."

And with the realization that his formula had worked, "eventually" might prove to be a very long time indeed.

* * * *

It was after sundown when they departed the restaurant. There was little enough light that Varanus did not wear her veil—part of a hereditary condition, she explained to Friedrich, but one that he had no fear of inheriting. It was curious, but Friedrich knew better than to pry.

They left by way of the Wenzelsplatz, where there were still some people taking in the pleasant, if crisp, evening air. There was an old man outside the restaurant drawing pictures in charcoal, and Friedrich, feeling charitable, gave him a few coins as they passed by.

"This was…well, quite fun, Mother," he said, as he helped her into a cab.

"Quite fun," Varanus agreed with a smile.

"Would you care to take breakfast tomorrow?" Friedrich asked hopefully. "I believe Aunt Ekaterine is having another sitting with Zoya. You could join her."

Varanus considered this and sighed. "I fear I am likely to be staying in tomorrow morning. Perhaps a late lunch?"

"I would like that," Friedrich said.

"Lunch it is," Varanus agreed. "Come by at around two."

After seeing his mother off, Friedrich returned home by a circuitous route, more from habit than concern for secrecy. All points indicated that Stanislav's misinformation had already done the trick. According to reliable circles, all of the talk about Stanislav and Erzsebet had it that they had already quit Prague in favor of some more distant place.

Upon returning to his house in Zizkov, Friedrich found a party in full swing, no doubt celebrating that very same liberation from outside scrutiny that so relieved his nerves. Zoya was irritated, of course, and he found her sitting by the window trying in vain to paint Erzsebet as the young woman lounged in Stanislav's arms. The revolutionaries were in good spirits, drinking and laughing their concerns away. They were used to hiding from the authorities, but hiding from some aristocrat with a vendetta was ignominious.

Friedrich quickly joined the party, sharing drinks with Stanislav and the others. He even joined Karel in an impromptu poetry recital, though he only half understood what they were saying. Through it all, he saw that Zoya remained at the parlor window, painting the scene of their revelry and every so often looking out through the glass. Presently, Friedrich joined her, bearing two glasses of the stiff spirits that Wilhelm had provided the company.

"Thirsty?" he asked.

"Parched," Zoya said, taking the glass with a smile and sipping it.

"And what has you so enthralled over here?"

Friedrich looked at the painting and saw that it was more a conceptual study than a rendition of fact. It showed all of them in a state of revelry, but the focal point was Erzsebet seated before the fire, surrounded by an aura of light.

"Radiance," Zoya replied.

"You and your light," Friedrich said, taking a drink. He grinned. "And I thought that Aunt Ekaterine was your muse."

Zoya sighed, taking the comment far more seriously than it had been intended. "Erzsebet is fire. Your aunt is light. If I could have the two of them together, it would be marvelous." She shrugged. "Alas, the best I can manage is a few hours with either."

"I could be your muse," Friedrich joked.

"You lack the necessary qualities," Zoya replied, though she smiled.

"Ah."

Zoya glanced toward the window again and frowned. "Friedrich...."

"Yes?"

"There are a couple of men at the end of the street," Zoya said. "They have been there at least an hour. I think they're watching us."

"What?" Friedrich asked.

He leaned against the window and peered through the glass. Being dark, there was only a little that he could make out, but the stars were bright, and they showed enough for him to see. There were two men at the end of the block, a little distance from the house. They had settled in beneath an overhanging room, and Friedrich almost dismissed them as vagrants seeking shelter from the elements. But as Friedrich watched for a few minutes, he saw one of the men strike a match and light a pipe. His blood chilled as he recognized the artist who had been situated in the Wenzelsplatz only a few hours earlier.

"My God..." he murmured.

"So I haven't lost my mind?" Zoya asked. "They *are* watching us?"

"I think so," Friedrich said.

Who could it be? Von Steiersberg's men, surely. Or possibly some in league with Count Erdelyi. But it was simply mad to think that such men were there watching them. Hadn't Stanislav's friends done their job already and misled anyone on his trail? And how had these men found the house? Had they been following him all day? Was that it?

"What do we do?" Zoya asked softly.

"I...am not sure," Friedrich said.

"I don't want to cause a panic."

The calm in Zoya's tone had surprised Friedrich, but as he looked into her eyes, he saw the very real fear there. She was simply keeping cool under pressure, but she was terrified. Terrified like any sensible person would be.

Friedrich finished his glass in a single gulp. "It could just be a coincidence," he said. "Best not to jump to conclusions."

"Is it a coincidence?" Zoya asked skeptically.

Friedrich hesitated. "No. No, it's not." He quickly stood as an idea came to him. "We are going to leave. What we should have done after the incident in the cafe."

"Where are we supposed to go?"

"Um." Friedrich considered his options. "We will stay with my mother. I am certain she would…well…tolerate the company. And Aunt Ekaterine would enjoy having guests, I think."

"What do you want me to do?"

"We can't leave on foot," Friedrich said. "They will follow us if we do. Keep everyone here and get the lads armed. Well, anyone who's close to sober at least. I'll sneak out the back and get help. We will need at least two carriages to transport everyone. I am certain there is at least one at Mother's house, and even if we must hire a cab, I don't think I would trust one lurking around the corner just now."

"Agreed."

Friedrich bit his lip. Perhaps he was panicking unnecessarily. Perhaps it was all absurd. But surely Mother wouldn't say no. She might even like the company.

He glanced at his reflection in the window and shook his head. No, Mother would not like the company. But she would tolerate it for his sake. Hopefully this was only paranoia, and tomorrow morning he would wake up and feel an absolute fool.

Again his reflection shook its head at him.

It was not paranoia, and he was not being foolish. They were all still in danger, and he needed to get them out of it before something terrible happened.

CHAPTER EIGHTEEN

Varanus lay against Julius, held tightly in his arms, her lips pressing against his. She smiled softly as Julius caressed the back of her neck with his fingertips. Julius was a delightful distraction, and Varanus enjoyed being distracted by him.

"What is it, *Fräulein?*" Julius murmured, smiling back at her. He looked into her eyes, his own lit with admiration and desire.

Varanus grinned and ran her fingernails along Julius's cheek. "I am simply admiring a particular *objet d'art*," she said.

"Mmm."

Julius sat up and kissed Varanus again. Varanus held him tightly and pressed against him, breathing deeply as the intoxicating sound of Julius's heartbeat echoed in her ears. It was a delicious sound that tickled some slumbering part of her mind, making her warm with excitement, warm with hunger. But she could not allow herself to partake of him, and the longing for him, the longing for his blood, made the hunger all the stronger.

It made the hunger almost pleasurable.

Julius rolled sideways and pushed Varanus onto the bed. Startled, Varanus laughed in delight. Torn away from her pleasant thoughts of blood and indulgence, she ran her fingers through Julius's blond hair and kissed him again.

She was broken from the pleasure of the moment by a sudden, sharp knock. She jerked away from Julius and snapped her head around to look at the door, her hands immediately clenching into fists, ready for whatever threat had intruded upon them.

Sudden noises always meant danger. She had learned that five years ago, and that understanding had never left her. It had burrowed down into her very bones and lurked there still.

Beneath her, Julius gasped and then exhaled. He fell back against the pillows and muttered, "Damn them all, what is it?"

"What?" Varanus asked, looking back at him.

Julius stroked her cheek and let his fingertips trace the soft skin beneath her chin.

"I instructed the servants to leave us in peace," he said, sounding irritated. He was breathing heavily, just as she was. "It must be some emergency to have disobeyed my orders."

Varanus sighed and rolled sideways, flopping onto the bed. Damn the servants indeed, she thought, as the knock sounded again. She quickly brushed her hair with her fingers to make herself more presentable. Not that it much mattered. She was still more or less clothed—neither she nor Julius had had the patience to fully disrobe—but being caught in a gentleman's bedroom was scandalous, no matter how pronounced her state of undress.

Nor, of course, did Varanus much care. That was the great advantage of being Shashavani sojourning in the mortal world: if things became too problematic, one could always leave.

Julius stood and put on the dressing gown that hung near the door. He was too shirtless to be seen, even by the servants. The knock sounded a third time.

"Your Lordship?" called a very intrusive voice from the adjoining chamber.

"What is it?" Julius demanded, pulling open the door.

Varanus saw one of the footmen standing beyond the threshold, carrying a small parcel in one hand. As he began to speak, he caught sight of Varanus and turned slightly pale.

Julius cleared his throat and repeated, "What is it?"

"My apologies, My Lord," the footman said softly, regaining some measure of his composure, "but there are some gentlemen who must speak with you on a matter of importance."

Julius's mouth tightened in annoyance, and he glanced at Varanus. She smiled at him, but she suspected that her expression still managed to convey more than a measure of irritation.

"Can it wait until the morning?" Julius asked.

"I am told that it cannot."

The footman handed Julius the parcel. Julius sighed again and examined the papers inside. After a few pages, he nodded to the footman.

"Yes, very well," he said. "Tell them I will be with them momentarily."

"Yes, My Lord."

"And offer the men a drink," Julius added. "In deference to the hour."

"I was already instructed to do so, My Lord."

"Oh," Julius said. "Well, carry on." As the footman withdrew, Julius turned back to Varanus and gave her an apologetic look. "Forgive me, *Fräulein*. I shall be but ten minutes. Twenty at most."

Varanus flashed him an amused grin. "I am not known for my patience."

Julius coughed and rubbed his chin, unable to hide a smile. "Five minutes."

"I shall be counting," Varanus told him. She arched an eyebrow and pointed toward the clock on the mantle.

Julius exhaled and repeated, "Five minutes."

He backed into the adjoining office and closed the door behind him. The door did not quite catch, and it remained ajar just enough for Varanus to hear Julius searching through the desk in the office.

Varanus lay back on the bed and stared at the ceiling. She slowly closed her eyes and listened to the ticking of the clock.

Tick, tock. Tick, tock. Tick....

"Enjoying yourself, *Liebchen?*"

Varanus's eyes opened to see Korbinian's pale, beautiful, blood-stained face gazing back at her from above. She gasped in fright and covered her mouth with both hands to keep from crying out. Korbinian merely smiled, and a few droplets of blood fell from his eyes, fading into smoke before they touched Varanus's face.

Regaining her composure, Varanus sat up and glared at Korbinian.

"As a matter of fact, I was," she said angrily. It was the first time she had actually responded to Korbinian's oft-repeated question, and she was curious whether he had a reply.

"How strange that your new friend has deserted you at this hour," Korbinian said. He walked around the end of the bed, never looking away from Varanus. "Were it me sharing your company on a cold evening, I could not be dragged from your embrace by armed men and wild dogs."

"You have become very dramatic of late," Varanus noted.

"I have always been dramatic, *Liebchen*. I am from Fuchsburg. We are a passionate people."

"I know this to be true," Varanus murmured, tinged with the memory of Korbinian in life.

Korbinian walked to the door and gently eased it open. Varanus could just barely hear voices speaking in the suite of rooms beyond the office.

"What I wonder, *Liebchen*, is what business can be so pressing that it could possibly lure a man away from you for as long as...." Korbinian looked at the clock. "Four minutes and thirty seconds."

"I do not know," Varanus replied, "nor do I care. Business, politics, war? It is none of our concern."

Korbinian paused in the doorway and smiled at her. The flickering firelight twisted the shadows about his face, transforming his mirth into something hideous and unsettling.

"Oh, but *Liebchen*, I am such an inquisitive creature. How could I not intrude into another man's affairs?"

He turned and stepped into the office. Varanus was on her feet in an instant, following him with a hurried pace. He was up to some mischief, and she had to stop him. Why, she could not imagine: no one else could see or hear him. But she could not allow him to go wandering about the house doing God knew what in Julius's absence.

And besides, even if others could not see him, it did not mean he could not touch them. She had seen him kill before. What if he planned to kill again?

There was a ringing in Varanus's ears as she crossed the bedroom and entered the office. The blood sang in her temples and her mouth felt dry. The shadows followed in her footsteps and clung to her skirt like the grasping hands of children afraid of losing their mother.

She saw Korbinian at Julius's desk, idly searching through its contents. The desk was in impeccable order, but almost maliciously Korbinian poked at its contents with his fingertips, knocking over the neatly stacked papers and rummaging through the drawers.

"What are you doing?" Varanus demanded, though she kept her voice very low so that she would not be heard by Julius and his guests in the adjoining room.

"Being inquisitive," Korbinian replied, as he picked up one of Julius's pens and dropped it onto the floor.

"Stop it!" Varanus hissed.

She felt that she should charge across the room, grab Korbinian by the arms, and drag him away. How dare he behave in such a manner! But she could not. The grasping shadows were too heavy as they clung to her, dragging her back toward the bedroom. It was all she could manage to cross the office with slow and deliberate steps until she stood on the far side of the desk, watching Korbinian angrily as he continued his impetuous display.

"But *Liebchen*," Korbinian said, smirking horribly, "we must answer the question. What could possibly drag a man from your arms at such an hour? For I find in that a thing most curious."

He tried the last drawer on the desk. It was locked.

"Mmm. Curious indeed."

"Stop this now!" Varanus demanded. "We are guests!"

Korbinian took a letter opener from the chaos he had created on the top of the desk and forced the locked drawer open. He took out the parcel that Julius had been given and began to examine its contents, which proved to be sheets of coarse paper now that Varanus looked at them properly. Seeing them from behind, she did not know what they contained, but whatever Korbinian read in them made a fresh tear of blood trickle from his eye.

"Oh, *Liebchen*," he murmured, "what man could not be jealous of you?"

"What are you talking about?"

Without a word, Korbinian held up the papers for Varanus's examination. Varanus took a step closer and suddenly realized that they were sketches, drawn variously in pencil and charcoal with a practiced hand. The first was of some people seated in a cafe: Friedrich and his friends.

"No…" Varanus murmured.

"Yes, *Liebchen*," Korbinian replied.

He dropped the first drawing. The next was Friedrich again, on his own, reading a book over breakfast in a small restaurant.

"Julius has been following our son?"

The paper fell away from Korbinian's fingers, revealing another of Friedrich, another of his friends, another and another until the floor was littered with drawings of Friedrich being watched in secret. Korbinian smiled as he held up the last few sketches.

Varanus saw herself and her son standing in the Wenzelsplatz outside the restaurant they had dined at that very night, smiling and talking. Varanus felt cold. She shuddered and the shadows drew in all around to comfort her. She saw a hideous light in Korbinian's eyes as he smiled and held up the very last page.

It was a simple, hurried sketch of Friedrich's house, with her son just about to enter.

"What is this?" Varanus whispered, finding her throat dry and her voice hoarse. She took the sketch from Korbinian and stared at it.

"Don't you see, *Liebchen?*" Korbinian murmured in her ear. Suddenly he was behind her, his bloody cheek caressing her hair. "Your new friend is going to murder our son."

"No.…"

It could not be so simple, Varanus told herself. There was something going on, truly, but she could find a solution. She only had to think! Why couldn't she think?

Korbinian opened the office door and, taking Varanus by the hand, led her through a small corridor toward the adjoining parlor. The voices were louder, but they were unclear, a chaotic torrent of words that Varanus recognized but did not understand. She stepped into the parlor and saw Julius standing around a table with a group of men, all of them examining a map. Von Steiersberg was among them, but she did not recognize the others.

"Now remember," Julius was saying, "make sure you capture the girl and the violinist."

"Leave no witnesses," Von Steiersberg added.

"No witnesses," Julius agreed after a moment's hesitation.

As they spoke, Von Steiersberg looked up and caught sight of Varanus approaching. He gasped and swore. The other men turned, and Varanus saw the blood drain from Julius's face.

"Varanus…" he said, taking a few steps toward her. "I said I would only be a few minutes. We are just discussing—"

"My son," Varanus finished.

Julius's eyes fell upon the sketch that Varanus still held in her hand. A look of regret crossed his face.

"I am so very sorry," he murmured.

"I demand an explanation, Count von Raabe!" Varanus snapped. "You have had men following my son! Following me! And now this?"

Von Steiersberg drew alongside Julius. "You know what must be done," he said.

Julius exhaled and nodded. He took a few steps toward Varanus, who quickly withdrew a pace.

"Julius, let us be reasonable," Varanus said.

"I am sorry," Julius replied, shaking his head. "I do not know what else you have seen. What else you have heard. And I know that you are not a fool. But I promise I will be quick."

"Get on with it!" Von Steiersberg shouted.

"Julius…" Varanus said, withdrawing again and slowly raising her hands.

But Julius did not answer her. He lunged forward and grabbed Varanus by the throat, choking her with his strong, smooth fingers. His grip was more powerful than Varanus had remembered, perhaps invigorated by desperation. Had she still walked in the Shadow of Death, she might soon be in its darkness.

But she was Living, and the Living had little to fear from mortal strength.

Varanus broke Julius's grasp easily and tore his hands away. Julius stared at her, shocked to see such power in the body of someone so small.

"How…?"

Varanus did not answer. Instead, she grabbed his robe and pulled him down to her level, kissed his soft lips one last time—for even marred by treachery, they were still quite pleasant—and slammed his head against the door frame. She heard and felt the side of his skull fracture from the blow.

"Good God!" someone exclaimed.

"Kill her!" Von Steiersberg shouted, backing away and grabbing a revolver inside his coat. "Kill her now!"

The other men rushed at Varanus. Some of them came barehanded while others had the sense to draw knives or pistols, but all of them moved close too quickly for the weapons to be useful. Now all thoughts of reason and discourse were gone. The darkness in the corners of the parlor loomed high, painting the walls and the ceiling black as Varanus flung herself into the mob, kicking and punching.

Varanus killed two men outright as they came at her with knives, crushing the throat of one and striking the other hard in the chest until his heart gave out. Another man was suddenly upon her, and Varanus ducked low and threw him into a fourth man armed with a revolver before the gunman could fire.

The headiness of violence had taken her, and Varanus laughed as she fought. Across the room, Von Steiersberg aimed his pistol at her; Varanus, lacking another body to throw, grabbed a book from a nearby shelf and hurled it at him. Von Steiersberg shied away, turning so that the book struck him in the arm.

Laughing again, Varanus dispatched a third man as he collapsed in front of her, snapping his neck with a single twist. Everywhere she turned, Varanus saw Korbinian watching her amid the looming shadows, a smile on his bloody lips.

"Behind you," he whispered, though Varanus still heard him clearly.

Varanus spun about, expecting another one of Von Steiersberg's men. Instead she saw Julius standing with ease despite his injury, as blood slowly pooled into one eye, transforming it to a bright crimson.

"How…?" Varanus gasped.

As she spoke, her eyes caught a flash of steel. She grabbed for Julius and flung him away again, but not before he plunged a knife deep into her neck and tore a long slice across the side of her throat.

Varanus grabbed at her throat as blood spurted across the wall and the carpet. Were she mortal she would be suffocating too, but breathing was the least of her concerns. Varanus felt her head swim and her limbs go heavy. A few moments later, she collapsed to her knees and finally fell onto the floor, her eyes darting about in a desperate search for something to staunch the blood.

Even the Living were vulnerable to blood loss, which sapped their strength and finally paralyzed them until their wounds could heal.

Varanus had seen Shashavani far older and stronger than she rendered helpless by nothing more than a slit throat or a sword through the heart.

Nearby, Julius picked himself up again and clutched his head. The other men were getting up too—those that had not been killed outright.

"A fine mess of things this is, Julius," Von Steiersberg grumbled, hurrying to help his friend. "And all over the carpet too!"

"I will buy you a new carpet," Julius grumbled. He looked down at Varanus, who he surely assumed was dying as her limbs grew numb and her body stopped writhing. "Such a shame. She would have been a marvelous addition to our society."

"There is always the husband," Von Steiersberg noted.

Julius shook his head. "No, it is too much of a risk. Who knows how he will react to his wife's death. Best to leave it. Or perhaps kill him too. He is dangerously inquisitive regarding the tenets of our faith."

Von Steiersberg gave a nod of agreement. "That is probably best." He snapped his fingers at a couple of the men. "You two, dress the body, make certain you take all of her jewels and valuables, and dump the body in the river. Make it seem a robbery. The servants will attend to our dead comrades."

"Yes, My Lord," came the reply.

"Where is the husband?" Julius asked. "He has something I would like to acquire before his grief drives him back to Russia and beyond my grasp."

"I have it on good report that he has been at the bookseller's all evening," Von Steiersberg said.

"Even better. Herr Mordechai is another dangerously inquisitive person. He may be a skeptic, but I fear he will eventually uncover something that will leave him unable to dismiss our faith as fantasy. Better to kill him now and prevent an unwanted epiphany."

Julius went to a nearby table with halting, uncertain steps and scribbled a list of names onto a piece of paper. Varanus counted it a miracle that he was still conscious and standing, but he was clearly suffering some effects from his fractured skull. He handed the paper to the nearest man and said:

"This is a list of books in Herr Mordechai's possession that I require. Go to the bookstore, kill the bookseller and Prince Shashavani, and retrieve these items. Then burn the place. Leave nothing to be found."

The man nodded and hurried for the door, quick about his business.

"I have some agents watching the bookstore!" Von Steiersberg called after him. "Gerhard and Schultz. They will help you." He turned to the others. "The rest of you, come with me. We go to retrieve my fiancée and punish the dog who dared to steal her!"

This was met with cheers. The men were eager for violence, Varanus noted, though it was only with great effort that she maintained enough consciousness to think such a thought. Her vision was clouded almost to blindness, and soon she would be unconscious.

She saw Julius kneel over her and stroke her cheek. She wanted to lunge at him and tear out his throat, but her body could not even twitch in reply to the impulse.

"Alas, my darling," Julius murmured, "what a shame this is. I was so certain you were touched by Her favor. Such life. Now but dead flesh."

Varanus tried to scream her rage, but her lungs had stopped working.

Von Steiersberg placed a hand on Julius's arm and helped him stand again.

"Are you certain you want to join us for the ritual?" he asked. "Perhaps you should rest."

Julius touched his temple, which gave slightly beneath his finger.

"Oh no, my friend, it is imperative that I am there and imperative that we have a proper sacrifice. Our Mother in Her mercy has preserved me for now, but without an offering and Her divine grace, I doubt that I will last the week. The violinist's death will be my salvation."

Von Steiersberg smiled and said something, but Varanus could no longer hear anything. The shadows closed in around her until there was nothing left but the darkness of dead senses and a corpse confining a living mind as it struggled blindly against oblivion.

CHAPTER NINETEEN

Friedrich was still waiting at the window when Stanislav joined him, alerted to the danger by a few quiet words from Zoya. Stanislav was pale with worry, and he kept his hand resting on the handle of his revolver as he looked out past the curtains.

"Yes, I know spies when I see them," he said, after a lengthy observation. "How long have they been there?"

"Couldn't say," Friedrich answered. "Some time at least."

"Over an hour," Zoya added.

"You saw them first?" Stanislav asked.

Zoya nodded. "At first I didn't think anything of it. You know we often get drunks around here."

Stanislav and Friedrich exchanged leery looks. The vagrant population in their particular little neighborhood often seemed to outnumber the other inhabitants.

"But I finally realized they were actually *watching* the house," Zoya continued, "so I alerted Freddie."

"Freddie before me?" Stanislav asked. He made it a joke, but Friedrich knew he was annoyed.

"Of course. It's Freddie's house."

"Wilhelm's the one the landlord deals with," Stanislav said.

"Freddie pays for it," Zoya countered.

Friedrich cleared his throat and raised a finger. "Back to the spies."

"Right," Stanislav agreed. "What to do."

"Obviously we must leave," Friedrich said. "It's not safe for you or Erzsebet."

"You reckon it's Von Steiersberg?" Stanislav asked. He sounded surprised, still holding confidence in the idea that they had given Erzsebet's fiancé the slip.

Friedrich almost mentioned that he recognized the spies, but he stopped himself. Mentioning that would mean revealing that he had seen the sketch artist earlier that day. They must have followed him home. If only he had shown better sense, if only he had been more alert, none of this would be happening. And he could not bring himself to reveal that, however hard he tried to form the words. Guilt held fast his tongue and left the truth dead in his throat.

"Of course it's Von Steiersberg," Zoya replied. "You don't believe he was tricked by that nonsense about you fleeing the city, do you?" She sighed and shook her head. "A wily fox like that wouldn't go chasing halfway across Europe in search of you without leaving a few of his dogs behind to keep sniffing, would he?"

"You give his cleverness too much credit," Stanislav said.

"Who else would it be?" Friedrich asked, finding his voice again.

"Secret police, obviously," Stanislav answered. "It might not even be me they are after. It could be anyone: Wilhelm, Ilya, Nicolas, that Schmidt fellow who turned up the other day."

"Regardless, they are here," Friedrich said. "We must act quickly."

"Agreed." Stanislav looked out the window again. "If they're watching the front, we will have to go out the back, through the alleyway."

"And if more men are out back?" Zoya asked.

Stanislav drew his revolver for effect. "We go past them, one way or another. But at least we will escape them before they can come in force to our front door!"

Friedrich frowned as the implications of Zoya's question began to sink in. Why attack by the front door, down a street that was plainly visible from the windows, even if it was pitch dark outside? Why not take the alley in the first place?

"Why would they come in force through the front?" he asked.

Stanislav turned pale. "Why indeed?" he agreed, taking a step back from the window as he came to grips with the same realization as Friedrich. "There's no clear view of the alleyway from the house. They could approach that way and we would never see them!"

Zoya slowly stood and looked around the room. "Where is Erzsebet?"

"She and Nicolas went to fetch some more wine from the kitchen…" Stanislav began. There was a pause as his face grew paler still. "Oh God."

As he spoke, a loud thudding noise sounded from the back of the house. It was followed moments later by the loud bark of gunshots, and suddenly the revelry in the parlor was seized by panic. Some people began screaming. The revolutionaries, drunk though they were, grabbed for their weapons. Some had revolvers, others had knives, and one fellow even upended a mostly empty bottle to serve as a club. The guests were there for the party and did not know what to do, but Stanislav's men were used to danger and they acted accordingly.

Friedrich and Stanislav exchanged one look and bolted for the kitchen. As he ran, Friedrich heard Zoya calling after them:

"Freddie! More are coming down the street!"

"Wilhelm, the front door!" Stanislav shouted in passing before leaving the other revolutionaries to protect the front of the house.

Friedrich was the first one into the kitchen, which was small and cramped and smelled of burned meat and old vegetables. There was a narrow door that led out into the alleyway. It had been latched, but now it stood open, thrown almost off its hinges by some powerful force—probably the shoulder of the brawny man with whom Friedrich suddenly found himself face-to-face.

The big fellow held a smoking revolver, and he fired at Friedrich, who only just managed to throw himself to the side in time to escape the shot. The bullet buried itself into the wood of the door frame. A moment later, Stanislav burst in, and Friedrich lunged at the invader to pre-empt the next shot, which would have been for his friend.

A blow to the head with the revolver barrel followed by a punch in the gut sent Friedrich to his knees. His head swam with pain, but he struggled to keep his senses. He saw blood on the floor. Then he spotted Nicolas lying by the door, slowly dying from the three bullet wounds in his chest. Erzsebet knelt by the dying man, his blood staining her dress and her hands.

Given his opening by Friedrich, Stanislav barreled into the attacker at full force, pummeling the man with his revolver. He took a step back and shot the attacker point blank in the chest. The man winced but he did not fall. Instead, despite what could only have been a considerable amount of pain, he tore the revolver from Stanislav's grasp and prepared to return fire with both weapons.

"Wait!" someone shouted from the doorway. It was another ruffian, dressed and armed similarly to his companion. "Wait, that's the violinist! Take him and the girl alive!"

The big man nodded but said nothing as he lowered his guns. Taking the hesitation as an opening, Stanislav charged again, punching viciously. Again the big man did not seem to care. He caught Stanislav's right arm and, with a single sharp tug, yanked it from its socket. Stanislav's eyes widened and he screamed, trying to lash out with his good arm despite the pain. The attacker grabbed him by the throat and struck him in the head a few times until Stanislav finally succumbed and fell into a swoon.

"No, no, no!" Erzsebet cried. She struggled to her feet, slipping on Nicolas's blood as she ran at the big man, her eyes wide with desperation and hatred.

On the ground, Friedrich had regained his senses. He clambered to his feet and made another lunge for his friend's attacker. He punched the man across the face hard enough that he felt something give—whether it was bone cracking or merely meat being shifted from the force, he could not tell. The big man stumbled slightly, but again he seemed to take no notice of the pain. Friedrich punched him again, this time in the gut, as Erzsebet joined them from the side, kicking and clawing and biting.

Looking more annoyed than anything, the big man grabbed Erzsebet's collar and threw her clumsily across the room. Unable to keep her footing, Erzsebet tumbled backward and landed in a heap atop Nicolas's body.

"I'm coming, Erzsebet!" Friedrich shouted, as he landed another blow against his enemy's unfeeling flesh.

Having dispensed with one irritation, the big man turned to Friedrich. He tried to bring his two revolvers to bear, but Friedrich refused to give him so easy a solution. Friedrich knocked one hand away before it could aim properly and then snapped his forearms together around the man's other wrist, forcing him to drop the gun. Friedrich then drove in with his shoulder against the man's chest and swatted the second pistol away with a vicious blow from his hand.

And yet, the big man was not deterred, only annoyed, if even that sentiment could be discerned from his dull expression. He punched Friedrich in the chest, knocking the wind out of Friedrich and leaving him hunched over, gasping for breath. The man shoved him away to get a little space and then took his arm, giving it a strong tug just as he had done to Stanislav.

But despite the pain, Friedrich's shoulder refused to give, the joint held firmly in place by the muscles and tendons that seemed to actively resist the attack. Instead, the force of the pull made Friedrich stumble forward into his attacker with enough momentum that the man had to scurry back a step so as not to lose his footing. Taking advantage of his enemy's confusion, Friedrich grabbed the man by the collar and slammed his forehead into the man's nose.

Bleeding and snorting, the man returned the favor, hitting Friedrich just over the eye. Friedrich reeled backward as lights exploded in his head. He had not quite regained himself when the big man grabbed him by the collar, punched him again, and threw him into the adjoining hallway with enough force that Friedrich almost passed through the doorway into the parlor.

For the moment stunned, Friedrich heard gunfire followed by the sound of windows shattering. Wilhelm and Ilya were shouting something. The revolutionaries were returning fire. People were screaming. Jadwiga the cat was yowling as she scurried about, looking for a place to hide. Amid the chaos around them, Friedrich saw Zoya grab Karel and pull him away from the fighting, which neither of them was equipped to help with.

Erzsebet's cries snapped him out of his daze. The revolutionaries could handle themselves. Stanislav and Erzsebet were on their own. Friedrich pulled himself up and ran back to the kitchen. He arrived just in time to see the big man slap Erzsebet across the face to silence her, before shoving her into the waiting hands of his accomplice in the alleyway. Stanislav was on the ground struggling to rise, but the big man kicked him a couple of times, and he collapsed again.

"Bastard! Leave them alone!" Friedrich shouted.

He ran for the attacker and threw himself on the big fellow, punching and kicking and tearing. Amid the pain and panic, he felt himself grow mad with fury, suddenly seized with the impulse to bite and tear, to gouge and claw.

Snorting blood from his broken nose, the big man took Friedrich by the throat and began choking him, ignoring Friedrich's fingers as they tore at his face. Even as Friedrich grew dizzy from loss of oxygen, the intensity of his violence only increased, driven by some deranged instinct to drag his enemy to the grave with him.

But it seemed his death was not sufficiently interesting for his enemy to be bothered with it. Instead, as Friedrich's attacks grew clumsy from the dizziness, the man slammed him against the wall a few times and threw him again, this time across the kitchen. Friedrich struck the iron stove and went limp for a few moments. Satisfied, the big man lifted Stanislav's body with both hands and hauled him into the alleyway.

For what felt like the better part of an hour, Friedrich lay where he had fallen, screaming inside his head for his body to move. He heard more shouting from the front of the house, more gunfire, more cries of pain and fear. Jadwiga was yowling. Then the yowling suddenly stopped.

He finally willed his hands to move again, clenching and unclenching his fists. Then he could lift his arms. Then he could turn his head. Then he was on his feet, leaning against the stove. His body ached from the abuse it had suffered, but with the pain came the intoxication of adrenaline. The headiness of violence.

He stumbled to the back door, his footing growing more sure with each step. Reaching the alleyway, he realized that his hour of senselessness had been perhaps a minute or two. The two men were still there, one carrying Stanislav, the other restraining Erzsebet and forcing her into a carriage that waited in the street. When she was finally inside, despite the vigor of her struggles, the men shoved Stanislav in after her and then climbed aboard at the back.

Friedrich started to run, somehow crossing the length of the dark alleyway without stumbling more than once or twice over the refuse that had been left there. He reached the carriage as the driver cracked his whip and it began to move. Now the men saw him, for though the moon was dark, the stars were out, and the street was lit by a few feeble lamps. The accomplice riding on the back called out, and the big fellow reached for Friedrich, but Friedrich ignored them. He jumped up and grabbed onto the door. Shattering the glass of the window with his elbow, he looked inside, searching for his friends.

He found them and the men who had taken them. The unconscious Stanislav was slumped in the seat on one side as his hands were being bound by a handsome, middle-aged man with very fine blond hair. On the seat across, he saw Erzsebet, her eyes wide with terror and hopelessness. Beside her sat a man Friedrich recognized from photographs as her unwanted fiancé, Count von Steiersberg. Von Steiersberg held Erzsebet's wrist with one hand while the other gripped her firmly by the back of the neck, making it clear that he did not intend to let her escape him again.

"Let go of her!" Friedrich shouted, as he struggled half to tear open the door and half to climb in through the window.

From the injury, the adrenaline, and whatever instinct of violence had taken him, his sense of reason had more or less fled, leaving behind a confused muddle of action that drove him forward, onward, seeking his friends, seeking his enemies, seeking their blood.

The breaking of the window made Von Steiersberg and the blond man look up. Von Steiersberg was alarmed, startled even. He had sent men to retrieve his prize, and he clearly did not anticipate having to become personally involved. The blond man was more composed. He looked at Friedrich and tilted his head, a slight smile playing on his lips.

"Now that is interesting," he murmured, reaching into his coat. "Quite a resemblance. Such a pity."

There was a flash of steel in the darkness, and suddenly the blond man was at the window, though Friedrich had not seen him move. Another flash and Friedrich felt fresh pain blossom in his chest, just below his heart. Startled, he looked down and saw a knife protruding from his chest.

Suddenly the carriage jolted as it struck some uneven paving stones, and Friedrich's grip slipped. He grabbed wildly for another handhold, but his fingers found only air as he tumbled backward into the street. He struck the ground painfully and felt his will to rise again ebb.

As the rattling of the carriage receded into the distance, he stared at the knife protruding from his chest. His head lolled backward against the stones, and he gazed up at the moonless sky until the darkness took him.

CHAPTER TWENTY

In the back room of Mordechai's bookstore, Iosef sat with a small glass of wine in his hand, periodically sipping as he compared passages from three books that his host had kindly provided for him. Mordechai sat nearby in much the same state: a little wine, several texts, and a collection of curiosities waiting to be identified. They had spoken little since Iosef's arrival several hours ago, save to exchange thoughts on a point of mutual interest or to offer a query from one scholar to another. But, Iosef reflected, Mordechai did not seem to mind the silence any more than he did.

Presently, Iosef finished his glass and went to a nearby table to refill it. As he did, a thought came to him and he paused.

"Mordechai," he said, "the Hoffmann artifact came from a tomb in Poland, is that correct?"

Mordechai looked up from his work and removed his spectacles. "Yes, near Poznan, I believe. I am told it was a remarkable find with all manner of ancient relics. Alas, I was not privy to it myself."

He stood and joined Iosef at the table as Iosef refilled both their glasses.

"So you would not know about the tomb's other contents?" Iosef asked. "Its layout? Composition? For whom it was built?"

"Well, the latter I can surmise," Mordechai replied. "From what I was told, it was quite clearly built for a Slavic chieftain. And having seen some of the more commonplace items taken from the excavation, I am certain of it. You recall several items from the Hoffmann estate came into my possession."

"Of course."

Mordechai looked off into the distance as he recalled the list. "Two swords," he said. "I still have one. The other was recently acquired by a gentleman from Salzburg. Several pieces of jewelry. I believe that was the extent of it."

"Were there any statues?" Iosef asked.

"Statues?"

"Idols," Iosef clarified.

"Ah." Mordechai gave him a knowing smile. "You want to know whether the tomb was for a worshipper of the Horned Serpent."

"Indeed."

"Count von Raabe asked me the same thing some time ago," Mordechai said, chuckling softly with genuine amusement. "Unfortunately, in that regard, I can only answer with ignorance. Having never inspected the tomb myself, I can only surmise from the artifacts I acquired. But I suppose it would not surprise me. The region where the tomb was found does have a long-standing association with the cult—if certain rather esoteric legends are to be believed."

"Kaminskus Magnus," Iosef said.

He sipped his wine and tried to ignore the whispers in the shadows. They always troubled him late at night, but recently they had become more pronounced. It was possibly the result of some impending madness, but that fear was fanciful. It was more likely stress and long hours coupled with the overhanging guilt at Sophio's death, a guilt that grew worse and worse the more he pursued his studies into her final area of scholarship.

"Kaminskus Magnus indeed!" Mordechai exclaimed happily. "An excellent scholar, if a little political in his motivation."

"When one serves at the pleasure of the king, one cannot easily avoid that," Iosef noted.

"Perhaps not." Mordechai smiled. "But that is why I labor in a bookstore and not at court."

"Much more sensible."

"Kaminski's account of witchcraft in Poland almost certainly uncovered a very real, persistent cult of the Horned Serpent," Mordechai said, "in addition to countless benign practitioners of the old Slavic faith or various folk traditions."

"Certainly," Iosef agreed.

"The problem we face is in clearly separating the one from the other, as so much of the varied and nuanced practices of pagan worshippers have repeatedly been dismissed in favor of a rather absurd notion of some monolithic 'devil worship'. Kaminski's observations are generally more objective than most, but he too falls under the sway of simplicity."

Iosef gave a thin smile. "It is a dark temptation."

"I hope that is not a touch of sarcasm, Your Highness," Mordechai replied, though his tone was jesting. "We might enjoy our tidy libraries and reading rooms—"

Iosef coughed softly. Mordechai might be regarded as *organized*, but he was anything but tidy.

"—but the world is messy with nuance. Whenever we scholars accept simple answers for complicated questions, we fail in our task. Religion pretends that things are simple. We know better."

"You reject the notion that one of those many simple answers might be right?" Iosef asked.

"Without hesitation," Mordechai said, sounding very pleased. "There was a time when I was a religious man, but in my youth I traveled and I encountered a great many religions and a great many religious people who very eloquently explained why their faith and theirs alone was unquestionably correct." Mordechai frowned for a moment, remembering a pang of disappointment. "Eventually they began to sound more or less the same and none of them very convincing."

Iosef paused for a moment, considering whether to voice the question that tickled his curiosity. It was quite a presumptuous thing to ask, and he still enjoyed having access to Mordechai's books and knowledge and to Mordechai himself, whom Iosef found to be an agreeable study companion.

Mordechai must have read the sentiment in Iosef's eyes, for he said, "You want to ask me something."

"It is…very forward, I fear," Iosef replied. "I do not wish to be rude to a new friend."

"Ask it anyway," Mordechai told him, smirking a little. He did not seem troubled by the ambiguity of Iosef's statement. Perhaps he already anticipated the question.

"Are you an atheist, Mordechai?" Iosef finally asked.

"Ah.…" Mordechai nodded with understanding. "A worthy question. I would say that I am a deeply religious man still waiting for a revelation from God rather than the dubious claims of men. Though perhaps 'religious' is not the proper word for it. I distrust anything that demands obedience when it ought to demonstrate merit."

"God demands faith," Iosef countered. He did not really believe it, but Mordechai's philosophical revelation intrigued him.

"Man demands faith," Mordechai said. "The docile acceptance of unproven things. It guides the peasant to obey his lord, the wife to obey her husband, the laity to obey the clergy, and all people to obey their divinely appointed king. And when obedience fails, faith sooths the conscience of the survivors when the rebellious have been put to death." He paused and gazed into his wine as it gently swirled inside his cup. "I do not trust faith, young Iosef. By its power, I have seen atrocities proclaimed as good deeds and justice condemned as heresy."

Iosef snickered under his breath at being referred to as "young", but he did not allow his amusement to show. Mordechai looked perhaps ten or even fifteen years his senior. Of course the man regarded him as some untested youth. It was almost as bad as Julius, but not quite.

His amusement slowly faded as he felt the shadows lengthening, murmuring "Sophio, Sophio, Sophio" in his ear. Iosef quickly shook himself.

"After all," Mordechai continued, "what is religion but a conspiracy between the warrior class and the intellectual class to exploit everyone else? The warriors protect the priests, and the priests legitimize the warriors' rule. Those who do not fight and do not pray must work…and they must work so that the other two need not."

"A rather cynical view of things," Iosef said.

"Perhaps," Mordechai agreed. "I often suspect that cynicism is the logical result of age and experience. But then, I have been told that I am far too cheerful to be a cynic, so perhaps not."

Iosef smiled a little. "I suspect that to be true."

He paused as he heard the bell above the front door ring.

"Ah! Customers at this hour?" Mordechai asked. He set his glass down and hurried to the front room.

Iosef followed him a few paces back. "Are you still open for business?"

"I suppose I never really close," Mordechai replied. "Customers simply stop visiting for a few hours each day."

"Indeed," Iosef murmured.

He found the bookstore very dark. The gas lamps burned low, and there was precious little light. Despite the darkness, Iosef had little difficulty in seeing a group of men who had just entered. Mordechai raised a hand in greeting as he turned the gas knob on the wall. The lamps blossomed to life, but in the claustrophobic confines of the bookstore, they did little good.

"Good evening, gentlemen!" Mordechai exclaimed. "Welcome to my humble store. What do you req—"

Iosef saw three men, by now spread out a few paces. One was inspecting the contents of a nearby case, another stood by the door, and a third approached Mordechai with a friendly smile and an outstretched hand. It was only as Mordechai began his final sentence that Iosef noticed a fourth man, lurking in the shadows, aiming a pistol at Mordechai's head.

In the few seconds it took for Iosef to see the threat, to turn and lunge, the man fired twice. Mordechai seemed to notice too, in the moment just before the pistol's report. He snapped his head around just as the bullets entered through one eye and the bridge of his nose, tearing apart his brain and shattering his skull. He gasped a noise that might have been a surprised "Oh!" and collapsed in a heap.

"Kill, kill, kill," whispered the shadows.

Iosef did not need the prompting of grief-borne delusions to know what his instincts already told him. The man with the gun turned his aim on Iosef, but Iosef was already leaping through the air. Iosef's chest stung as he was shot twice, but it did not stop him. The weight of impact threw the man back into the nearest bookshelf. The pistol dropped to the floor with a clatter and was lost in the darkness.

To his credit, Iosef's opponent tried not to succumb easily. He grabbed a knife from beneath his coat and would have driven it into Iosef's flesh, but Iosef was not inclined to give him such satisfaction. He grabbed the man by the throat and hoisted him into the air, slowly choking him. The man lashed out with his knife, but Iosef knocked it away with a sweep of his hand.

He expected the others to come at him in defense of their accomplice or at least in pursuit of their unknown task, but they did not. Iosef glanced over his shoulder and saw that the bookstore was empty. Or at least empty as far as he could see. Despite the lamps, it was extremely dark: darker than he remembered it being before the fighting began. But surely that was merely a trick of memory. Had the other attackers fled?

He was answered a moment later by a flicker of movement in the shadows beside him. The steel of a blade stung him in the side, just below his ribs. Glancing down, he saw that a knife had been driven through his waistcoat and into his flesh. But as Iosef grabbed for his new attacker, the man withdrew into the darkness, and Iosef's hand closed on air.

Confused, Iosef quickly killed the man still in his grasp and dropped the body. He turned and regarded the room, his eyes darting about and his ears straining to catch the slightest hint of danger. He managed to hear scraps of noise scattered around, lurking behind the bookshelves and lingering in the shadows upon creaking floorboards, but everything was muffled like sound underwater.

Another flash of movement made Iosef turn again. Another knife was driven deep into his forearm. Iosef lashed out at the man who had attacked him and felt ribs break beneath his fist. The man gasped in pain. It was a wet, strained sound. But before Iosef could follow up with a second blow, he was stabbed again, this time from behind. The knife tore the back of his neck just under the edge of his collar. It hurt, but it did not manage to sever any of the major blood vessels.

Iosef spun around with inhuman quickness and again found himself facing shadows. A slow panic began to creep over him. What impossibility was this? Three mortal men stabbing at him in the darkness could not possibly be a threat. He had faced far worse countless times before, and though he was often injured, his enemies fell quickly and did not rise again. But now his senses betrayed him? He could not even see or hear or smell the men who came at him clumsily, wielding brute force with little art? It made no sense.

Poison, he realized. *The knives must be poisoned.*

Not that poison often affected the Living, and never for long when it did, but that was the only explanation. Something had dulled his senses and slowed his reaction time: some vile toxin that his body could not quite resist.

But even that explanation, logical though it was, sounded feeble to him.

His thoughts were broken as another attack came from the shadows, which had grown up all around him until there seemed to be a haze of darkness over his eyes that almost blinded him. He could see the bookstore and its chaotic accouterments of knowledge, but as if through smoked glass.

Iosef backed away into the center of the room, putting distance between himself and the furniture. Part of him hoped that he might fare better if his enemies had no hiding places from which to strike. Another part of him suspected that it would not make a difference.

Steel flashed from the shadows, and more of Iosef's blood spilled upon the floor. He lashed out again, feeling his first blow land solidly, only to be followed with emptiness. Iosef inhaled once to calm himself and then halted his breathing. There was a pattern to be found, a rhythm that he could adapt to his purposes. His enemies were only men.

And slowly he found the pattern he searched for. He could not detect the men as they lurked in the shadows, though his senses strained to do so. The fleeting rustling of cloth or the creak of floorboards were more a distraction than a help, so he put them from his mind. But in the moment just before a knife was driven into his flesh, Iosef could feel his attacker slip from the shadows. It was all that he required.

When the next strike came, Iosef did not bother to block the attack. Something as small as a knife would not kill him. Instead, he struck with both hands, feeling the satisfying shudder of meat and bone beneath his touch. He almost fancied that he heard a whimper of pain. The next attack came from his flank, and he responded with the same tactic, placing his fists where he was certain the attacker would move in order to strike.

And so it went, Iosef spinning around in a circle to meet each new thrust, amid the twisting shadows and the heady scent of his own blood. He punched and lunged and bled over and over again until it seemed impossible that his mortal attackers were still standing. Eventually the attacks ebbed, his enemies slowed by newfound caution and their own injuries.

Suddenly the darkness receded as Iosef's mind cleared. His senses, no longer muffled and confused, were almost deafened by the loud thud as two more corpses fell to the floor beside him, their bodies twisted and broken. But Iosef could not take satisfaction in victory, for even in his triumph, he saw that he had failed.

Before him stood the last of the attackers, whose bruised face and limp right arm showed that he too had suffered several of Iosef's blows. In his left hand the man held a revolver, which he had leveled directly at Iosef's head, just out of arm's reach but still close enough that even one of the Living had little hope of escaping a bullet. And while the old could suffer such head trauma and eventually recover, Iosef knew that he was far too young. A bullet through his brain was likely to kill him, just as it would a mortal.

The man sneered even as he gasped for breath. He had not expected such a hard fight, and he seemed much relieved at holding Iosef at gunpoint.

"Why?" Iosef asked softly.

"Count von Raabe sends his regards, Your Highness," the man replied, scoffing as he spoke.

Iosef gazed at the man's finger, watching as the muscles in his hand twitched. He tried to anticipate the shot in a vain hope that he might evade it, all the while knowing he would not.

As he watched his enemy, waiting for the inevitability of death, he saw Mordechai's corpse rise, partly obscured behind the gunman. Half of Mordechai's face remained shattered grotesquely by the bullet holes, but his remaining eye glinted in the lamplight. Iosef stared at him, and Mordechai rewarded him with a smile.

In a flash, Mordechai grabbed the gunman from behind, pulling his arm back and throwing his aim away from Iosef. The man cried out, but his cries were quickly silenced as Mordechai tore open his throat and drank deeply of the blood that sprayed from the wound.

Iosef watched in silence, unmoving as Mordechai fed on the dying man. He was grateful for the unexpected reprieve from death, but he had no reason to believe that his good fortune would last. Mordechai was Shashavani. And while he might be a loyalist sojourning in the world, he might just as easily be a Basilisk, one who had turned renegade and been cast into exile. If Mordechai felt it necessary to enforce Iosef's silence, it would be a hard fight.

Presently, Mordechai dropped the body he held and stretched his back. Taking a handkerchief from his pocket, he began to wipe the blood from his face until he was more or less clean. The bullet wounds quickly closed, sped along by the recent meal, and as Mordechai blinked a few times, his missing eye reformed and swiveled around to right itself.

"Well," he said to Iosef.

"Indeed," Iosef agreed.

"Now we know each other."

"As only the Living can," Iosef said.

Mordechai smiled at Iosef. "I am no threat to you, if that is what you fear Brother Iosef. I am simply a wanderer too busy to return home."

"That is…reassuring," Iosef told him.

Mordechai knelt beside the body and began searching through the man's pockets. When he found nothing of interest, he moved on to the next one.

"The question we must now answer," he said, "is why these men wished to kill you. Or me. Or *us* perhaps." He glanced up at Iosef and smiled. "What a nice thought."

"Isn't it," Iosef agreed dryly, phrasing it as a statement rather than a question. "Your recent meal told me that Count von Raabe sends his regards."

"Is that what he said?" Mordechai mused. "I heard him speak, but I was slightly muddled at the time. I fear I am less experienced with head injuries than some of my friends."

"Friends?" Iosef asked.

Mordechai dismissed the question with a wave of his hand. "Curious that Julius von Raabe would want either of us killed, unless something quite extraordinary has occurred between the two of you."

Iosef shook his head.

"Hmm." Mordechai moved on to the third man and made an "Ah!" noise as he pulled a piece of paper from the man's coat pocket. "This is interesting.… A list of books, all in my collection."

"They were sent to rob you?" Iosef asked.

"They were sent to kill us and then rob me," Mordechai said. He read the list and frowned. "An original volume of Kaminski. Not a surprise. Two manuscripts by Algirdas. Fair enough. Ah…but this is odd. Al-Kazani's account of the rituals in the lands beyond Yugra? Vychegdov's *Hymns to the Zlata Baba*? These are Antlered Maiden texts. And the rest?" He held the list out to Iosef as if Iosef would understand the significance of the names. "Half of these texts have nothing to do with Julius's area of study, and most are more fantasy than scholarship."

"Not books worth killing over?" Iosef guessed.

"No, not at all," Mordechai answered. He stood and suddenly he blinked rapidly as a thought came to him. "Of course! I should have realized it!"

"What is it?" Iosef asked.

Mordechai frowned with genuine disappointment and said, "I fear that Julius is a true believer."

"A true believer? You mean to say that he *believes* in the Horned Serpent?"

Mordechai nodded. "And he believes in the Antlered Maiden too, at least to the extent that he is willing to kill for a collection of prayers written in her honor. He probably believes that they are one in the same, along with the Black Goat. I see a text by Kiril of Ryazan listed here. He is either a fanatic, or he is a collector with no sense of morality and little fear of the law."

"One wonders which is the more far-fetched possibility," Iosef mused.

"Brother Iosef," Mordechai said, putting a hand on Iosef's arm, "I suggest that you return to your house at once and make certain that Julius's madness has not fallen upon your companions as well as on us. If he is simply a mad collector, I suspect that I and my bookstore are the only things in danger. If he is a fanatic…. Well, one wonders what else he intends to do in the name of his horned god. The devout are so very unpredictable at times."

"What about you?" Iosef asked. He motioned to the dead on the floor. "What about the bodies?"

"I shall attend to them, do not fear," Mordechai answered cheerfully. "I have had ample time to become familiar with the disposing of corpses." He frowned and surveyed the bookstore. "Still, I suspect it is no longer safe for me to remain here. A pity, but one becomes accustomed to travel. I think it would be prudent to vacate the city for a few decades. Let my face be forgotten."

"Where will you go?"

"A friend tells me that America is quite nice at the moment," Mordechai said. He shrugged. "Honestly, these things decide themselves most of the time. Perhaps I should take a walk beyond the Urals, see if there truly is something in these stories."

"Do you believe you will find anything?" Iosef asked.

"Doubtful," Mordechai said, "but I have always enjoyed brisk walks." He smiled and pointed toward the door. "Now then, off you go, young man. I have corpses to attend to, and you have a family that might still be in danger."

Understanding the wisdom in Mordechai's words, Iosef went to the door, but before he departed he looked back and asked:

"What if your fears are mistaken? What if there is no danger, and this was all just about some old books?"

Mordechai chuckled. "Then by all means, come back. These old books will not organize themselves, and I could do with another set of hands." He grew serious again. "But mark my words, Iosef: this is not about old books, and your family is in danger."

Iosef nodded and hurried from the bookstore, knowing with all certainty that Mordechai was right. As he hurried down the street in search of a passing cab, Iosef felt his hand in his pocket, his fingertips tracing the lines of the amulet as the night's gentle breeze tickled his cheeks and whispered:

"Sophio, Sophio, Sophio."

CHAPTER TWENTY-ONE

Varanus opened her eyes and sat up slowly, overwhelmed by a sense of apprehension that she could not quite explain. Something was terribly wrong, but she did not know what.

She found herself reclining on a long bench at the far end of a broad stone balcony. She stood and slowly approached the railing. Below her, she saw a quiet reading room filled with books and tables and robed scholars busy with their work. Across the room, a pair of tall windows were shielded against the day by heavy curtains, which blotted out all but a halo of sunlight that flickered around their edges.

The place was familiar. She knew it, though that familiarity did not comfort her for a reason she did not remember. But this was home: the Shashavani castle. Everything was as it should be. The scholars were studying; the sunlight was kept at bay. She should be at peace. What troubled her?

"A pleasant sight," murmured a voice beside her.

Varanus looked and saw a tall, bearded man looming over her, his dark hair woven through with gray. His was a kind face, warm and grandfatherly.

"Father Vaclav," Varanus said, startled by the sight of him. "I thought you were...."

Her voice trailed off. She could not quite bring herself to speak her thoughts.

"You thought I was dead," Vaclav answered.

"Yes." Varanus looked at him for a few moments before looking away again. "I suppose I was mistaken."

"So it seems," Vaclav agreed.

"It was so vivid," Varanus told him. "We were here." She paused and shivered at the memory. "We were *here*. We were fighting. And then you were killed by Thoros of Yerevan. He...."

"He cut my head from my body," Vaclav said.

Varanus's heart fell. She sighed and looked down. "You're not real, are you?" she asked.

Vaclav laid a hand on her back and smiled. "I am as real as you believe me to be."

"That is not an answer."

"It *is* an answer, Doctor," Vaclav replied, his tone deeply amused. "It is simply not the answer you wanted."

Varanus looked around and asked, "Are you a ghost? None of the others seem to see you."

"You are a woman of science," Vaclav said. "Tell me: do ghosts exist?"

Varanus paused and looked around again, this time more thoroughly, searching for Korbinian. But she did not see him anywhere. A pity. She could have asked Vaclav if he saw her dead fiancé now or if Korbinian could see Vaclav.

"I am not yet certain," she said, her voice more distant than intended. She quickly rallied herself and looked back at Vaclav. "I had a curious dream while I slept."

"Oh?"

"I dreamed that I was in Prague. It was very vivid, and yet I can barely remember it now."

"But you are certain it was Prague?" Vaclav asked.

Varanus thought for a moment to be certain of her memories. Finally she nodded. "Yes, that part was very clear. I remember the castle, the Old Town, the view of the river. I dined with my son near Wenceslas Square."

Vaclav sighed sadly. He rested his arms on the railing and leaned forward, gazing across the reading room at the sun-rimmed curtains.

"It saddens me that you were not able to visit my homeland until after my death," he told her. "I would like to have shown it to you myself, though it has been many years since last I was there, and I fear it must be very different from how I remember it."

"It was very beautiful," Varanus told him.

Vaclav nodded, his smile tinged with longing. "Yes, it was."

"It was so vivid," Varanus said, pressing a hand to her temple in the effort to remember, "but now it is like a haze, like a sunrise viewed through fog."

There was a pause.

"Have you ever been to Prague before?" Vaclav asked.

"No...." Varanus frowned. "No, never."

"Then how do you know what it looks like?"

Varanus exhaled as she felt her heart sink. Suddenly things made sense. She placed her head in her hands and sighed. She had not dreamed of Prague.

"*This* is the dream."

"Is it?" Vaclav mused. He smiled at her. "Once Zhuang Zhou dreamed that he was a butterfly. When he awoke, he did not know whether he was

Zhuang Zhou who had dreamed of being a butterfly, or a butterfly dreaming that it was Zhuang Zhou."

"Neither of us is a butterfly," Varanus said.

"Neither of us is Zhuang Zhou," Vaclav added.

Varanus laughed. "True."

She closed her eyes and forced herself to remember that this was a dream. This was not real. Prague was real. Prague had not been a dream.

I am not a butterfly.

"You certainly are not a butterfly," agreed a deep, rumbling voice behind her.

"Grandfather!" Varanus gasped, knowing the voice in an instant.

She spun about and saw her grandfather, William Varanus, striding across the balcony toward her and Vaclav, a narrow smile upon his lips and a twinkle in his pale blue eyes. Despite herself, she ran to her grandfather and embraced him. Grandfather held her tightly and brushed her hair with his hand, like he had done when she was young.

"Now I know this is a dream," she murmured, tears brimming in her eyes, "because I know that you are dead."

Grandfather knelt before her and touched her cheek.

"This being a dream," he said, "you should try to wake up."

"No!" Varanus protested. "No, I do not wish to—"

"Wake up."

* * * *

"Wake up, *Liebchen*. You must wake up."

Varanus jerked awake, one hand grabbing at her throat while the other reached out to ward off the next blow that she knew would come.

But there was no other blow. There was no wound at her throat. The fight was over. Julius was gone. Instead, she saw Korbinian looming over her, his pale face dripping with blood. He smiled at her and extended his hand. Though there was still a darkness in his eyes, the malevolence that Varanus had witnessed for months had finally lifted. He was almost as she remembered him.

Almost.

"Julius tried to murder me," Varanus said.

"I know," Korbinian replied, his tone filled with regret. "If I could have stopped him, I would have. I did try to warn you."

Varanus frowned. "You could have been more eloquent."

"It is not always easy for me, *Liebchen*," Korbinian said. "I speak as best I can, but my words are not always clear."

"That is true," Varanus agreed. "All this time I thought that you were jealous."

Korbinian chuckled, but a shadow fell across his face as he asked, "Ah, but *Liebchen*, what man could not be jealous of you?"

Varanus frowned and sat up. "Please do not start all of that again."

She sat up and tried to get her bearings. She was in the back of a wagon filled with crates and rubbish, much of which had been piled around her to conceal her body. The wagon sat in a stone chamber that smelled of mold and hay and manure, possibly an adjacent stable. This might be the carriage house of Von Steiersberg's mansion.

A horse was already harnessed to the wagon. It whinnied softly as Varanus stirred, frightened by the smell of blood and the movement of the dead.

"Visitors," Korbinian murmured.

Varanus turned her head and saw two of Von Steiersberg's men enter the room, carrying a long sheet of canvas—presumably to finish hiding Varanus's body from prying eyes. Varanus quickly lay back in the wagon and played dead. She had lost a tremendous amount of blood, and the men probably had firearms. She could not risk a fight until they came within arm's reach of her.

"Dump her in the river and then what?" one asked the other.

"Return here and await orders," his companion said.

"We're not to help with the violinist?"

"By the time our business is finished, all that will be done with," came the reply. "And besides, what hope do any of them have?"

"None, I suppose. Even armed, they haven't our mettle."

They rounded the side of the wagon, and the first man asked, "You were sure to take all of her jewels?"

"*Ja*. Weren't many of them, but I took what was there." The man patted his pocket. "Fetch a nice price when all this is done."

"Good."

The men reached Varanus and spread out the canvas sheet. As they laid it over Varanus, she tensed her body and pulled into a crouch. She had to be sure to kill both of them before one could flee. Julius and Von Steiersberg thought she was dead. She needed them to keep thinking that until she intercepted them at Friedrich's home and killed them both.

As the sheet drifted down not quite on top of her, Varanus lunged forward, catching it with one hand and holding it below the level of her eyes. The men did not understand what was happening for the first few seconds as Varanus tore the sheet from the grasp of one and threw it over the other. But they caught on quickly enough.

"What?" came the startled gasp.

"Chernobog!" swore his companion, as he struggled to free himself from the sheet. "What is happening?"

Varanus lunged at the first man as he drew a revolver from his belt. She knocked it away with a sweep of her hand. She struck him a blow upon the side of the head and he reeled from it, but a moment later he had rallied and pulled a knife from inside his coat.

"Sorcery!" he cried.

"Science," Varanus replied.

Finally, the second man freed himself from the sheet and stared at Varanus with equal parts of astonishment and horror.

"Not dead?"

"Sorcery!" the first man repeated. "Run for help!"

"*Science*," Varanus corrected again, this time with greater emphasis. She spun around and dove at the second man as he turned to flee. She caught him by the arm and shattered his knee with a solid kick to make sure he wouldn't be running anywhere. "Stay."

To her surprise—and to her enemy's credit—the man only whimpered from the pain. He grabbed Varanus's wrist and held her fast as he too drew a knife. With unexpected speed, he thrust the blade into Varanus's side, the sharp point managing to penetrate the layers of her clothing and strike flesh between two ribs.

"Sneaky," Varanus admonished.

She grabbed the man's throat with her hand and drove him against the ground, strangling him. A sudden pain blossomed in her lower back, and she arched her body. Glancing back, she saw the first man standing over her, having just driven his blade into her. Varanus hissed as he drew it out again and brought the knife down for another strike. Varanus kicked backward with her foot and hit him in the shin, making him stumble and miss his target.

The man glanced toward his revolver where it lay on the ground and then looked back at Varanus.

"No…" Varanus ordered, without really expecting him to listen.

The man hesitated a moment longer and then ran for the pistol. Varanus swore and bashed his companion's head against the stone floor to put him out of the fight. For a moment she was distracted by the pulse in his throat as it jumped frantically. She was dreadfully parched, but at least she had a meal readily available.

As the first man scooped up the revolver, Varanus rose to her feet. As he aimed it at her, she lunged for him, one hand outstretched, the other curled tightly into a fist. She reached him as he fired his first shot, and a moment later the world erupted into a haze of pain and blood.

Delicious, delicious blood.

CHAPTER TWENTY-TWO

Friedrich's first indication that he was not dead came when he heard himself groan in pain. As a doctor, he knew that was a good sign. Not a wonderful sign, as his aching body told him, but a good one all the same. He was alive, his limbs still had sensation, above all he could still *feel*, and while the night air was cold, his body remained warm enough that he knew he was not bleeding to death.

Friedrich opened his eyes and gazed into the dark sky. He was alive. That was something. He looked at his chest and saw the knife still protruding from his body, just below the heart. The stab ought to have killed him. It was meant to have done so, certainly. But as he felt the wound, he noticed that there was very little blood. Somehow it was a flesh wound. He reached beneath his vest and found that the point of the knife had struck his rib and stopped there.

Thank God, he thought.

Only a little higher and the blade would have gone in cleanly, probably to the hilt. And that would have been a very different matter.

Acting on impulse, Friedrich pulled the dagger free. A moment later he remembered that this was a very bad idea, but to his relief, he found that the flow of blood was only slight. The knife had cut meat alone. Indeed, with the obstruction removed, the wound seemed to clot over almost immediately.

Friedrich sat up and rolled onto his knees, groaning again as every part of his body groaned with him. He was bruised and battered, but at least nothing was broken, and he had stopped bleeding. It took him a few moments to collect his thoughts and remember what had happened. There had been a fight. There had been gunfire. Stanislav and Erzsebet....

Friedrich gritted his teeth at the memory. He had failed them. He had been so close. They had needed him. He could have saved them if only he'd been more careful, if only he had kept a better grip on the carriage. Now they were gone.

The others.

He grabbed for a nearby wall to steady himself as he rose. The others were in danger too. He had to get back home and save them. Because he *could* save them, he told himself. There was still time. He just had to run.

Running proved to be more than his body could manage at the moment, and he stumbled after the first few feet. Instead, he settled for a brisk shamble, forcing his legs to move aching step after aching step. As he went, his adrenaline began to rise again and hurrying became easier and easier. The pain drifted away into some hidden part of his brain, forcibly ignored by his conscious mind.

He remembered this feeling. It had come to him before, after that unfortunate rock fall in Asia....

The house, he reminded himself. *Your friends. Hurry!*

As Friedrich retraced his steps to the alleyway, he heard the rattle of a carriage and horse's hooves clattering along the street ahead of him. Friedrich tensed, clutching the knife in his hand. Who could be out at this hour? Was it Von Steiersberg or his blond friend returning to finish what they had started?

But no, that was a mad thought. They had fled, and it would be a determined hunt to find them again—a hunt that he had every intention of carrying out, and the Devil take anyone who got in his way.

Ahead of him, he saw a simple, horse-drawn wagon barrel down the roadway and turn onto the street leading to his house. Though it was dark, he could just make out a tiny figure at the reins, and in the faint starlight, he almost swore that it was his mother!

Perhaps he'd lost more blood than he thought.

Hurrying along, Friedrich rounded the bend onto his block and saw the wagon pull up outside his front door. The small figure jumped down from the seat, and in the light of the open front door, he saw that his eyes had not lied to him.

"Mother?" he exclaimed, rushing toward her as fast as he could manage.

Though he had not spoken loudly, Varanus seemed to have heard him. Perhaps she simply noticed the approaching footsteps, but either way she spun around to face him.

"Alistair!" she gasped.

She ran to meet him, and Friedrich, with his longer stride, met her not far from the door. He held her tightly, ignoring his body's disgruntled murmurs of pain as his mother almost crushed him with her embrace. It was as though she had feared him dead.

"Mother, what are you doing here?" he asked.

"Men are coming to kill you," Varanus answered, her tone both desperate and relieved. "You must get away from here immediately!"

"How do you know that?" Friedrich demanded.

He broke from the hug and held his mother at arm's length. Her clothes were rumpled and chaotic, quite unlike her. And there was blood all across her chest and one shoulder, almost as if her throat had been cut. But there was no wound.

"Oh, God, Mother!" he cried. "The blood!"

"It's not mine," Varanus said quickly. "But I…I overheard men plotting to come here and kill you and your friends. They…um…found me and…and there was a struggle before I could get away."

Friedrich narrowed his eyes. Mother was hiding something from him, as usual. But he could not stay angry with her for that.

"They have already come," he whispered.

"What?" Varanus demanded. She looked Friedrich up and down and, curiously, sniffed the air. "You're bleeding!"

"It's mine," Friedrich confirmed, his brain too muddled to make an excuse about the blood. He looked toward the doorway.

Varanus caught Friedrich's chin and pulled his attention back to her. "What do you mean 'they have already come'?"

The question jogged Friedrich's memory and renewed his confused sense of panic. He pulled away and backed up a step. Then, as Varanus hurried to follow him, he turned and ran for the house.

"They're still here!" he gasped. "My friends.…"

"No, Alistair, wait!" Varanus called after him.

But Friedrich did not heed her words. He reached the door and rushed inside. He smelled blood and gunpowder. He heard nothing. There was blood on the floor and bullet holes in the walls. He was too late. Again.

Friedrich stumbled into the parlor, somehow finding the presence of mind to avoid the worst of the blood that pooled on the carpet. The parlor was a scene of carnage, filled with bodies that lay where they had fallen. Some had been shot in the midst of fleeing or where they cowered behind whatever fleeting cover the furniture could provide. Wilhelm's revolutionaries had mostly died fighting, with guns or knives in their hands, but they had died all the same.

Near the fireplace, Friedrich saw an unmoving pile of blood and fur. Jadwiga the cat. In the midst of so many corpses, the corpses of his friends, the body of the dead cat seemed almost to take on a special significance.

The bastards had killed the cat. Of course they had killed all the people. "No witnesses" or some horrible nonsense like that. It made a deranged sort of sense, the kind that men of violence would accept without question. But the cat? Why in God's name kill the cat? Because it yowled too much? Because it was there?

He turned as Varanus entered the room. At the sight of the bodies, she grew pale and pressed herself against the wall, a hand balling into a fist as if she expected the killers to be there, lurking just around the corner. But of course they were not there. They had done what they set out to do, and then they had left, tracking the blood of their victims into the street as they went. The house was empty and silent.

Almost silent.

Friedrich cocked his head as he heard a muffled sound coming from the back hallway. Though the sound was faint, Varanus seemed to have heard it too, for she snapped her head in its direction. Indeed, she seemed almost to have heard it *before* Friedrich, though surely that was impossible. How could one person hear a sound before another?

Friedrich held up a hand for his mother to wait while he investigated, and then saw that she was doing the same thing. Mother and son shared a tense smile, but neither of them could take amusement in the symmetry of their actions under such circumstances.

Walking carefully to avoid making a sound, Friedrich entered the hallway and slowly approached the kitchen. Varanus followed just behind him. A glance into the kitchen told Friedrich that it was empty, inhabited only by the body of Nicolas, who by now was most definitely dead. The back door stood open. There had been no one to close it. But that was not where the noise had come from. It was from inside the house.

There was a small pantry adjacent to the kitchen. The door was closed, and Friedrich had almost forgotten it in passing, but now he turned toward it and slowly raised his knife.

Had someone remained behind in ambush in case they had missed someone? A glance at Mother told him that she was thinking the same thing. Friedrich yanked the door open and made ready to lunge at whomever might be lurking there.

He was met by Zoya, looking terrified and disheveled, as she prepared to meet him with a cleaver in one hand. At the sight of him she screamed, a sound that he almost echoed such was his surprise. Friedrich quickly lowered his knife, and a moment later Zoya lowered hers.

"My God, Freddie…" Zoya said, exhaling in a long sigh. "I thought you were dead."

"I thought the same of you," Friedrich answered.

Behind Zoya, he saw Karel poised to strike, holding a length of sausage like a club. He slowly relaxed as well and, giving his improvised weapon an embarrassed look, he quickly dropped it.

"Where is Erzsebet?" Zoya demanded, pushing her way into the hallway. She stopped short when she nearly collided with Varanus, who gave her an irritated look.

"Taken," Friedrich answered sullenly.

"And Stanislav?" Karel asked as he joined them.

"The same." Friedrich sank against the wall, feeling his adrenaline and his earlier determination ebb from him, unsustainable in the presence of the atrocity his home had witnessed. "My God, what are we to do?"

Varanus had returned to the parlor and was looking around, gently sniffing the air. She looked back at them and addressed Zoya and Karel:

"Are you the only two survivors?"

"As far as I…" Karel began halfheartedly, caught between the impossibility of optimism and an unwillingness to fall totally into despair.

Zoya was far more direct and matter of fact. "Yes," she said without hesitation. She glanced at Karel. "We would have heard someone."

"But—"

"They are all dead," Zoya insisted. Her tone sounded heartless, but Friedrich understood. It was the emotionless monotone of someone on the verge of utter collapse who simply refused to succumb. He knew it well.

"And the attackers are all gone?"

"Dear God, I hope so," Karel said, his voice shaking just like his hands. "Oh God, oh God, oh God…."

"You're safe now, Karel," Friedrich snapped, perhaps more harshly than he intended. But at least it stopped Karel's panicked ramble. "We need to get the authorities. We need to tell…well, *someone*."

"We are doing nothing of the kind," Varanus interjected.

"What? In Heaven's name, why not?"

Varanus motioned to the corpses in the parlor and asked, "Do you recognize everyone in this room?"

"Well, yes," Friedrich answered.

Of course he recognized them! They were his friends! Or friends of his friends at least.

"Then your attackers have either all escaped alive, or they have at least carried off the bodies of their comrades," Varanus said, "which means that you have absolutely no proof of what happened here. And what will you tell the police? That a highly placed and respectable Austrian nobleman sent a gang of murderers to kill you and kidnap your friends? To carry off his fiancée who *just happened* to be staying here with the radical you claim she willingly ran away with?"

"Well, I mean…" Friedrich stammered.

"It's what happened," Zoya said.

"The police will not believe a word of it," Varanus told them. She sounded absolutely confident of the fact. "Allow me to hazard a guess: all or at least most of your dead friends are wanted men, is that right?"

"I…suppose so," Friedrich admitted. Perhaps not Wilhelm, but Ilya, Nicolas, Schmidt, indeed most of the revolutionaries. And Stanislav too. They had all hidden out there to avoid the authorities.

"So we have a house in this decrepit working-class neighborhood filled with wanted criminals, socialists, and radicals bent on overthrowing the Empire," Varanus said. "A house being used as a hideout for the man who *abducted* the daughter of a Hungarian count, for that is surely how the authorities will interpret your friend Erzsebet's presence here all these months, which means that all three of you will be seen as their accomplices."

"But…but the murder!" Karel protested.

"You mean a probable power struggle within the revolutionaries' own ranks?" Varanus mused. "At best, they will ignore it. More likely, they will use it as an excuse for a fresh round of arrests and repression."

Friedrich fell silent as a creeping dread came across him. She was right. The police would not care about them. They might even be jailed for collusion with the revolutionary movement. He looked at Zoya and Karel and saw the same expression on their faces.

"Alis…Friedrich," Varanus said, "who knows that you live here?"

"Um…. You. Us. Aunt Ekaterine. Constantine." Friedrich turned his eyes toward the parlor and shuddered. "Everyone else is either dead or gone."

Varanus seemed to be mulling some thoughts over in her mind.

"Von Steiersberg and Von Raabe know," she murmured, "but they will not act on it. They must believe you to be dead. And besides, why implicate themselves in all of this?" She looked back at Friedrich. "Your neighbors? Do they know?"

"I've never dealt with them," Friedrich replied. "They may have seen me once or twice, but people around here keeps to themselves."

"What about the landlord?"

"I never dealt with him either," Friedrich said. "It was through a middleman like every house on the block, and Wilhelm handled all of that anyway. I just paid for it."

Varanus snorted. "You allowed one of your 'friends' to take your money and expected him to pay for your house? And no doubt after taking a sizable cut to help pay for the Revolution."

"It wasn't like that," Friedrich protested.

He saw Zoya open her mouth to correct him, but she evidently thought better of it and said nothing.

"What about Prague society?" Varanus asked.

"I have a far more respectable address for my correspondence and that sort of thing," Friedrich explained. "I could hardly tell my peers about my laboratory, could I? I only gave the address to Constantine in case he found time to visit. Otherwise, as far as anyone knows, I live in a good part of Prague."

"If only you actually *resided* there," Varanus said. She sounded angry, but perhaps it was just worry. "So no one whom the police would actually believe knows that you are here?"

"I suppose not..." Friedrich answered cautiously. "Why...?"

This seemed to be what Varanus wanted to hear. "Good," she said. "Then you are packing your things, and we are leaving at once."

"Mother, no!" Friedrich exclaimed.

"*At once*," Varanus repeated. She looked at Zoya and Karel, weighing something in her mind. "The two of you as well, I suppose. Ekaterine would be very angry with me if I allowed her pet painter to be arrested or killed." To Karel she added, "And you're...here...at the moment, so you can help carry my son's bags."

Friedrich was appalled. "Mother, we can't just leave! The bodies—"

"The bodies are precisely why none of us are going to be here in the morning when someone reports the gunshots to the police," Varanus said firmly. "So you are going to pack what you can carry, you are going to burn anything that could even *possibly* connect you to this place, and then we are leaving." She pointed at Zoya and Karel. "That goes for the two of you also. When the police arrive tomorrow, I do not want there to be any reason for them to suspect that there are survivors still alive, am I understood?"

Such was the severity of her tone that Zoya and Karel quickly nodded their heads.

Varanus continued, "And I expect neither of you to breath a word of this to anyone, not even your families. If I am given cause to believe that you have endangered my son's life with idle talk, you will learn precisely why a worried mother is the most dangerous creature alive."

CHAPTER TWENTY-THREE

Upon returning home, Iosef was relieved to find things in a state of peace. The lights were dimmed, and most of the servants had retired, following Iosef's customary instructions. The footman was still up to meet him at the door, but otherwise things were quiet. That meant that whatever his earlier misgivings, Julius had either not elected to move against the household, or his ruffians had not yet arrived. The second possibility was unlikely. A sensible man would have attacked Iosef's family at more or less the same time that they attacked him, and Iosef considered Julius a sensible man.

Sensible, that is, until he had mistakenly decided to murder one of the Living; though being mortal, he could hardly be faulted for his ignorance. It seemed that Mordechai truly had been the target, and there was no further cause for alarm.

"Good evening, Highness," the footman said, taking Iosef's hat and cane.

As Iosef's suit still bore the knife holes from the fight, he chose not to remove his overcoat. Pravec surely noticed this, but he was a good servant and said nothing of it. As was customary with sojourning Shashavani, mortal servants, when they were necessary, were always selected for their ability to "forget" or "overlook" any eccentricities among their employers.

"And you, Pravec," Iosef replied, heading for the stairs. "Where are the Princesses this evening?"

"I believe your sister is reading in the upstairs library, Highness," Pravec answered. "The mistress of the house has gone out for the evening. She did not say where."

Iosef froze for a moment. "Has gone out?" he asked. "Or is still out?"

Varanus had left to visit her wastrel son before Iosef made his visit to Mordechai's bookstore. If she had not yet returned....

"To my knowledge, she has not returned from her earlier outing, Highness. I could inquire of the other servants if you wish."

Things began turning over in Iosef's mind. A chaotic torrent of probabilities, possibilities, and unlikely events that might still come to pass twisted and mingled into endless lists that quickly ranked a series of outcomes until he finally fixed on the best course of action available to him.

"Pravec, is Mister Luka still awake?" he asked.

"Yes, Highness," Pravec replied. "He is in the east drawing room." Pravec coughed slightly. "Attending to his firearms. I served him some wine at his request only a quarter of an hour ago."

"Excellent," Iosef said. He reached out and retrieved his hat and cane. "Fetch him for me and instruct him to ready the carriage. I have some business to attend to."

"At once, Highness," Pravec said. He bowed his head and quickly hurried from the foyer.

Iosef heard someone approaching on the upstairs landing a few moments before Ekaterine appeared through the doorway. She looked down at him, appearing both surprised and pleased to see him.

"Oh! Lord Iosef," she said in Svanish. It would not do for the servants to hear her addressing her alleged brother in unfamiliar terms. "I thought it would be the Doctor."

"It seems that Varanus is still at large in the city," Iosef answered. "But I am concerned for her safety. Where has she gone?"

"She had supper with Alistair...er...Friedrich," Ekaterine told him. "And I believe she then intended to spend the evening with Count von Raabe."

Iosef felt the muscles in his face tighten into an expression of displeasure that might almost have been noticeable to a casual viewer, such was the severity of his discontent. It was as he had feared. Varanus had gone to see her lover, the same man who might have tried to murder Iosef and might now try to murder her.

"Did I say something wrong, My Lord?" Ekaterine asked, quickly descending the stairs. She was very familiar with the enigmatic expressions of the Living, and of course she recognized Iosef's distress.

"Men in the employ of Von Raabe attacked me and Herr Mordechai this evening," Iosef said. He did not say that they were dead. He did not need to. "I do not know if I was the intended target, but if I was, Varanus may be in danger."

Ekaterine grew pale and ran down the remaining steps.

"I am coming with you," she announced. Only as an afterthought did she think to amend the statement, "With your permission, My Lord."

"Of course," Iosef said. Were their situations reversed, he would have demanded the same, and possibly without the decorum of asking permission afterward.

Ekaterine stopped at the bottom of the stairs as a thought came to her. "I should get a gun," she said, spinning on her toes and making for the stairs again.

Iosef glanced toward the adjoining hallway as he heard and smelled Luka and Pravec approaching. As an afterthought, he grabbed Ekaterine by the arm to stop her from leaving, without bothering—or needing—to look toward her.

"That would be best," he agreed, "but Luka has weapons aplenty for us to use."

"Oh, yes, of course," Ekaterine said quickly.

Luka arrived a few moments later, his moustache twitching, either from excitement at the prospect of some as yet unannounced adventure or out of irritation at being interrupted by one of the servants. The latter was most likely. He was coatless and his sleeves were rolled up. There was gun oil on his fingertips, and he carried a half-full glass of wine in one hand.

"What is it, Brother?" Luka asked Iosef, also speaking Svanish. "The man in the starched collar said it was urgent, but as usual he had nothing useful to tell me."

"Thank you Pravec," Iosef said to the footman. "You may retire."

"Very good, Highness," Pravec answered. "Shall I rouse the coach-man about preparing the carriage?"

"No need. Luka will attend to it."

"As you wish, Highness."

When Pravec had left, Luka raised an eyebrow at Iosef and opened his mouth to speak.

"Why am I—"

"Julius von Raabe attempted to kill me tonight," Iosef explained, un-buttoning his overcoat to show the knife wounds. Now that the servants were gone, there was no further need for concealment.

"*What?*" Luka exclaimed.

"Well, either myself or Mordechai," Iosef amended, leading the way across the foyer in the direction of the attached carriage house. "But I understand that Varanus intended to visit Von Raabe this evening, so if I was the target, she may be in danger."

"I most certainly was," announced Varanus as she stormed into the foyer from the servants' passage.

"Doctor!" Ekaterine exclaimed. She ran to Varanus and embraced her friend tightly. "I thought you might be dead!"

"I am perfectly fine," Varanus said. There was a pause. The front of her dress was covered in blood. "Now," she added. "I am perfectly fine now."

"You have blood on your dress," Iosef noted dryly.

"It's mine," Varanus answered. "Your shirt has holes in it."

"I did not put them there," Iosef said.

"What happened to you?" Varanus asked.

"Julius von Raabe attempted to murder me," Iosef explained. "And you?"

"What a strange coincidence," Varanus said. "Julius von Raabe attempted to murder me as well. And my son."

Iosef did not comment on this last point. He had always regarded young Friedrich as something of an unfortunate distraction.

Varanus hesitated for a moment and added, "And on that note...."

"*Varanus*...?" Iosef asked. "What have you done?"

"Alis...Friedrich and his friends had nowhere else to go," Varanus told him. "Or rather, his friends had nowhere else to go, and he refused to leave them."

"What?"

Varanus turned toward the passage and called out in German, "Come in!"

Iosef's eyes narrowed as Varanus's son entered the foyer, followed by a young man and woman. All of them were disheveled, exhausted, and frightened, and carrying heavy bags of luggage or medical equipment. To Iosef's irritation, Friedrich smiled at the sight of him. For some reason, during their first meeting in London ten years ago, Friedrich had gotten it into his head that they were somehow friends. But then Friedrich's expression turned to one of bewilderment. Iosef looked no older than he had at their previous meeting.

Before Friedrich could ask any annoying questions, the girl next to him caught sight of Ekaterine and gasped aloud, not quite with delight and not quite with relief. She dropped the bags she was carrying and threw herself into Ekaterine's arms, clinging to her like a drowning woman would cling to driftwood.

"Muse!" she exclaimed.

Though confused, Ekaterine smiled and took it all in stride. "Hello Miss Chromoluminarist. There, there, you're safe now."

"I was afraid they had taken you too," the girl rambled, clearly on the verge of losing her wits.

"Too?" Ekaterine asked.

Friedrich was the one who answered, as he stormed up to Iosef and Varanus:

"Stanislav and Erzsebet have been taken, and I mean to find them. We must do something immediately before those men get away!"

Iosef looked at Varanus and asked in Svanish, "What is he going on about?"

"Two of his friends were kidnapped by Von Raabe's men," Varanus explained. "I fear he is insistent about rescuing them."

"Of course he is." Iosef sighed. "To be honest, I am more than a little annoyed at my recent treatment by our once friend."

"As am I," Varanus agreed. From her tone, Iosef knew she understood what he was getting at, and he suspected her sentiments were much the same. "A shame, really. He was *very* pretty."

"So I recall," Iosef said. "And a good conversationalist. Very learned."

Varanus nodded. "A pity, but certain things simply cannot stand."

"Indeed."

Luka looked at them, his eyes shifting from one to the other. "To be clear," he said, "we are talking about hunting him down and brutally murdering him, yes?" He emptied his glass in one gulp. "Because if everyone here is alive and well and we are *not* plotting revenge, I have an elephant gun in need of cleaning and a bottle of wine that I would like to finish."

"Brutal murder, yes," Iosef told him. "Revenge aside, Von Raabe must surely have his reasons for trying to kill us."

He paused, thinking better of mentioning Mordechai's cultist theory in front of Ekaterine, who would surely become unnecessarily excited and insist on investigating it herself. He would inform Varanus and Luka privately once they had departed.

He continued, "If Julius learns that we are not dead, he will simply redouble his efforts until the deed is done. In addition to his original motives, he now has self-preservation to inspire him to deeds of violence. I would prefer to resolve that little problem now before he can recover and try again."

"Agreed," Varanus said. Her voice carried a hint of regret, which did not surprise Iosef. Julius had been a very pleasant diversion for her until now.

"I will ready the coach," Luka said, excusing himself and making for the carriage house.

Iosef addressed Ekaterine: "Sister Ekaterine, would you be so good as to take Varanus's...*guests* upstairs and secure them someplace quiet until we can decide what to do with them?"

"Of course!" Ekaterine replied. She detached one arm from the enthusiastic girl's grasp and held it out to Friedrich and his other friend. She addressed them in German, "Welcome to our home. I understand you've all had a bit of an ordeal, so I want you to be sure to make your-selves comfortable during your stay."

"Not too comfortable," Iosef reminded her.

"Sufficiently comfortable," Ekaterine said cheerfully. Taking Fried-rich's hand, she gently led the mortals up the stairs. "Now then, come along and I'll get you some nice hot baths and a little sherry. Just the thing after whatever's happened to you."

Iosef turned to Varanus and resumed speaking in Svanish. "Julius is residing at Count von Steiersberg's house in Prague, is that correct?"

"Yes," Varanus said. "I know the way."

Iosef had expected as much, but he did not consider it polite to say so.

"Good, then once Luka has readied the carriage, we will depart. With luck, we will find Julius and his associates and attend to the problem they have imposed upon us." Iosef considered another thought. "Oh, and if your son's friends are imprisoned there, I suppose we might rescue them too."

"Magnanimous of us," Varanus noted dryly. "But I suppose that would be best. Until they are found, Friedrich will insist on looking for them, and it may get him into trouble."

A common enough occurrence in the best of circumstances, Iosef thought. But he wisely chose not to voice the comment.

CHAPTER TWENTY-FOUR

Iosef was disappointed to find Count von Steiersberg's house dark and all but empty. Not surprised. Disappointed. He had always known that his quarry might prove a more difficult thing to chase, but he had harbored a certain hope that the matter might be concluded quickly and easily. Of course, it was still possible that the household had simply retired rather than fled, but in light of the evening's events, he very much doubted it.

He and Varanus abandoned their transport a block from the house. It was a horse-drawn wagon that Varanus had apparently "borrowed" from Von Steiersberg and was now eager to return. Iosef thought it very good of her to return the stolen property before setting out to kill the owner.

They entered through the stables. The door was poorly secured, and a quick listen told Iosef that it was empty. As he entered, he smelled the lingering scent of dried blood. A moment later, he saw the places where it had pooled on the floor. But he did not see the bodies from which it had come. Someone had removed them.

He noticed Varanus look around for the corpses, and he recognized the subtle hint of concern on her face. She had been the one who spilled blood here.

"Was this where it happened?" he asked her.

Varanus shook her head. "In the house. Upstairs." She glanced at the dried blood. "This is where I awoke. They planned to dump my body in the river, so I expressed to them my distinct wish to remain alive and dry."

"Very prudent," Iosef said, hiding a smile.

He went to the door and glanced into the adjoining passage, which led into the house. He knew that there was no one nearby—he neither heard nor smelled anyone—but it was best to be cautious. Crossing through the dark passage, he and Varanus eventually reached the main hall of the house, which was feebly lit with lamps that had been turned down.

Iosef felt the shadows close in around him, twisting in the darkness, plucking at his fingertips, whispering incoherently at the very fringes of perception. He shuddered and closed his eyes, willing himself to keep ahold of his senses.

Voices on the upstairs landing caught his attention, and he opened his eyes again. Looking beyond the threshold, he saw an older man in livery talking to two footmen and another man in plain clothes. Though their words were hushed, Iosef's keen hearing could just make out the conversation.

"And be certain to wash the stable floor," the butler said to the footmen. "When His Lordship returns, it must be to a house that is clean and in order. Flushed from such jubilation, it would be a grave insult for him to be met with...." The butler grimaced. "Pollution."

"It is only a little blood, Herr Haas," one of the footmen said.

The butler stopped immediately and spun about. Both footmen froze as if they knew what was to follow. Without pause, the butler struck the impudent footman across the face. The young man reeled backward and caught himself against the wall to keep from falling. He quickly bowed his head in obedience even as he wiped blood from his nose.

"Do not speak back to your masters, boy!" the butler snapped.

"No, Herr Haas."

In the darkness beside Iosef, Varanus murmured, "A bit of a harsh hand below stairs."

"Indeed," Iosef agreed. "And unwise, I feel. I have always found violence to be a poor maintainer of discipline."

On the landing, the butler seemed to take satisfaction both in the beating and in the subservience it produced.

"Good," he said. Then he sternly added, "And it is *not* only a little blood. It is the blood of the faithful spilled without cause. I will not allow such a thing to greet His Lordship when he returns from the ritual."

"No, Herr Haas," the footman repeated, his words echoed by his companion.

The butler nodded approvingly. "And the bodies have all been accounted for?"

"Yes, Herr Haas. In the cold cellar," the second footman answered.

"Good," the butler repeated, sounding pleased at having his instructions carried out. "Herr Grauss, I will leave it to you to deal with our unfortunate brothers."

"I will have them properly disposed of," Grauss said.

The butler smiled slightly, again pleased. All things were in order, it seemed. He looked at the two footmen.

"Go and clean the stables," he said. "Now."

"At once, Herr Haas."

Varanus and Iosef exchanged a glance and quickly crept into the front hall, drawing toward the back with as much stealth as they could manage, until the footmen had descended the stairs and passed them, none the wiser. On the landing, the butler turned briskly and resumed his walk as if nothing had happened. The man called Grauss fell in beside him, and the two resumed their conversation. Iosef and Varanus hurried up the stairs, their footfalls all but silent, no louder than the shadows that tugged at Iosef's coattails.

Ahead, he heard the butler continue, "Herr Grauss, is there any word on what became of the woman? I was quite certain she was dead. This is clearly not the case."

"Not having seen the body, I cannot speak to that," replied the man in plainclothes. "But I find it unlikely that she was responsible for our brothers' deaths. Someone so small and feeble could not have accomplished it. More likely, another party killed them and stole the body. After all, the wagon was taken."

"True," the butler agreed. "That must be attended to as well."

"I shall set my men to it once they return from the bookseller's," Grauss said. He frowned and checked his pocket watch. "It seems they are delayed."

"Surely they have a great many books to search through," the butler offered.

Grauss grunted and nodded, though he did not seem convinced.

The two men turned into a side room. Iosef glanced at Varanus and she nodded back. It seemed that all of the household might be implicated in the conspiracy, but certainly these two were. And to hear the butler talk, he too was one of Mordechai's "true believers". Iosef found it difficult to imagine modern people actually believing such fantastical nonsense, but clearly it was so. Then again, he reminded himself, the further man was drawn away from the basic concerns of food and shelter, the more his mind was free to wander. Their ancient ancestors might have looked to the sky in ignorance and granted godhood to a bolt of lightning, not understanding its cause. But so often modern folk, knowing the truth, were that much more determined to find Zeus or Apollo *somewhere*. *Anywhere*. If not in thunder and sunlight, then in coincidence and shadow.

Perhaps Von Raabe, Von Steiersberg, and their cohorts had grown bored with the dull reliability of reason and had cast it aside in favor of more thrilling occult ideologies.

Iosef hurried along the hallway with Varanus at his side. They took up positions on either side of the door, pausing a moment to ready themselves. There was an exchange of nods, and then Iosef tried the door.

It was unlocked, and he quickly entered the room, allowing his eyes to dart about wildly to give him as broad a sense of the layout as he could manage. His mind worked heavily for a second or two, weaving together each fractured glimpse into a concrete whole so that he could have closed his eyes and drawn the room perfectly from memory.

It was a useful skill. A useful skill that Sophio had taught him.

And at his urging, the whispers started again:

Sophio. Sophio. Sophio.

"By the god, who—" exclaimed the butler.

Iosef opened his eyes again. The butler and the man called Grauss stood midway across the room, in the middle of examining some papers on a table. They stared at Iosef and Varanus. For a moment, Iosef felt the shadows creeping in around him, suffocating him.

Paranoia. It had become so familiar. So comfortable.

"Restrain the butler," Iosef instructed Varanus.

He lunged at Grauss before either man could fully react. He took the ruffian in his grasp and threw him to the floor. Grauss tried to struggle, but Iosef struck him several times in the chest until the man's enthusiasm broke, along with a rib or two. The butler started shouting for help, but Varanus grabbed him and hit him against the wall, grinning slightly at the catharsis of violence. Only a few moments later, the two cultists were both lying on the floor, pinned and gasping for breath. It seemed they both lacked the vigor of their companions who had been sent forth into the world. Perhaps there was a reason for that.

Iosef leaned over them and allowed the flickering lamp light to catch in his eyes, reflecting back like the devilish glow of a cat's eyes.

"Now then," he whispered, "I am searching for Count von Raabe and Count von Steiersberg. I have some business I eagerly wish to share with them. Where are they?"

"Say nothing!" the butler cried, though the force of Varanus's hand on his throat kept him from raising his voice too loudly.

But Grauss was the wiser of the two. "To Vienna," he replied. "They have gone to Vienna."

Grauss was not a good liar, Iosef could tell. The quiver in his tone, the hesitation in his breath, the dilation of his eyes, and the change in pulse all gave him away. One could not always tell truth from falsehood by the physical signs, but it was much easier for the Living. And it was very easy with the unfortunate Grauss.

Iosef placed one hand over Grauss's mouth to muffle any screams that might result and then bent his finger backward until just before it broke. Grauss shuddered and struggled and whimpered in pain, but to his credit, he did not cry out. Though perhaps that was only a ploy to make

Iosef relax enough to allow a proper shout for aid. Fortunately, Iosef did not intend to take any chances on that account.

"One of you will tell me," Iosef said.

Again he allowed the light to catch in his eyes, its reflection shimmering hypnotically as he gazed at his victims. He clenched his throat to both soften and deepen his voice until it was a rumble sounding almost at the same tone as a beating heart. It was pageantry, but it might prove effective all the same. The weak-minded and weak-willed alike were sometimes coerced more through animal suggestion than through reason or fear, and he very much doubted that either reason or torture would move the "faithful" in time to be effective.

He listened carefully as he heard the butler's breathing slow, even as his heartbeat quickened with excitement. Grauss remained unmoved, still snarling viciously. Iosef kept his hand over Grauss's mouth and turned his full attention to the butler, his glistening eyes inviting the man to become lost in the instinctive dread of darkness.

"You are going to tell me, aren't you?" he asked.

"N-no," the butler answered, but the conviction of the word was not supported by the listlessness of his tone.

"You are going to tell me," Iosef repeated.

"N.... N-no…" came the reply, even less certain than before.

Iosef smiled. He had his man.

"Where have they gone?" he asked softly.

* * * *

"They've fled to Valkenburg," Iosef told Luka, as they met him at the carriage a few blocks from Von Steiersberg's house.

Luka raised an eyebrow and asked, "Prussia? At this hour?"

"Naturally," Varanus said, climbing into the carriage with Iosef. "Julius's home ground. His ancestral seat. What better place to bring his captives?"

"Any place that does not involve crossing a border," Luka ventured.

He set the carriage in motion, but for the time being he kept their pace slow, partly to avoid attention and partly so that they could still converse.

"Borders are notoriously porous things, Brother," Iosef said. "You know that."

Luka chuckled knowingly. "Indeed. And are we to follow them?"

"I have a thirst for revenge and a passion for not leaving alive a man who wishes to kill me," Iosef replied. "We will return to the house and wait until the morning train. We will obtain horses in Königsberg and proceed to the Von Raabe house from there."

"And our quarry?" Luka asked.

"Either they managed an overnight train or they go by carriage," Varanus said, "though I suspect it is the latter. Two unwilling prisoners are likely to attract attention. And if they have gone by carriage, we shall arrive days ahead of them. Ample time for us to survey the land and lay a trap."

"Sneaky of you, Doctor," Luka said, laughing. "I daresay you ought to have become a hunter rather than a surgeon."

"Thank you, Luka, you are too kind."

As the carriage picked up speed, Iosef leaned back in his seat. He turned to Varanus and said, "I suggest that we leave Ekaterine to manage your son's...*guests*. She will also be ideal in assuaging the suspicions of the staff. We will have her make excuses of a family outing or some such thing."

"A visit to the countryside," Varanus agreed. "Quite innocuous." She frowned. "Ekaterine will not be happy at being excluded. She adores ruined castles."

"She will persevere," Iosef said. "But short of locking your son's guests in the cellar, there is no alternative."

"Alistair can look after them," Varanus said. She then considered her own words. "Though I am not certain if leaving him alone would be a good idea at such a time."

"Regarding that..." Iosef murmured.

"My son?" Varanus's eyes flashed. "What of him?"

"Much as I am displeased to say it, we must bring him with us," Iosef replied. "For your sake."

"For *my* sake?" Varanus demanded.

Iosef sighed softly. "Varanus," he said, "if we vanish without explaining anything to him, he will begin to make inquiries, which is the last thing we want when our intention is to murder someone."

"Agreed," Varanus replied cautiously. "But if we tell him...."

"If we tell him and do not bring him, he will rush off to rescue his friends on his own. He will be clumsy and unsubtle about it. He will ask questions. He will attract attention. And this may well get him killed if Von Steiersberg's allies take notice of him."

Varanus inhaled and exhaled very slowly. She was not pleased.

"If we bring him, he may die," she reminded Iosef.

Iosef did not regard that possibility as any great concern, but he did understand why it was important to his student.

"If we do not bring him, he will be angry with us," Iosef said. "That does not trouble me, but I know that it will trouble you."

"True...."

"And worse," Iosef continued, "if we do not bring him and his friends die, he will be furious with you, and it may take him years to forgive you because he is young and that is how young people behave."

Varanus frowned and gazed out of the window.

"I suppose that is true," she admitted. "Or at least plausible."

"Believe me, Varanus," Iosef said, "I am not pleased by the thought of having your son accompanying us, as I have yet to witness him being particularly reliable under any circumstances." He paused as Varanus exhaled angrily at his description of her son, and he raised a hand to show that it was not his intention to make an argument of it. "But he is important to you, and therefore, I would prefer to keep him alive. If he intends to go chasing after his abducted friends, he will be much safer in our company than on his own."

Varanus sighed. "I suppose you are right, My Lord."

"Indeed," Iosef said. "I have been known to speak reasonably from time to time, though I shall not make a habit of it."

Varanus laughed at this, and Iosef joined her, enjoying the brief reprieve from the disquiet of the night's events. And he enjoyed the laughter all the more knowing that things would only grow worse in the coming days.

CHAPTER TWENTY-FIVE

It was late evening by the time they reached Königsberg, but even so, Varanus and Iosef agreed that it would be best if they ventured out to the Von Raabe house and appraised the situation. If Julius and his cohorts had gone by carriage as Varanus suspected, it would be a few days before they arrived, even at a rapid pace and under ideal circumstances. That gave Varanus enough time to survey the land, identify the best place for an ambush, and prepare for the inevitable confrontation.

Julius's home was the logical place to start: if the conspirators managed to slip past them in Königsberg, that was likely the ultimate destination. Where better to keep prisoners than a secluded mansion in the countryside? And it was important to determine whether the rest of the Von Raabe family were in league with their patriarch. That would influence the lay of the land when Julius finally arrived.

They had all dressed inconspicuously to avoid attention, but given how distinctive Varanus and Friedrich looked, mother and son did their best to stay out of the public eye, as did Iosef, leaving Luka to manage whatever arrangements were necessary: rooms, food, transportation. After about an hour of searching, he returned to them with a horse and buggy that he claimed had been purchased outright from its former owner. Varanus thought it best not to ask for details.

Under cover of darkness, they drove out into the Prussian hinterland, following the road that Julius had taken during their last visit. Despite the moonless night, Luka seemed confident of the route. Varanus suspected that it was one part memory, another part deduction, and a tremendous amount of bravado. But as long as they arrived with the Von Raabe household still abed, she did not feel inclined to comment.

Next to her, Friedrich rubbed his hands against the cold. There was a sharp wind blowing in from the Baltic, bringing with it a northerly chill more suited to the past winter than the new spring. As one of the Living, Varanus barely noticed it.

"Here," she said, pulling the shawl from her shoulders and wrapping it around him.

Friedrich pushed the shawl away gently. "I am perfectly well, Mother. Just a little chill. Nothing I cannot manage." He smiled and nudged her. "I daresay you need it more than I do."

"Nonsense," Varanus retorted, though she returned his smile. It pleased her to spend time with her son, even under such unfortunate circumstances. "I only have the thing to make foolish onlookers mistake me for a peasant woman."

Friedrich laughed. "You would never be mistaken for a peasant, Mother."

"Even so," Varanus said. "I doubt that the German authorities will have any cause to investigate us when all this is over, but I would prefer to avoid any possibility of being recognized."

"I will drink to that," Friedrich said, reaching into the pocket of his overcoat, no doubt for a flask of spirits.

Varanus placed her hand on his arm and stopped him. Her son was welcome to be a drunk on his own time, though she did not like it one bit. But she was not about to have him drinking at a time like this.

She glanced at Iosef and saw him frowning ever so slightly. It was an expression typical of the Living, and Varanus doubted that Friedrich noticed it—if he could even make it out in the dark. But Varanus saw it and it troubled her. She knew that Iosef harbored unfounded concerns about her son's reliability. They were wrong, of course, but did Friedrich have to be giving those fears more credence all of the time?

"Reaching for the wine, no doubt," Iosef mumbled in Svanish.

"Certainly not, My Lord," Varanus replied. There was an uncomfortable pause. "More likely it will be brandy."

Iosef smirked a little. "Brandy is a kind of wine."

"It is medicinal," Varanus said.

"Of course it is." Iosef did not sound convinced.

Overhearing them, Luka leaned back in the driver's seat and asked, "Did someone mention wine? I could do with a bottle."

"Keep your eyes on the road," Iosef told him sternly. "If we lose our way, we will have lost a day, and we do not have many of those before our adversaries arrive in force."

"I can see perfectly well," Luka retorted.

"No you cannot," Iosef corrected him.

And with that, the two of them promptly launched into a good-natured argument about the road, the night, and the frigid weather. It was not often that Varanus witnessed such disagreements between them, but they occurred. Such was to be expected from comrades who had lived as brothers for two lifetimes or more.

"What is happening?" Friedrich whispered in her ear. "What are you all talking about?"

Varanus quickly returned to German and replied, "We are merely... um...discussing how best to get your *friends* back to Austria-Hungary. I doubt that either of them will be in particularly sound condition. A journey on the train might prove difficult."

Friedrich nodded, evidently relieved to hear her speaking in such a way. It comforted him to hear her talk about his friends both being alive now and surviving to return home. And Varanus was skeptical about both of those possibilities, especially where the violinist was concerned. She was confident that the girl Erzsebet would be largely unharmed until she could be married to Von Steiersberg and could begin producing heirs. That was usually how these things happened. But the one called Stanislav was certainly traveling to his death, if he had not been killed already, either for spite or for expediency. Though perhaps he was being kept alive just long enough to make Erzsebet docile for the wedding, Varanus mused. It seemed like the sort of thing such people would do.

Then again, it was their fault that all of this had happened, Varanus reminded herself. If Friedrich hadn't known Stanislav, there would have been no attempt on his life, no attempted murder by Julius, none of it. So there was still that to consider. Varanus did not intend to feel callous about such things, but she was certainly *annoyed*. And she had noticed that empathy for mortals grew harder and harder as the years passed. They would all be dead one day, wouldn't they?

"That is rather hardhearted of you, *Liebchen*," said Korbinian.

His voice gave Varanus a start. She had not seen or heard from him since their encounter at Von Steiersberg's house in Prague. Now he was back, sitting on the driver's seat next to Luka and leaning over to speak with her. His face was pale, and crimson tears glistened at the corners of his eyes, but he was far more himself than he had been for the past several months.

"I am merely acknowledging the truth," she murmured, turning her head so that the conversation would go unnoticed by her companions. "The girl should not have run away with the violinist. Another nobleman, one with the standing and influence to placate her father, certainly. But a penniless musician? A socialist?" Varanus shook her head. "Within a few years she would be dead in the street or...*ill* from her lover's recklessness."

"Perhaps," Korbinian acknowledged sadly. "But is that so much worse than to be married to a bully and a tyrant? I know such men well. The girl's flesh and bones would have told the history of her marriage by the time she gave birth to her first child."

Varanus frowned at this, knowing that it was true. The realization made her angry. And it also frightened her a little to know how easily she could have found herself in the same circumstances. If she had been forced to marry a brute like Alfonse des Louveteaux, she knew that her back would have been inscribed with each instance of her husband's displeasure, at least until she had found an opportunity to kill him for it. Fortunately, her circumstances had been immeasurably different.

"In Fuchsburg such things are not tolerated," Korbinian said, his tone clouded with the same anger that Varanus felt. "We have old laws and better men."

"We are not in Fuchsburg, my love," Varanus reminded him. "Nor are we among the Shashavani. We are in the world, and in the world women are seldom given a choice between good and bad. Rather the choice is between tolerable and worse."

"It was not so with us, *Liebchen*," Korbinian ventured.

Varanus frowned. "No. You died." She looked into Korbinian's eyes as blood began to trickle across his lips. "I was given a choice, and my choice was stolen from me."

"I am sorry, *Liebchen*," Korbinian said sadly.

"Why are you sorry?" Varanus asked. "You did not kill yourself."

"No," Korbinian agreed, as tears of blood rolled down his cheeks. "But I did not remain alive. And for that, I will always be sorry. I would have fought God Himself if it meant I did not have to leave you alone, but the coward would not give me the chance."

Varanus felt her chest tightened. She tried to speak and suddenly found her lungs empty of air. She took a deep breath and began to reply, but Korbinian interrupted her as he pointed his finger toward the coast.

"I wonder," he mused, "why there are fires burning at Castle Valkenburg."

This observation surprised Varanus, for surely it was not possible. Valkenburg was a deserted ruin, the sort of place to be visited by sightseers and the curious only during the daytime for a picnic or some other outing. And yet, as she turned and looked across the dark countryside, she saw that his words were true.

The remains of Castle Valkenburg loomed against the black sky, its stones illuminated here and there with scattered fires that burned behind its empty windows. To anyone but the Living, it might have gone unnoticed, for the lights were faint and well obscured by the remains of the castle's walls, but Varanus's eyes saw them clearly, just as Korbinian's had. This was no trick of starlight.

"Iosef..." she said softly, pointing toward the castle.

"Hmm?" Interrupted from his argument with Luka, Iosef looked toward the castle, and his eyes widened ever so slightly, barely enough for Varanus to notice. But she recognized his astonishment. "There are people at the castle," he murmured. "But why?"

"Vagrants, perhaps?" Varanus suggested. But even as she spoke, she doubted it.

"There is little shelter to be had there for a vagabond," Iosef replied, echoing Varanus's sentiments. "And there is too much light for it to be a wanderer's humble campfire."

"Julius, perhaps," Varanus said, though the very suggestion sounded false to her. "Though if they went by horse and carriage, they should be days behind us."

"Indeed," Iosef agreed. "And yet, who would have cause to be among the ruins at this hour?"

"I suppose we have but one way to answer that question," Varanus said.

Iosef considered this and then nodded. He patted Luka on the shoulder to get the man's attention and then motioned toward Valkenburg.

"Luka, we are making a detour. Take us to the castle."

CHAPTER TWENTY-SIX

Without the aid of moonlight, it was difficult going once they left the road, so after a few minutes of careful plodding along the winding dirt path, they abandoned the wagon and continued on foot, leaving the horse hitched by its reins to the branch of a tree. Varanus tried in vain to convince her son to remain behind to safeguard their transportation, but Friedrich flatly refused. He would not wait patiently in the dark while his friends were in danger, he said; and while it angered Varanus that her son insisted on endangering himself, she was not surprised by it. Nor was there much that she could do. Better to keep him in sight than to risk him rushing off into certain danger on his own.

They approached the castle on foot, careful to avoid the dips and falls of the landscape. Drawing nearer, Varanus saw clearly the fires burning within the castle walls. There were torches standing in rows along the ruined halls, their flames flickering in the cold breeze. And somewhere at the heart of the castle burned bonfires. Varanus smelled the rich fragrance of the burning wood as it drifted past on the wind.

"Do you smell that?" she asked Iosef as the two of them crouched in the shadows next to the castle's crumbling outer wall. The wall had suffered badly at the hands of the elements, leaving breaks and gaps that could no longer keep out the wind or conceal the fragrance of burning that flowed through the halls within.

Iosef nodded. "The fires? Wood smoke…and in great quantity."

"Why would anyone be burning firewood here?"

"My mind suggests vagrants but finds that solution untenable," Iosef replied.

"Vagrants would set one fire for warmth and no more," Varanus said, "lest they be discovered."

"Perhaps some of the local folk engaged in a tradition of great antiquity," Iosef suggested.

"Perhaps," Varanus agreed, "but then who? The nearest people are the Von Raabes. Do you suppose they set candles and burn torches in their patriarch's absence?"

Iosef shrugged, admitting his ignorance to the answer.

Behind them, Luka crouched down and murmured, "We are in Europe, Doctor. Half of the time I do not understand anything that you people do."

It was spoken as much in jest as in sincerity, and Varanus snickered slightly. "Were Ekaterine here, she would no doubt explain it as a manifestation of 'Latin paganism' and suggest its origins in 'uncharted Kent'."

"I have always found the inhabitants of Kent to be unrepentant pagans," Luka mused.

Iosef snorted with distain at his comrade's words. "You have never even been to Kent, Brother."

"I have heard stories about it," Luka replied, his moustache twitching.

"Ekaterine's stories no doubt," Varanus said.

Luka's moustache twitched again.

Friedrich joined them and knelt beside Varanus, looking very puzzled. Of course, as they spoke in Svanish, he could not understand what they were saying.

"What are you all going on about?" he asked.

Iosef and Luka exchanged a glance, and Varanus noticed a very thin smile creep across Luka's lips.

"Kent," he said.

Varanus shook her head at him. She placed a hand on Friedrich's arm and whispered, "We are attempting to ascertain who is burning a fire in the ruins at this hour and why they are doing it."

"Vagrants?" Friedrich suggested.

At his words, Luka almost laughed aloud, and Iosef glowered in reply.

"Possibly," Varanus answered. "Still, we will not get our answer waiting here." She motioned toward the nearest gap in the broken exterior wall. "Shall we?"

She crept into the castle ruin, her ears carefully searching for any hint of activity nearby. She heard no footsteps nor anything she could count as voices in the vicinity, although truly it was hard to make out any sounds at all aside from the moaning of the wind as it blew through the roofless corridors. There was a distinct saltiness to the breeze that made Varanus cringe. The bothersome influence of the nearby sea, of course.

Crossing through an outer passage, Varanus entered a crumbling hall near the entrance. To her surprise, she saw two parallel rows of torches leading from the empty doorway into the shadowy depths of the ruin. This was not merely some temporary haven for the dispossessed. Someone had come here with a purpose and put great effort into arranging things. The meticulous placement of the torches was as elegant as it was ominous, each one the same distance from the ones before and after it.

The sound of loud applause echoed from the flickering darkness further down the hall. Varanus almost jumped in surprise, afraid that someone had spotted them. But she relaxed a little as she saw Korbinian advancing toward her down the row of torches, clapping his hands as if enjoying a private performance.

"How very theatrical!" he announced. "I do so enjoy pageantry."

"It is rather *dramatic*," Varanus agreed softly.

"Dramatic!" Korbinian exclaimed, as the hint of scarlet tears formed in the corners of his eyes. "But why should it not be a drama, *Liebchen?* Surely you can see that this is a scene set for a tragedy."

Varanus eyed the torches and said, "Nonsense. Torches at midnight in a ruined castle? It is assuredly farce."

Korbinian smiled. It was not a pleasant expression. "Of course, *Liebchen*," he said. "I am laughing already." And with that, he withdrew back into the darkness.

"What are you looking at, Varanus?" Iosef murmured, startling her. He and the others had joined her in the hall.

"I am pondering where this illuminated path leads," Varanus said.

"Indeed," Iosef agreed. "This is not happenstance. This is meant to be seen."

"Yes, but not by us," Varanus replied.

"By whom, then?" It was as much a question spoken by Iosef to himself as to her.

Varanus sniffed the air, searching for some distinctive smell that could be separated from the salt. There was a brief respite as the wind died down, and Varanus managed to discern the distant scent of burning wood.

"That I do not know, My Lord," she said, "but that way is the bonfire."

"The bonfire and our answers," Iosef replied.

With the wind now quiet, Varanus heard the sound of voices speaking just outside the entrance to the castle.

"You hear something?" asked a man's gruff voice.

There was a pause.

"No.... Maybe?"

"Luka," Iosef said, putting a hand on his comrade's shoulder and nodding toward the door.

"Of course," Luka replied, a smile tugging at the corners of his mouth.

He detached himself from the group and hurried across the hallway toward the door just as a pair of men standing guard rounded the corner. Luka lunged forward into the darkness outside, grabbing each of the men by the throat so they could not cry out for help as he knocked them to the ground.

Nearby, Friedrich turned to watch Luka pass and then took a step backward at the sight of the confrontation. He quickly drew a pistol from beneath his coat and rushed to offer Luka his assistance—which was neither needed nor wanted. Varanus caught her son's hand and pulled him back.

"Nothing to worry about Alis…Friedrich," she said, smiling to reassure him. "Only some interlopers. Luka will handle it."

"Oh…. Right." Friedrich frowned but he did not protest.

Presently, Luka returned, cracking his knuckles with a satisfied half smile. He exchanged a knowing nod with Iosef.

"Is it done?" Iosef asked.

Luka shook his head. "That you should even need to ask…."

"Unconscious?"

"It is a kind of sleep," Luka replied.

"Any indication of who they were or why they are here?" Varanus asked.

In reply, Luka held out two pistols, which he had obviously taken from the men. "I cannot say for certain, but they carried weapons."

Friedrich, unable to understand what was being said, nevertheless started in shock at the sight of the guns.

"Those men were armed?" he asked.

Varanus gave Iosef and Luka a pointed look and said in Svanish, "For the sake of my son, we should use German until we are done here. If the men who lit the fires hear us, we will be discovered whether or not they understand our words."

Iosef sighed softly but he nodded. "Agreed."

"Not merely men with arms, but men on guard," Luka said, in comfortably fluent German. "It seems clear to me that they were left there to restrict entry through the main gate."

"Thank God the outer wall is so decayed we were not forced to use the door," Friedrich said, "or else we would have been discovered by them when we made our approach."

Luka cleared his throat. "No. We would not have been discovered."

"But then the men might not be unconscious," Iosef noted sardonically.

"It is a *kind* of sleep," Luka repeated.

Friedrich frowned and interjected, "Those men are dead, aren't they?"

At this Iosef smiled slightly and said in Svanish, "The boy is not completely stupid."

"He remains a drunk," Luka said, also lapsing back into Svanish.

"He remains my son," Varanus reminded them. And having made the admonishment in defense of her blood, she returned to German. "If they were here with weapons in this place and at this time, I doubt that their intentions were good. Likely they work for Julius's family and are here preparing the way for their lord."

"I suppose that is…reasonable," Friedrich admitted. "But still, my friends are in danger. We ought to hurry."

"Indeed," Iosef said. "We ought to hurry for the sake of your friends."

And the mess they have gotten us into, Varanus added silently.

"I am glad that we agree," Friedrich said, Iosef's sarcasm evidently lost to him. That much was not surprising: it was difficult to discern the subtleties of humor and emotion among the Living unless one was very familiar with them, or the Shashavani in question made a special effort for their sentiments to be recognizable.

Iosef nodded toward the rows of lights leading into the darkness and said, "Come, we have dallied long enough. Let us determine what is happening here and just who is responsible. I do not wish to alert our quarry. If we have already disturbed the scene here, it is better we silence things before our disruption can be reported."

There was no argument to this, neither from Varanus—who quite agreed with Iosef's assessment—nor from Luka or Friedrich. As Iosef headed into the depths of the castle, Varanus took her son by the arm and led him along too, determined to keep him close. There was no telling what they might discover, and she did not intend for him to be put in any greater danger than he had already insisted upon.

The path of torches led through the castle in a serpentine route, certainly intended more for show than for practicality. The entire ambiance of the place—if one could even call it such—seemed almost calculated to be ominous. Deeper into the crumbling halls, Varanus saw more bits of pageantry. There were wreaths of flowers and holly cast by the wayside, and the skulls of animals were placed on poles where the torchlight could make the most of their presence.

Ekaterine would indeed be sad she was not there.

Midway along the length of the castle, a noise suddenly caught Varanus's attention. It was the gentle cough of a man suffering the torments of the cold sea air. She quickly threw out her arm to stop Friedrich and Luka, who followed along behind. She was about to reach for Iosef when she saw that he had stopped as well. And of course he had. He must have heard the sound too, for his hearing was easily as keen as hers.

"More watchmen," she murmured.

"Indeed," Iosef agreed. "To be expected."

Varanus glanced about them and saw an adjoining passage a few feet back, which split off from the torch-lit path and led into darkness. She nodded toward the passage and led the way into the darkness, only just able to see in the dim starlight. She felt Friedrich stumble several times as she led him along, but he trusted her enough not to protest. Indeed, Varanus almost found herself anticipating the lay of the floor and the curve of the walls as she went along, as if she was being guided by a stick that touched each protrusion or uneven stone a moment before she reached it.

After a minute or two of the oppressive near-darkness, the passage opened into something familiar: the great hall that Varanus had visited with Julius during her first journey to the castle. Open and roofless, the room was better lit by starlight than was the passage, though it remained oppressively dark. Varanus glanced toward the balcony that overlooked them, half expecting to see Korbinian there, gazing down at her amid a cloud of malice and black feathers.

Instead, she saw lamplight.

Curious, Varanus narrowed her eyes and allowed them to adjust to the unexpected brightness, stripping away the darkness around its unpleasant halo. She saw Count Erdelyi and young Erzsebet standing together in the company of Julius and a couple of armed men. In the lamplight, she could see that Julius and Erdelyi had covered their normal clothes with long black robes, which were woven through with delicate embroidery and golden thread. Each man wore a long bejeweled necklace adorned by the skull of some small creature, and on his head each man bore a wreath of holly and the skull of a ram. It was like some perverse transfiguration of their equinox festival.

Erzsebet, in contrast, was dressed in the manner of a May Queen, with a simple dress of white linen and a crown of flowers in her hair. She was sullen and hostile, her eyes downturned and her expression caught between resentment, resignation, and abject terror. Erdelyi held her by the back of the neck like she was an animal being taken to slaughter, rather than his own child.

"Will Augusta and the children be joining us?" Erdelyi asked Julius, his tone pleasant and jovial despite his callous attitude toward his daughter.

"Alas not," Julius replied, sounding genuinely disappointed, as if his loved ones were missing some pleasant summer outing to the seaside.

"We have guests from Berlin visiting for the week. I fear it would arouse suspicions if anyone was absent."

"But not you?" Erdelyi asked. He chuckled, his question some manner of joke.

Julius shook his head, and as he did so, the light fell upon the other side of his face, and Varanus saw the one eye—where she was certain she had broken his skill—was purely crimson and gently leaking blood like teardrops.

"I fear my presence would raise more suspicions *before* our business tonight," he explained, "though I shall be 'arriving on a late train' once I am whole again."

"Of course," Erdelyi said, as though this was a perfectly normal thing to say to a man whose eye was slowly leaking blood and who should not even have been able to stand in light of his injury.

In the darkness below them, Varanus was silent as her mind worked to process what she was seeing. Behind her, she sensed that same astonishment in the others.

"Von Raabe," Iosef noted, his voice barely above a whisper. "That is unexpected."

"How could they have arrived before us?" Varanus asked.

"By the light of the moon," Iosef murmured, though from his tone it sounded like a half-hearted joke born of uncertainty. With more confidence, he replied, "They must have secured a private train last night. They would have arrived hours before we did."

"On such short notice and without raising any questions?" Luka asked. "That suggests influence."

"Influence is the last thing I would expect such men to have in short supply," Varanus noted.

Beside her, she sensed Friedrich leaning forward, his eyes straining against the darkness to be certain of what he saw.

"My God!" he breathed. "Erzsebet!"

In a flash, Friedrich had drawn his pistol and taken a step forward, rushing to the aid of a friend he could neither reach nor rescue. Varanus grabbed him and pulled him back. As an afterthought, Luka and Iosef did the same, so that, together, their ability to restrain him did not arouse his suspicions. Varanus clamped her hand over Friedrich's mouth.

"No!" she hissed in his ear.

"But Erzsebet!" Friedrich protested through her fingertips, though he showed enough sense to keep his voice quiet despite his agitation, which only grew and grew as he struggled against the hands that held him.

"You cannot reach her," Varanus whispered. "Not yet. And if we give ourselves away now, we will never be able to save her, nor will we discover what has become of your other friend."

It took Friedrich only a moment to register the wisdom in her words, and he quickly gave up fighting. He holstered his pistol and was rewarded by being released.

"Well, the boy has some sense," Luka said in Svanish.

"The boy *listens* to reason," Iosef replied in the same tongue. "But it must be told to him first."

"True."

Varanus took Friedrich's hand in hers—partly to comfort him and partly to prevent him from drawing his pistol again—and gave him a reassuring squeeze.

"We will rescue them," she said. "But we must judge the situation calmly or else we will be undone."

Friedrich nodded slowly, though he did not look pleased with inaction.

On the balcony above them, the conversation had continued:

"Are you certain you are well enough for this, Julius?" Erdelyi asked.

Julius laughed. "If I do not do it now, I suspect I will not last to see the sunrise. Certainly not the week." He turned to Erzsebet and smiled at her, lovingly like an uncle. "But you will see to my salvation, won't you, my dear?"

He touched Erzsebet's cheek with his fingertips, and she cringed away from him.

"I will not do it," she snarled.

"Wicked child!" Erdelyi snapped. He struck her across the face with his open palm. "Do not speak to your elders so!"

Erzsebet whimpered in pain and tears flooded her eyes, but her snarl did not abate. "I will not do it!" she repeated.

Erdelyi raised his hand to strike again, but Julius caught him and smiled.

"Patience, Istvan, patience," he said. "Erzsebet is simply frightened. But she is a good girl. She will do as she must when the appointed hour arrives."

"I will not," Erzsebet protested. "I refuse!"

"You should have thought of that before you ran off with that mongrel!" Erdelyi roared. "Sullying yourself with him, letting him pollute your body! It is a disgrace! How dare you bring such shame upon me? In the eyes of my friends, my brethren—"

Again, Julius interrupted his friend with a soothing tone. "Patience, patience. Give the girl a chance to redeem her soul." He touched

Erzsebet's cheek with his hand. His motion was tender at first, but as she pulled away, he took her firmly by the jaw and held her there. "But it must be done, child, to undo the wrong that you allowed to be visited upon your family and upon your husband."

"He is not my husband!" Erzsebet cried.

"Not if your ill judgment has any say in the matter," Erdelyi said disdainfully. "But thankfully, Count von Steiersberg has generously agreed to forgive your shameful transgression and welcome you back into the fold, which is welcome news for our family. But you must be the one to carry out the ritual that you might plead with God to restore your…your *tainted virtue*." Erdelyi stuttered over the words and finally spat them out, seething with rage. "After allowing that peasant to defile your body, this is the only way to make you whole again. So you will do it, and you will be grateful for our mercy."

"I will not!" Erzsebet insisted.

Erdelyi tightened his grip on her neck. "We will see if you are so impudent when the hour has come and the knife is before you," he growled as he dragged her off toward the next set of rooms.

Julius and the guardsmen fell in behind them and departed into the shadows.

For a few moments, silence filled the hall. Presently Luka spoke, his moustache twitching at having seen such virulence directed at one so meek.

"I am permitted to kill them, am I not?" he asked.

"Not if I reach them first," Friedrich said, his hand on the grip of his pistol.

"I think we will all kill them for the manifold things they have done," Varanus noted, "as soon as we are able to catch them unawares and kill them without any of them escaping."

"A sensible voice of pragmatism," Iosef noted, sounding pleased.

"Justice is pragmatic, if nothing else," Varanus replied.

"But I will get to kill *someone*, yes?" Luka asked.

Iosef looked at him with pronounced seriousness and asked, straightfaced, "Don't you mean, 'put them to sleep'?"

The corner of Luka's mouth twisted upward.

"It is a *kind* of sleep."

CHAPTER TWENTY-SEVEN

Friedrich understood the wisdom in remaining hidden until they located both prisoners and had a proper advantage over their enemies, but it chafed him to watch silently as Erzsebet was so abused by her father and Count von Raabe. Once it was safe to move again, he followed Iosef and his mother through the hall and into the adjoining passage. Luka took up the rear, carefully checking the bullets in his revolver.

Friedrich was not certain what to make of the man. He had presented himself in London as a sort of ill-tempered good Samaritan, protecting the poor in the East End from the local gangs that troubled them. But Friedrich suspected that Luka's motivation was as much a thirst for violence as an eagerness to see justice done.

And Iosef was even more of a peculiarity: the same fair youth that Friedrich had met a decade ago, almost unchanged by the passing years. It was yet another peculiarity, just like Mother and her perpetual youth, or indeed like Aunt Ekaterine for that matter. Ten years seemed to have passed the entire household without effect. Of course, Friedrich had unlocked the secret to that mystery, only to have lost it yet again.

But now was not the time for such thoughts. Erzsebet was in danger, and Stanislav was yet to be found. As Friedrich followed Iosef through the darkness, he kept his Mauser ready, his fingers flexing around the pistol's handle to be certain of their grip. He would not fire until the moment was right, but when that moment came, he would not hesitate and he would not miss.

As they passed beyond the great hall, Mother seemed to have a much clearer sense of where they were and where they were going. And though she tried to hide the fact, Friedrich noticed that this troubled her. She had been here before, it seemed, and she had reason to suspect what was afoot. This troubled Friedrich as he wondered how she had come to be here and what she knew, but he did not inquire. Now was not the time for unnecessary talk.

They soon came to the main corridor again, which was wide and still lit by the two rows of torches. There were more men here, standing guard attentively but without any real indication of concern. And why should they fear intrusion? Who in his right mind would be poking about in a decrepit ruin at such an hour? But they were armed and it would not do to draw attention, so Friedrich and the others made their way through another side route that passed through a collection of abandoned rooms that might once have been private chambers.

After a tangle of darkened chambers, Friedrich and the others passed into a cloistered court that ran between the castle keep and the outer wall. Friedrich gazed up at the keep and saw tall windows of stained glass above him. They were broken and weathered, but their meaning was plain: this was the castle's chapel, where knights praised God before sallying forth to kill those who sang praises to another.

There was another man on guard just inside the side door to the chapel, but again he seemed present more as a precaution than for the expectation of intrusion. Either way, the man would soon have cause to regret his unfortunate placement. Friedrich went to deal with the guard himself, but Luka was the quicker. He darted past Friedrich and the others and drew alongside the doorway. Pausing and listening for a moment, Luka pulled a knife from inside his coat. He stepped into the doorway and took hold of the guard, plunging the knife into the man before he could cry out. Turning in a flash, Luka stabbed again several times for good measure and then threw the body into the darkness of the courtyard.

With one bloody hand, Luka motioned for the others to follow him inside. The chapel was tremendously large, rather the size of a proper church, though like the rest of the castle it was in horrible disrepair. Friedrich saw the stars through the broken roof, and the pillars that lined the nave were like stone trees in a bare forest. And like a scene in a forest, the chapel was distorted into a hideous display of pagan fantasy. A great bonfire in the center of the transept lit the chapel, and piles of flowers and skulls had been heaped about the pillars and at the base of the altar in profane ornamentation.

Friedrich stared speechless at the display while the others did the same. Varanus in particular seemed to be disturbed by what she saw, and her eyes darted around, taking in every detail, comparing it to some unspoken memory.

As Friedrich watched, he saw Count Erdelyi pass by the bonfire, pulling Erzsebet along with him. Erzsebet went unwillingly but obediently, her head downcast and her expression resigned. Friedrich clenched the Mauser in his hand and took a step forward, preparing to run to his friend's rescue. He felt a hand grab his arm and hold him fast. A glance told him that it was Iosef, who looked at him with disapproval.

"Calm yourself, young man," Iosef said.

"But—" Friedrich protested, though he found enough reason to keep his voice low.

"We must proceed with caution," Iosef told him coolly. "These men are armed and they are capable, and it would be unwise to lose our advantage. We must take them by surprise and kill them all at once, or else this will be an unpleasant fight."

Friedrich might have protested again, but he heard voices passing nearby. Julius von Raabe had arrived, and he walked toward the altar along the nearest row of columns with Von Steiersberg. Both men were strangely casual in their manner and speech, a most curious thing given their garments and adornments, for Von Steiersberg was dressed the same as his cohorts, in a black robe, a holly wreath, and a skull.

The two men paused a moment near one of the columns, temptingly close, but still too far away to strike without sounding the alarm. Friedrich saw the others weigh the situation and hold back, and against his instincts, he did the same.

"How is your eye?" Von Steiersberg asked Julius.

As if in answer, Julius touched his temple. "It fares poorly. I have lost all sight in it, and the dizziness is becoming more frequent."

"You may soon die," Von Steiersberg noted. His tone made it almost sound like a friendly joke.

"I may indeed," Julius agreed. Though he seemed to tolerate Von Steiersberg's humor—perhaps even share it—there was a far greater sense of urgency in his voice.

"Best we hurry then." Von Steiersberg rubbed his hands together, either in anticipation or against the evening's chill. "Is my fiancée prepared to do her part?"

"It matters little whether she is or she is not," Julius said. "She has no choice." He touched his head again. "And I fear I have no choice either, so she had damn well better find her sense of piety."

Von Steiersberg laughed. "I suppose if the girl refuses to through with it and remains sullied, there is always your Mechtilde."

Julius frowned slightly and said, "Franz, I neither need nor desire an Austrian alliance as dearly as Istvan does and certainly not dearly enough to give you my daughter."

"You do not want me as your son-in-law?" Von Steiersberg asked, his good humor undiminished by the rejection. "Not after our years of friendship?"

"No, I do not," Julius answered pointedly. "Tell me Franz, have you ever considered taking a wife nearer your own age? I have a sister in Italy who will soon be recently widowed. Wouldn't you enjoy a wife with a Tuscan villa all her own?"

Von Steiersberg paused a moment to consider this, seeming rather pleased by the suggestion. "Not the one outside Arezzo with the grotto of the Faunus Ater?"

"That is the one," Julius said. "Why do you think she agreed to marry him?"

"Tempting," Von Steiersberg admitted. "But alas, I require a young and fertile wife. Children, Julius: they are a blessing from the god." He paused a moment and looked away, gazing into the bonfire. "And I have great plans for all of my children."

"I am certain you do, Franz," Julius said, his tone neither approving nor disapproving, but merely a man's acceptance of fact. He touched his eye, and his hand came away with blood. "Come. We must hurry."

"Yes, of course," Von Steiersberg replied, and the two of them continued on to the chancel and the altar.

With the way now clear, Friedrich and the others advanced quietly into the chapel, each lurking behind one of the columns to avoid being seen. A few cautious glances told Friedrich that the other guards were in place near the bonfire, as much worshippers as soldiers. They were all armed, and memory reminded him that there were also two more men in the main corridor. They would surely come running once the gunfire started.

Friedrich looked back at Varanus and mouthed the words, "I am going to get a closer look."

All of the activity seemed to be concentrated around the altar, so Friedrich waited until he was confident he would not be seen and dashed for the next column and then the one after that, approaching the chancel with as much stealth as he could manage. He needed to see what was happening, and it seemed reasonable that if everyone was gathering at one end of the chapel, he could best take them by surprise from that end.

Looking back at his companions, he saw Varanus glaring at him in exasperation and motioning for him to return. Friedrich tried to pantomime his plan without drawing attention, though it did not work very well. Behind Varanus, he saw Luka slipping away to the far end of the chapel, no doubt to secure the door and deal with the men waiting outside. That was good thinking, Friedrich reasoned. They were outnumbered, but provided they managed to take the enemy by surprise, they could bring down the armed guards before a pitched fight could ensue. And with that done, rounding up the three unarmed noblemen and rescuing Erzsebet and Stanislav would be a matter of simplicity.

Friedrich tried very hard to convince himself of that as he studied the chapel and made an accounting of who had a gun and where they were standing. In the meantime, he saw that Von Raabe, Von Steiersberg, and Erdelyi had all met together at the altar. Erdelyi kept Erzsebet by his side, holding her firmly by the back of the neck. As Friedrich watched, he saw another man dressed in much simpler regalia fill a bowl with ashes from the fire and kneel beside Julius, holding the bowl up for his master's approval.

"It is good," Julius declared, reaching into the bowl and removing a handful of ashes, which stained his hand almost black. The blood trickling from his eye slowly ran along his cheek and dripped onto the floor.

Von Steiersberg nodded. "Let us begin."

He motioned toward the back of the chapel, and two more men in simple robes advanced out of the shadows, dragging Stanislav between them. They had him pinned by the arms, but he had been severely beaten and was barely able to struggle.

In the shadows, Friedrich very nearly started shooting at the sight of his friend in such a state, but he stopped himself. There were still armed guards across the chapel who were not quite in his line fire. He would need to wait until he either had a clear shot at them or he could be certain that Luka was in position behind them. And a glance toward the narthex told him that Luka had only just returned. Friedrich caught his attention and nodded toward the other side of the room. Luka seemed not to notice him—at least the man gave no sign of acknowledgement—but he dashed to the shadows on the far side of the chamber all the same.

Friedrich waited impatiently, every muscle tensed and ready to charge and start shooting. His thoughts churned violently, trying to decide in what order he should take his targets. He needed to keep Stanislav and Erzsebet from harm, so it seemed logical to attack the company at the altar first, especially if Luka could dispatch the men across the chapel on his own. But then again, the light was inconsistent and the situation around the altar chaotic. Friedrich was a good shot, but at this range there was still a risk of hitting one of his friends. He would have to wait until the ideal moment and then make a run for the altar until he was close enough to begin shooting safely. After that, nothing was certain.

As he watched and waited, he saw Julius von Raabe raise his ash-covered hand high into the air and call out in a voice like thunder:

"Hear me, Oh Mother! Oh Father! Hear me Creator, Destroyer, Deliverer, Devourer!"

At that moment, the wind blowing off the shore picked up again, bursting through the cracks in the windows and churning overhead with moans and groans.

"Hear me Serpent! Hear me Ram!" Julius continued. "Hear me Blood of Sky and Night!"

Fed by the wind, the bonfire began to twist and dance, fading and then growing again with each torrent of the salt-stained breeze. The amber light it cast upon the chapel stones ebbed and flowed like the tide, and at its touch, the shadows cavorted in obscene merriment.

Julius shouted to be heard over the roar of the wind, but his voice was clear despite the cacophony:

"Blood of Sky and Blood of Earth, He Who Hungers, She Who Feasts, by the light of Darkest Moon, I beseech you: hear my prayer!"

Julius raised both hands heavenward as the frenzied wind battered down the bonfire until it was little more than coals, burning orange and crimson in the dark.

"Black Goat! Black God! Chernobog!" Julius cried. "Your wretched servant begs your grace! For you are mighty, we are weak, but what we have we gladly give: a simple gift to ease your hunger, if you will only cast your shadow down upon this sacred earth!"

Panicked by the sudden darkness, Friedrich abandoned caution in favor of action. He tried to run for the altar, but the press of the wind was somehow too much for him, beating him back and holding him in place as the shadows wrapped about him, cavorting with him as if possessed of life.

A final gust of wind flooded through the chapel, killing the remains of the bonfire and leaving only burning coals and thick black smoke.

And in the darkness, Erzsebet, terrified but defiant, could be clearly heard to shout, "No! No, I will not do it!"

And just as suddenly as it had come, the wind died away, leaving behind the stench of salt and smoke. There must have been some life left in the bonfire, for it burst alight again, though the flames burned low and scarlet, painting the chapel the color of blood.

In this feeble light, Friedrich saw Erzsebet and Count Erdelyi behind the altar, standing next to the limp body of Stanislav, still held by the two robed attendants. Erdelyi had an old and ornate knife in his hand, which was stained almost black as if by some kind of lacquer. He was struggling to force the weapon into Erzsebet's hand, and the girl fought back with all vigor, her eyes wide and her face desperate.

"You *will!*" Erdelyi shouted. "You *must!*"

"I will not!" Erzsebet cried. "I will not kill him!"

Even in the absence of the wind, Friedrich found his feet heavy and his body dull, as he fought to race across the chapel and rescue his friends. All thought of planning was gone. Now panic drove him onward, fueled by fear and anger, growing with each step he struggled to make. The press of the shadows and the shifting scarlet firelight ignited a heat within him that clouded his senses save for the sight and smell of his friends at the altar and the men who held them captive.

"Sacrifice him!" Erdelyi yelled, forcing the knife into Erzsebet's hand. "Do as I tell you, you impudent child!"

Erzsebet shuddered violently at the touch of the knife in her hand. Her gaze fell upon it, and what little color remained in her face drained away. Slowly, she looked up at her father and breathed one word.

"No."

And what that, she plunged the knife into Erdelyi's stomach.

Erdelyi opened his mouth to scream, but all he managed was a sort of throaty gurgle. Still staring wide-eyed, Erzsebet twisted the blade inside the wound before finally tearing the knife free from her father's body. Erdelyi made a feeble grab for her, but the effort made him stumble, and his legs abandoned him. Pitching forward, he fell against the altar, his blood spilling out across its surface and down one side.

Erzsebet dropped the knife and fell to her knees, staring at her bloody hands.

Erdelyi clawed at the top of the altar and looked back at his companions. He reached out for them, gurgling as he pleaded for help. Von Steiersberg merely sneered at him and said nothing. Julius said nothing either, though his expression was one of uncertainty and doubt. This had not gone according to plan. He slowly lowered his ash-covered hands and blinked a few times as his eye continued to weep blood.

"This is not good," he said.

"His blood is on the altar," Von Steiersberg replied. "One sacrificial lamb is as good as another."

Julius looked around, his good eye searching the darkness above them for something he did not seem to find.

"No," he said. "Not as good. Not good enough."

He reached down and grabbed the knife from the floor. With an unceremonious kick, he pushed Erdelyi's body off the altar, despite his friend's pleading noises. Taking Stanislav by the hair, he pulled the man's head back and exposed his throat.

Friedrich screamed into the shadows as he struggled through the invisible mire that clung to him, dragging him down, pinning his footsteps, holding him back from his purpose. He had to get to the altar. He had to save Stanislav. If he could only move! If he could only raise his pistol and shoot!

With the ease of experience, Julius drew the knife across Stanislav's throat, cutting through skin and flesh in a single stroke and spilling Stanislav's blood upon the altar in a violent spray of crimson.

CHAPTER TWENTY-EIGHT

Varanus was not surprised to see her son creep his way forward toward danger, though she was both disappointed and exasperated by it. She had done her best to coax him back before he could be seen or could do anything foolish, but she had been answered with nonsensical hand waving.

As the wind grew and the shadows plunged the chapel in darkness, Varanus found herself transfixed by the ritual unfolding before her. A curious numbness fell upon her shoulders, and her ears tickled to half-heard whispers in the dark. As if in a dream, she watched the proceedings unfold with fascination, almost overwhelmed by a kaleidoscope of miniscule sights and sounds that, were she not Living, would surely have escaped her notice. The very air seemed to glisten. The fire smelled of roses. Unseen hands tugged at her hair.

And then suddenly the oppressive darkness fractured and fell away. Erdelyi lay on the ground, bleeding from his stomach. Friedrich's friend Stanislav slumped between the two men who held him as blood spurted from his throat. Julius stood next to the dying man, holding aloft a bloody knife.

Varanus heard her son screaming and turned in time to see him rush toward the altar, firing his pistol wildly. The cloud that had hung about Varanus's senses was gone, leaving behind a hideous mixing of sounds and smells that dizzied her: salt and sulfur, roses and the groaning wind, the crackling of the fire and the scent of lotus blossoms. She glanced at Iosef and saw him slowly blink and shake his head. He had been overcome just as she had been.

But the immediate concern was Friedrich. His mad rush took Julius and the others by surprise, and some of his wild shots hit one of the men holding Stanislav. The man fell, clutching his chest, and Stanislav's body tumbled onto the ground beside him. Still, the moment of surprise would not last. The second attendant released Stanislav's arm and reached inside his robes for a weapon, as did Von Steiersberg.

Without thinking, Varanus charged into the center of the chapel and made for the chancel, turning her path to intercept Friedrich. Men behind her started shouting. She looked back and saw the remaining guards rushing to meet her, firing their pistols. Then she saw Luka and Iosef counter-charging toward the men and left the matter to them.

Friedrich reached Julius a few moments later and aimed his pistol at Julius's head. Julius blinked a few times, and he smiled as Friedrich pulled the trigger on an empty magazine. Julius lunged forward and stabbed with the bloodied knife. Startled, Friedrich stumbled backward, step after step, as Julius advanced at him, thrusting and slashing with such rapid movements that Friedrich could not even block most of the attacks, though he tried desperately to do so; it was all that Friedrich could do to dash backward and save himself the same fate as Erdelyi and Stanislav.

Varanus reached them and threw herself against Julius, knocking him to the ground. Hot with anger and confident that she had him within her power, she loomed over him for a moment and raised her fist, ready to pummel him into pulp. But she paused as she caught Julius gazing back at her, his expression triumphant and his eyes bright.

Both eyes. Both whole. Both bloodless.

"How…?" she began.

The sting of metal in her side caught her attention, and she looked down to see the sacrificial knife buried to the hilt in her body. It burned like fire, and the sight of it made her strangely dizzy. And had she been mortal, it would certainly have been a fatal blow.

How foolish of her to let her guard down. She had not even noticed him draw back his arm to strike….

Then she heard gunshots and felt bullets tear into her back. One of the attendants had reached them, a smoking revolver in his hand. Varanus had not expected such an immediate response. As the attendant shot at her, Varanus leapt upon him, striking, clawing, and gouging until he stopped firing and his pistol fell limply to the ground.

The scent of blood was pleasant. Varanus's head swam and she licked her lips. The fog that had overwhelmed her before had been reduced to a haze, but that haze still dulled her senses. Only the brightness of blood was clear, but that was all the direction she required.

She was drawn away from her fury by the sight of someone running past her in a flurry of black and crimson. Gasping for air, Varanus looked up, and her eyes focused on Julius as he dashed for a doorway on the far side of the chapel. He paused a moment just before the threshold, and his eyes grew wide as Varanus stood and gazed at him. Strangely, a smile crossed Julius's face, and he looked at her with the same desire he had shown her so many times before over the past months. Then Julius was gone, fleeing into the darkness.

Varanus stood and swayed a little as the shadows whispered around her. Through the blood fog, she formed the thought of her son. She turned and saw Friedrich standing too. There was a gash along his forearm where Julius's knife had struck him, but he was otherwise unharmed.

"Stay out of sight," Varanus growled at him.

"But I—" Friedrich protested.

"Stay out of sight!"

Varanus needed to know that her son would be safe from his own impetuousness, but she was not about to let Julius escape her vengeance. Nor was she ready to risk him reaching home and raising the alarm.

Still muddled by whispers and bloodthirst, Varanus ran for the door and into the darkness beyond.

* * * *

Past the chapel, Varanus followed Julius through a tangled series of chambers and passages, tracking her prey by smell as much as by sight or sound. Despite the fragmentary starlight that crept in through the crumbling roof, the way was incredibly dark, even for the Living. Varanus thought it a miracle that Julius could see well enough to keep ahead of her without stumbling, but perhaps this was a route he had planned beforehand, and he knew the way even blind.

Varanus tried to follow him by sound as well, but the air was thick and her ears were clouded. Even running, Julius's footsteps were all but silent. Only the dull thumping of his heart could be heard, and it echoed from the very stones, surrounding Varanus and pressing against her with every beat.

But by smell she knew him and she could track him. His pleasant fragrance drew her onward through the castle, drawing a great circle that was surely intended to elude her. It was not enough. She smelled him clearly, and she followed him without pause. He would not escape.

At last, Varanus came to the great hall. She wondered if Julius intended to flee all the way back to the chapel, but it was not so. As she crossed into the hall, she saw Julius waiting for her, standing in the center of the room, lit by a haze of starlight that shone out against the darkness. The sight of him standing there made Varanus halt a moment. When she approached him, it was with caution. Something was not right here.

Julius smiled at her. He slowly removed his headpiece and ran his fingers through his hair. For a little while they stood there, watching one another across the room, their eyes slowly entwining, gaze with gaze, until there was nothing in the empty space but the two of them.

"Well, here we are, *Fräulein*," he said softly.

"Indeed, here we are, *Fremder*," Varanus agreed.

"I feared that you would not be able to follow me," Julius told her. "I had begun to hope…. And I was afraid that hope would be unfounded."

"A curious thing to hope for: dying," Varanus noted.

"There are worse fates."

"True," Varanus admitted, "but none so final."

Julius ran his fingertips along the top of the horned skull he held.

"I knew that there was something special about you," he said. "I knew from our first meeting. I saw you atop the stairs and I…I saw *Her*."

"Her?" Varanus asked. She was not entirely certain what he meant, but she could hazard a guess, and it was not one she cared to make. Not after the display in the chapel. "Pronouns are dreadful things, Julius. Whom did you see when you saw me?"

Julius's smile grew a little wider. "I think we both know of whom I speak, *Fräulein*."

"A lady prefers not to comment on idle speculation," Varanus replied.

She took a step toward him, and Julius matched it with his own.

"A pity," Julius said. "There are such things I had planned to show you." He sighed. "But Franz and Istvan have ruined all that with their plotting and foolishness."

"*You* are the one who tried to murder me," Varanus said.

"True." Julius frowned. "I regret that. But I suppose it is just as well that I did." His frown softened and he smiled again, genuinely pleased. "That was what showed me my suspicion was correct."

"Trying to kill me?" Varanus asked, taking another step forward. Again, it was matched by Julius.

"Oh yes," Julius breathed. "You should have fallen before us and died in a moment. And yet, you killed three men and shattered my skull with your bare hands before you succumbed." He absently touched the side of his head where it had been injured. "If not for the grace bestowed upon me, I would have died. That you savaged us so brutally before your death was incredible enough, but then *you rose from the dead*! A miracle among miracles!"

Julius advanced toward her now, his empty hand outstretched as he gazed at her longingly, his eyes filled with wonder and admiration.

"You rose from the dead," he repeated. "You followed me here in time for the ceremony, like one who is called to a greater purpose. You were shot and stabbed, and yet you stand here before me whole and alive! There is but one way that can be."

Varanus shook her head, astonished by the madness in Julius's words and the seductive fervor in the voice that spoke them. Finally, they reached each other and stood there within arm's reach. Varanus wanted to take him there and then and slaughter him for all that he had done, but something stayed her hand: something in his eyes, that glinted as if in moonlight as they looked into hers.

"I am not your god," she told him coldly.

This only made Julius smile all the more. "I think you do believe that," he said. "And yet, clearly do I see Her in you and you in Her. All my life when I have sung praises and shed blood, it has been to you, only I did not know it until tonight."

Varanus exhaled deeply and said, "I am going to kill you, Julius. You tried to murder me, and you tried to murder my son. You do not harm my blood and live."

She had expected her words to shake him out of his maniacal adoration, but they seemed to delight him even more.

"I know," he said. "I am honored, Goddess, to have been chosen for such a blessed end."

"I am going to kill you because of what you did," Varanus insisted. "This is not a blessing. This is retribution."

Julius chuckled and touched her cheek tenderly. "You speak your words, Goddess, but with Her voice. In this moment, you might believe that this is your revenge. I another moment, you will remember your true intention." He grinned at her, showing his teeth. "To live for you has been an honor. To die for you will be doubly so. May my death sate your hunger, and may your blessing fall upon my house and all those who shall come after me."

A shiver ran along Varanus's spine as the room returned to her and with it her senses. She grabbed for Julius, but he darted backward into the shadows. Varanus advanced further, knowing that he would be there, but she found nothing but air. Confused, she turned this way and that, searching for him.

She found him behind her as she heard him murmur in her ear, "And do not fear, I will not go quietly. I will give you sport before I give you my blood."

Julius kissed her on the cheek, and as he did, Varanus's body jerked as she felt him plunge his knife into her lower back and then rip the blade out again. She turned and grabbed for him, but again she was met with shadows. Turning around and around, Varanus stared into the darkness, searching every corner of the hall, but still there was nothing. The shadows crowded around her, smothering her and tugging at her. In the feeble light she could see nothing.

She felt a sharp pain blossom in her side. She saw Julius's smiling face inches away from hers a moment before he withdrew again. Again she grabbed for him, and again there was nothing but emptiness between her fingers. Then came another stab, another smile, another retaliatory blow that found only shadows.

"How is this possible?" she gasped, lashing out blindly as her ears and eyes strained to catch a hint of anything in the dark, any indication of where Julius might be and from where his next attack would come.

Instead of Julius, Varanus saw Korbinian appear from the shadows. His face and body were drenched in blood, and he looked at her sadly, forlorn at his inability to help her.

"All things are possible, *Liebchen*," he said, "as long as we have faith." Blood trickled from between his lips with each word. "It is in faith that the impossible becomes possible."

"You are not helping," Varanus growled.

A moment later, Julius appeared from the shadows beside Korbinian. There was a flash of movement, and Varanus felt the knife cut her across the cheek, slicing almost to the bone. She jerked back and grabbed for her face, startled as much by the surprise of seeing Julius and Korbinian standing next to each other as from the pain. By the time she recovered, Julius had disappeared again.

Then she realized that Korbinian had vanished too.

"I am doing my best, *Liebchen*," Korbinian said from behind her.

Varanus turned to address him just in time to see Julius appear again and drive his knife into her chest, plunging it upward beneath the ribs and only just missing her heart. Having seen Julius as he came at her this time, Varanus recovered from the surprise quickly enough to strike a solid blow against Julius's temple as he drew out his knife. His eye began bleeding again and he grinned at her.

"What you give, you take away," he said happily. "As it should be."

Varanus lunged at him, but he backed into the shadows and again vanished.

"I am doing all that I can, *Liebchen*," Korbinian said, appearing a few paces to her right. "What more can I do?"

Varanus glanced toward him and she understood. Indeed, what more could he do? And what more did he need to do? He told her all that she needed to know.

She reached out with her hand as Julius appeared from the darkness where Korbinian had been standing and charged at her, his knife held overhead ready to be plunged into her neck. The force of his charge carried him right into her grasp, and Varanus grabbed him by the throat. Julius gasped and froze as her fingers tightened. He smiled and dropped the knife.

Hungry and tired from injury and exertion, Varanus flung Julius onto the stone floor. She knelt over him and snatched up the knife. The blood was pounding through his body, and its intoxicating rhythm surged through his warm flesh and into her, his heart beating against her thighs.

"I said I would give you sport," Julius murmured. "What I would not give to die for you a thousand times, but once will be enough."

Varanus pressed the knife to his throat. She was trembling with hunger and excitement. Her pulse was almost strong enough to feel. In the empty space between her own slow heartbeats, Julius's heart pounded quickly, and together their blood and bodies met in a kind of dance, beat for beat.

"*I am not your god!*" Varanus snarled, though she found herself almost breathless.

"I think you do believe that," Julius repeated, his eyes wide with awe and admiration. "But I see you now as I have only ever glimpsed you before! That which I have seen hinted at through smoke, now it is before me in moonlight and it is glorious."

Varanus shook her head as Julius's eyes became unfocused as he gazed at her and through her and beyond her. His fractured skull had taken his reason just as it would soon take his life. But Varanus did not intend to let him escape so easily. She plunged the knife into his throat. The blood that spurted out smelled sweet and tantalizing, more pleasant than any she had ever smelled before. An illusion born of hunger, surely.

But as Varanus placed her lips against the wound and drank, she found that the taste was better still: sweet and strong and dizzying, a liquid ambrosia that sated a hunger she had not known until tasting its cure. She drank and drank, feeling Julius's warmth flowing through her as her flesh tingled with delight at its touch. She realized that she wanted nothing in the world as much as the taste of that blood, that life, that death.

Filled but not yet sated, Varanus sat up with a moan and threw back her head, gasping for air she did not need to breath. Blood stained her lips and throat, and her hair fell about her shoulders, writhing in the shadows that clung to her. She loomed over Julius and looked at him, licking her lips and struggling to fight off the delicious dizziness that had taken her.

She saw Julius still smiling at her, delighting in his own slaughter. As the light in his eyes faded into oblivion, he whispered:

"I see you, girl in sable. I see your horns of starlight and your eyes of night. Take me...."

And then Julius died and there was only silence.

CHAPTER TWENTY-NINE

Through the haze of firelight and the whispers of the shadows, Iosef saw Julius flee the chapel and Varanus give chase. There was a moment when his instinct was to protect his student, but it soon passed. Varanus was Living; Julius was mortal. Varanus could easily catch and kill him. Iosef thought of his own difficulty during the encounter in Mordechai's bookstore, but he had been caught unawares and poisoned by a lucky knife-blow. The chances of Julius enjoying such advantages were few.

The greater worry was Varanus's son. Friedrich had backed away from the fighting at Varanus's urging, but once she was gone, the foolish boy ran headlong back into the fray. Iosef watched as Friedrich reloaded his pistol with a fresh clip and ran at Von Steiersberg, firing with all the abandon and as little accuracy as he had before. Iosef sighed. If something happened to the boy, Varanus would be distraught for years. Iosef himself felt the unbearable weight of losing his wife of nearly two hundred years; the loss of one's only son was surely as harrowing, and Varanus was far younger and far less capable of withstanding the loss.

As Iosef pondered these things, he heard a familiar voice behind him whisper his name.

Iosef.

Iosef spun around, searching for the one who had spoken, yet could not have done so. As he turned, he saw one of Julius's acolytes rush at him from the choking, red-colored darkness, aiming a revolver at Iosef's head. Iosef was suddenly reminded of the chaos in Mordechai's store, of the whispering shadows that spoke in such familiar tones.

Without thinking, Iosef struck the gun with his open hand to force it away. The acolyte froze with astonishment for a moment. He had not expected Iosef to notice his approach, much less to react to it in time. Iosef did not bother himself with the thoughts of mortals. He took the acolyte's arm with both hands and shattered it with a single vicious blow. The acolyte gasped and tried to scream.

Kill, the voice whispered.

Obediently, Iosef grabbed the acolyte by the throat and snapped his neck with a hard twist. Despite the shock and fear, the acolyte resisted until the final twist broke his spine, and Iosef shuddered from the visceral sensation of the kill. He inhaled deeply, scenting death and smoke. His head swam as the voice continued to whisper, drawing him toward the lusty lure of carnage.

No, he reminded himself, there was the boy to consider. Friedrich did not matter but Varanus mattered, and Friedrich's death would destroy Varanus. Therefore, the boy had to be saved.

Iosef turned back toward the altar. As he did so, he saw his brother Luka struggling with two of Julius's guards, beating back one with blows from his pistol while he gutted the other with a dagger. Despite the chaos of the fight, Luka was enjoying himself. And let him, Iosef thought. Luka had contented himself with quiet and inaction for months at Iosef's unspoken request. Let him sate his passions now among men who were both mortal and party to murder.

Iosef's gaze reached Friedrich as the boy came to the altar, firing bullet after bullet at Von Steiersberg. The Austrian laughed as the shots missed him, tearing through the edges of his robe or passing close by his head. It was an astonishing thing to see a man miss so nearly so many times. Whether Friedrich was a terrible shot with astounding luck or an astounding shot with terrible luck, Iosef could not say, but either way left him with an empty pistol and a whole enemy.

Swearing loudly, Friedrich stumbled backward, still pulling the trigger of his empty weapon while Von Steiersberg closed the distance between them. Von Steiersberg bounded forward and reached Friedrich with a hideous snarl and knocked the boy to the ground. Iosef slowly approached, as if in a daze, as Friedrich struggled against his attacker. Von Steiersberg knocked aside Friedrich's defensive blows as easily as one might those of a child, which was an absurdity given Friedrich's much greater size and youthfulness. But as Von Steiersberg closed his fingers around Friedrich's throat and began choking, Iosef reached them.

The boy must live, he reminded himself.

Iosef leaned down and caught Von Steiersberg's neck in the crook of his arm. Von Steiersberg was taken by surprise, and he lashed out, striking backward to free himself from Iosef. Iosef did not give him the courtesy of reacting as the man hit and kicked him in the chest and legs, thrashing like a madman in an attempt to escape Iosef's grasp.

Kill, the voice whispered again, and Iosef obeyed. He squeezed Von Steiersberg's throat, just as Von Steiersberg had intended to do to Friedrich. Iosef both heard and felt the man's heart as it beat frantically and then finally grew still. He waited until the tremors had left his enemy's body and Von Steiersberg's breathing had stopped entirely. Then, disinterested, he let the body fall to the ground.

He looked down at Friedrich. The boy was staring at him, probably astonished at what he had seen. Iosef did not much care. He was tired and hungry from exertions he did not realize he had made. The body of his enemy smelled sweet to him, for it was full of blood and nourishment. But Iosef could not partake. He was in clear view of both Friedrich and the girl, Erzsebet, who sat by the altar, sobbing and cradling the body of her fallen lover. If either of them saw Iosef tear open Von Steiersberg's body and drink his blood, it would be a grave revelation. Iosef would be obliged to kill them, and again, Friedrich's death would be Varanus's great distress. And for that, the two mortals were allowed to live, and Iosef forced himself to go hungry.

A faint sensation of electricity tickled the back of Iosef's neck. He smelled blood and heat, though the bonfire was too far away to be the cause. Iosef turned toward the altar, his movements slowed and incoherent. In a daze, he watched as the blood that had spilled across the altar began to boil and hiss, like water over a roaring fire. The blood of Erdelyi and Stanislav blended together as it lifted into the air in a kind of ruddy vapor that smelled deliciously of iron and intoxication. Iosef took a few hesitant steps forward, one hand reaching out toward the cloud of blood that had formed, suspended in the air. None of the others seemed to notice it—Luka too occupied with fighting, Erzsebet with grief, and Friedrich with the struggle to recover from his near murder at the hands of Von Steiersberg. So Iosef alone watched the vapor as it coalesced into a heavy mass suspended in the air, lit by the firelight and framed by dancing shadows.

It was then that he noticed the most curious thing of all. Amid the blood vapor, Iosef saw a shape begin to form: a vague impression of a figure reaching back toward him, like one seen through smoke. There was a fissure, a break, a division in the very air before him, like a crack in a pane of glass.

Iosef reached into the bloody cloud and extended one fingertip toward the sliver. As his fingertip touched the space, he heard the ever-present voice whisper his name.

"Iosef," Sophio murmured, in a voice so soft and distant that it was almost certainly imagined. Almost certainly.

Light erupted behind Iosef's eyes and consumed everything: the cloud, the blood, the chapel, the world. Everything but Sophio's voice, still whispering over and over again:

"Iosef, Iosef, Iosef."

* * * *

"Brother?"

Iosef felt a hand strike him across the cheek, and he jerked awake. He sensed a shape hovering over him. Had he not recognized the voice as Luka's, he would have struck out blindly, and that would have been unfortunate. But he shuddered violently as he held back his impulse of self-defense, and a few seconds later, his eyes focused on Luka's face where it hovered over his.

"Luka," Iosef said, exhaling.

"Ah, you live," Luka replied.

"I do," Iosef agreed. "What happened?"

"You collapsed," Luka said. "One moment you were standing. When next I looked, you were on the floor. I did not see the cause. I was preoccupied with other concerns." He nodded toward the corpses that lay near the bonfire.

"Of course." Iosef frowned. He could not clearly remember what had happened to cause his unconsciousness. A head injury, perhaps. That was the most likely. "Still, no matter. I am recovered from whatever took me."

Iosef accepted Luka's hand and stood. He stretched and looked around. Von Steiersberg and his men were dead, their bodies scattered about the chapel. Iosef vaguely remembered strangling Von Steiersberg, but the memory was clouded and indistinct. Something about the memory made Iosef look toward the altar, expecting to see something he did not find. Instead, it was absence that proved the most intriguing.

The altar was empty and clean.

"Where is all the blood?" Iosef asked aloud.

"The blood?" Luka glanced at the altar and frowned. "Ah, I see. That is strange."

Blood from Count Erdelyi had pooled on the floor, and a spattering of droplets from the late Stanislav dotted the stones all around, but the altar itself was untouched. A curiosity, but not one that Iosef had time to investigate.

"Where is the boy?" Iosef asked.

Luka pointed past the altar. Iosef advanced a few steps and saw Friedrich seated on the ground next to Stanislav's body, cradling Erzsebet as she sobbed into his shoulder. Friedrich was silent, but his face, too, was wet with tears. He had bandaged his wounded forearm with a piece cut from his shirt, but having attended to his injury, he now seemed to have lost all concern for his own condition as he comforted his friend.

"And Varanus?"

"Did someone call my name?" Varanus asked from behind him.

Iosef turned and saw her approaching from the bonfire. It seemed that she had returned from her chase by the main door. Varanus's dress was torn open in places, and it was covered in blood, but she did not seem troubled. Her wounds were closed, and she walked with a kind of meandering gait, like someone caught in a haze of intoxication. Perhaps the struggle with Julius had proved more taxing than expected. Iosef was suddenly reminded of his own ordeal in the bookstore, but if Varanus had been poisoned, it would soon pass.

"Are you well, Varanus?" Iosef asked, hurrying to meet her.

Varanus took his hand and looked into his eyes, smiling. "I am marvelous!" she answered. "I feel like I am floating on a cloud. A delicious cloud made of...." A thought interrupted her and she suddenly asked, "Where is Alistair?"

"Friedrich!" Iosef called to the boy.

Friedrich and Erzsebet slowly stood, leaning on each other for support. Iosef was reminded of the great fragility of mortals. Even after Sophio's death, *he* had managed to trek from the Kazakh Steppe to the Caucasus in order to warn the Shashavani before he finally succumbed to the wages of his grief. But then, mortals were mortal. That fact might be tiring, but it could not be helped.

"Mother?" Friedrich exclaimed. He hurried to meet her, his expression pale with horror. "Oh, God, Mother, the blood!"

"Hmm?" Varanus mused. She looked down at her dress and blinked a few times. "Oh, yes, of course." She gave her son a very serious look and said, "It is not mine, I promise you."

Friedrich sighed with relief. "Oh, thank God."

In Svanish, Varanus said to Iosef, "It is my blood, actually."

"Yes, I know," Iosef murmured. "Is Julius dead?"

"Dead and delicious," came the reply. Then Varanus reverted to German and touched her son's cheek. "Oh, but Alistair, you're not hurt, are you? Those bruises!"

"I am unharmed, Mother, I swear it," Friedrich protested. As he spoke, Erzsebet joined the group and, shuddering, wrapped her arms around him, like one trying to hide from the world. Friedrich held her and gently brushed her hair. He looked back at the others and asked, "What are we to do now?"

"Hide the bodies?" Luka suggested.

Iosef exhaled. "No, that is an unnecessary exercise. We could put them in the fire, but truly I am more inclined to leave them as they are, to be discovered in their full regalia."

"Why?" Varanus asked, tilting her head with pronounced interested.

"Because then the family will have great reason to conceal the whole thing," Iosef said. "They will not want a proper investigation lest details of this peculiar witchery become revealed."

"Do you think the family is also a part of this?" Luka asked.

Iosef looked at Erzsebet and smiled. The girl drew back and quickly looked away.

"I suspect that Friedrich's friend knows the answer to that," he mused.

"What do you mean?" Friedrich demanded, looking at Erzsebet and then back at Iosef.

"Her father was one of them," Iosef explained, "and he clearly expected her to play a role in all of this."

"Now look here!" Friedrich snapped, rushing to Erzsebet's defense.

"Alistair, hold your tongue," Varanus told him sternly.

"Hold my...? Now look here—"

"It is not important," Iosef interrupted. "We do not have time for such a conversation now. It will wait until we are in Prague, safely away from this place and any association our presence might create should we be discovered."

"You wish to simply leave, brother?" Luka asked. He sounded disappointed, which did not surprise Iosef. "That is, if the family is complicit too...."

"We came to kill Julius and to rescue the girl," Iosef reminded him. "Our work done, I wish to be away from this place before sunrise and before anyone can investigate the sound of gunfire."

"What about Stanislav?" Erzsebet asked softly.

"What about him? He is dead," Varanus remarked. "We cannot rescue him now."

"We leave him, obviously," Iosef said.

"What?" Friedrich cried. "No!"

The boy's impertinence tickled Iosef's ire, but he calmed himself. Instead, he simply asked, "Do you propose to carry your friend's corpse all the way to Prague? Do you think that, perhaps, might raise a few suspicions?"

"Well...I..." Friedrich stammered.

Erzsebet blinked a few times to dispel her tears. "He is right," she said, her voice shaking. "We cannot take him home for burial. He is dead and he must be left here and it is all my fault!"

"No, no, no, not your fault," Friedrich murmured and held her tightly as she cried into his shoulder.

With the boy and the girl thankfully distracted, Iosef returned to the immediate concern: how to return home without being either identified or connected with the deaths.

"Shall I fetch the wagon?" Luka asked.

"It's probably safest if we walk to it," Varanus noted, though her attention was elsewhere. She was gazing off into the distance beyond the altar.

"True," Iosef said. "I prefer not to trouble the horse in the dark any more than is necessary. We must ask it to go a long way."

"Königsberg is not so far," Luka reminded.

"We are not going to Königsberg," Iosef told him. "Consider: a group of strangers arrive in the city the same night that Julius von Raabe is killed, and then that same group departs the following day? No, better we disappear and are forgotten. We will take the wagon west and return to Prague via a different railway from a different city."

"Prudent," Luka agreed. "And we should obtain some new clothes before we are seen too much in public. Blood and holes do not make inconspicuous clothing."

Varanus blinked a few times and lifted her skirt slightly to study it. "Oh!" she exclaimed. "I thought it looked rather nice."

"Are you certain you are feeling yourself, Varanus?" Iosef asked.

"Why, I have never felt better," Varanus replied. She took Iosef hands and grinned at him in a manner that gave Iosef an uncomfortable turn. "And I can tell you truly, My Lord, I think that I should very much like to feel this way again. You must try it!"

Poison, Iosef confirmed to himself. *There can be no doubt.*

But at least that would pass soon enough, even if she had been subjected to a greater dose of the substance than Iosef had suffered in the shop. However virulent, all toxins eventually left the Living. Eventually.

"Thank you, no, Varanus," Iosef said to her. "Perhaps another time."

"Mmm," Varanus agreed. Still smiling, she glanced toward the altar, and her expression became puzzled. "Wasn't there blood on the altar?"

"There was and yet now it is gone," Iosef answered. "My curiosity would bid me stay and examine it fully to determine the cause, but my good sense counsels otherwise. Better to escape now and return later, in smaller company."

"Sensible," Varanus agreed.

A thought occurred to Iosef and he asked, "Varanus, where is Julius's body?"

"In the great hall," Varanus replied, pointing toward the door. "Why?"

"Because I suspect he has something on his person that I wish to retrieve," Iosef told her. "It was the reason for our coming to Prague in the first place, so it would be foolish to leave here without it."

* * * *

Iosef arrived in the great hall, finding his way by the light of a torch. He would meet the others at the castle gate shortly, but first he intended to retrieve Julius's amulet. It would have been his had Hoffmann not died before Iosef could take possession of it. He would now correct that error.

The hall was dark as pitch as Iosef entered, darker than he remembered from their arrival. Glancing upward, Iosef realized that he could no longer see the stars. It was like a stain of ink spilled across the sky.

Julius lay in the center of the room, surrounded by blood. It had pooled around his head and shoulders like a dull crimson halo. More blood had been splattered across the floor stones all around, spilled by violence and likely not from him. Iosef knelt and smelled one of the drying clusters. It belonged to Varanus. That was not surprising given the state of Varanus's clothes. She had fought Julius, and he had wounded her time and time again before she finally bested him.

It was strange to think of the Living being almost undone by mortals, but again Iosef remembered the fight in the bookstore. Only three mortals had managed to very nearly kill him. Julius must have used the same toxin on Varanus that his men had used on Iosef.

The sacrificial knife lay next to Julius, also covered in blood. Iosef picked it up and sniffed at it cautiously. He smelled both Varanus and Julius, but no discernable poison. Still, that meant nothing. The toxin might be odorless, or it might have been wiped clean by its successive uses.

Iosef looked at Julius and saw traces of joy in his lifeless eyes and a grin on his unmoving lips. Despite all reason, he had died happily, even while being bled to death. And Varanus had drunk deeply of her enemy. What little blood remained had formed the peculiar near-perfect circle around Julius's head, but there was little of that. Otherwise, the corpse was completely bloodless. Varanus had drunk her fill and more, until nothing remained.

She must have been severely injured in the fight to have needed so much blood.

But there were more important matters to consider. Iosef reached into Julius's robe and began searching for the amulet. It was impossible that Julius would not have it with him during the ceremony, being so plainly a devoted follower of his imagined god. And indeed, it was there, concealed in a pocket just over Julius's heart.

How sentimental, Iosef thought.

As he reached for the amulet, his torch flickered in the breeze, and the chaos of the feeble firelight made it seem that the shadows were closing in around him. He touched the amulet's metal, and he heard the wind whisper his name.

Iosef.

Iosef froze and closed his eyes. It had been a long and harrowing two days. But it was foolishness to let the superstitions of his enemies cloud his own judgment. Wind was wind, fire was fire, and shadows were shadows.

He took Julius's amulet and tucked it into his coat pocket, where it rested next to its twin. Iosef stood and walked from the hall as the shadows parted before him.

CHAPTER THIRTY

"Now then," Iosef said to Erzsebet, as he sat in the chair across from her, "I would like you to tell me, in your own time and in your own words, about your family's cult."

The girl fidgeted and stared at the sitting room wallpaper as she nervously played with her fingertips. Iosef gave her a smile that he meant to be reassuring but which might not have been so. It was an unaccustomed expression, especially in recent years.

"Must we do this?" asked the one called Zoya. Both she and Friedrich had insisted on being present for the interview, and as their presence seemed to calm Erzsebet, Iosef had allowed it. Still, he did not like how crowded the sitting room had become as a result. If they proved an impediment, he would have them removed without a second thought.

"Yes," Iosef answered coldly.

There was a lengthy pause as Zoya waited for more, perhaps expecting an explanation that neither she nor the boy had the right to demand.

"Oh," she finally said. Turning her attention to Erzsebet, she put her arm around the girl and told her, "You do not have to do this, you know." "She does," Iosef corrected.

"You cannot force her to speak if she isn't ready, Iosef," Friedrich insisted.

To be addressed in such familiar terms by the boy made Iosef bristle, but at least it was his proper name. Ten years earlier in London, Friedrich had repeatedly mispronounced it as "Joseph", so this was some improvement.

"Come now, Friedrich," Iosef replied, smiling a little more, "surely the correct term is 'Father', as your mother and I are married. *My son*."

Now it was Friedrich's turn the bristle, which Iosef allowed himself to enjoy. But he was surprised when Friedrich did not lose his temper. The boy simply nodded politely and said:

"Of course, *Father*." But tact and politeness were not to be interpreted as passivity. "You cannot force her to answer your questions if she is unready or unwilling to speak."

"I marched to the far side of Poland to rescue her from her father, Friedrich," Iosef answered sternly. "I risked my life against armed men to free her from a pagan ritual that she clearly understood." He turned his gaze toward Erzsebet and said, "I am quite within my rights to demand an explanation, especially while she remains hidden from her enemies in my house."

Erzsebet looked away from the wallpaper and met Iosef's eyes. She nodded slowly. "He is right, Friedrich," she murmured. She took a deep breath and looked at Iosef again. "What do you want to know?"

"Everything, of course," Iosef told her.

There was a moment of hesitation as Erzsebet gathered her thoughts. "My family belongs to a…a *society* that believes in the existence of a god older than any recorded religion. It has been known by many names. You might have heard it called the Dark Faun or the Black Goat. My father said that when the Slavs discovered the god, they called it the 'Horned Serpent' and tried to banish it to the underworld, but in the end they could not escape its reach: the faithful of the Horned Serpent simply chose the Slavs' own god Veles and worshipped their master under that name. My father said that this has been done in every faith and in every tongue. Even he did not know how many of us there are, all worshipping the same god through different guises all across the world."

"Have you ever met followers of a different guise?" Iosef asked.

"No," Erzsebet admitted, sounding embarrassed. Perhaps she realized how far-fetched the tale was; though, having been told it since childhood, she had no doubt accepted the story as true. "I only ever met members of our own society. The Von Steiersbergs, the Von Raabes, the Petrescus—"

"I would like a full list of the names you remember," Iosef told her, "but we will come to that later."

"There were not many…that I recall," Erzsebet said evasively, her gaze again shifting away from him and to the walls, hovering somewhere in the vicinity of a darkened corner where there was nothing to trouble her.

"As many as you remember," Iosef insisted. "But later." He paused. "When were you inducted into the…society?"

As that was the term she had used, he used it as well rather than the dismissive title of 'cult'. This seemed to calm her slightly, and she answered with only a little uncertainty.

"I am told I was inducted as soon as I was born," Erzsebet told him. "Something like a baptism, but I do not remember it."

"A baptism?"

Erzsebet nodded a little. "So that the god might know me, even before I could take the vow of faith."

"Vow of faith?" Iosef asked, intrigued.

Erzsebet shuddered and wrapped her arms around herself, staring at the corner again. Zoya hugged the girl tightly and whispered in her ear, trying to sooth her.

"We will address details of ritual later," Iosef said in his reassuring voice. Preferably when there were no extraneous distractions. "But there *was* an induction ritual?"

"Yes," Erzsebet replied softly.

"When?"

"When I turned thirteen," Erzsebet said. "The first new moon after my birthday. It was a…festival of sorts. The faithful came from all across Europe. I believe there was even a Turk. I fear I do not remember much."

"Was there any form of regular service?"

"There were prayers," Erzsebet answered. "Every month we would celebrate the fading of the moon. And there were certain yearly festivals—the Solstice, the Equinox. Sometimes we held them by ourselves, and sometimes other people came to celebrate them with us."

"People like Von Raabe and Von Steiersberg?" Iosef asked.

Erzsebet nodded.

"Did you ever travel to a festival somewhere else?"

"A few times," Erzsebet said. "We sometimes went to Austria to celebrate with Count von Steiersberg and his family or to Romania to be with Colonel Petrescu and his. But mostly I celebrated at home in Hungary. Father said that I would travel more once I was married."

At her own mention of marriage, she shivered and held herself tighter.

"And how did you come to be betrothed to Count von Steiersberg?"

"Good God!" Friedrich exclaimed. "It has only been four days! Don't make her think about *him* again!"

Iosef turned his head very slowly and looked at Friedrich. "Be quiet," he said in a soft yet forceful tone.

Before Friedrich could protest further, Erzsebet answered the question.

"My father is…was an ambitious man," she said. "He was well regarded in Hungary, but his influence was only marginal in the Empire, whereas Count von Steiersberg has…*had* the ear of the Emperor himself. The Count wanted a young wife from within our community of faith. My father wanted to draw our families closer together and gain his influence. I was the obvious choice."

"So you fled?"

"I did not wish to marry him," Erzsebet replied. "He was old and cruel, and when my mother told me what I was expected to do on my wedding night…*before* our wedding night…to secure the grace and favor of the god...." She shivered and her hands gripped Zoya's arms, pulling the woman around her like a blanket to ward off the frightening memories. Finally, she composed herself enough to continue, "I realized that I could not bear to be one of the faithful any longer, not if it meant doing the things I have seen my mother do. And then there was Stanislav. He was on the run from the police in Bohemia, and he came to work in the stables under a false name. And he was kind to me and he was handsome and he was young, and when he told me who he was, I realized that I had another choice. So I fled with him."

She clenched her eyes shut against tears that trickled down her cheeks despite all efforts to hold them back. Finally she gasped in desperation and said, "I thought we were safe."

"You are safe now," Zoya assured her, whispering in her ear as she pressed her cheek against the girl's hair, enfolding herself around Erzsebet in a desperate attempt to shield her against the world.

"None of us are safe!" Erzsebet protested, her voice little more than a hoarse whisper.

Iosef had little patience for sentimentality, but the girl could not be blamed for her fear. Indeed, her composure under the circumstances was remarkable. Kidnapped by the cult she had fled, forced to kill her father by her own hand, her love murdered before her eyes: it was enough to break any mortal. And to the girl's credit, though struck to the core by her ordeal, she had not broken.

But it was an academic point. There were more immediate things that demanded his interest.

"You *are* safe," Iosef said gently, speaking in a tone calculated to resonate with the mortal mind. He took Erzsebet's hand, and she looked up at him, her eyes wide with fear. "No one will harm you while you are under my roof."

"You do not understand!" Erzsebet protested. "The faithful are everywhere!"

"They are not in my house, child," Iosef assured her. "And should they enter some night in search of you or anyone else, I will destroy them. And there is nothing that they or their god can do to stop me."

As Iosef had calculated, the resonance of his tone and the mixed warmth and intensity of his gaze calmed Erzsebet enough for her to relax. Her frantic heartbeats slowed, and her breathing grew normal again. She was still afraid, but the moment of panic had passed.

Iosef smiled and patted her hand. "Now then," he said, "are you ready to answer more questions?"

Erzsebet nodded after a little hesitation.

"Good."

After the interview, Iosef sat in his study, examining the two amulets side-by-side, one in each hand. It gave him a sense of triumph to have the prize finally in his possession, but with that task accomplished, he was now faced with the same quandary as before. He still had an artifact that could not be authentic, yet was; made of aluminium long before the metal could have been easily acquired in sufficient quantities and inscribed with a message in a language Iosef did not know or even recognize. The only difference was that now he had two of them.

But that in itself was progress. The study of the Black Goat's followers had been Sophio's last unfinished work. Each piece of knowledge Iosef acquired brought him closer to some kind of legacy he could assemble in Sophio's memory. Perhaps that would give him some resolution to his grief. Likely not, but it was something for him to cling to in her absence.

He heard the door open slightly, and he recognized the sound and smell of Luka.

"Good evening, brother," he said, setting the amulets down on his desk.

Luka joined him, carrying a bottle of wine and a half-filled glass. He took a drink and asked, "How went the interrogation?"

"The girl is terrified, which is of little surprise," Iosef answered. "I would be more concerned if she were less affected than she is. But she answered what questions I put to her. After she has recovered further, we will speak again."

"About the sacrifice?" Luka asked.

"Among other things, yes. I touched on the matter, but it troubled her greatly so I did not press. Not this time."

"Surely you were curious," Luka said. "Why the restraint?"

"We cannot allow curiosity to incite cruelty," Iosef answered. "That is the road of the Basilisk, and I know better than to dare even a few steps along its path. The girl will give me all the answers I require. It is only a question of time. Indeed, talking about the cult and her upbringing in it will probably help the girl more than it distresses her. To voice one's ordeal is cathartic."

"So is watching a play," Luka noted dryly.

Iosef smiled a little. "Are you volunteering to give us a theatrical performance, brother? I am certain Ekaterine would be eager to assist."

Luka made a noise and took another drink of wine. "Do not joke about such things," he said. "One day spent entertaining a couple of artists, and she suddenly fancies herself a poet. It will be a playwright next."

Iosef chuckled and asked, "How is your cousin?"

"Displeased at having missed our adventure, or so she says." Luka scoffed and then sighed. "I foolishly mentioned the bonfire and the skulls, and now she will not give me a moment's peace about it. Apparently it sounds 'profoundly romantic and sublime'."

"Did you mention the human sacrifice?"

Luka sighed again and drank more wine. "I did. While distraught at the fate of the victim, she claims it proves her thesis about the Latins."

"That Europeans are all fundamentally pagans?"

"That is the one," Luka said. "Evergreens and blood sacrifice, such is the nature of the West, she says."

Iosef looked at the amulets that lay on his desk and frowned. "I sometimes wonder if that is not, in fact, the nature of mankind, whether in the West, the East, the North, or the South," he murmured, half to himself. "Murder and idolatry seem to be our most fundamental instincts, whatever pageantry we use to clothe them." He quickly dispelled such melancholy thinking. "Regardless, your cousin reads far too many novels."

"Far too many," Luka agreed.

There was a lengthy silence as Luka refilled his glass and drank again. In the quiet, Iosef heard the shadows murmuring to him, whispering hints of Sophio's name. He was exhausted again. He could not remember whether he had properly meditated since their return from Germany. Long hours spent in research were good for learning but not for sanity.

"Brother," he said softly, "did you see me when I collapsed in the chapel?"

"When it happened? No," Luka answered. His voice was tinged with a half-thought of guilt and worry at having not been at hand to safeguard his friend. "I saw you standing, I turned away in the fight, and when I turned back, you were on the ground."

Iosef closed his eyes and spent a few seconds reconstituting the fragmented memory.

"I imagined that I saw Sophio," he told Luka.

"What?" Luka exclaimed. "You saw her? How?"

"I did not see her," Iosef clarified. "I *imagined* that I saw her. I imagined a shape…a figure in smoke hovering above the altar. It whispered to me in her voice, and then I lost consciousness."

"How is that possible? Do you mean to say you saw her ghost?"

"Ghosts are not real," Iosef said.

Luka shook his head. "I would not be so certain of that, brother. When I was a boy, my grandfather told me a story—"

"When you were a boy, your grandfather told you *many* stories, Luka."

Luka grinned. "That he did, and it is my duty to pass them along to a younger, even more impressionable generation."

Iosef smiled at this. It felt good to smile, especially with Luka.

"You are as bad as your cousin and her tales of Kent," he said. He returned to the question of his vision. "I did not see a ghost. I did not see anything. I believe I was poisoned, possibly by a weapon, possibly by something in the air."

"Poisoned?" Luka grew pale. "It must have been strong to affect the Living."

"Possibly," Iosef agreed. "It is difficult to say. Most poisons are too weak to do us much harm, but sometimes certain substances can produce unforeseen afflictions that do not occur in mortals, who inevitably die before any other effects are allowed to set in. When I was attacked in Mordechai's bookstore, I was stabbed several times, and I found myself becoming…confused."

"Confused?"

Iosef searched for the words. "The shadows grew darker and sounds became dull. I repeatedly lost track of my enemies in the darkness. I even heard voices. Something affected my senses, and I suspect it was a toxin."

"And you believe that is what happened in the chapel?" Luka asked.

"I am certain of it. Just as I am certain that Varanus was also poisoned. You recall her behavior when she returned from killing Julius von Raabe."

"Drunk," Luka said, not at all tactfully.

"Severe poisoning," Iosef replied. "I think there was something we both encountered that distorted our senses. But alas, I do not know what it was or how we were both exposed."

"Or why the rest of us were not affected," Luka added.

"Indeed," Iosef agreed. "That is the most puzzling question. Why the Living were affected and those in the Shadow of Death remained unharmed."

* * * *

"And there truly were skulls everywhere?" Ekaterine asked Friedrich, as the two of them walked along the upstairs hallway. "Truly?"

"More than I care to remember," Friedrich said.

He could not imagine how Ekaterine could speak of such things in so excited a tone. She sounded genuinely excited at the prospect of pagan witchery and sacrifice. But surely that was the comfort of distance speaking. Had she been there, she would have recalled it as Friedrich did: a horrifying, bloody ordeal that he wanted simply to erase from his memory.

"And they wore crowns, you say?" Ekaterine pressed. "Of flowers?"

"Holly, I think," Friedrich answered. "And they had horns. No...no, skulls with horns. They wore them on their heads."

Ekaterine took Friedrich's hand and held it tightly, her eyes lit up with excitement. The sight of her warmed Friedrich a little. As he gazed into her eyes, he felt himself smiling. He was seized by the urge to tell her more, to relate every last lurid detail he could remember—and as many others as he could invent—simply to delight her. Which was foolish, he knew. No one should be delighted by such stories, nor should he find it so infectious to witness her delight.

"You *must* tell me everything, Friedrich," Ekaterine said. "Luka told me a little, but now he refuses to relate any more. And he said there was a bonfire. *A bonfire!* Who builds bonfires in ruined castles? You tell me that."

"Um.... Sorcerers?" Friedrich ventured.

Ekaterine's eyes lit up yet again at the suggestion. "Sorcerers!" She paused as they passed a mirror and took a few moments to examine herself and adjust her hair. "I could be a sorcerer, don't you think? I would be very good at it."

Friedrich gazed at her reflection in the mirror and found himself still smiling, even though he knew that she could see it too. But what of that? He had nearly died in Germany. Life was fleeting. Why should he hide the fact that Ekaterine made him smile, that her delight was his delight?

Not that life was fleeting any longer. As he studied himself in the mirror, he saw yet again the youthful face he had not known for almost ten years. His face was younger, fitter, healthier. Even the gash on his arm had almost faded away, though admittedly a certain celerity of healing was not unfamiliar to him even before subjecting himself to the treatment. But now his very youth frightened him. He had hit upon something on that mad and frantic night, just as he had destroyed it. And now he had to live with the realization that he might never be able to reproduce it, though he silently swore to himself that he would try.

"A marvelous sorcerer," he murmured to Ekaterine, remembering himself. Best not let her notice him drifting away into such frantic thoughts. "The best of sorcerers. Though as I recall, sorcerers are expected to have a long white beard."

This paused Ekaterine only for a moment. "Spirit gum," she said firmly, with an accompanying nod. "A little spirit gum and I shall have the longest beard you have ever seen. And a skull to match it."

For a moment, Friedrich almost imagined her as she described, her reflection dressed in the regalia of Von Raabe or his cohorts. He pictured Ekaterine in dark robes, bedecked with skulls, drenched in sacrificial blood, and holding a dagger above her head. He shut his eyes against the vision and turned away.

"I am certain it would suit you well," he said, trying to play off his sudden distress. "A goddess of the harvest. You should wear it to a ball sometime."

Ekaterine smiled at him and gently touched his arm, perhaps sensing his distress.

"No, I think not," she murmured. "It is always more fun in novels than in life, isn't it?"

"Significantly," Friedrich agreed. "Not that it is so unfamiliar to me…. My travels in Asia held their own share of bloodshed. But I fear that I shall never become accustomed to it."

"You will," Ekaterine said sadly. "Eventually, we all do. We must. A cruel world will not permit otherwise, not if we face it and refuse to turn away. The more you see, the less it will trouble you." Her voice grew a little distant. "Which is troubling in itself."

"I hope so," Friedrich confessed. "I suspect that I will see much more of this cruel world than I ever thought I would. It sometimes feels like I am drawn to it, unable to escape. Unwilling to look away."

"Evil does not vanish simply when we ignore it," Ekaterine said. "When we look away for our own sake, we betray those who need us most. When the world horrifies us, we must confront it and make it better, not flee in fear."

Friedrich grinned at her. "I will never flee in fear." Then his voice fell as a certain memory from his travels rose to trouble him. "Never again," he whispered.

Ekaterine touched his cheek with her hand and looked into his eyes. Friedrich gazed back and found himself suddenly dizzy, falling away into the marvelous uncertainty he saw there.

"Friedrich," Ekaterine murmured, "promise me that you will not rush to harden yourself against the evil in this world. Courage in the face of cruelty is splendid, but I think your aversion to violence is far more admirable than a callous disregard for cruelty. Stay as you are and promise that you will not lose that gentleness."

It was such an odd thing to say and said with such seriousness that Friedrich laughed with uncertainty and felt an awkward grin cross his lips. He quickly drew back and coughed a few times. Surely he had looked a fool just now.

"What a curious thing to ask," he said.

"Will you promise me?" Ekaterine asked.

Friedrich quickly rallied from his earlier uncertainty and answered, "I would promise you the world, if you asked it. And I would deliver it, were it in my power."

"I do not want the world," Ekaterine told him, smiling a little but not quite approving. "And it is not right for you to speak to your aunt in such a way."

"My aunt by marriage," Friedrich reminded her.

Ekaterine sighed and shook her head, but she did seem at least amused by what had been said. Friedrich counted that as a success. He was about to say more when a door along the hallway opened, and Karel rushed into the hallway, carrying the one piece of luggage he had brought with him. He was quite disheveled, more than Friedrich had seen before, which was saying something given the state of their previous lodgings.

"Oh, Karel!" Ekaterine exclaimed, rushing to intercept him. "Just the person I wanted to speak to."

"What?" Karel stammered.

"Are you familiar with Mister Chambers?" Ekaterine asked. "He's an American."

Startled and confused, it took Karel a few seconds to manage a simple reply of, "Not personally. Should I be?"

"You must!" Ekaterine insisted. "You see, he's written a book about a play that drives people mad!"

"A what that does what?"

"But you see," Ekaterine continued, "Mister Chambers only wrote a little bit of the play down, so I thought it would be tremendous fun if you and I wrote the rest of it and then performed it. I've always wanted to be a theater producer, you know."

Karel's bloodshot eyes widened, and he shook his head. "No, no, no! I am finished with plays! I am finished with poetry! I am finished with artists and romantics and revolutionaries!"

It was then that Friedrich noticed the dark circles under Karel's eyes and asked, "I say, have you been sleeping properly Karel? You look dreadful."

"Of course I've not been sleeping properly," Karel answered frantically. "Freddie, our friends are dead! Men came into your house and killed them! I might have been killed myself! And now Erzsebet says that Stanislav was carried off and murdered too!"

Friedrich nodded and placed a hand on Karel's shoulder. He had suffered bad dreams too in the wake of recent events. It was only to be expected.

"I am not surprised, Karel," he said. "Now don't you worry. I have just the thing for restless nights: laudanum, and lots of it."

"What? No!" Karel exclaimed. "You may dull yourself with drink and opium if you want, Freddie, but I have had enough. I am leaving!"

"Leaving? But Karel—"

Karel pushed past them and carried his luggage toward the front stairs.

"You can't stop me, Freddie!" he called back. "My father wants me to join the family business, and that is what I am going to do! I am going to pretend that none of this ever happened and, God willing, I will never see any of you again!"

And with that, Karel stumbled down the stairs to the foyer and was gone.

"Should we give chase?" Ekaterine mused. "He might talk."

"Doubtful," Friedrich said. "Poor fellow, he's terrified. I suspect he'll be silent about the whole business simply out of fear."

"Some people are simply not ready to be artists," Ekaterine said lightly.

"True."

"But what if he does tell the police?" Ekaterine asked.

"Then more's the pity for him," Friedrich replied. "I may only be a baron, but legally I am answerable only to His Majesty the Kaiser. Even in Austria, I suspect that the police would be more willing to take my word over that of a factory owner's son. Besides," he added, "Karel might be afraid, but he's a good fellow. I trust him."

Ekaterine sighed at Friedrich and shook her head, but she did not comment. Without another word, they continued on to the upstairs sitting room where Friedrich's friends had been sequestered, sheltering them from the outside world while also sheltering the rest of the house from them. It had been the best compromise Friedrich could bargain from Mother.

Friedrich found Zoya painting a portrait of Erzsebet, who sat by the curtained window, slowly twisting a flower in her hands. Erzsebet looked toward Friedrich as he entered, and her face lit up. Friedrich found it only right to return her smile with one of his own. She was still shaken by her ordeal, but at least she was recovering in peaceful surroundings. Friedrich saw red around her eyes: she had cried recently, most certainly in memory of Stanislav.

"Hello all," Friedrich announced. "How are you?"

Zoya glanced away from her work and said, "Well, Freddie, well. Ah, Muse!" she exclaimed at Ekaterine. "A most welcome addition."

"Hello Miss Chromoluminarist," Ekaterine replied, joining Zoya at the easel. "What a delightful painting. Most chromoluminary."

Zoya sighed. "The compliment is appreciated, Muse, though undeserved. I fear this latest work does no one due credit: neither my subject." She motioned to Erzsebet. "Nor my audience." She waved her hand to indicate Ekaterine.

"Still, though, lovely colors," Ekaterine said brightly.

"It is the surroundings," Zoya grumbled. "Utterly bourgeois. I will be content as soon as I have a factory or a field to surround my model. Until then, I am stumbling in darkness!"

Erzsebet seemed distressed at Zoya's reaction to her own painting, so Friedrich approached her with some words of reassurance.

"Ignore Zoya," he told her. "It looks lovely, as do you."

Erzsebet smiled a little and looked down at the flower. "Thank you," she murmured.

Friedrich knelt beside her and asked, "How are you?"

"I am…better than I was?" Erzsebet ventured, sounding uncertain that it was the looked-for reply.

Friedrich gently took her hand, careful to stop in case being touched caused her distress. But the physical contact seemed to comfort her, and she put her other hand on his.

"Good," Friedrich said. "You are safe here, I promise. And you may stay as long as you like."

"Ah…" Ekaterine began, raising a finger to correct him.

"We are not staying, Freddie," Zoya said. "Erzsebet and I are leaving Prague soon, and I do not think either of us will return."

"What?" Friedrich asked, very surprised and rather disappointed to learn that he was to lose even more friends in the same day. "When?"

"As soon as I have answered all of the Prince's questions," Erzsebet said, looking back at the flower. "Once all of our business here is done, I must be away from this place. Zoya is very kind and has agreed to join me."

"But where? Why?"

"Paris," Zoya answered, punctuating the name with a firm dot of her brush. "It's far away, much safer than here. And I understand that Montmartre is a splendid place for artists. It seems the logical place to go."

"You could join us!" Erzsebet told Friedrich, holding his hand tightly. "You would be most welcome."

"And so would you, Muse," Zoya told Ekaterine, smiling at her slyly. "I am certain you would be very popular."

"I have always wanted to be an artist's model," Ekaterine admitted. She tilted her head and smiled at the thought.

* * * *

That evening, Iosef was roused from his studies by a knocking at the front door. The sound was unobtrusive, but it carried well enough that Iosef heard it clearly from the room where he had been reading. Under normal circumstances, he would have ignored it altogether and allowed the servants to attend the matter unaided, but he did not recall expecting anyone at that hour, and in light of recent events, it seemed prudent to be aware of any persons leaving or entering.

Perhaps it was young Friedrich's poet friend, returning to trouble Iosef's door again. Or perhaps the boy had revealed them to the authorities, and now Iosef would be obliged to dirty his hands with mortal blood. That would be most inconvenient.

To his great surprise, Iosef found Mordechai waiting in the foyer, having been just let in by the footman. He carried a pair of large and over-filled carpetbags, which he placed on the floor with a heavy thud. Smiling at Iosef, Mordechai stepped forward and offered his hand.

"Herr Mordechai," Iosef said, unable to completely conceal the astonishment in his voice. "Why ever are you here?" As an afterthought, he nodded to the footman, who waited attentively nearby. "Thank you Pravec, you may leave us."

"Yes, Highness."

"Why am I here?" Mordechai repeated. "In your house? Forgive me, I had assumed I would be welcome."

"*In Prague*," Iosef clarified. "Of course you are welcome here, but in light of...*events*...I assumed that you had left our fair city days ago."

"Ah, that." Mordechai grinned in his usual jovial way. "I have been liquidating my properties and accounts in Prague in preparation for my journey. Twenty years of meticulously assembled assets do not make themselves portable simply overnight."

Iosef nodded in understanding. "Of course. Is there any assistance I might render...?"

"It is all done," Mordechai replied, "though I do thank you for the offer."

"Where do you go? Yugra after all?"

Mordechai laughed. "It is tempting and I do so enjoy brisk walks, but in fact I have decided to take up my friend's offer and visit him in America. It has been some time since I was there. I am given to understand that it is an interesting place."

"That is a word for it, yes," Iosef agreed.

"In fact," Mordechai continued, reaching down and patting one of the carpetbags, "I am here to conclude my last piece of business before I quit the country."

"What do you mean, Mordechai?" Iosef asked cautiously.

Mordechai's expression became devilishly mirthful as he knelt and opened each of the bags. Inside, Iosef saw a collection of old books, carefully packed so that each one reinforced its companions, and together they withstood their jostling journey unharmed.

"I have sold off most of my store's books," Mordechai explained. "Most texts of true significance that I possess are far from here, kept safely out of the public eye, but there were a few pieces in my local collection that I felt deserved the consideration of a true scholar rather than soaking in dust on the bookshelf of an ignorant collector. And so, I have brought them to you."

Iosef was astonished at Mordechai's generosity, for among the Shashavani all knowledge was treasured, and the gift of a book of quality was counted far better than silver or gold. "This is most kind of you, Mordechai," Iosef said, dropping to his knees in excitement as he began to rummage through the books, examining each one in turn. Their languages and subjects varied widely, but all of them were authentic, original, and of great academic interest. "I know not what to say!"

Mordechai chuckled and flexed his fingers as he and Iosef knelt together beside the books. "I am certain you will enjoy them," he said. Coming to one in particular, he exclaimed, "Ah, yes! And I made a special point of including all of my texts pertaining to the Cults of the Black Goat. I think you will find them most interesting." He paused. "That is, provided our recent encounter with *men of the faith* has not soured you from its academic study."

"Quite the opposite, Mordechai, I assure you."

"Nothing quite like attempted murder by cultists to prick one's intellectual curiosity, eh?"

Iosef smiled a little. "That is certainly a way of putting it, yes."

* * * *

In the pleasant stillness of the parlor, Varanus sorted through the mail that had accumulated over the preceding days. It was difficult to imagine that more than a week had passed since the unpleasantness in Prussia, and still they had all allowed the correspondence to pile up again. At least they seemed to have escaped without repercussion. There had been no inquiry by the police, though Varanus remained ready to quit the country at a moment's notice. There was little reason to remain.

"Anything of interest, *Liebchen?*" Korbinian murmured in her ear.

As they were alone, they sat together in adjoining chairs, enjoying the pleasant fire as it burned low. Varanus smiled and kissed him on the cheek. With Julius's death, he seemed to have returned to his old self. How strange that jealousy could incite such a change in him.

"Little at best," she said, tossing an invitation aside. She would let Ekaterine decide whether it was for an event worth attending. "And I am very pleased that you have stopped moping about the place. You were most unnerving, my darling. Please never do it again."

Korbinian raised the back of her hand to his lips and said softly, "But *Liebchen*, I was only trying to warn you. I simply lacked the proper words."

"I think you were jealous," Varanus replied. "And jealousy is most unbecoming."

Korbinian grinned. "But *Liebchen*, what man could not be jealous of you?"

"Don't start that again," Varanus admonished, waving a finger. She turned to the next letter and frowned at the inscription. "Oh my. From our friends the Von Raabes."

"Oh dear," Korbinian said, his tone almost humorous, but still taut with curiosity. "And what have they to say?"

Varanus opened the letter with her knife and read the contents. She almost laughed. Under other circumstances that would have been horrible, but in light of recent events, it seemed fitting.

"With a heavy heart, dear Augusta informs us that poor Julius and several of his friends were killed in an unfortunate motoring accident while returning home late one night."

"Goodness!" Korbinian exclaimed, his tone mirthful.

"As Iosef and I were such good friends of his, we are invited to attend the funeral and to perhaps stay a little while to commiserate." She scoffed and threw the letter into the fire. "I think not."

"You suspect a trap?" Korbinian asked.

"Possibly," Varanus admitted. "And even if they are sincere, I do not consider it a risk worth taking. I fear that the message shall have been lost in the mail."

She leaned against Korbinian and rested her head on his shoulder as he in turn rested his head on hers.

"But was it?" she heard him ask.

"Was it what?"

"Sent by mail," Korbinian clarified. "It seems very quick to have arrived in time, especially sent from another country. What if it was hand-delivered?"

Varanus cast her gaze toward the letter where it lay in the fireplace, slowly decaying into ash amid the flames.

"What if indeed…" she agreed.

That would mean an agent of Julius's family was in Prague at that very moment, possibly in the vicinity of the house. If their interest was sincere, there was no cause for concern. But if they suspected what had transpired, if somehow they had deduced that night's events, their intentions would be hostile indeed.

Her eyes turned toward the mantelpiece. It was a rash assumption, but still it gnawed at her. And perhaps it was better to be safe, at least until they made arrangements to quit the city.

So, as the clock struck midnight, Varanus rose, took the shotgun from above the fireplace, and set it beside her chair.